"THIS IS A. W. GRAY COUNTRY,
SIZZLING WITH TEXAS SLEAZE,
VIOLENCE, AND CORRUPTION . . .
delivers all the dark wit and kinetic style that
the author is quickly becoming famous for,
making the comparisons to Elmore Leonard
more reasonable every time out."
                                        —*Booklist*

"RIVETING . . . COMPELLING . . .
When A. W. Gray describes a place, you see
it; when he creates a perilous situation, you
feel it."
                                        —*Orange County Register*

"Plenty of suspense and excitement."
                                        —*Abilene Reporter-News*

"ROUSING, HARD-BOILED SUSPENSE
. . . tough, energetic . . . packs disturbing
crime scenes, salty language and cynical
working-class views of the power elite."
                                        —*Publishers Weekly*

PRIME SUSPECT

A. W. GRAY

AN ONYX BOOK

ONYX
Published by the Penguin Group
Penguin Books USA Inc., 375 Hudson Street,
New York, New York 10014, U.S.A.
Penguin Books Ltd, 27 Wrights Lane,
London W8 5TZ, England
Penguin Books Australia Ltd, Ringwood,
Victoria, Australia
Penguin Books Canada Ltd, 10 Alcorn Avenue,
Toronto, Ontario, Canada M4V 3B2
Penguin Books (N.Z.) Ltd, 182–190 Wairau Road,
Auckland 10, New Zealand

Penguin Books Ltd, Registered Offices:
Harmondsworth, Middlesex, England

Published by Onyx,
an imprint of New American Library, a division of Penguin Books USA Inc.
Previously published in a Dutton edition.

First Onyx Printing, August, 1993
10 9 8 7 6 5 4 3 2

 REGISTERED TRADEMARK—MARCA REGISTRADA

Printed in Canada

PUBLISHER'S NOTE
This is a work of fiction. Names, characters, places, and incidents either are
the product of the author's imagination or are used fictitiously, and any resemblance to actual persons, living or dead, events, or locales is entirely coinci-
dental.

For Daniel Malcolm Gray
and John Edward Gray,
3.2 college material.
From the old man, who,
when *he* was in college,
thought that 3.2
was Oklahoma beer.

1

On the Third of June, Nineteen Hundred and Seventy-three, J. Percival Hardin III graduated from Berlyn Academy in Fort Worth, Texas, in the upper third of his class. There were forty-nine graduating seniors. The entire baccalaureate assembly, relatives and all, filled less than half of Landreth Auditorium on the TCU campus while a Van Cliburn protégé played "Pomp and Circumstance" on a concert grand piano. The graduating class had voted to forgo the traditional caps and gowns; the men wore plum tuxedos while the female seniors made do with the same formals they planned to wear to the following month's Debutante Ball.

Ross Monroe, whose daughter Marissa was a Berlyn senior, held the postbaccalaureate get-together at his home. The Monroe digs overlooked the seventeenth fairway of Colonial Country Club, and inside the mansion were nine bathrooms and a sixty-foot den. A parlor ensemble from the Fort Worth Symphony provided the music. Percy Hardin got high on Purple Passion, which was grape juice mixed with 180-proof Everclear, and rejoiced over his graduation present from his father, which was a brand-new yellow Grand Prix. He danced every dance save one with Marissa Monroe; the lone dance without Marissa he endured with her mother, Luwanda Monroe the hostess. During a break in the music, Marissa took Percy by the hand and led him outside. The couple strolled along stone pathways through the gardens, talking of college plans while they gazed upon azaleas and impatiens in livid shades of red and yellow and blue, and finally sat down together in the vine-shielded gazebo. There Marissa rewarded Percy with her own graduation present, a blow job which curled his toes into knots.

On the same Sunday, June 3, 1973, and in the same city of Fort Worth, Texas, Lackey No-Middle-Name Ferguson graduated from Richland High, 427th in his class. Lackey's baccalaureate took place in the Tarrant County Convention Center, which boasted the only auditorium in the county large enough for the 736 Richland seniors along with parents, siblings, current wives and husbands of parents, and children of some of the seniors, legitimate and otherwise. The class wore gray caps and gowns rented from Arnold's on the Loop for twenty-six dollars plus a fifty-buck security deposit. The New York Philharmonic Orchestra played "Pomp and Circumstance," though there was quite a lot of static on the convention speakers, and the tape, which was rerecorded from a pirated cassette, lacked a bit in the quality department.

Mr. Hale, the Vice-Principal and Chief Disciplinary Officer at Richland High, called the men of the graduating class aside just prior to the service. "Look, guys," he said, "this may be the end of the line for you, but it's old hat to me. Every year the same shit, so listen up. We've got three thousand people out there, three thousand hardworking folks that came down here to give their little dumplings a send-off, most of them tickled to death 'cause after today they don't have to support you any more. They deserve a nice ceremony. So what I'm saying here is, the first guy I catch playing grab-ass in line, I'm tearing up his diploma and he can just figure on having to fuck with me again next year. Any questions?''

The baccalaureate itself went off pretty smoothly, though Lackey had a hard time accepting his diploma with a straight face after receiving a well-timed goose from Ronnie Ferias just prior to Lackey's walking across the stage. And a secretly pregnant girl named Lucy Martin retired from the service with a bout of morning sickness and had to get her sheepskin by mail. The highlight came shortly after the service ended, when the fathers of the valedictorian and salutatorian went after it with broken beer bottles in the parking lot.

Lackey Ferguson's graduation gifts, which came in the form of cash from uncles and aunts, with ten bucks kicked in by his father, totaled fifty-two dollars. He spent part of the money on a six-pack of Lone Star Beer and the balance at the Jackson Hotel, a whorehouse on South Main.

The following day, while Percy Hardin completed his acceptance letter to Princeton, and while Lackey Ferguson nursed his hangover in the US Army Recruiter's office, the Texas Education Agency entered both young men on a percentage-of-high-school-grads statistics ledger. Aside from their names on the same TEA printout, the two had nothing in common at that point in their lives.

2

with nervous, in you there receiving a million and a half loans already resting; this was one of these a million loans. Trouble was that application that Larry Mickle a loan officer that came into the office, into a form for making a million it would be anytime good as for them. His appearance know... and... the service oaths around the limits of the loan structure and relationship Larry and only known them enough as the future.

Merlyn Graham, whose opinion it was that the only bad loan decisions were the result of bad information, and who attributed his success to prudent use of his time, couldn't figure out who'd screwed up and sent *this* customer in. The young guy was obviously flying by the seat of his pants without the slightest idea what the business world was all about.

"I'm not sure I understand," Graham said. "Our people couldn't show you how to fill out the application?"

The young man fidgeted, then stood and offered the application form across Graham's desk. "That's not exactly it," the young guy said. "No, everybody was really helpful, it's just that none of this applies to me." He seemed earnest enough, around thirty-five with a self-confident way about him, and Graham thought that if the young man would dress in a suit instead of faded jeans, hard-toed lace-up shoes, and an off-white T-shirt, he wouldn't make a bad impression at all.

Graham put on his glasses, snugged the caramel-colored plastic frames up on his nose, shot his snow-white cuff, and pretended to study the form carefully. Rudeness was something that Merlyn Graham wouldn't tolerate in his people, and he believed that courtesy began right up there with the man in charge. "Well, you're not showing much information here," Graham finally said.

"Hey, it's not that I'm being hard to get along with."

The young guy settled back and crossed his legs. "It's just that there are a bunch of questions on there that I don't have any answer to."

Graham was beginning to understand why the people out front had referred the customer. A good-looking guy like this would be one that the loan officers (particularly the token female who'd just come on board) wouldn't have the heart to turn down. No matter, the buck at Ridglea Bank stopped with Merlyn Graham. "Your middle initial is 'X'? What's that, Xavier, or . . . ?"

"It doesn't stand for anything. Lackey X. Ferguson. See I was in the army. If you don't have a middle initial, half the time you don't make payroll. So I added the 'X.' "

"I see," Graham said. The far wall in Graham's office was plate glass; visible beyond Lackey X. Ferguson were secretaries typing, loan officers loaning, and rows of paying and receiving windows. Look busy even if you're not, was Graham's motto. "Well, say, Mr. Ferguson—"

"Lackey. Last names make me nervous, tell you the truth." Lackey X. Ferguson had a full head of center-parted brown hair and a neatly trimmed beard and mustache. His gaze was steady and his manner of speaking, Graham had to admit, was straightforward and pretty impressive. Graham instinctively liked the guy, but reminded himself that liking someone had nothing to do with a loan decision. Letting one's feelings interfere was a sure way to get burned in the long run.

"All right, Lackey then. I've got to tell you that your name and address by themselves don't give us much to go on. Not for a loan of a hundred thousand dollars. I'm not familiar with this street where you live. Is it . . . ?"

"North Richland Hills. You know, on the far north side."

Christ, North Richland Hills. Predominantly blue-collar with a few department store clerks and school teachers thrown in. "That's another problem, as I see it," Graham said. "Ridglea Bank is a long way from home for you. Here we service mostly westside folks. Have you tried one of your banks over there?" Graham was getting just a tad nervous, picturing a conversation he'd had with a fellow CEO at the Petroleum Club. Seems a person such as this young guy had cornered an officer at NCNB recently on the pretext of getting a loan, then had pulled a gun and robbed the place. Christ, could this be the guy?

"No, I . . ." Lackey Ferguson swept the room with his blue-eyed gaze. Could be that he was only nervous, but he might be casing the joint as well. "You see," Ferguson said, "I didn't even know I was going to need the loan until this morning. A guy sent me here."

A referral? Graham flipped to the reverse side of the form. Oh. He sat up straighter, his attitude friendlier. "I should have noticed. Have you known Percy Hardin long?"

"I just met him. I saw his ad in the paper."

"What kind of an ad?"

"Construction. He wants to build a bathhouse which is twice the size of the place I live in. But hey, if these rich guys over here want to piss their money off, who am I to say? I just build things."

"Now we're getting somewhere," Graham said. "You're looking for an interim construction loan. I've got to tell you, Lackey, Mrs. Hardin was by and showed me the plans last week, and I don't think you're wanting to borrow enough money. The quote I saw on the work was a hundred and a half."

"You see that all the time. Somebody's living in one of these rambling castles, everybody wants to hijack the guy. I don't believe in that, plus I've got ways to cut costs that none of these westside contractors have."

"Oh?"

"Yeah," Ferguson said. "See my partner, that's Ronnie Ferias, he's a guy I went through high school with. Ronnie supervises the crews himself so we've got no superintendent to pay. Plus we hire convicts."

"You use convict labor? What's that, some kind of new work-release program the county's got?" Christ, Graham thought, they're paroling all these guys in no time, now they're wanting to put them on the streets while they're still in jail.

"No. *Ex*-cons. Look, it's a federal deal. For every releasee we hire we get a tax deduction. We can pay the guy full wages but save money overall."

Graham pictured a group of felons, all driving nails through their fingers so they could make workmen's compensation claims, and then walking off with half the material on the job while the boss wasn't looking. "Sounds interesting," Graham said. "But let's get back to Square One. The application. Besides the name and address, there's nothing here. What about credit references?"

"That's how I wound up talking to you. It's what I was telling the guy out there, I got no credit references."

"Now hold on," Graham said. "Everyone in business has credit references, good *or* bad. How long have you been in business?"

"Six months, me. Ronnie's been doing it longer. I joined up with him when I got out of the army."

"A serviceman," Graham said. "That's a mark in your favor."

"You'd think so, wouldn't you? I was in seventeen years, resigned as a Master Sergeant."

"Three more years," Graham said, "and you could've had full military retirement. That's unusual, someone getting out after seventeen years." Maybe a Section Eight, Graham thought. Mental Disability.

Lackey Ferguson was beginning to relax, the signs

evident, a man now talking about things familiar to him. "A lot of people tell me that. I got sort of disillusioned, tell you the truth. You know about the Panama invasion, the one where we went after General Noriega?"

"Of course. Who doesn't?"

"There's a lot of things about it you *don't* know. Like charging around invading a bunch of civilians. You should have seen us, running around asking everybody directions, looking for a drug dealer. One guy told me, 'You want to find a drug dealer go to New York City.' "

"An international thug," Graham said. "Masquerading as a military leader."

"I can't argue about that," Ferguson said. "I don't like drug dealers any more than the next guy. But really. I'm standing there in the middle of Panama City, right outside the Panama Hilton Hotel it was, and suddenly it comes to me that this just isn't what it's supposed to be about. I enlisted to *defend* my country. I'm a soldier, not a DEA agent. Anyway, when I got back stateside I put the paperwork in motion to get out. Took another six months."

"We're getting pretty far afield," Graham said, checking his watch. "Why you got out of the army is really your business. But people in the service have credit records. Didn't you ever have any credit cards?"

"Not me," Ferguson said. "One-and-a-half percent on the unpaid balance I can do without."

"And you don't even have a bank account." Graham was really pushing to get rid of the guy now; he had a lunch appointment and this was a waste of precious time. "Any cash on hand?"

"I had fifteen thousand dollars when I got out. Mustering out pay plus this poker game."

Wonderful, Graham thought. We make the loan, he goes to Las Vegas with the money. "That's a lot of cash for someone to carry around."

"I didn't carry it far. I bought my pickup."

"Well, that might be some collateral," Graham said.

"I wouldn't do that," Ferguson said. "What I'd want to do is pay the money back as soon as this Hardin pays me. Say, you know this guy, huh? I guess we could depend on getting paid."

"Well, certainly," Graham said. "We handle Percy Hardin's trust fund. My God, man, you saw the house he's living in."

"Yeah. That's why I was sort of worried about my money. You got any idea what the monthly nut on that place is? What I think is, these westside guys are humping to pay the bills every month just like me, only they got a lot more bills to pay."

Christ, Graham thought, a guy flying by the seat of his pants questioning Percy Hardin's ability to pay. "I'm not seeing much hope in this application, Lackey. Maybe you've got some personal references. Someone who could—"

"Oh, I got a lot of those."

"—cosign for you."

"I wouldn't want anybody doing that."

"It's a lot to ask of someone," Graham said. "But at some time everyone needs a little help. Who do you know that might . . . ?"

Ferguson's brow furrowed into an earnest look of concentration. "Well, there's Ronnie. My partner."

"The guy you went to high school with," Graham said.

"Yeah. He stood right behind me in graduation line. You know, Ferguson, Ferias. *F*."

Graham resisted the impulse to roll his eyes. "Anyone else?"

"Nancy. Nancy Cuellar, my fiancée."

Graham's pulse quickened slightly. Now here was something that might . . . "Cuellar?" he said. "Is she part of the restaurant family?"

Ferguson appeared confused, clearly not getting the point, and didn't say anything.

"The Cuellar family," Graham said. "El Chico Mexican Restaurants. They've got quite a name."

"Oh," Ferguson said. "Nancy's a legal secretary. She put herself through college, I guess that's something to say for her."

"Commendable," Graham said, checking his watch again. "Commendable. Different line of Cuellars."

"I don't see anything wrong with that. Hey, we eat at El Chico's a lot. Under four bucks you can get two chicken enchiladas with sour cream. Nancy's got an uncle, Geraldo, I think he waited tables at El Chico's a few years ago."

"Speaking of enchiladas," Graham said, putting the application aside, straightening up his desk, "I've got a luncheon engagement. I do hate to cut this short."

"Hey, well, don't let me keep you." Ferguson rose and went over to stand by the door. "I guess I'm not getting the loan."

"A few years ago we could take some flyers," Graham said. "But not in the nineteen-nineties atmosphere. These regulators today . . ." He wanted to let Ferguson down easy; success was, in part, never leaving a bad taste in anyone's mouth.

"Well thanks for your time," Ferguson said. "And, tell you what, no hard feelings. We'll be working over at Hardin's house. Can I send my men to you? These guys all got records, and it's, you know, tough on them to find somebody to cash their paychecks."

3

Lackey Ferguson decided on the way over to J. Percival Hardin's house that he wouldn't like living on the west side. Lackey thought that walking around on the lawn and making sure the gardener wasn't fucking up the rosebushes, or sitting out by the pool and reading the *Wall Street Journal* while Nancy sunned on a raft in her string bikini and drank mint juleps, well, that kind of stuff would be kicks for a while. But if a west-side guy wanted to take off his shirt and shoes and lay around watching the ball game, his wife would be all over him about it. Lackey and Nancy had rented a movie, *War of the Roses,* with Michael Douglas and Kathleen Turner, and in the movie Douglas and Turner had been living in a house sort of like the ones in this westside neighborhood. One thing Lackey had noticed (and hadn't mentioned to Nancy for fear she'd start getting ideas) was that Michael Douglas had come to supper in a coat and tie. Duding out for supper was something that could get old in a hurry.

Hardin's home was a ten-minute drive from the bank, down the red-brick paving on Camp Bowie Boulevard with its fancy dress shops and cutesy French pastry restaurants, north on Hulen Street, past clipped lawns the size of polo fields and houses with fountains in their yards, and finally east on a winding, tree-shaded boulevard which offered glimpses of Colonial Country Club. As he pulled his blue and white GMC supercab to the curb in front of Hardin's, Lackey wondered briefly whether Percy Hardin carried his deposits to the bank, or if maybe the worried-looking guy (Graham? Yeah, Merlyn Graham) came over in person to save Hardin the trouble. Lackey couldn't understand why the banker had seemed so worried; it was pretty obvious that Ridglea Bank didn't lend any money to anybody who needed the loan to begin with. If a guy really needed some money he could try and get it from his brother-in-law.

The pickup was spotless and its chrome gleamed like polished sterling. Lackey and Nancy had spent part of Sunday afternoon washing the truck and vacuuming out the inside, taking extra care with the windows to be sure there weren't any smudges; Lackey couldn't afford to show up in search of a contract on the bathhouse in a dirty pickup. Like he'd told Ronnie Ferias, getting the bathhouse job wasn't a matter of life and death, but it was pretty important. Remodeling kitchens and enclosing back porches into extra bedrooms put food on the table and paid the rent, but something like this bathhouse job was pure gravy. Lackey and Nancy had set the date—August 15th—and the westside job would give them a nice honeymoon in San Francisco three months from now. San Francisco was the one place that Nancy had always wanted to go. Lackey had been there when he was in the army, and picturing Nancy strolling along on Fisherman's Wharf with the seabreeze whipping her dark hair made Lackey want to take her. He was going to get this bathhouse job, bank loan or no. He'd just have to figure something out. He climbed down from the pickup and crossed the lawn toward the house.

Hardin lived in a two-story gothic of dark red stone. The house was seventy-five years old if it was a day. During the brief meeting he'd had with the Hardins in their parlor that morning, Lackey had done some looking around. He'd decided that the parlor furniture alone had probably cost more than Lackey and Ronnie had made in the past six months, and the paintings that hung over the mantel were probably good for a couple of years' worth of remodeling jobs. The house appeared enormous as seen from the street; as Lackey drew nearer the structure loomed like Texas Stadium.

He passed the gardener, a Mexican guy in overalls who was clipping a hedge. Lackey nodded and winked, and the gardener smiled. He'd tried talking to the gardener that morning and found that the guy didn't speak any English, which made Lackey wish he'd brought Nancy along. The gardener paused in his hedge-clipping to mop his forehead with a handkerchief. The noon mid-May temperature was nearing ninety degrees, and Lackey decided that he wouldn't take the job as Percy Hardin's gardener unless they'd let him work in his bathing suit.

He went up a stone walkway between twin two-story pointed spires and skirted a fountain on his way to the front porch. The fountain showed thick green plants waving gently beneath the surface of the water, and maybe a thousand trout-sized goldfish that wriggled about and flicked their tails among the leaves.

Percy Hardin waited on the porch. Hardin was fretting about something, pacing back and forth with his hands clasped behind his back. He was a tall, slender blond, wearing baggy navy pants with pockets in the legs, and a blousy pink Remert knit shirt whose hem was snug around his hips. His sleeves hung to his elbows. Nancy watched the fashion pages like a hawk and wanted Lackey to try the oversize look; Lackey personally thought that guys dressed like Percy Hardin looked as though their clothes didn't fit. Lackey climbed the three steps up on the red-stone porch and said hello.

Hardin's lips were thin, and his eyes were hidden behind black sunglasses with silver wire frames. He reached up under his shirt to scratch his ribs, at the same time snapping the fingers of his free hand as he said, "Let's see, you're the . . ."

It took a couple of seconds for Lackey to get it; it had only been two hours since he'd talked to this guy. Finally Lackey said, "Contractor. We talked about the bathhouse you want behind your pool. You sent me over to your bank to talk about interim financing, remember?"

The fingers snapped again. "Sure. Sure, of course. Merlyn Graham fix you up?"

"Well, not exactly. He didn't have the interest rate I was looking for."

"I know just what you mean," Hardin said. "The bastards really stick it to you for money these days. For a hundred thou, though, what the hell. I don't know as I'd be shopping around that much."

"Yeah. Yeah, a lousy hundred," Lackey said. "But all those points, well, it just rubbed me the wrong way is all. Tell you the truth, I got an alternate plan to run by you."

"Hey, I like that. A man that lives by his principles. Look, do you mind? I'm running way late." Hardin went over to lean on a set of golf clubs, Ping Eye irons and woods with fuzzy headcovers inside a big pink leather bag like the touring pros had.

Lackey thought, Do I mind what? No, the guy wants to lean on his golf clubs, I don't mind. Percy Hardin seemed a little weird to begin with, and if Hardin wanted to lean on his golf bag, then Lackey Ferguson sure as hell didn't have anything to say about it. "Suit yourself," Lackey said.

"No, I mean"—Hardin flashed a plastic smile—"would you mind carrying these out to the curb for me? My regular help took the day off."

Lackey permitted himself one blink, then decided that if he was going to get this bathhouse job he'd better do what Percy Hardin wanted. Just think of Nancy on Fisherman's Wharf with the wind in her hair. Better yet, picture Nancy without any clothes, that should do the trick. "Sure, no problem," Lackey said. Then he hefted the golf bag and slipped the strap over his shoulder and followed Hardin down the steps and around the fountain. Hardin walked with long strides, his hands swinging loosely by his hips, his head moving slowly from side to side like a guy used to giving orders and having everyone jump when he said the word.

"Wouldn't you know they'd pick this morning to be late," Hardin said. "Fucking *years* I've been trying to get in the group with Norman. Finally I'm in and stand a good chance of missing my practice round."

Lackey wanted to say, Norman who? But he had enough to do carrying the golf clubs, so just struggled along without saying anything. The golf equipment must have weighed seventy-five pounds with all those extra wedges and crap in there, and Lackey wondered whether he could carry the bag for eighteen holes, reading the break on putts and telling Percy Hardin what club to hit. Be a tossup.

"Of course, the real thing's not till Wednesday," Hardin said, "and usually the club's closed on Monday. But NIT week they let us get in extra practice rounds."

Lackey said between huffs and puffs, "I thought the NIT was in Madison Square Garden." He quickened his pace, doing his best to keep up with Hardin as they crossed the yard. The tiff grass was the color of pool-table felt and, Lackey knew, required tons of water in the Texas heat to keep it from burning out.

Hardin stopped and looked around. "Madison . . . ? Oh, you're talking about basketball. Hey, pretty funny, I like that. Colonial. Colonial National Invitational, that's what I'm talking about. I'm getting ready for the pro-am. Do you play golf?"

"Yeah, some. Me and Ronnie Ferias and a couple of other guys go out to Rockwood sometimes on Sat-

urday mornings. Say, you'll meet Ronnie if we do the
bathhouse. He's my partner.''

"Oh. Rockwood Muny," Hardin said, as though he
was saying, Oh, what a pile of shit. Which Rockwood
was, Lackey supposed, big patches of bare ground in
the fairways and greens so bumpy you'd miss a four-
footer about half the time. Then Hardin said, "Give
me a minute, huh?" and went over to say something
to the gardener in Spanish.

Lackey set the bag down; the clubs shifted and made
hollow thunking noises. A towel hung from the bag
ring, and Lackey used the towel to wipe the sweat
from his forehead. Not only was it hot as hell, the
humidity must be ninety percent or so, and Lackey
decided right then and there that no way would he be
a caddy. He was pretty impressed that Hardin could
speak Spanish; in fact Lackey himself had thought
about taking a night course at Tarrant County Junior
College so that he and Nancy could speak Spanish to
one another. But on second thought, Hardin's Spanish
wasn't lilting and musical like Nancy's; Hardin spoke
Spanish like a guy who'd taken the language in school
and liked to try it out on Mexican waiters. Lackey
decided that if his own Spanish was going to sound
like Percy Hardin's, then he'd as soon not learn to
speak Spanish at all. Whatever Hardin was saying to
the gardener must have been pretty good; the guy
stopped clipping the hedge and took off for the corner
of the house with a big pass-the-enchiladas grin on his
face. Come to think about it, Lackey thought, how
come that gardener's not carrying these golf clubs instead of me? At least the guy's getting paid.

When the gardener had disappeared from view, Hardin gave Lackey a come-on motion and continued on
his way toward the street. Lackey sighed, shouldered
the bag, and took off after Hardin like Gunga Din.
Hardin said, "That's one way to keep the help in line.
Give them the day off every once in a while, then when

you ask 'em for a little extra they don't have any argument.'' As Lackey was wondering if he was included as one of the help, Hardin paused, hands on hips. ''Well, it's about time. About fucking time,'' Hardin said.

Lackey followed Hardin's gaze. A white Lincoln stretch limo had come abreast of the house and was angling to the curb behind Lackey's pickup. The limo was every bit as spotless as Lackey's truck, and its windows were one-way black. ''Yeah,'' Lackey said. ''You'd think people would be more considerate. Listen, about the bathhouse.''

Hardin's lips twisted in thought. Then he said, ''Oh, yeah, the bathhouse. I thought we had that settled this morning.''

''Well, I did, too. But that was before I had the problem at the bank.''

Lackey realized that Hardin wasn't really listening; the slender blond guy was in a hurry to make his tee time, and anything as pissant as a hundred-thousand-dollar bathhouse was something he didn't have time to fuck with. The limo's trunk lid sprung open with a metallic *pop,* and a uniformed chauffeur hopped out and hustled to the rear. The backseat window slid down with an electric hum, and a man of about fifty stuck his head outside. He wore a snow white golf shirt and had silver curly hair combed straight back. ''I get four strokes a side,'' he said. Then, glancing at Lackey, ''Got you a new man, huh?''

Hardin jerked a thumb in Lackey's direction. ''This guy? No, this guy's . . . what's your name again, guy?''

Lackey said, ''Huh?'' then got it and said quickly, ''Lackey Ferguson,'' and then said to the silver-haired guy, ''How you doing?''

''He's here to talk about the bathhouse,'' Hardin said. ''You know, *that* fucking deal.''

The silver-haired man climbed out to stand on the

curb. "Yeah, a honey-do. 'Honey, do this and honey, do that.' My old lady's wanting a doghouse that some guys wish *they* could live in." In addition to the golf shirt he wore gray slacks, and he was round shouldered with a protruding belly. "Well, listen, Lackey. Slide them sticks over to my man back there. We got tracks to make."

"Hold it," Hardin said. Then, as Lackey was wondering, What sticks? Hardin came over and unzipped one bulky side pocket on the golf bag. He took out a pair of pale pink golf shoes, held them pinched together in one hand and said to Lackey, "Give the clubs to the chauffeur. That's a good man." Then Hardin walked past the silver-haired guy to sit sideways on the limo's back seat and take one sneaker off.

Lackey was beginning to do a slow burn, but thought about the bathhouse job and decided that Percy Hardin was something that he was just going to have to put up with. He lugged the clubs back to the trunk where the chauffeur waited. The chauffeur was a thin guy of about forty who looked as though he knew which side his bread was buttered on. He rolled his eyes at Lackey as he loaded the clubs into the trunk. Lackey went back to stand beside the limo and said to Percy Hardin, "Listen, on the bathhouse deal, I got to have some answers. I hate to push you, but me and my partner got to make some plans."

Hardin paused, then winked at the silver-haired man. "What's to talk about?" Hardin said, then bent over to tie the laces on one golf shoe. On his other foot he wore only a white sock.

"Well," Lackey said, "it's the financing. I'm going to—"

"Wait a minute." Hardin yanked the laces into a bow, then eased his stockinged foot into the other golf shoe. "Let me make sure you get the big picture here. That bathhouse. I don't care about that bathhouse. I don't give a *shit* about that bathhouse. My *wife* wants the bathhouse, not me. I want to play some golf. So what you need to do is, you need to talk to my wife. Okay? Now if you're going to do the job, I'll see you around. Let's get cracking, Sam.'' Then, as the silver-haired guy climbed into the front seat beside the chauffeur, Hardin swung his legs inside the car and slammed the door. The limo moved slowly and smoothly away from the curb as the rear window beside Hardin hummed and slid upward.

Lackey cupped his hands to his mouth. "Hey. Hey, well, is your wife at home?''

"She was the last time I checked,'' Hardin said loudly. He disappeared from view as the window closed. The limo picked up speed.

Lackey watched the limo round the corner, then stalked away in the direction of the house. He was pissed, but forced his emotions down to a low boil. Bitching at Hardin's wife wasn't going to help. As he moved between the spires and went around the fountain, Lackey wondered if Percy Hardin was into something crooked. Everyone Lackey knew who did nothing but hang around Rockwood and play golf all the time was either dead broke or dealing dope, and it was a cinch that Hardin wasn't broke. Lackey decided that if he was going to do the bathhouse, he needed to keep his eyes and ears open.

Lackey stood on the porch with the fountain at his back and rang the doorbell. Chimes played four high notes from within the house, the sound muffled by the thick oak door. Lackey waited first on one foot and then the other, picturing himself saying to Nancy, Look, Ronnie and me got a tee time, how about taking care of this little bathhouse deal for me? Nancy would probably tell him to jump in the lake. He turned around, folded his arms and gazed across the street. Directly across from Hardin's was a white two-story Colonial; next door to the Colonial was a brick Spanish house with a red tiled roof and a verandah. Lackey pressed the button a second time; the four chimes played one more set.

Static emitted from a speaker camouflaged into the carved doorframe, and Lackey jumped slightly as a soft and cultured female voice said, "Who is it?"

Lackey couldn't come up with much of a mental picture of Mrs. Percy Hardin; Hardin had done all of the talking in his sitting room that morning while his wife had run back and forth in a terrycloth robe with a bandanna around her head, bringing coffee. In fact, Lackey couldn't remember Mrs. Hardin having said a word. He leaned close to the doorframe and said, "Lackey Ferguson, Mrs. Hardin. Your husband said I should talk to you about the bathhouse."

There was a *pop* from the speaker, then she said, "You're yelling and you're too close. I can't understand you, just speak normally."

Lackey put his hands on his waist and said as though she were standing right beside him, "Lackey Ferguson, the contractor. About the bathhouse. That better?"

"Sure. Sure, just a minute." Chains rattled, dead bolts slid, and the door opened halfway. "Everybody does it wrong," Mrs. Percy Hardin said. "I'm going to have a sign printed. 'Speak normally,' or something." She was wearing a flouncy white pleated tennis dress, and her skin was the color of a Brandy Alexander. Her legs were long and slim, and the hair she'd hidden earlier under the bandanna was honey blond, combed straight down on both sides of a center part and cut into a measured line midway between her ears and the base of her neck. At first glance she could have been a college girl; a closer look revealed little crinkles around her brown eyes. Her gaze swept him head to toe. "Well, are you going to do it?" she said.

"Huh?" Lackey said. "Excuse me, but do what?"

She showed a strange smile as though she had a

secret and blinked. "The bathhouse. What did you think I was talking about?" Then, as she stood aside, "Hey, come on in. I'm Marissa, and if you ever call me Mrs. Hardin again I'll fire you." Lackey caught a whiff of perfume mixed with bath oil as he went by her and entered the house.

The entry hall floor was stone tile. A six-foot grandfather clock stood in the foyer. Its pendulum was the size of a basketball, swinging back and forth, back and forth, ticking and tocking. The hall was about twenty feet long and opened into a mammoth den complete with floating staircase. The den's vaulted ceiling was two stories overhead and held six curtained skylights. The staircase was around twenty feet wide and ascended to a second-floor balcony with a carved wood railing. As Lackey followed Marissa Hardin into the den, the stone floor gave way to rich brown carpet with foam padding underneath. "I'm having a shake," Marissa Hardin said. "Come on."

On the way through the den they passed a long, low sofa, a baby grand piano, and a Sony rear-projection bigscreen TV. The sitting room where Lackey had talked to Percy Hardin was on his left, through yawning double doors. Marissa Hardin walked like a majorette on parade, the hem of her skirt popping from side to side in rhythm with her hips, and she threw two quick, hey-are-you-watching-me glances over her shoulder. Women who made sure that everyone was watching their fannies were turnoffs to Lackey; Nancy handled the looks from men as though she didn't notice them. Lackey followed Marissa around the foot of the stairs, down a narrow hallway and into the kitchen.

The kitchen might have been as big as the living room at Lackey's own house, he wasn't sure. There were what seemed like a hundred feet of counter space, an island stove, a mammoth stained oak table with chairs whose legs were carved into lions' paws. Also there was a built-in double oven and microwave, and matching refrigerator and standup freezer. Marissa's hands were soft as a teenager's; Lackey doubted that she'd ever operated the stove or ovens.

On the counter stood a ten-speed blender half-full of what looked to be orange juice. Marissa pressed a button; the blender's motor buzzed and the juice whipped instantly into white-orange foam. "There's a raw egg in it," Marissa said, "and I dumped in a little powdered sugar. Want some?" She pressed the switch again; the frothy liquid settled and fizzed. Marissa watched Lackey over her shoulder, her lips parted and her eyes widened slightly. *Hey, are you watching me? Don't I look good?* Lackey's cheeks flushed and he averted his gaze.

"Yeah, I'll try a little," Lackey said. Then, as she looked as though she was going to laugh he said quickly, "Some orange juice ought to hit the spot. About the bathhouse, Mrs. Hardin." He sat down at the table and folded his hands in a businesslike posture.

"Marissa, I told you." She stood on the balls of her feet, rummaged in a cabinet, found two squatty glasses and set them on the counter. As she poured the drinks, Lackey kept his gaze riveted on two huge brass cooking spoons, crisscrossed on the wall above the sink. Marissa carried the now full tumblers over, set one in front of Lackey, then sat in the chair nearest him so that their knees practically touched. "What about it?" she said.

"About the bathhouse?"

She sipped, regarding him over the rim of her glass, then licked her lips daintily. "What else?"

He shifted his legs away from her so that he couldn't feel her body heat through his jeans. "Well, there are a couple of things," he said.

"What things? You saw the plans and said you'd take the job. What else is there? You're built like a weightlifter.'' Marissa's nose was slender and there was a back-East finishing-school tilt to her pointed chin.

Jesus Christ, Lackey thought, this is all I need, her husband fucking around on the golf course. He had a sip of the orange juice concoction. It wasn't bad; reminded him of Orange Julius. ''I'll level with you,'' he said. ''We need the job, me and my partner, and there's a problem with money.''

''Not with Percy,'' she said. ''That's one thing he *doesn't* have a problem with.''

''I'm not talking about *your* money. It's us. Look, we've got quite a few remodeling jobs going that are paying the rent, but to tell you the truth we don't have the money to do this job for you without an advance. I went over to your husband's bank this morning and asked for a loan. They wouldn't even talk to me.''

She picked up her glass and ran her finger around in the circle of moisture left on the table. She wore clear lacquer polish on her nails. ''You didn't answer me,'' she said. ''Are you a weightlifter?''

He nervously scratched his Adam's apple. ''Mrs. Har—''

''Marissa, dammit.''

''Okay, whatever. I need this job because I'm getting married in a couple of months.''

She leaned back and supported her elbow with the palm of her opposite hand, holding her glass off to one side. She smiled. ''Why?''

''Why am I getting married?''

''I've had fourteen years of it and it's a pile of shit,'' she said. ''Back when Percy and I were both in college—he was at Princeton and I went to Stephens College in Missouri—back then we'd only see each other during the summers and we used to screw like rabbits. Take it from me, marriage is a pile of shit.''

''Now look, Mrs.—''

''Marissa. I'm telling you, if you won't call me Marissa I'm through with you. Say it.''

He couldn't help looking her over. Most guys Lackey knew would jump at this. What the hell, if it wasn't for Nancy . . . ''Say what?'' Lackey said.

''My name. Yours is Lackey, I don't have any problem with that. Now you say mine.''

He swallowed. ''Marissa.''

''That's better. It will do for starters, anyway. Now, are you a weightlifter?''

''I did some in the army. Hey, I don't think it'll take much. I can get the slab poured and the water and electrical in for fifteen thousand dollars, less than that if it wasn't for the spa you want.''

She propped her knee against the table and touched her own tanned thigh. ''Oh, I couldn't do without that. My muscles get sore. I do a lot of stair walking and bicycling.''

Lackey took another drink and forced himself to look away from her leg. He had to have the bathhouse job. ''You don't think the fifteen thousand would be a problem?'' he said.

She moved her jaw slightly to one side and arched an eyebrow. ''None at all. If you can convince me.''

''Convince you?''

She leaned over to gently touch his forearm. ''That you need it. Come on, Lackey, how badly do you need it?''

Jesus, he thought, talk about anything. He said, ''Well, we could live without it, but I wouldn't have much of a honeymoon.''

She pursed her lips and gave the air a smacky kiss. ''Poor baby.''

His jaws tensed. ''Look, I'm not sure what you've got in mind—''

''You're not?''

''—but I can guarantee you you won't find anybody to do a better job.''

She brushed her own thigh. ''I certainly hope not.''

''But that's all there is, Mrs. Hardin. A new bathhouse and a damn good one.'' He folded his arms and met her gaze squarely.

''Maris—'' She paused and studied him, caught something in his look, lowered her eyes. ''How much of an advance did you say?''

''Fifteen thousand dollars. And, tell you what, I'll get you a receipt for every nickel. It's just to pay for labor and materials, Ronnie and me won't take a dime for ourselves till the job's finished.''

Lackey supposed that he'd sort of put her down, and he felt a slight twinge of guilt about that. But he had to let her know that all he was interested in was the job, and that the job didn't include any screwing around. She sure was one nice-looking female, and nine guys out of ten would have taken her up on it. He wondered how it would feel to have a pile of money, own this monster of a home and all, and be married to a woman who kept herself in shape and who came on to guys who dropped by to talk about building a bathhouse. Lackey decided he'd take Nancy and a one-bedroom in North Richland Hills any old time. His breath caught just a fraction as he waited for her answer.

''Wait here a minute,'' Marissa Hardin finally said. ''I'll have to get my checkbook.''

Marissa stood with the door open and watched Lackey Ferguson go, watched the broad shoulders move under the fabric of his T-shirt, his tapered waist and strong buttocks and legs in faded jeans, as he paused for a moment by the fountain to watch the goldfish, then continued on between the spires and disappeared from view in the yard. She leaned her forehead against the frame, felt the roughness of wood on her skin, sniffed the fragrance of stained oak. *Christ, Marissa Monroe Hardin. Jesus H. Christ, the guy must think you're a thousand kinds of an idiot.*

She closed and secured the door, turning the knob

to slide the deadbolt raspingly into place, rattling the chain as she moved the metal catch into the slot, then slowly retraced her steps toward the kitchen. A stack of mail was on a table beside the grandfather clock; she picked up the letters and thumbed through them. It was the third time that morning she'd gone through the mail, not really seeing a thing that was printed on the envelopes—using the mail as a pacifier to keep from screaming out loud and kicking her feet. She absently laid the mail aside and continued on through the den, a lithe, smoothly tanned woman whose tennis dress hugged her figure, moving silently in L.A. Gear sneakers with hot pink laces, thinking things over and deciding that Edna Rafferty was totally full of shit.

Edna Rafferty was Marissa's tennis partner at Colonial Country Club—they were to play a doubles match in an hour and a half—and to hear Edna tell it, she was banging half of the men on Fort Worth's west side along with the front four on the Dallas Cowboys football team. If hubby's too busy to take care of you, Edna said, then you've got to get it somewhere, honey. Edna's husband Donald was a film distributor and spent a good part of his time on the coast, which, Edna said, fit right in with Edna's sex life. Edna said, Edna said, Edna *said*. Marissa wondered how much of what Edna said was real and how much was fantasy. She pictured Edna alone in her bedroom with a row of vibrators, naming one Tom, another Charley, still another Troy Aikman. The image of Edna and all those electronic lovers caused Marissa to giggle out loud as she went into the kitchen.

The problem was that Marissa really didn't *want* an affair, never had and never would. She knocked herself out keeping her body in shape—two miles of jogging three times a week, workouts with ankle weights while Twisted Sister blared from the stereo, endless hours of tennis even though in truth she despised the game—for one reason and one only: She wanted her god-damned husband to quit screwing around and become her lover.

In the past three years Marissa had had sex with her husband fourteen times. Exactly fourteen, and anyone who wanted to bet her that it was really *approximately* fourteen would be wasting their money. She vividly recalled each time—could give the date and time of day, in fact—and each time she'd gotten the feeling that Percy was forcing himself. Jesus Christ, *forcing* himself, as though making it with his own wife was something he was *required* to do.

So. Was Percy screwing around? Definitely, though with whom she didn't know, and the thought of him in the sack with another female made Marissa sick to her stomach. And if her husband was screwing around, did that give Marissa the right to do the same? Of course it did, but there was this one little problem. It had been so many years since she'd been with another man—a total of two times, in fact, and those had been in high school—that she didn't have the slightest idea where to begin. And here she'd gotten up the nerve to make some moves on this contractor guy—not that it had taken all that much effort, the guy was quite a hunk and Marissa really wouldn't have minded following through with it—and the guy had *rejected* her. Had rejected Marissa Monroe Hardin right there in the kitchen of her million-dollar home. Just who in hell did he think he was messing around with?

Marissa sat down at her kitchen table, took an angry gulp of her orange-juice-and-egg shake, picked up the phone and pressed the buttons. She listened for a moment, then said, "Edna?" Then listened some more and said, "I did it. This contractor guy came over, and Christ, was he a *hunk*. Four times we did it, can you believe it?" And felt a twinge of conscience as she hunched over the table to hear Edna Rafferty tell a lie of her own.

4

Lackey decided that he wasn't going to talk about the rich lady sort of coming on to him. There just wasn't any point in telling anyone, half of them wouldn't believe it had happened to begin with, and the other half wouldn't believe that Lackey had turned her down.

He pictured Ronnie Ferias's reaction: "You're telling me that there she was, this good-looking rich broad and she was offering it and you were turning it down? You are one dumb *chingarro,* you know that?"

Or Nancy's: "Come on, you expect me to believe that? I mean, we're both adults, Lackey. And by the way, you can forget about building any bathhouse over there. Turned her down? What a bunch of *caca.*" *Caca,* that's what she'd say. Nancy never cussed unless it was in Spanish, where Lackey would have to go and ask Ronnie Ferias what she'd said. And then half the time Ronnie would tell him wrong, and then Ronnie and Nancy would get a big laugh over it.

No way. Lackey Ferguson was going to keep his lip buttoned and go on about his business. But done it he had, walked right into that Astrodome of a house, turned down the lady's damn-near-straight-out offer, and now he was leaving with her fifteen-thousand-dollar check in his pocket.

Jesus H. Christ.

He stopped in his tracks near the curb, twenty feet from the nose of his pickup, put his hands on his hips and lowered his head. The check. He'd been so glad to get her to write the check that he hadn't even noticed when she'd asked him to spell out his name. She'd made the check out to Lackey Ferguson, personally, and Lackey Ferguson didn't have a bank account. Dammit, he should have had her make the check payable to F&F Construction, for Ferguson and Ferias.

Well, he still had time to fix it. She was right behind him, standing there in her doorway, wondering how this dumb construction worker from North Richland Hills had walked out without taking her up on her offer. All he had to do was turn around, retrace his steps to the porch, ask her to . . .

But he couldn't take the chance. What if the lady changed her mind? Odds were that she might, once she thought it over.

Nope, he was going to have to take the check as it was, carry the check over to the Ridglea Bank and cash it at the window. Lackey pictured the look on the snooty banker Merlyn Graham when the contractor turned up with a fifteen-thousand-dollar check from Mrs. Percy Hardin. Eat your heart out, Mr. Graham, bet you'll think twice before you turn the next guy down for a loan. Lackey didn't like the idea of carrying all that cash around, but later he could get with Ronnie and deposit the cash in the construction company's account. He dropped his hands to his sides and went around the pickup's nose to the driver's side. His and Nancy's wash job was perfect; even the edges of the sideview mirror were spotless. There was one mote of dirt beneath the doorhandle; he bent to clean it with his sleeve.

Lackey got in and started the engine. There was a pop from the stereo speakers, then Kenny Rogers and Dolly Parton filled the cab's interior with perfect off-key harmony: "Islands in the Stream." He pulled slowly from the curb and picked up speed, his thoughts on the check in his pocket and the reaction from the highbrow banker when Lackey showed up at the pay window. He was so caught up in his thoughts that the white Volvo bearing down on him from the opposite direction didn't register until it was almost too late. Jesus, he was going to . . .

The Volvo was speeding and was hogging the road, its tires a good foot over the median. Lackey reacted on pure instinct; he whipped the steering wheel to the right. His full weight slammed into the door with an impact which jarred his neck muscles. Rubber squealed as he fought to keep from jumping the curb. The Volvo flashed by on his left, and for a fleeting instant the Volvo driver's face was scant feet from Lackey's nose: bulldog face with a pinched expression, thinning brown hair combed straight back from a sloping forehead, a big bent nose like a parrot's beak. The face disappeared as the Volvo rushed past with a draft that rocked the pickup slightly on its springs.

The pickup came to a jarring halt. Lackey's breath escaped his lips in a relieved whoosh as he shifted his gaze to the sideview mirror. The Volvo hadn't even broken stride. Its window was down; a long arm extended and a bony hand clenched into a fist, relaxed, then formed the universal fuck-you sign. The guy in the Volvo was shooting Lackey the finger.

Lackey gripped the wheel, shook his head and gained control of himself. What an asshole the guy had to be. Lackey gave the pickup a little gas and moved on. This west side of town was dangerous. He needed to get on back to North Richland Hills.

Everett Wilson's sentiments were that the yokel in the pickup could get out of the way or get run over, and if the dumb prick didn't like it he could step the fuck out on the curb. Everett Thomas Wilson was one full-growed man that you didn't want to fuck with, and he'd just as soon the guy in the pickup find it out the hard way. The truck had made one helluva racket, fishtailing and squealing its tires, so Everett decided he'd better make the block before going in the house and killing the woman.

Which was what made Everett different, to his way of thinking, from the ignorant bastards in the Texas Department of Corrections. Most of those fucking morons would have gone on in and done the woman with the neighbors gaping out their windows, which was one reason they were still in lockdown while Everett was breathing the free.

There wouldn't be no more accidents like the last time. And a pure accident it had been, no doubt about it, the dumb-lucky patrol car happening by the house in Houston's Bel Aire district just as Everett was climbing in the window. Probably the two cops had been driving up and down the street hunting a place to take a nap and had happened on poor unlucky Everett Wilson instead. Well, that shit's over with, Everett thought.

Absolutely no way had Everett known the little girl was sleeping in that bedroom. He'd known it was the child's room, sure he had—Everett Wilson never did no job without staking out the territory. But how could he have known the little girl was in there copping z's? He'd pled guilty to Attempted Burglary on a pretty cushy plea bargain, but the cop's notation in his file about the girl in the room had caused the Texas Department of Corrections to house him with the sex offenders. Jesus Christ, who'd have believed it? A bad motherfucker like Everett Thomas Wilson sleeping with a bunch of lousy *perverts*. Two extra years in the joint it had cost him, because Everett Thomas Wilson hated perverts so much he'd beat the crap out of two or three of the bastards, and had spent most of his time in solitary. Which hadn't set too well with the parole board, a guy in the hole all the time, even though he'd never have gone to solitary to begin with if it hadn't been for the stinking perverts.

And the perverts? Why the lying slimy bastards had

gone and spread the word that the real reason Everett
had gone to the hole was that he'd been giving it to a
guy up the ass, had gone berserk and had nearly killed
the guy. What a bunch of bullshit. Hell, the guy had
wanted to get roughed up a little. Had practically
begged for it.

Everett made the block slowly, like a guy who might
be interested in buying a house, or maybe a hick from
the sticks who'd heard about these Fort Worth westside
mansions and was getting an eyeful. He was hoping
he didn't run into another dumb bastard like the guy
in the pickup who'd make him lose his cool; he had to
do the job in a hurry and get away from the neighborhood. He took the final turn and parked in front of the
gothic house with the twin spires guarding the fountain. The automatic sprinkler system had come on.
Fine sprays shot upward at intervals; the droplets glis-
tened and made rainbows.

Everett's hands trembled slightly as he pictured the
woman. Jesus, but that broad was put together. He'd
watched her twice on the country club tennis court,
running, serving, her legs moving like supple pistons,
and once he'd watched her from the top of the wall
behind her pool as she'd sunned herself. He couldn't
decide which way he liked her best, in flying action
on the tennis court or stretched out on the bank in her
maroon bikini. Either way she'd make a man's balls
ache. You're really lucky, girl, Everett thought. Really
lucky that it's old Everett coming by and not one of
those lousy perverts from the Texas Department of
Corrections. One of those sex perverts would do
something awful to a woman with your shape. Not old
Everett, though. Everett Thomas Wilson knows how
to treat a woman.

A dozen yellow roses wrapped in waxpaper lay on
the seat, and now he picked them up and sniffed. He
flashed a crooked-toothed grin. Roses for the sweet,

he thought. Not a woman in this world doesn't like roses.

His grin fading only slightly, Everett climbed out of the Volvo and went up the stone pathway in an odd, side-canted gait, a man with heavy stooped shoulders and arms the length of an orangutan's, his swinging fingertips on a level with his kneecaps. The guards at TDC had called him Monkey Man, the lousy bastards. One bad motherfucker like Everett Wilson locked up in a solitary cage and all these spick and nigger guards calling him Monkey Man. "Hey, Monkey Man, want a banana? We having oranges today, I'll give you one if you don't throw it at me." One of these days he was going back down to Palestine, Texas, and catch one of those Eastham Unit guards off duty. Show the bastard a fucking Monkey Man.

Everett wore a dark blue shirt with sleeves that quit a good six inches above his wrists, and khaki work pants whose cuffs were rolled up. His thick legs were as short as his arms were long, and he'd never found a pair of pants in his life whose waist fit him—size 36—unless the pants legs dragged the ground. It was a joke that God had played, and Everett hated God just as much as he hated the dirty bastards who called him Monkey Man.

He ignored the mist thrown by the sprinklers as he went up the pathway, passed between the spires, and skirted the fountain. He could have made the trip with his eyes closed. The last time he'd come up the path had been at two o'clock the previous morning, and he'd sat down on the steps leading to the porch and had smoked a cigarette. He had a pretty good idea of the house's interior layout as well, having been on all four sides and having peeked through every downstairs window and once even having perched on top of the wall behind the pool in broad daylight, sweeping the upstairs windows with a pair of binoculars. He'd seen the woman through the binoculars as she'd passed a window. She'd been wearing shorts and a halter, and there had been an instant tightening in Everett's crotch. He'd resisted the urge to unzip his fly and play with himself, more proof, to his way of thinking, that Everett Thomas Wilson was no lousy stinking pervert from the Texas Department of Corrections. One of those fucking guys would have pulled it out right there on top of the wall.

Everett whistled softly as he ascended the steps with a little hop-and-skip, then paused before the door. After a final quick glance behind him, he clenched the flowers between his teeth through the waxpaper. Then he fished a pair of thin latex surgeon's gloves from his hip pocket. He hated the fucking gloves, absolutely despised anything that interfered with his sense of touch. Like putting on a rubber, though the gloves kept a man out of trouble. He worked his fingers in one at a time, then stretched the ends of the gloves above his wrists and released them with sharp elastic *pops*. The .44 Bulldog was heavy in his right hip pocket; he touched the gun through the fabric of his pants and adjusted the handle upward. He smoothed his thinning hair back with his palm, then took the roses in his left hand and ran his tongue over his crooked front teeth. Smiling, feeling the bulge growing in his crotch, Everett Wilson stepped forward and rang the doorbell. Get ready for the time of your life, girl, Everett thought. Your man is coming to call.

Marissa Hardin was switching the receiver from one ear to the other, wanting to interrupt Edna Rafferty's lie with one of her own. The chiming of the doorbell gave Marissa the chance. "Hey, someone's here," she said. "I think he's coming back for more."

"Well, don't forget we're playing tennis." Edna's voice was nasal, her tone just a little bit jealous.

Finally got one-up on her, Marissa thought. "I won't," she said. "We've got over an hour. 'Bye now.'' As she hung up, Marissa wondered how many other women in the neighborhood spun yarns about their own affairs while their husbands were out doing the real thing. She left the kitchen and headed for the front of the house.

It was probably a salesman at the door, and Marissa felt a twinge of irritation with Percy for letting the maid off. Or if he was going to let the maid have a free day, he should have at least given the gardener inside duty. Answering one's own doorbell was something a westside person never did. A lack of servants was the first sign of a dwindling bankroll, and a westside wife coming to her door in person was sure to set the tongues awagging. *Guess what. I went by Marissa Hardin's to talk about the Fort Worth Symphony Fundraiser, and she let me in her ownself. You don't reckon they're in trouble, do you? Be a rotten shame.* Marissa detoured through the den and crept into the parlor and peeked through the drapes. If the person on the porch was someone she knew, Marissa was going to pretend that she wasn't home.

A delivery guy or a handyman looking for work, that's what the man had to be. Slope-shouldered and powerfully built, a man with a big nose and a weak chin, standing on the porch holding what looked to be a bouquet of flowers wrapped in waxpaper. So he was making a delivery. Well, if the contractor won't come across, Marissa thought with a fierce giggle, what's wrong with the deliveryman? *Jesus Christ, Marissa, have you completely lost your mind?* She went quickly through the entry hall to the door, pressed the intercom button and said, ''Yes?'' Then released the button, pressed it once more and said, ''Just speak normally, you don't have to yell.''

''Got roses here for Mrs. Hardin.'' The voice was deep and hoarse, with an uneducated manner of speech, but sounded friendly.

Marissa might have been thinking of her tennis

game, might have had Percy's suspected screwing around on her mind. For whatever reason, she didn't act normally, didn't check the man out with a phone call before letting him in. She quickly undid the locks, tugged on the handle, felt the rush of warm outside air. "Flowers from who? Whoever would . . . ?"

The man's face was a foot from her own. The odor of cheap after-shave—Old Spice or Mennen, one drugstore brand or the other—assaulted her nostrils. He had a sloping forehead and thinning hair, and under his big crooked nose his lips were parted. There were gaps between his teeth. There was something . . . sinister? Yes, something sinister about him; his gaze bored into her like twin drills. Marissa gasped and started to close the door.

He stepped quickly forward. "For you, ma'am. They're for you, nobody else." His gaze lowered. "Man, you got them legs. You damn sure do."

Panic clogged her throat. She grasped the edge of the door in both hands and tried to force it closed. She was wasting her time; the man's shoulder hit the door like a battering ram and it crashed open. Marissa stumbled backward on the stone tile, righted herself, lowered into a half-crouch, her gaze darting from side to side. The man grabbed the door handle and shut out the world with a solid thunk of oak wood. He dropped the roses, dug in his back pocket, came up with a pistol whose bore was the size of an archery bullseye. He leveled the gun at her midsection.

Stay calm, Marissa had heard. If it happens, above all stay calm. She covered her windpipe with the palm of her hand. "Take what you want. Just don't hurt me." Her voice sounded to her like a thin croak.

"I ain't here to hurt nobody, girl. I ain't no pervert. Just come over here and get down on your knees."

"What? What do you want me to . . . ?"

"On your knees. Over here in front of me. Yeah, come on, that's what I'm saying." He gestured with the pistol, pointing first at the floor near his feet and then again at her stomach.

Like just about every other woman in this world, Marissa had thought of moments like this. She'd discussed her fantasies with other women in the safety of the Colonial Country Club. *I'd let him kill me first,* she'd say, or, *I'd scream so loud it would scare him to death.* Not two months ago she'd attended a seminar given by the Fort Worth Police Department, and she recalled the detective's get-tough advice. *These guys are just as nervous as their victims. Keep the upper hand on him.*

But this wasn't fantasy, and the wild-eyed man who was holding the gun didn't appear nervous at all. Sheepishly, her eyes downcast, her limbs tingling with growing numbness, Marissa Hardin crossed the entry hall and sank to her knees like a sinner before the altar.

"Look at me," he said.

She obeyed. A single drop of spittle bled from the corner of his mouth and clung to the flesh beneath his lower lip.

Gently, lovingly, he caressed her cheek with the barrel of the pistol, moved the gun slowly down the side of her neck, and placed the barrel against the point of her breastbone. Her throat constricted and there was no feeling in her legs. What she'd told the ladies at Colonial was wrong; she wouldn't rather die first and she wasn't going to scream. Whatever he wanted. Whatever he wanted, if only he wouldn't . . .

"We're going to get along, girl," he said. "And you're going to like me. You going to like me? Huh?"

Mutely, she nodded.

"That's good. That's real good you're going to. Now take me to your room. It's on the second floor, so don't try going noplace else. I know my way around here, case you don't know it."

She rose, hesitated—Was she doing it right? Sweet

Jesus, she thought, don't let me do anything wrong—
then turned and led the way through the den to the
staircase. At every other step he prodded her between
the shoulder blades with the pistol. His ragged breathing was deafening in the stillness, the scent of his after-
shave strong in her nose. "High ceiling," he said.
"Great big high ceiling you rich people got."

"Thank you," she said in a monotone. Great God
in heaven, just like giving a tour.

As they noiselessly ascended the carpeted stairs,
there was a sudden churning in Marissa's stomach, and
an uncontrollable retching welled up in her throat.
God, was she going to be sick? She was sure that she
was. Right there on the magnificent staircase of her
home, with this crazy man as an audience, Marissa
Monroe Hardin—late of Stephens College and cur-
rently of Fort Worth's Upper West Side—was going to
puke. She staggered sideways and gripped the banister
as vomit rushed into her mouth.

There was suddenly a callused hand on her arm, a
painful grip around her bicep as he spun her around
to face him. He shoved. Her nausea subsided in an
instant as she sprawled upward on the steps. The padded carpet jarred her backside. Air whooshed from her
lungs.

He put the gun against her forehead and aired back
the hammer with two sharp *clicks*. "None of that, none
of that shit, girl. I don't like that shit, you understand?" His voice was guttural and his words slurred.

She nodded—*Anything, I'll do anything, just don't
let me die*—then struggled to her feet and led him up
to the landing, then along the rail toward the master
bedroom. There was a suit of sixteenth-century armor
on the landing holding an antique battle-ax pointed
upward between folded arms. She'd had the piece
shipped over during a trip to England, and there was
a spot of tarnish near the tip of the ax blade. Strange
she'd never noticed the tarnish before. She moved like

a robot past the armor and entered the bedroom. For an instant she considered slamming the door in his face and making a dash for the bedside phone; both the moment and the thought passed as he came inside and closed the door with his foot.

His dull gaze swept the bedroom, lingered on the canopied four-postered kingsize bed, the twin dressing tables, the side-by-side oils, Marissa in a strapless evening gown, Percy in jeans and boots leaning on a ranch-style wooden fence with thoroughbred horses in the background. "Nice," the crazy man said softly. Then, his tone a sharp command, "Get out of that laundry."

Her own voice sounded to her like someone else's voice, someone small, weak, and faraway. "I beg your pardon? Get out of that . . . ?"

"That laundry. Them fucking clothes, girl, take them off."

Oh. Her clothes. Sure, her clothes. She sat on the edge of the bed; the tassels on the snow-white spread dug softly into her fanny. Her gaze never leaving the pistol, she removed first one shoe, one sock, and then the other. His face was a caricature, a humorless cartoon of an ugly man. She stood docilely, raised the hem of her tennis dress, and started to take it off over her head.

"Not like that," he said. "Not like that, girl. Turn around. I want to watch you from behind."

Sure. Sure, of course. From behind. She turned her back and stripped, not certain how he wanted it, not certain whether to take her clothes off slowly or in a hurried frenzy. However he wanted. Naked, she dropped her dress and lacy pants off to one side. The air-conditioning cooled her flesh and hardened her nipples. She was conscious of the odor of incense burning on the dresser.

Behind her he murmured, "Christ. Let me see you, girl."

She turned. Oh, sweet God, he'd taken his pants off. There he stood, still in his blue work shirt, black socks, and shoes, but naked from ankle to waist. He was still holding the pistol. His thick hairy legs were spread; his penis—she couldn't help it, she did look— and, oh, Jesus, sweet savior, his cock was . . .

Her nudity forgotten, she stared at the hideous thing. He had an erection, but midway down the shaft his hardness ended in a mass of bone-white scar tissue. In front of the scar the head dangled limp and flaccid. An accident? God, did he have an accident? She struggled to take her gaze away from it. She couldn't.

"The fuck you lookin' at, girl?" he said. "Goddammit, what you *lookin'* at?"

She opened her mouth. She couldn't speak.

He came forward and slapped her with the back of his hand. Neckbones crunched as her head rocked. Her front tooth dug into her lower lip and there was an instant wetness. She touched her lip, stared numbly at smeared redness on her fingertip.

'On the bed.'' He gestured with the gun. "Get up on the bed.''

Marissa obeyed. God, yes, she obeyed, she would have obeyed anything, would have . . . She put her knee on the bed, then her hand, and her buttocks quivered as she rolled onto her back. Like this? God, did he want her like this? She raised her head in an unspoken request for approval. Like this?

He bounded onto the bed beside her and straddled her ribcage. The hard portion of his cock lay on her breastbone, its head flopped loosely between her breasts. His breathing quickened. "Do me," he said. "Do me with your hands." The barrel of the pistol waved unsteadily over her nose. Overhead, the quilted underside of the canopy was off-white silk.

Anything, Marissa thought. "Yes," she said. "Yes, just please don't . . .''

She closed both hands around the hard portion of

his cock and pumped. If only he wouldn't make her touch the end of the thing. God, if only he wouldn't.

"Harder. Faster, goddammit." He placed the gun against her forehead, at the same time reaching with his free hand to one side, grabbing, then raising a pillow aloft. "Just do it, girl, you don't have to look at me." The pillow covered her face.

The linen on the pillow was soft and smelled of lemon. Yes, she thought, that's better. *I'm doing what he wants*. Her hands moved faster. *I'm doing it for him, and once I've finished he'll go away and—*

The muffled gunshot sounded like a faraway Chinese firecracker, a strange noise that Marissa didn't comprehend. In fact, she was wondering what that strange noise could be even as the safety slug tore its way through her skull, exploded its copper Teflon-filled jacket, and sent its payload of number-twelve shot blasting through her brain.

As the .44 Bulldog jerked in his hand, Everett Wilson came. The dead woman's hands tightened convulsively around his erection and her solid body tensed beneath him as semen spurted onto her breasts like liquid paste. It was good. Christ, it was good. He shuddered, closed his eyes, and rocked with climax. As her body relaxed, he let the pistol rest on his thigh and stared dumbly at the burnt edges of the hole in the pillow. He smelled singed gunpowder.

You're really lucky, girl, he thought. If one of them perverts had gotten ahold of you, no telling what they would have done.

To Joe Eddie Moore's way of thinking, J. Percival Hardin III qualified as Prick Number One of all the pushy members at Colonial Country Club. Prick Number Two was Hardin's playing partner for the day, the paunchy silver-haired guy who stood beside Hardin as the two of them hovered over the starter's table

and acted like the pricks that they were. All part of
being an assistant pro, Joe Eddie supposed, right in
there with parking lot attendants and department store
clerks, putting up with a bunch of pricks all the time.

"I don't care what's on the list," said Percy Hardin.
"We've had a standing one-thirty tee time since time
immemorial, and if I have to see the head pro about
it I'm going to get the board of governors involved."
He took off his sunglasses, held them by a sidepiece,
and brushed the lenses across the front of his pink
Remert shirt. Hardin's eyes were pale blue. The fish-
white skin around his eyes contrasted with his tan.
Visible beyond him, the clipped Bermuda of Number
One fairway stretched one-fifty from the tee, then
dipped into a swell. A burly fat man in a white knit
shirt posed between the members' tee markers. He
gripped the shaft of his driver as though he was strangling a chicken, then lunged at his teed-up ball as
though he was afraid it was going to run away from
him. The clubhead made uneven contact; the ball
sliced weakly down the right side of the fairway and
disappeared into a grove of trees. The fat guy teed up
another one and prepared to take a Mulligan. Further
away, parked on the concrete path, two electric carts
sat one in front of the other. Big leather pro-line bags
were strapped to the rear of the carts; the bags held
Ping, Titleist, Wilson Staff, and Hogan irons and
woods. Colonial members went first class; the only
exceptions were their golf swings and their attitudes
toward the assistant pros.

Joe Eddie Moore had drawn starter's duty under protest; the Colonial assistants called the detail their "day
in the barrel." He was seated at a folding table to one
side of the tee. Spread out before him was the day's
list of starting times; Hardin and his playing partner
leaned over the table as Joe Eddie studied the sheets.
Joe Eddie was a tall, lanky youngster of twenty-two.
The previous spring he'd led TCU to second place in

the Southwest Conference Tournament, and at the moment he was wondering whether having a shot at the tour was worth putting up with pricks like Percy Hardin. Joe Eddie tried a little diplomacy. "The pro's off today, Mr. Hardin. Normally the club's closed on Monday, and the only reason we're out here today is to let you guys get in a few licks before the pro-am. An off-day like this we don't keep the regular tee times. You were supposed to call in and make a reservation." He checked his watch. "After two the course is reserved for the pros to take practice rounds."

"Well nobody told *us* that," Hardin said. "How about you, Sam? Anybody tell you that?"

Hardin's playing partner scratched his pot belly and shifted his weight. "Hell, no. Sounds like a bunch of shit to me, treating the paying members like this."

"It's been posted at the register in the pro shop for more than a month," Joe Eddie said. "But if you fellas will wait a minute, I'll slip you in between this bunch on the tee and the next group." And then, Joe Eddie thought, listen to the *next* group bitch. I should have been a beach bum or something.

"Well, if that's all you can do," Hardin said, "that's all you can do. But I'm taking it up with somebody." He reached over and tore a corner from one of the time sheets, took a pencil from the pile beside the score cards, and prepared to write. "Exactly what time is it?" Hardin said.

Joe Eddie squinted at his watch. "One-twenty-seven."

"Okay. Now, what I'm writing down is, that Sam and I were right here on the first tee at one-twenty-seven, and you folks had given away our regular tee time." Hardin finished his scribbling and pushed the torn paper over in front of the assistant pro. "Sign this. Now when I talk to the board of governors I'll have proof of what time we were here. You got any problem with that?"

Joe Eddie hesitated, pencil in hand. What the hell, he needed the job. For the time being, anyway. "I don't guess I do, Mr. Hardin," he said, and signed his name.

"I don't guess you'd better," Hardin said, folding the slip of paper and putting it away, "if you know what's good for you."

What an asshole, Joe Eddie Moore thought.

5

On Monday nights, Lackey liked to take Nancy to Big
Ed's down in Haltom City. There he could have a few
beers while sitting close to Nancy in a booth, tickle
her leg every once in a while, and crane his neck occasionally to watch the baseball game on the TV,
which was mounted on a platform high above the bar.
Lackey was a nut about baseball and argued all the
time with Ronnie Ferias over whether paying Jose
Canseco and guys like him all that money was ridiculous. Ronnie always said, "Why pay the guy three
million a year when he'd do the same thing for a hundred thousand? What's the guy going to do, be president of General Motors or something?" But Lackey
took the opposite view, thinking that it wasn't so much
what Jose Canseco did as the number of fans that he
drew to the ballpark. Tonight Big Ed's was extra
crowded because the Rangers were playing. There was
only one empty stool at the bar, and the ceiling ex-
hausts were chugging like crazy to get rid of the
smoke. There was action on both pool tables, and rows
of quarters were lined up on the rails over the coin
slots. The quarters belonged to people who were chal-
lenging the winners. Sometimes there'd be an argument over who was next in line for the pool game, and
Big Ed would have to lumber over from behind the bar
to straighten things out. As usual, the Rangers were
stinking it up in front of a national audience.

"That's three," Lackey said, settling down after

raising up for a look at the TV. "Three errors in five innings. They don't play that way behind Ryan. They know the schedule way in advance. Looks to me like every time they're going to be on national television, Valentine would go with Nolan Ryan."

"Go where?" Nancy said. She shifted in the booth, brushing her olive-complexioned leg against Lackey's thigh. She wore baggy thigh-length shorts and an over-size green cotton shirt whose tail hung loosely about her hips. Lackey liked that about Nancy, that she dressed neatly but modestly, didn't go around bars in shorts that showed the cheeks of her ass.

"Pitch the guy. You know, put him on the mound. Looks like on national TV they'd want to put their best foot forward, and lately Nolan Ryan's the only foot they got."

"He's the guy with five million strikeouts or some-thing," Nancy said. "Nice-looking guy, he's always on, telling kids to say no to drugs."

"Five thousand. Three hundred wins. That's more wins than the Rangers'll probably get in the next five years." Lackey took a pull from his Pearl longneck. He was drinking slowly so he wouldn't get too much of a buzz. The bottle was half full and the beer was getting warm.

Nancy was having plain club soda with a lime wedge. She stirred with a swizzle stick; the liquid swirled in the glass and the ice tinkled. "Well, if he's that good," she said, "why doesn't he pitch every night?"

Up and down the bar, men in jeans and women with beehive hairdos hunkered over their beers and grum-bled about the way the Rangers were playing defense. If the Rangers won, they'd all hang around until two o'clock closing time and party. If the Rangers lost, the men were likely to go out cruising in Haltom City, catch a biker or two on the prowl and try to whip the bikers' asses for them.

"You can't pitch every night," Lackey said. "He'd throw his arm out."

"Out where?" Nancy said.

"He'd ruin his shoulder muscles. Hey, you check on the furniture?"

Nancy lowered her gaze, long dark lashes moving downward as she encircled her glass with both hands. "Yeah, I did. I don't know, Lackey, going in so much debt."

"Not with this bathhouse job. I'll pay cash for it. What, a couch and a couple of chairs?"

"Three thousand dollars," she said. "And you're counting your chickens before you've even started the job. Plus there's your tuition we're going to pay."

Lackey ran his thumbnail down the side of his bottle, splitting the wet label in half. He guessed that they weren't supposed to get along on every little thing. "I've got twenty-one hours," he said. "I don't know I'm going to have time for college."

"We've talked about this."

"Sure. Sure, yeah, I just don't know that a degree's going to help me any. Like, 'Look, lady, I'm raising the price of your sheetrock 'cause I'm an educated installer.' " He glanced over to where a guy in a plaid work shirt was hunched over his cue stick, lining up a shot. When it came to college, Lackey never felt as though he and Nancy were talking on the same level. "The army was paying for those courses I took," he said. "That was okay, but if the money's coming out of my own pocket I don't know that it'd be worth it."

"It'll mean something someday," Nancy said. "When you're talking to businessmen."

"If you'd go ahead and move in with me, we could start banking your check and have the tuition money by the time we got married."

"Sure. And wake up some night with a couple of my uncles over there to beat you up. Mama's already got people driving by my apartment at two or three in the morning to make sure my car's there and your pickup isn't.'' Nancy spoke with just the barest trace of a Spanish accent, a slight rolling of her r's that one wouldn't notice unless they were listening closely. She had a wealth of glossy black hair cut into bangs which overhung her forehead and an elegant neck like Audrey Hepburn's. Her nose was slim, her lips full, and her light olive complexion didn't require much makeup. ''You don't want the Cuellars stirred up,'' she said. ''Make Pancho Villa look like the Cisco Kid's buddy.''

Until he'd begun going out with Nancy, Lackey had never dated a woman who couldn't spend the night since he'd joined the army, and having to climb out of bed to take Nancy home was a pain in the ass at times. On the other hand he sort of liked it that she hadn't done a lot of sleeping around. That Mexican-American families were so conservative took some getting used to; the first time Lackey had taken Nancy over to his own folks' house, Lackey's old man had called him aside and asked if that was any good. Lackey said to Nancy, ''I talked to a guy today that thought you might be rich.''

''He hasn't seen my paycheck,'' Nancy said.

''He was a banker over at Ridglea. I said, 'Cuellar,' he said, 'El Chico?' ''

''I wish.''

''I don't. We'd have to eat tacos every meal.''

''To tell you the truth,'' Nancy said, ''they could be cousins. One El Chico brother is named Gilbert, mama had a cousin named Gilbert in Tampico and a few years ago she called El Chico's corporate offices to try and find out if there was a connection. It hurt her feelings that nobody ever called her back. What were you doing at Ridglea Bank?''

''This rich guy, the one with the bathhouse job, that's his banker. The guy sent me over there to talk about interim financing. They wouldn't even talk to me, but the rich guy's wife went ahead and gave me a check. I took it back to Ridglea Bank and cashed it.''

Nancy blinked. ''Is she good-looking?''

''Huh? Is who good-looking?''

''The rich lady.''

Lackey thought, How 'bout that, huh? Not, 'How much of a check?' or, 'When do you start on the job?' Just, 'Is she good-looking?' Women were something else. ''She's okay,'' Lackey said. ''Nothing to write home about.'' And pictured Nancy after she'd gotten a load of Marissa Hardin, Nancy's eyes widening as she said, ''I thought she was nothing to write home about.'' Women never forgot what a guy told them.

''I'll bet she's got a tan,'' Nancy said. ''Laying around by the pool. How old is she?''

''I can't tell. Maybe thirty-five, about my age.''

''Probably pretty firm,'' Nancy said. ''Those women over there get a lot of massages and spend half the day at President's First Lady. At thirty-five I probably won't look so good.''

''That's only ten years from now,'' Lackey said. ''You won't look any different than you do right now. Forty, forty-five, that's when it begins to show.'' He was picturing the crow's feet around Marissa Hardin's eyes and thinking that Nancy was right, that Hardin woman got a lot of exercise. Nancy had the kind of shape that wouldn't go downhill, even after a couple of babies.

''Are you going to be working around her house with just her there?'' Nancy said.

''There's servants. This gardener guy, I met him, this gardener doesn't speak any English.''

''Run, you bastard,'' a guy at the bar yelled, and a couple of the pool shooters edged up for a look at the TV. Lackey rose halfway up and turned his head. On the screen, against a background of pale green Astroturf, the Oakland shortstop glided to his left, knocked a hot grounder down, scooped the ball up, and tossed a floater toward second. The second-sacker, legs flying, caught the toss barehanded, then vaulted over the sliding runner and pegged a clothesline over to first. The relay got Pete Incaviglia by half a step. Incaviglia trotted to the dugout to retrieve his glove as though he didn't give a shit; the double play had ended the inning. The guy at the bar said loudly, "Choker," while the beer drinkers and pool players groaned as one.

Lackey sat down and swigged from his beer. "Lazy bastard. Guy's got all that talent."

"Who?" Nancy was looking toward the pool tables.

"Pete Incaviglia," Lackey said.

"He's a baseball player," Nancy said. "I guess her husband's gone all day."

"Mrs. Hardin?"

"Of course Mrs. Hardin. What's her first name?"

"Marissa." Lackey winced. He'd come up with the name too quickly; he should have pretended to think it over.

"So you're already using her first name," Nancy said. "When's she having you over for a swim?"

"Look, Nancy. It's the way I'm making my living, doing home improvements. The woman of the house is usually home. Plus my whole crew's going to be there."

"Those convicts? You can tell them to take a long lunch."

"Hey, what is this? I built those cabinets in Mrs. Turner's kitchen all by myself. You didn't say anything about that."

"Mrs. Turner's got five kids and lives in a two bedroom," Nancy said. "She's not laying around by the pool crooking her finger."

"Well, you go down there every day with all those lawyers. I don't say anything about that. That guy Brantley, I bet you spend a lot of time with him, taking dictation."

"Mr. Brantley's sixty," Nancy said.

"So? That's when all those guys start looking for a little young stuff."

Nancy picked up her glass and sipped through the swizzle straw. She didn't say anything, but her eyes were shooting sparks.

"Well, isn't it?" Lackey said.

"Isn't what?"

"Isn't that about the age when they start to like 'em young?"

"Oh, I suppose," Nancy said. "His wife's thirty-eight. About the same age as Mrs. Hardin. Excuse me, Marissa."

"Look."

"And while we're on the subject, yes, Mr. Brantley's got a young wife, and Mr. Brantley happens to live over on the west side. And Mr. Brantley's wife is sleeping around when he's out of town. It's common knowledge. So don't tell me." Nancy folded her arms.

"Whose common knowledge?" Lackey said. "Bunch of women talking."

"*And* knowing. One of her—lovers I guess you'd say, he's a young lawyer they just hired this year from the University of Houston. Guy's about twenty-two."

"Sounds like he's more your speed," Lackey said.

"No. No, *my* speed's a guy going over on the west side to work so nobody over here will know what's going on."

Lackey's beer held only a couple of inches in the bottle; he thought about going to the bar and ordering a fresh one, then changed his mind. A couple of times in the service he'd gotten rowdy when he'd had a few too many, and the way this conversation with Nancy was going he didn't want anything stirring him up. "Well," he said, "your speed is also a guy trying to make some good money so we can have a few nice things, buy some furniture and maybe take a honeymoon. That's mainly what I'm up to." He studied the table, then had a thought that was funny to him, hesitated, then couldn't resist saying, "Course, I guess she is pretty good-looking at that. She'll be easy on the eyes, working over there every day." And then he waited for Nancy to really let him have it. He wanted to grin but kept a straight face; Nancy would get over it in a little while, and after they'd had a little spat she went really wild when they had sex together.

Just then a guy at the bar—the same guy, Lackey recalled, who'd called Pete Incaviglia a choker—said loudly, "Well how about that?"

Lackey turned his head to see what was going on in the ballgame. But the TV was showing a news break, the front of a home, a bunch of cops standing around, paramedics wheeling a shrouded gurney out and lifting it down the steps. Some kind of stabbing or something. Lackey relaxed, started to look away, then did a double-take as the paramedics wheeled the gurney around a fountain and in between two tall brick spires. The scene shifted to a newswoman interviewing a paunchy silver-haired guy. Lackey blinked. Hell, wasn't that . . .

Sure, the same guy who'd been riding in the limo that morning, the guy who'd picked up Percy Hardin for the golf. The guy looked really serious answering the newswoman's questions. Lackey went up to the bar and said to no one in particular, "What's going on?"

Big Ed leaned a beefy elbow on the counter. "Some guy's wife getting croaked. The Rangers finally got a man on third, they're showing this shit. Can you believe it?"

Lackey went back to the booth, slid in beside Nancy and studied the ceiling.

"What's wrong?" Nancy said.

"I don't know for sure," Lackey said. "We might've just lost the bathhouse job. I'll have to check on it."

6

There was a problem with three guys nailing up roof board: Only two men could work at a time, one holding the board in place and another driving the nails, while the third guy sat on his ass and watched what the other two were doing. So, Lackey Ferguson thought as he stood on the ground by the ladder, hands on hips, how come there's not *four* guys working up there? He adjusted his hard hat and climbed the ladder—one rung near the top felt as though it might buckle under his weight, and Lackey made a mental note to get the ladder repaired or buy a new one—then crawled up the slanted framing to where the three workmen were doing the work of two.

"Hey, Frank," Lackey said. "Where's Junior?"

The black man who was driving the nails paused with the hammer in midair. He took four nails out of his mouth long enough to say, "Parole officer," then stuck three of the nails between his lips, steadied the fourth on the board, and raised the hammer and brought it down with a long bang. He had a square chocolate-colored face and a broad flat nose. A burlap bag bulging with nails rode the curve of his hip.

"Wait a minute," Lackey said. "That was last week. Junior's parole meeting was last Thursday."

Frank rested the hammer on the board as he glanced first at Ricky Jackson, who was holding the other end of the board, then at Ramon Gomez, who was sitting on his ass, then finally back to Lackey. "Yeah," Frank said. "Last week he saw him, this morning, too. Then this Thursday. Twice a week from now on."

Lackey turned so that he was sitting upright and hugged his knees. "That dude getting in trouble?"

The three ex-cons exchanged looks. One thing all parolees had in common, Lackey had noticed, was that none of them liked to talk about another guy's business. One thing, Lackey thought, that people who'd never been to prison could take a lesson from.

Finally Lackey said, "Look, I don't give a shit what Junior's problem is. It's none of my business. But we got crews to run. A man off once a week, that's a problem we're living with 'cause we know the guy's on parole. But twice a week's a double problem. What's the deal?" A ball of sweat ran from under his hard hat and down his forehead. He wiped it away with the back of his hand.

"We all got problems, boss," Ramon Gomez said. "Twice a week from now on this fucker's having us come. Tomorrow I got to be off, next day Frank and Ricky plus Junior. Ain't none of us done shit, but we got a new parole officer." Gomez couldn't have weighed more than a hundred and thirty pounds, small and wiry with a Fu Manchu mustache. He lay on his side, propped up on one elbow.

"What happened to the old guy?" Lackey said.

"Ain't no old guy," Frank said, laying his hammer aside. "Ain't none of 'em stay around long enough to get old. The guy that just left, we had him for two months. This new guy's about twenty-five, got a hard-on for everybody. Way he talk we lucky we ain't reporting every day."

"Well, we can't put up with this," Lackey said. "We got work to do."

"That's what we told him," Frank said. "That he fuck with us, he's fucking with our job. But I tell you, boss. You go over there you better carry papers prove you ain't on parole yourself. This dude, you give him one word of bullshit, he's going to try to put your ass in jail.''

Ronnie Ferias was around to the side of the addition when Lackey found him. Ronnie looked up, then used a trowel to spread mortar on top of a row of bricks. ''Don't say a word,'' Ronnie said.

''I *got* to say a word,'' Lackey said. ''Otherwise you won't know you're not any bricklayer.''

''Well I'm better'n nothing,'' Ronnie said. ''Fucking parole officer's got these guys trotting back and forth twice a week we won't never get anything finished. *Cabrón.* They get rid of one asshole they get another *pindejo.* That's a prick to you gringo fuckers.''

''Well I'm going over to see the parole guy,'' Lackey said. ''This kind of shit can break us.''

''I thought that westside bathhouse job going to make us rich,'' Ronnie said. ''How we going to get rich if we broke first?'' He dipped in the wheelbarrow and brought the trowel up dripping with mortar. Ronnie was around five-ten, a couple of inches shorter than Lackey, with narrow shoulders and the beginnings of a belly. He wore a paint-stained T-shirt, khaki pants, and an apron with pockets. ''Them Rangers blow another one last night,'' he said.

''I watched it at Big Ed's. They leave too many runners stranded.''

''It's no different than construction,'' Ronnie said. ''Pay 'em all that money they going to sit on they ass.''

''The bathhouse job might be a problem,'' Lackey said.

Ronnie concentrated on the brick in his hand as he set it carefully in place and then dabbed on more mortar. The row on which Ronnie was working was chest high and ran about half the length of the wall. A pile of cleaned brick lay on the ground beside the wheelbarrow. "Woman's check bounce or something?" Ronnie said.

Lackey patted his own rump, feeling the thick wad of bills through the fabric. "No problem with that, I got the cash right here. But that woman got murdered sometime after I left."

"No shit?"

"Yeah. Didn't you see they interrupted the ball game to show that news break?"

"No shit? That was her, huh? I was thinking when I saw that, bet her old man did it. All them westside people, Cullen Davis and all that shit."

"He was gone playing golf," Lackey said. "I carried his clubs out to the car for him."

"Nice of you." The trowel went back to the wheelbarrow, scraped the leftover mortar off, dipped in for more. "Maybe after the funeral we talk to him. With his old lady gone maybe a new bathhouse take his mind off of it."

"Not this guy I don't think," Lackey said. "It was her wanted the bathhouse, not him. I don't think they were getting along too good, tell you the truth."

Ronnie brushed dirt from his arm with the hand that held the trowel; a couple of drops of mortar fell onto his sleeve. "Why? She give you some pussy while you was over there?"

"Naw. Naw, man, I don't screw around on Nancy."

"Come on, bro'."

"Hey, Ronnie, what everybody else does is their own business. I just don't believe in it."

"You believed in it back in high school you was going steady with Edie Farr."

"That was different."

"Bullshit," Ronnie said. "What's different about it?"

"It's different, that's all," Lackey said. "I'm not sure what to do about this money I got."

"The fifteen thousand?"

"Yeah."

"Well," Ronnie said, "maybe we go ahead and take a crew out there tomorrow. Show up like we never heard of no murder. Then if the guy tells us he changed his mind we got something to argue about giving back the money."

Lackey considered it. Ronnie was always thinking, Lackey liked that about his partner, but sometimes Ronnie's thinking was just a little bit haywire. "We'd be screwing the guy," Lackey said.

"So? Everybody screws everybody. You think that rich dude wouldn't screw us, he had the chance?"

"Well we're not," Lackey said. "Not on this deal, the guy's wife just got murdered. What kind of shape we in for crews?"

"Oh, we got plenty on the payroll. This job here, we're fifty percent complete and it's the only big project we got right now. All we got besides this is three kitchen remodelings and that new bathroom out in Keller. All our supplier invoices paid except for this brick I'm laying here, and I ain't sure about that. I think he give us B-grade brick or something, this shit don't lay too good. I'm going to have a talk with him before I pay the guy. We in pretty good shape except for this parole officer fucking with our people." Ronnie adjusted his hard hat back with his forearm.

"That's where I'm going right now," Lackey said. "Out to the Board of Pardons and Paroles. What's this new guy's name?"

"Lincoln, the guys say," Ronnie said. "Probably a black dude, got a chip on his shoulder."

Lackey said, "See you in a couple of hours," then started to walk away over a little hill of dirt left over from when they'd excavated for the foundation on the addition.

"You watch your ass out there," Ronnie said. "They say this guy, he'd as soon put you in jail as one of them parolees."

* * *

Lackey drove past the parole office on Meadowbrook Drive without even noticing the place, even
though he was keeping his eyes peeled. Meadowbrook
was a two-lane asphalt street with big leafy trees lining
both curbs, and the parole office was in a one-story
white building set back from the road behind a small
parking lot. Lackey was a full block past the building
when the sign reflected in his rearview mirror; he
cussed under his breath, wheeled into the lot of a
MacDonald's to turn around, then went back to the
parole office and parked nose-on to the building beside
a ten-year-old Buick. In the front seat of the Buick a
black girl was nursing a baby. She favored Lackey with
a bored stare. Lackey got out of his pickup and entered the building.

In the lobby, parolees waited on imitation leather
couches and chairs which lined both sides of the room.
One guy—a boy, really, in his early twenties, wearing
a T-shirt that featured a cartoon of six girls with their
pants down, showing their asses, below the caption,
''We Be Crack Free''—was handcuffed, seated beside
a uniformed Tarrant County Sheriff's Deputy. On a
couch to Lackey's left, a black man with a beard and
a white pregnant girl with a grimy T-shirt stretched
over her belly were asleep. The guy was snoring.
Lackey went up to a sliding window and asked to see
Mr. Lincoln. A sleepy-looking woman in her forties
reached through the opening to hand him a form.
''Sign the register,'' she said. ''Then have a seat and
fill this out.''

''Excuse me,'' Lackey said, ''but this is business.''

''It's all business,'' the woman said. ''And as soon
as you fill out the form and give it back to me I'll take
it to Mr. Lincoln. No form, no visit. That's the rules.
Pencils are right there on the table beside the register.
Mr. Lincoln's got two people already waiting, so he'll
be a while.''

Lackey shrugged and went over to the table, where a register on a clipboard lay beside a pile of stubby yellow pencils. He picked up five pencils before he found one whose point wasn't broken off, then filled in the columns on the register with his name, the time—he checked the wall clock; 9:42—and Lincoln's name. The only empty seat was beside the kid in the handcuffs. Lackey sat down and studied the form the woman had given him.

The form wanted to know Lackey's full name, address, phone number (or message phone if he didn't have a number of his own), who he was living with, where he was working, and whether or not he'd been questioned by the law in the past month. He almost went back to the window and told the woman that this was ridiculous, then he changed his mind. If he rocked the boat he might never get to see the guy. He scratched his beard, thought, and began to write.

At 11:04, Lackey was the only one still waiting. About an hour earlier, the deputy had led the handcuffed guy through a swinging door, then five minutes later had emerged with the guy not only handcuffed but with his feet shackled as well. The boy had been crying. The deputy had taken him out into the parking lot, locked him into the rear of a van, and had driven away. The black man and the pregnant white girl had gone in to see their parole officer together, stayed less than a minute, and had left giggling with their arms around each other. Visible through the glass inserts on the door, they'd gotten into the Buick with the black girl who was nursing the baby. The Buick wouldn't start. The man had come back inside and used the phone, and now sat on the Buick's trunklid, apparently waiting for a tow truck while the girl with the baby and the pregnant girl slept in the front seat.

Lackey's joints were stiff; he stretched his arms and legs and yawned. Jesus, how could somebody on pa-

role keep a job if they had to go through this all the
time? Just as he was about to go to the window and
ask the woman—for the fourth or fifth time—how much
longer until Lincoln was free, the inner door opened
and a young black man marched into the waiting room.
He was tall, thin, and clean-shaven, with skin the color
of a chocolate malt. He wore navy slacks, a white shirt
and a dark tie. "Ferguson?" he said. "That you?"

Lackey sat up and looked around. "Well, I'm the
only one left. Yeah, I guess so."

"I'm Lincoln. Follow me." He turned on his heel
and marched back into the inner office.

Lackey followed down a corridor past open doors of
cubbyhole offices with men and women inside hunched
over telephones, through a small open area with secretaries typing and file clerks filing, into a small conference room with a scarred wooden table. Lincoln
walked at a fast clip, like a man in a hurry to get things
over with. On the wall of the conference room was a
sign reading, "Need a job? See the Texas Employment
Commission." Lincoln sat down at the table and
looked up expectantly. Lackey hesitated, then had a
seat and handed his form to Lincoln. As Lincoln studied the page he said, "I don't find your file. You just
get out of the joint? Sometimes it takes a week or two
for your records to catch up."

Lackey propped his knee against the edge of the
table and smoothed his hair back with his palm. "You
won't find any file on me. I'm not on parole."

Lincoln's narrow jaw dropped. The form drifted out
of his grasp, swooped slightly in a current of air, and
came to rest face-up on the table. "Then why you
filling the form out?" Lincoln said.

Lackey wondered if a mustache might make the parole officer appear any older. He doubted it. Recent
college grad, Lackey thought. He said, "The woman
told me to, the woman out front. I just follow orders
when I'm not sure what's going on. Besides, it was

kind of fun. I couldn't remember my license number, had to go out to the parking lot.''

''You know, we're pretty busy,'' Lincoln said, ''without people coming in here because they think it's funny. Somebody dare you or something?''

''No, I've got legitimate business. I came to see you about why you're having all these guys report twice a week.''

''Oh. You've got a brother on parole. Cousin or something,'' Lincoln said.

Lackey folded his arms. His hard hat was outside, on the front seat of the pickup, and he felt slightly lightheaded without the hat. He hadn't had anything to eat, and his stomach was grumbling. ''I'm an employer,'' he said. ''And tell you the truth, having my people gone all the time is putting me in a bind.''

''Well that's part of the deal,'' Lincoln said. ''When you hire a parolee, there's consequences.''

''It wouldn't be so bad if it was just one,'' Lackey said. ''But my whole company is parolees, except for my partner. And sometimes I wonder about him.'' He smiled at his own joke. Lincoln didn't look as though he thought anything was funny. Lackey coughed into his own cupped hand.

''Damn. Your whole company?'' Lincoln folded his hands. ''Ferguson, Ferguson. I don't remember hearing that name.''

''It's F&F Construction. My partner's Ronnie Ferias.''

Lincoln snapped his fingers and pointed. ''Sure. F&F, I got some . . .'' He got up, circled the table and stopped by the door. ''Don't move a muscle, I'll be right back. I've got some things to talk over with you.'' He disappeared down the hall.

Lackey got up and squinted at the Texas Employment Commission sign. The sign pictured a hungry-looking man shaking hands with a grinning man who was seated behind a desk. A couple of Lackey's bricklayers had tried the Texas Employment Commission before they'd come to F&F. One of the bricklayers had gone on interviews set up by TEC for six months without any luck; the other guy had gotten part-time work on a garbage truck. Lincoln came back in with a stack of bulging file folders and dropped them on the table. Lackey sat down. So did Lincoln.

"We've been wondering about that company of yours," Lincoln said. "I'm going to need your social security number. Your partner's, too."

"Whoa, hold it." Lackey held up a hand, palm out. "I'm not looking for a job. I got work."

"That's not the point," Lincoln said. "Guy's hiring all these ex-convicts it makes us wonder. Most people wouldn't hire one of the bastards on a bet, but here's you with nothing *but* ex-cons. Makes us wonder if you got a record yourself. If you do, all these guys got to find another job."

"You can do that?" Lackey was getting a little warm around the collar, and it took some doing for him not to raise his voice. "You can tell a guy where he can work?"

Lincoln didn't bat an eye. "We can tell 'em whatever we want to tell 'em. We got the power of God where parolees are concerned. Now. What's that social security number?" He took a ballpoint from his breast pocket, a small pad from his hip pocket, and got ready to write.

Lackey decided he'd better not risk any trouble with this guy. He gave his social security number—Lincoln tucked his tongue into the corner of his mouth as he wrote it down—then said to Lincoln, "I don't know Ronnie's offhand. I'll have to check."

"Yeah, well you do that. By Friday, huh? That's as long as we can wait." Lincoln put the pen and pad away.

"Wait for what?" Lackey said. "Suppose you don't get it by Friday?"

"Suppose you show up Monday without any employees," Lincoln said. "That's what to suppose."

"Well okay, then. I'll get it." Lackey showed a smile which he hoped looked as though he was dying to help this bastard. "But hey, Mr. Lincoln. You got no reason to be so tough on our people."

Lincoln twisted his lips into a smirk. "We don't?"

"No. No, you sure as hell don't. These guys are making damn good workers for us."

"Yeah, I bet," Lincoln said. He reached over for one of the folders, opened it, leafed through a stack of papers and came up with a mug shot which had a lot of printing underneath the picture. "Here's one of your people right here. Frank Nichols, you know this guy?" He turned the photo so that Lackey could see it.

Lackey thought that Frank in the picture was thinner than he'd looked that morning, nailing up roof boards. "Sure," Lackey said. "Guy's never missed a day of work. Except when you people are dragging him down here for parole meetings."

"We got to keep these guys under our thumb," Lincoln said. "Frank Nichols done nine burglaries, you know that? Nine that we know of, all these people done a hell of a lot more than what they got caught for."

"Yeah, he was pretty good at it," Lackey said. "We got a little office you know, right off Loop 820 and Rufe Snow Boulevard in North Richland Hills. One morning I lost my key and old Frank got in there without even leaving a mark on the door frame."

"Keeping in practice," Lincoln said. "Most of 'em do."

"Yeah, whatever. I sure got no beef with Frank Nichols. I'd like a hundred like him."

"That's good," Lincoln said, "as long as he wouldn't like to have a hundred like you, you're letting him off during the day to steal a few TVs or something." He reached for another file. "Here's another nice one. We go from a burglar to a dope peddler, Ramon Gomez. You got a lot of Mexicans out in that neighborhood, don't you?"

Lackey thought of Nancy, and pictured himself grabbing Lincoln by the collar and hauling him across the table. And saying to Lincoln, "Yeah, and one of them is my fiancée." Lackey had lost his racial hang-ups in the service; he'd noticed, though, that black guys as a rule seemed to be more into race than the white people Lackey knew. He decided he'd better not start anything more with Lincoln than he already had. Lackey swallowed. "Well, yeah," he said. "Not a big Hispanic population, but some. Ramon sold some marijuana. So what? I think they ought to decriminalize it." Then he felt like biting his lip, and waited for Lincoln to let him have it with both barrels.

Lincoln didn't change expressions. "It's what marijuana leads to. Don't you know anything about drugs? You need to, in case one of your employees shows up high. This Ramon Gomez, he's likely to do that. Believe me, I can spot 'em."

Lackey's jaws clenched. "Ramon never took a hard drug in his life. Nothing but a little grass, and he was a teenager. For that he got to spend three full years in the joint, on a twenty-year sentence. Tell you the truth, I think that's ridiculous."

Lincoln stacked the two files together in front of him. "Well, we don't. We think these guys should do *more* time than what they're getting. Instead of putting them on the street for us to have to fool with."

"Murderers, yeah," Lackey said. "But not some guy selling grass."

"I don't know about your attitude, Ferguson," Lincoln said. "Don't know if a man with your attitude should be working convicts to begin with. They need somebody that'll keep an eye on 'em and let us know if they're fucking up."

Lackey was mentally kicking himself. Here he'd come to reason with the parole people, now he was arguing with the guy over whether marijuana should be against the law. "Hey, Mr. Lincoln, I'm not here to give anybody any trouble," Lackey said. "Our problem is pretty simple. If these guys start taking off two days a week it's going to murder our work schedules."

"That's something I can't do anything about," Lincoln said. "My duty's to keep the screws on these parolees. Every day in the paper there's something, one of these guys holding up a convenience store, raping a woman or something."

"We don't have any sex criminals," Lackey said. "We screen their record before we'll take 'em on the payroll."

"You just don't have anybody that's been convicted of it. Most of these guys get their kicks raping women. That goes with the other stuff."

Lackey couldn't believe the fucking guy. "Well listen," he said. "None of our people have ever been in trouble on parole. Can't we make a deal that, well, as long as they behave themselves they don't have to come but once a week? You think you could help us that much?"

"Oh, I'm making a change," Lincoln said. "After talking to you I'm making a big one. I'm going over every one of these files on your people. Then I'm going to have 'em come *three* times a week, all the ones I don't make quit your outfit altogether." He grinned. "How's that grab you, Ferguson?"

Lackey swallowed, not wanting to say anything to upset the guy further, but finally not being able to help it. Lackey's complexion reddened; the cords on his neck stood out. "Well, it doesn't grab me too good, tell you the truth. Tell you what, who's your supervisor around here?"

7

Lincoln's supervisor was a fat white guy named Sullivan. He told Lackey that it wasn't his policy to interfere with his people. Furthermore, Sullivan said, while what the Parole Board did wasn't always in the parolees' best interests, the Board's policies were best for the public in general. Sullivan then gave Lackey a business card and showed him the door.

Lackey drove back to the jobsite doing a slow burn, jamming a Ronnie Milsap tape into the player with an extra hard shove and turning up the volume on "There Ain't No Gettin' Over Me," all in an attempt to take his mind off of Lincoln the Parole Officer. A lot of people had told Lackey and Ronnie that they were asking for trouble when they began hiring ex-cons; what the people had forgotten to say was that the trouble wasn't from the parolees themselves.

Frigid air drifted from the pickup's vents as Lackey made the climb-and-bend to the left on Loop 820, crossing over Airport Freeway, then whipped across two lanes of seventy-mile-an-hour traffic to take the northbound exit onto Grapevine Highway, finally halting at the traffic light on the access road. There was a Kip's Restaurant on his right; in the restaurant parking lot the grinning statue of the Big Boy held a giant hamburger on a plate aloft. Directly in front of Lackey, across Grapevine Highway, two men wearing jeans walked around on Hudiberg Chevrolet's used car lot, kicking tires.

So what do we do now? Lackey thought. All of the parolees were doing too good of a job to let any of them go, and the budget wouldn't stand hiring any more people to take up the slack caused by the extra parole visits. Lackey had been planning to put on an extra crew for the westside bathhouse job, but Mrs. Hardin's killing had changed all that. For maybe the hundredth time since his discharge, Lackey wondered if he'd have been better off staying in the army. Nope, no way. He wouldn't have Nancy.

The traffic light flashed green. He turned right onto Grapevine Highway, then immediately fought across two traffic lanes to make a left, headed north on Davis Boulevard. He steered the pickup several more blocks, between a Taco Bell and a Big State Auto Parts, finally turning left on Lola Lane. The jobsite was on Lola, a couple of blocks west of Davis, across the street from a one-story grammar school in a neighborhood composed of small brick veneer and wood frame homes. The guy whose house they were remodeling was a plumber; Lackey figured that with the hourly rate plumbers were getting, the guy could afford it. He pulled to the curb at the jobsite, then paused with one hand on the pickup's door handle. What in hell was going on?

A Tarrant County Sheriff's car—a metallic blue four-door Impala with rooflights and a wire screen separating the front seat from the back—was parked in front of the house. Jesus, Lackey thought, now Lincoln's sending somebody over to hassle these guys on the job. Well, that was something that F&F Construction couldn't put up with, a cop standing by while the men were trying to work. Scare the neighbors to death is what it would do. No way could they put up with that, things were bad enough as it was. Lackey got out, slammed the door with a thud that rocked the pickup, then took long purposeful strides across the lawn and around to the back of the house, ready to give somebody a ration of shit.

Frank Nichols, Ramon Gomez, and three other men—a black named Daniels and two Hispanic guys named Begorria and Nunez—stood off to one side of the addition, talking in whispers and shooting glances toward the two plainclothes cops who were listening to Ronnie Ferias. Ronnie was standing on top of a mound of excavated dirt, his glossy black hair riffling in the wind as he held his hard hat in one hand and gestured with the other. His jaw was working nonstop as the two cops stood by, one with folded arms and the other with hands on hips. The county men wore white shirts and dark ties, were coatless, and had holstered pistols hanging from their belts. There were badges pinned to the holsters. Both of the cops were tall and rangy, one bald with a sunburnt scalp and the other with a full head of blond-going-to-gray hair. The bald guy wore mirrored sunglasses. The blond's complexion was fair, reddening in the sun, and he was squinting.

As Lackey approached, Ronnie was saying, ". . . and can't be more'n a half hour or so. I thought he'd be here by now, tell you the truth."

"We got enough trouble keeping these people occupied without all this," Lackey said. "So what are you guys after?"

The bald sheriff's deputy was holding a photo. Light flashed from mirrored lenses as he looked at the picture, raised his head to give Lackey the once-over, then lowered his gaze to the photo. "Ferguson? Lackey X. Ferguson, that you?" There was an I'm-a-county-man twang to his voice, and a slight hoarseness, as though he had a hangover.

Lackey bent his head for a look. Hell, it was his army release picture, taken at Fort Bragg. "Well . . . yeah," he said.

The blond beckoned with a crooked index finger.

"Come over here, Lackey," he said, then led the way about twenty paces off to one side, near the back porch of the main house. Lackey followed, wondering what the fuck was going on, conscious of the bald deputy falling into step behind him, of the stares from Ronnie and Frank and the other construction workers.

The blond folded his arms and waited for Lackey to catch up. Then, when he and Lackey and the guy with the mirrored lenses formed a triangle, the blond deputy said, "I'm Detective Morrison. This guy's Henley. Where were you at yesterday, Lackey?"

Normally, Lackey liked it when people called him by his first name, but Detective Morrison sounded like a guy talking down to the hired help. Lackey folded his arms, spread his legs, and looked at the ground. "Why you want to know?" A gnawing uneasiness was creeping up the back of his neck, a feeling as though he shouldn't say anything to these guys.

Henley, the bald deputy, snugged his glasses up with his middle finger. "We'll ask the questions here."

Lackey cocked his head. "Well, you might ask 'em. But I'm not answering any till I know what's going on."

The deputies exchanged looks, then Morrison said, "You know a Percival Hardin?"

"I might," Lackey said.

"Cute," Morrison said. "Maybe you'd answer better if we all went downtown."

"I might do that, too," Lackey said. "But unless you got a warrant we're not going to find out." All of his life he'd done his best to cooperate with the law, but that morning's session with Lincoln the Parole Officer had changed Lackey's attitude. He'd had it up to here with civil servants throwing their weight around.

Henley smiled a smile that appeared painted on, and that didn't make Lackey particularly trust the guy. "Say, Lackey," Henley said, "we're looking for help. Now I know you seen the TV, somebody killed

Mrs. Hardin yesterday and did some things to her that aren't very pretty. So you were out at that house yesterday, no point in denying it. How about it? Come on down and give us a statement. Unless you got something to hide, you got nothing to worry about.''

There was a sudden weight in Lackey's belly like a football-size rock. All in all, Lackey Ferguson had had better days. "I need a lawyer?" he said, then immediately wished he hadn't. If he hadn't done anything, why would he be worried about a lawyer?

"Calling your lawyer's up to you," Henley said.

"Aw, I don't guess I need one," Lackey said. "Sure, whatever's going to help. My pickup's out front. I'll follow you.''

"That'll be fine," Henley said, stonefaced.

Lackey went over to tell Ronnie where he was going. Ronnie's brow was furrowed and his worried gaze darted back and forth between Lackey and the two cops. "Nothing," Lackey said, then cleared his throat and said, "Nothing to worry about. I'm going downtown with these guys to give 'em a statement about what I saw out at the Hardins' house yesterday. Be back after a while." Ronnie pawed the ground with his foot and didn't look reassured.

Lackey led the cops toward the front of the house. As they passed by the construction workers, Ramon Gomez said, "Don't tell 'em chit, boss. Anything you say they just try to turn aroun' on you. I been there." He favored Morrison with a nasty stare.

"One thing about it, Lackey," Henley said. "You got plenty of advice without even calling a lawyer.''

The county coffee was lukewarm and too strong. Lackey had a couple of sips and set the cup aside. Instead of taking him to the sheriff's department, in the same building as the county jail, Henley and Morrison had led him an additional block down Belknap Street to the District Attorney's office. Lackey didn't know if that was good or bad. At the moment he was sitting at a conference table in a big room with bookcases filled with legal volumes—the *Texas Penal Code*, the *United States Code*, and the *Federal Reporter, Second Edition*—and Henley and Morrison were seated across from him. The bookcases were dusty and the beige walls slightly yellowed. Henley was smoking a filtered cigarette. Lackey didn't like the smell of smoke and was about to say so, but just then a man came in. The newcomer carried a smoldering cigar in one hand and a briefcase in the other. Lackey closed his nasal passages and kept his mouth shut.

The man with the cigar was around thirty years old and wore a navy blue suit. He was medium height—five-ten or so—with short sandy hair, was squarely built and had some baby fat in his cheeks. He found an ashtray on a file cabinet, set it on the table and balanced his cigar on the edge of the ashtray. Then he snapped his briefcase open, pulled out a file folder, and sat down. The folder bulged with papers and was held together by a jumbo rubber band. The new guy nodded to Henley and Morrison in turn, then said to Lackey, "I'm Assistant District Attorney Favor."

Lackey rose and extended his hand. "Lackey Ferguson."

Favor regarded the hand distastefully, then shook it weakly and let go in a hurry. "Sit down, Mr. Ferguson. Anybody tell him his rights?"

Lackey had started to sit down, but now froze with his hands on the arms of his chair. "Hey, I'm not under arrest or anything."

"No," Favor said. "We don't arrest anybody until we're sure. But I'm telling you that you don't have to talk to us. Any statement you give here is voluntary, and if you want your lawyer present you can call him." He had mild green eyes. Unlike the detectives, this guy wasn't giving out any bullshit.

Lackey sank down into his chair. "Does that mean I'm a suspect?"

Henley inhaled and blew cigarette smoke across the table. "Hey, Lackey, everybody's a suspect in something like this. Like I told you, nothing to worry about."

Favor popped the rubber band from the file, then rummaged through the papers inside. He dug in his briefcase and came up with a pocket-size recorder, set it on the table and turned it on. Seen through plastic, tiny reels began to turn. "The recorder's so we won't have to take notes," Favor said. "You got any problem with that?" He lifted thin blond eyebrows.

Lackey didn't believe Henley, that there was nothing to worry about, but if he balked at the recording things were going to look even worse. "No, I don't mind," Lackey said.

"Good," Favor said, then turned slightly so that he was speaking directly at the recorder. "It's May twelfth, Nineteen-ninety"—he checked his watch—"and it's one-forty-two p.m. This is Assistant District Attorney Wilson Favor, and I'm conducting an interview with witness Lackey"—Favor glanced at a sheet of paper from the file—"X. Ferguson, white male, D.O.B. three-fourteen-fifty-five. Also present are Detectives Charles Morrison and Roscoe Henley of the Tarrant County Sheriff's Department." He nodded to Lackey. "Okay, you ready?" Favor said.

Lackey shrugged and his lips formed what he hoped was an innocent-looking smile. "Sure. Shoot," Lackey said.

"Okay," Favor said. "Yesterday did you go to the home of Mr. and Mrs. J. Percival Hardin III?"

"Yeah. Yeah, sure, I went over there to see about—"

"That's my next question," Favor said. "Please don't anticipate. Now, what was the purpose of your visit?"

Lackey scratched his head. "I'm in the remodeling business. Me and my partner."

"Who is . . . ?" Favor said.

"Ronnie Ferias. We're F&F Construction. I was answering an ad in the paper. They said they wanted to build a bathhouse."

"It was Mr. and Mrs. Hardin's ad?"

"Yeah. Yes," Lackey said.

"And what time did you get there?"

"Well, the first time it was around nine in the morning."

Favor glanced first at Henley, then at Morrison. "You went there more than once?" Favor said.

"Yeah. The first time I talked to Mr. and Mrs. Hardin in their sitting room."

"Pretty nice place, isn't it?" Favor said.

"Yeah. Yeah, sure, it's nice."

"Ought to have made quite an impression," Favor said.

Lackey hesitated. He'd heard from Frank Nichols and the rest of the parolees that D.A.'s and detectives liked to say things that would trip a guy up. Finally, Lackey said, "Well, the impression was at first that all this must really cost a lot. I was wondering how those people could afford to live there, tell you the truth."

A half-hour later, Lackey was thinking that his interview had gone pretty well. Favor had asked all of the questions while Morrison watched with sort of a strange grin on his face and Henley lit one cigarette off of the other, grinding the butts out in an ashtray at his elbow. Lackey's eyes were watering from the smoke. He'd answered the questions thoughtfully and in a straight-out manner. He hadn't told any lies, but also hadn't mentioned that Mrs. Hardin had been sort of coming on to him.

"I guess that about wraps it up," Favor said. "Anything else you recall, anything at all that looked unusual to you?''

"Not that I can remember," Lackey said.

"Okay," Favor said. "End of interview." He switched off the recorder. "Now, Mr. Ferguson. You're off the tape. Now why don't you quit fucking us around?" He didn't change the tone of his voice, asked the question matter-of-factly, the same way he'd spoken during the recorded question-and-answer session.

There was a quick tightening in Lackey's throat. "Beg your pardon?"

Henley ground his cigarette out in the ashtray. "Come on, Lackey. Good-looking broad like that flouncing around in a tennis dress, you sat around and talked about building this bathhouse, huh?"

"That's what I was there for." Lackey's voice rose an octave; he couldn't help it.

Henley grinned, but his eyes were dead as unlit bulbs. "You ain't queer or nothing, are you?"

"No. No, I'm not."

"But you didn't even notice that this was a good-looking broad you were talking to. I'd have damn sure noticed it. Wouldn't you have noticed it, Mr. Favor?"

Favor made a pyramid of his hands and rested his chin on his fingertips. "No way I couldn't have."

"Well Lackey here didn't notice," Henley said. "He didn't have nothing on his mind but that fucking bathhouse."

Lackey swallowed. "Well, yeah. Sure, I noticed her."

"That's what I thought." Henley fished in his shirt pocket for his crumpled pack, popped another cigarette into his mouth, paused with a disposable lighter inches from the tip. "That's a good-looking bedroom." He flicked the lighter, applied bluish flame to his cigarette, dragged and inhaled. "Lot of expensive furniture. That's some four-poster bed, ain't it?"

Lackey shifted his position and regarded the table. He wanted to meet Henley's gaze, but was getting too nervous to think clearly. "I already told you, I only was in the kitchen."

"I didn't say you were anyplace else," Henley said. "I just said it was a nice-looking bedroom. But since you said, I thought you were in the sitting room, too."

"That was earlier. When I was talking to both of them."

"You know, that's funny," Henley said. "Mr. Hardin didn't say nothing about that, that they talked to you earlier. You sure it wasn't just you and Mrs. Hardin in the sitting room? While her husband was gone?"

"No, him, too," Lackey said. "That's where he told me I should see his banker."

Henley had taken charge now; it was as though it was just him and Lackey, one on one, and as though Morrison and Favor were a couple of store-window dummies. Henley laid his lighter on the table, regarded it thoughtfully, flipped the lighter over. "You fuck a lot of broads you was in the army, Lackey?"

"Huh?"

"Fuck a lot of women. Most guys do, you were overseas and all."

Lackey did his best to look casual, but his heart was pounding and his fingertips were shaking. "I guess I did. A few. Like you say, most guys in the service."

"Yeah, most guys. How you like to do it?" Henley said.

"I don't get what you're asking," Lackey said.

"I mean, me and my old lady been married nineteen years, we always do it the same way. Always her on top, she can get her jollies better. But guys like you do a lot of different broads, you try different shit?"

"Oh, I don't know. Maybe some. I'm engaged now, I don't mess around with other women."

"You maybe like to jack off on women?" Henley said. "Show 'em who's boss?"

"Jesus Christ." Nervous he was, but Lackey was getting a little bit mad as well. "Jesus Christ, I've had enough of this. I got to go."

"Where you got to go?" Morrison broke in, the first time he'd said anything since the interview had begun.

"Go to work," Lackey said. "Unless you guys got something else important to ask, not just a bunch of shit about my sex life."

"You got a point," Morrison said. "Henley's a horse's ass sometimes, don't let him bug you. But, hey, before you go, there's a couple of things we'd like for you to do."

"Yeah," Lackey said. "Sure, anything to help."

"Sure, you want to help." Favor's voice was higher-pitched, milder than either of the detectives', and Lackey blinked in surprise. He'd forgotten that the Assistant D.A. was even in the room. "And so we'll know you're not fucking us around," Favor said, "we need to gather some physical evidence. You mind giving us a pubic hair?"

"Huh?" Lackey swept all three county men with his gaze.

"A dick-hair, Lackey," Henley said. "So the lab guys can compare it with one or two we found on Mrs. Hardin. Since you're such an innocent guy we know you won't mind. We'll even furnish the tweezers, and it won't hurt but just for a second. One little ouch is all. The second thing we want, that'll take a little longer, but it won't hurt at all."

"What second thing?" Lackey said.

Favor cleared his throat. "We need a semen sample, too, Mr. Ferguson. Take a sperm count for comparison. You'll have to sign a form that you're giving us this stuff voluntarily, otherwise I'll have to get a court order. And that's a pain in the ass and might look to somebody like you don't want to cooperate."

"I don't know about this semen sample," Lackey

said, shifting nervously and crossing his legs. "How you going to take that?"

"We're not," Henley said. "What you're going to do is, you're going to jerk off into a bottle. I got to tell you I won't like it any more than you do, 'cause I got to watch you to make sure it's your own sweet love-juice we're getting. You got any problem with that?"

Lackey looked from Henley to Favor to Morrison, all three men watching him, all three looking as though they didn't believe a word he'd told them in the interview. Jesus, why did he have to see the ad for the bathhouse to begin with? He was really beginning to hate this Henley and was getting the idea he was going to hate the guy a whole lot more before this was over. He stood and leveled his gaze at Henley. "Naw," Lackey said. "I don't have any problem with that, as long as you're going to watch me. You act like that's something you're wanting to do."

It was something he'd never admit to Nancy, not if they were married for sixty years, but Lackey thought that the last time he'd masturbated had been when he was twelve. He'd done it in his bedroom, one time after Ronnie Ferias's older sister Toni had dropped him off from school. Lackey had been sitting in the middle of the front seat on the way home, between Ronnie and Toni. Toni had been sixteen at the time and had just gotten her driver's license; it had been in the late spring and she'd been wearing a bathing suit. When she'd pulled to a stop in front of his house, Lackey had climbed over Ronnie and run like hell through the front door so that Ronnie and Toni wouldn't know he had a hard-on. That particular time, picturing Toni's caramel-colored thighs stretched taut over the fabric of the car seat, Lackey hadn't had any problem jerking off at all. But here in the men's room at the D.A.'s office, seated in a chair by the sink while Detective

Henley leaned against a water closet and kept an eye on him, Lackey thought he was never going to be able to do it. The only way he finally did was the same way he'd done it the other time, closing his eyes, blotting out the image of Henley, and bringing up a picture of Toni Ferias in her bathing suit. When he was through, Lackey cleaned himself with toilet paper and offered the specimen bottle to Henley.

"Wrap a paper towel around it," Henley said. "I don't want to touch it."

"I sort of thought you did," Lackey said. "Seems like you and me, we both got the wrong idea about each other."

The last person that Lackey expected to see at the D.A.'s office, with all of the county lawyers, uniformed deputy sheriffs, and civil service people lurking about, was Nancy Cuellar. So when Nancy came up to him in the hall outside the men's room, Lackey didn't know what to say to her. She was wearing a beige pleated summerweight skirt and a white blouse. She came running, her brown high-heeled shoes clicking rapidly on the tiles, threw her arms around his neck and hugged him as though she hadn't seen him in a year. She'd been crying and there were a few streaks in her light makeup.

Lackey gripped her shoulders, held her slightly away from him as he said, "Hey. Hey, babe, nobody's died or anything. How'd you know where I was?"

"Ronnie," she said as though she was choking, and then said softly and tearfully, "Ronnie called the office. I've talked to everybody in the sheriff's office, it seems like, and nobody wanted to tell me where to find you. Mr. Brantley donated to the sheriff's campaign last election, finally he got on the line and pulled a few strings. What are they doing to you?"

He held the point of her chin between his thumb and forefinger and raised her face, looked over the soft olive-complexioned cheeks, the wide, dark eyes like a doe's eyes in hunting season. Lackey winked at her, and hoped he looked a lot more confident than he felt. "Nothing," Lackey said. "Not one damn thing, babe, and don't you worry about it. Let's get out of here." He put his arm around her and steered her down the hall to the elevator. On the way they passed two uniformed deputies who were wearing holstered pistols. Nancy put her arms around Lackey's waist and hugged.

"How can I not worry?" Nancy said. "The way this is happening."

"Because *I'm* not worried," Lackey said. "And the worst thing we can do is go around hanging our heads, making people think we got something to sweat about." He held her tighter. "Hey, Nance, you won't believe what I've just been doing. Never in a million years. Wait'll we get out of here, I'll tell you about it."

Lackey and Nancy left the coolness of the building, walked onto the baking sidewalk, and blinked against the glare of the sun. Midafternoon downtown traffic was sparse; a lowslung Mercury went by, its radials *click-click*ing on the red brick pavement of Belknap Street. Over near the curb, standing midway between two parking meters, Assistant D.A. Favor was holding a news conference. He was standing at attention, his fleshy jaw thrust forward, while a circle of newspeople—two young women, a blond and a redhead, both wearing business suits, and a thin, thirtyish man wearing a plaid sport coat and slacks—pointed cordless mikes and fired questions. Two guys in shirtsleeves held minicams up on their shoulders with the lenses pointed in Favor's direction. Detective Morrison, his blond hair waving in the light hot breeze, stood beside one of the cameramen. Morrison was sweeping the streets and neighboring building with his gaze like a guy on the lookout for snipers. He spotted Lackey, touched one of the camaramen on the elbow, and pointed. The cameraman spun around and aimed his minicam, at the same time saying something over his shoulder to the redheaded newswoman. Now her face turned toward Lackey as well. She left the group and approached Lackey with her mike held ready. Lackey recognized her, the good-looking redhead from the CBS affiliate, and thought she was thinner than she appeared on TV. Her hair was permed into tight ringlets. She said loudly, "Mr. Ferguson. Mr. Ferguson, any comment on these charges?"

Nancy's breath caught and she uttered a little sob. Lackey held her protectively around the waist and gave the newswoman a wide berth as he went past her. "No. Hell, no," Lackey said. "Leave us alone."

The newswoman moved the mike close to her own lips. "According to the District Attorney, you're the prime suspect in the murder of Mrs. Percy Hardin. I should think you'd want to comment." She thrust the microphone practically in Lackey's ear.

Lackey froze, and his jaw slacked. To Nancy he said, "Back in a minute, babe." He left her there and strode purposefully by the newswoman in the direction of Favor and Morrison and the reporters. Lackey's teeth were clenched and his hands were balled into fists.

The blond dish—Lackey recognized her as well, from the ABC station, a real head-turner with rumors floating through the local papers about her possibly going to the network as the five o'clock anchor—turned toward Lackey as he approached. She appeared flustered for an instant, then composed herself and said, "Do you want to make a statement?" Her lips curved into a smile that appeared painted on. Lackey ignored her. The second minicam pointed in his direction as he went by, looking neither right nor left, and headed straight for Detective Morrison.

Morrison watched Lackey approach, and the expression on the detective said that he sensed what was coming. He spread his stance slightly and raised his hands, then drew the front of his coat aside and started to go for his pistol.

Morrison never had a chance. Lackey grabbed the knot on the county cop's tie and yanked, thrust his own jaw forward and placed the end of his nose inches from Morrison's. Then Lackey shoved. Hard. Morrison stumbled backwards, flailed his arms for balance, then went over the curb and tumbled into the street in a tangled pile of arms and legs.

"You son of a bitch," Lackey said. He turned to the newspeople. "How's that? That enough of a comment for you?"

8

Everett Wilson knew good and well that he needed to ditch the gun in the creekbed and get the hell away from there, but he couldn't stop watching the girl. He remained still as a picture, crouched behind the thick trunk of an elm which stood tall over sycamores and weeping willows in the woods. Everett's lips were pulled back from crooked teeth in a half-smile, half-snarl, as he peered out at the soccer field.

The girl was around fifteen years old, and she was beautiful. Soft brown hair was tied at the nape of her neck and hung straight down her back nearly to her waist, bobbing and flying in the wind as she moved. She was practicing alone, dribbling a black-and-white soccer ball between dancer's feet, trotting a few steps, picking up speed, long lean legs flashing, smooth muscle rippling below the hem of her shorts as she thudded the side of first one foot, then the other, into the bounding ball. Firm buttocks tightened and relaxed in turn under blue satin fabric as she shifted her weight from one foot to the other.

In his hiding place, Everett breathed in rhythm with the girl's stride: one graceful step forward, inhale, one catlike hop to the side, exhale. Everett's organ was throbbing; he squeezed himself through his pants, first touching the flaccid head and then moving his fingers down to encircle the hardened shaft, finally stroking himself up and down, back and forth, in rhythm with the steps of the girl and his own breathing.

He hadn't noticed the girl as he'd left his Volvo on an adjacent side street, then scuttled crablike through the park with a plastic garbage bag—containing the .44 Bulldog, the rubber gloves, and the shirt and pants he'd worn into Marissa Hardin's house, along with a three-foot garden spade—slung over his shoulder like a troll headed for the treasure cache. Just as he'd been about to clamber down the earthen bank into the creekbed, the *thud-slap* of shoe against inflated leather had reached his ears, and he'd paused to glance in the direction of the sound. Then he'd set the bag aside and squatted behind the elm tree. He'd been rooted in place now for almost half an hour as he watched the girl.

But he had to be moving on. Had to. Couldn't sit here watching the girl, playing with himself like some fucking pervert with this murder evidence just inches from his knee. Not a smart guy like Everett Thomas Wilson, no way. He forced himself to rise and hefted the bag onto his shoulder, walking in an embarrassed crouch to shield his hard-on from view—though no one was watching. At least he was *embarrassed,* which to Everett's way of thinking proved that he wasn't any fucking wacko. He went down the bank and stood beside the creek.

He'd chosen the park some time ago, had even come to the murky creek and tested the softness of the soil on the bank. The park was in Arlington, a good thirty-minute drive from where Everett lived. The odds against anyone finding the gun, gloves, and clothing were a hundred to one, minimum, and even if someone should stumble onto the buried sack—and even if they should match the gun to the Hardin killing—they'd never tie any of it back to Everett Wilson. Never in a million years.

He opened the bag to remove the shovel, then refastened the twist-tie and went to work. Sweat beaded and ran down his sloping forehead. In less than ten minutes he had dug a hole a foot-and-a-half wide and

two feet deep. Everett was a tireless worker—one of
the few times in prison when he hadn't been in solitary
for whipping ass among the perverts, he'd picked two
hundred pounds of cotton in a single day—and he was
as strong as an ox. The TDC guards had known about
his strength and had kept their distance when calling
him Monkey Man.

He raised up, panting, rounded shoulders hunched,
and allowed himself a few seconds to admire the hole
he'd made, sniffing the odor of fresh-turned earth.
Then he dropped in the sack and refilled the hole. The
covering up took less than half the time that the digging had taken; Everett packed the soil by tamping it
with the flat side of the shovel, then stood back and
studied. Only a small mound was visible, and after
one good rain there would be nothing. Grinning with
satisfaction, he half-ran back up the bank to stand on
level ground among the trees.

The girl was still there, still dribbling the soccer
ball, seemingly no more winded than she'd been a
quarter of an hour ago. Everett liked it that the girl
was strong. Christ, how could she keep that up? Everett needed to be on his way. Had to go, but couldn't.
Acting like some fucking . . .

He carried the shovel tucked under his arm and left
the trees at a slow trot, approaching the girl from the
rear, his hands going to his zipper, pulling it down,
exposing himself as he moved in closer. He stopped a
scant five yards from her, just as she aimed a kick in
the direction of the goal. He tried to speak but
couldn't, his gaze frozen on her flashing legs.

Finally he cleared his throat and said, hoarse-voiced,
''Hey. Hey, you like this?'' His hand was moving rapidly back and forth along the shaft of his penis; soft
flesh moved over swollen hardness between his fingers.

She was smiling as she turned. The smile froze; her
lips pulled back from her white teeth in a grimace of

fear. Her eyes widened. She raised her gaze to look at his face, then looked back down at his erection. Her lips parted; she threw back her head and screamed at the top of her lungs.

Everett bolted. Back to the shelter of the woods he ran, in a shuffling, side-canted gait that was much faster than it appeared. Behind him, the girl screamed and screamed again.

He charged among the trees, breath whistling between crooked teeth, his own heavy footfalls jarring him as he picked up speed. Brown, bark-covered trunks flashed past on either side. He reached the street, dashed to the Volvo, threw the shovel into the back seat, climbed in and drove away. His erection was enormous; two blocks away he pulled into an alley and finished himself.

What the hell's wrong with me, Everett Wilson thought. I'm acting like a pervert or something.

Tom Earl Peterman, the afternoon shift detective-at-large in the Crimes Against Persons Division of the Arlington Police Department, thought at first that the park and playground on West Division Street were in the City of Grand Prairie. The mid-cities area between Dallas and Fort Worth were like that, city limit boundaries crawling here and there like the edges of jigsaw puzzle pieces, half the time no one sure what the fuck town they were in. Peterman sipped black coffee, ran his finger west on the map along Division among red, blue, and yellow pinheads, until he reached the intersection of Walden Street. He frowned. "Shit, it's ours. I guess I got to take the fucker."

"Lady's pretty excited," Detective Smitty Anderson said. He tore the top sheet from a ruled pad. "Mrs. Jackson. Here's the address." Anderson was tall, skinny, and red-faced with a big protruding Adam's apple, and at the moment appeared glad that he'd drawn telephone duty and didn't have to drive to the scene and investigate the call. Pain in the ass, Peterman thought.

Tom Earl Peterman was twenty-four, slim-waisted and broad-shouldered, a former defensive back from Fort Worth Southwest High who'd made detective less than a month ago. "Goddam parks are crawling with these wackos," Peterman said. "He do anything to the girl?" He set down his coffee, held his finger in place on the map, and inserted a red pin at the intersection of Division and Walden, right beside his third knuckle.

"Nope," Anderson said. "Not that she told her mother about. According to the woman the girl started screaming and the guy hauled ass."

Peterman went to the coat tree, took down his service revolver and shrugged into the nylon holster rig. "So I'm going out and ask some questions and make a report. The girl won't remember if the guy's tall or short, but I bet she can tell you what his dick looked like. They all remember that much. Think there's a message there?"

"You know, Peterman," Anderson said, "you are one sexist son of a bitch. Someday it's going to put you in a world of hurt. To hell with it, we got to do a report. But I wouldn't waste a lot of time with it. Guy going around waving his pecker's not going to hurt anybody anyhow. They're all afraid of their shadows."

Samuel Lincoln trusted psychologists even less than he trusted parolees, which was about as far as he could throw 'em, and the way this Dr. Anna Matthews was acting made him trust her even less. Lincoln had never heard of such a thing, a psychologist coming all the way down to the parole office just because he'd terminated her counseling contract with one lousy ex-convict. Jesus Christ, the woman was acting as though she was losing her entire practice. What the hell, in no time she'd have two or three more parolees to counsel and could bill the state even more than she'd been billing them up to now. A hundred and twenty-five bucks an hour, Lincoln thought, that's what *I* ought to be getting just for putting up with this obstinate woman. Samuel Lincoln was having a bad week; first the F&F Construction Company guy, now this pissed-off psychologist. Lincoln leaned forward and touched his fingertips together on top of his desk. "What's the man's name again?" he said. "I've got a couple of hundred files to keep up with here."

Dr. Anna Matthews, Lincoln had to admit, was a pretty cool customer, a tiny, businesslike lady with short dark hair, her expression friendly but inquisitive, never flustered no matter what, just the way they taught 'em in psychologist's school. "Wilson," she said. "Everett Thomas Wilson. His last session with me was a week ago Monday."

"Wilson, Wilson." Lincoln scratched his chin, then snapped his fingers. "Oh, yeah." He opened his bottom drawer and thumbed through the file folders, all the way back to the letter *W.* "Ugly guy," Lincoln said. "Looks like a gorilla. Yeah, sure, I remember him." He found the folder and lifted it out of the drawer.

"His physical makeup is one of his problems," Anna Matthews said. "Just one of many."

"They've all got some problems, ma'am," Lincoln said. "Otherwise they never would have gone to prison. According to my chart you're paid up to date. I approved your last statement April twenty-ninth."

"That's true," Dr. Matthews said. "That's not why I'm here. As I said, I want to talk about why he's not coming back."

"Well, that's an easy question to answer," Lincoln said. "Twenty-six counseling sessions, that's enough to take care of anybody's problems. We're working on a short budget here." Money's what it's all about, he thought, no matter what this woman says.

She primly crossed her legs and smoothed her lime-green skirt. "Are you familiar with this man's history, Mr. Lincoln?"

Familiar? Lincoln thought. Two hundred assholes, I'm supposed to be familiar with this one guy. "Sure," he said. "We're familiar with everybody's history down here." He snapped open the file. "Guy's done three burglary beefs, last one ten years, did twenty-six months, paroled to Fort Worth eleven-fourteen-eighty-nine." What the hell's she think a parole officer is for? he thought. "The board recommended counseling, Dr. Matthews. That's why we sent him to you. Now we feel that he's had his counseling, he needs to get on with his life." Lincoln favored Anna Matthews with his best That's-the-way-it-is-and-that's-final expression.

She didn't even blink. "Does your file show that a condition of his parole was that he not return to Houston to live?"

"It's probably in here. A lot of these prosecutors, well they get . . . get it in for these guys." Lincoln had almost said, "get a hard-on for these guys," then had considered who he was talking to. He cleared his throat. "I got quite a few of 'em that can't go back to their home towns, usually it's something personal with the prosecutor or judge. They've all got to justify their existence." Including you, Lincoln thought. Wonder if she's got it in for blacks.

"Does your file show *why* he can't go back?" Anna Matthews's expression remained calm, as though Lincoln was one of her patients, as if even though she was a high-priced doctor she didn't look down on people who had to work for a living. Give me a break, Lincoln thought.

"Probably," Lincoln said. "Most of 'em got some reason or other, these prosecutors have to put something down. Concern for the victim or some such, they can't just restrict the guy without giving a reason. If they didn't say something the board wouldn't go along with their request that the guy live someplace else. We don't just rubber-stamp 'em, you know.''

"I'm sure you don't,'' Dr. Matthews said, adjusting her position in the chair, one hand dangling loosely from the end of the armrest, showing manicured and polished nails. Clear lacquer. "And that's comforting. But in any system there are a few who slip through the cracks, and the real purpose of my visit is to impress on you the kind of animal you're dealing with. This man needs more counseling. A great deal more. He's a victim of some pretty serious child abuse, and the odds are pretty slim that he'll ever get over it.'' On the wall behind her, visible over the top of her head, the small round clock showed 4:05. Twenty-five more minutes, Lincoln thought, then I can get out of here and have a few cool ones.

"Hey,'' Lincoln said. "I remember talking to this guy. He grew up in an orphans' home in Houston. Come to think about it, I talked to him about it a long time, and he didn't say anything about anybody mistreating him. Seems like a pretty friendly guy, tell you the truth. Well adjusted, most of these parolees won't look you in the eye.''

"Oh, he puts on a good front. That I'll grant you. The abuse, that came before the home. His foster father. Everett never knew his mother. She was a lesbian, and I suspect strongly that Everett was conceived during a rape in the Harris County Jail. She wouldn't have submitted to a man on a voluntary basis.''

You ought to know about that, Lincoln thought. He said, "A rape? What, some guards or something? That happens.''

She calmly shook her head. "Inmates. There's no documentation, of course, I've had to piece the scenario together. His mother was called Mikey D. Dalton, and I say 'called' because she didn't even have a birth certificate that anyone's been able to locate. She's got—*had,* she's dead now—a long record in Harris

County. Solicitation, drugs, you name it. She acted and dressed the part of a man, made solicitations for oral sex to men who thought she was male and were themselves of that persuasion. Every time she was booked into the jail she refused to acknowledge her gender and wound up on the male side. I suspect the rape happened in one of the holding cells, before they undressed her and discovered what they had.''

Lincoln drummed his fingers, tried his best to appear interested, figuring that the pay was the same for listening to this woman as doing anything else. He raised his eyebrows and didn't say anything.

''According to records at Ben Taub Hospital,'' Anna Matthews said, ''—and keep in mind that these are very *old* records, and as such, must be taken with a grain of salt—but according to the records, she checked in to have the child aborted. She met a man there, an orderly with a long criminal history himself, named Eli Wilson. Mikey backed out on the abortion and later had her baby and turned the child over to Eli Wilson. *Sold* the child, more than likely, but there's no proof of that. What *is* documented is that Eli Wilson made his money in child pornography. That and worse things.

''Eli Wilson took the boy home and named him. Kept him locked in the closet mostly, then took him out for . . . for photo sessions. Also for paid sexual sessions, most of them arranged by Eli's wife. Lovely couple, what?'' Anna Matthews looked down at her lap, then raised long-lashed eyes, slightly hesitant in her manner for the first time since she'd entered Lincoln's office. She flicked her tongue quickly over her upper lip and went on. ''When Everett was four years old he resisted once. As punishment, the wife held Everett down while Eli nailed the boy's penis to a board.''

''Jesus Christ.'' Lincoln sat up straighter, interested now, wondering whether this woman could be putting him on so that she could keep on treating the guy. Anna Matthews looked to be in her early thirties, just a few years older than Lincoln himself, and Lincoln wondered how she got up nerve enough to talk to men about things like this. Might get her kicks that way, Lincoln thought. "Jesus Christ," Lincoln said again. "Did you look at his . . . ?"

Dr. Matthews smiled slightly. "I don't make a habit of examining my patients' private parts, Mr. Lincoln. You're his parole officer. Have you? Seen it."

"No. No, why would I be looking at the guy's . . . ?"

"Urinalysis, perhaps. Drug testing."

Lincoln said, "This guy's got no drug history, people with his record we don't U.A. Sometimes these guys make things up."

"I'm trained to spot that," Anna Matthews said, her calm returning, her hesitancy gone. "Besides, this is documented. That's how he wound up in the orphans' home, a neighbor heard the child screaming and called the police. Eli drew a thirty-year sentence, the wife ten. He never made his release date, incidentally. Stabbed in the exercise yard by another inmate. People like Eli are not very popular even in prison, it's my understanding. I deal with sex offenders every day, Mr. Lincoln, and people who were abused as children are classic cases. Everett Wilson, though, is more than classic. He actually seems to *admire* Eli."

She enjoys it, Lincoln thought, sitting around talking about all these sexual nuts. He forced himself not to smirk and searched quickly through Wilson's file. "I don't remember any sex offenses on his record," Lincoln said. "We watch pretty close for that stuff."

"No *convictions*, Mr. Lincoln. Everett Wilson—he legally took the last name, which is strange in light of what Eli did to him—Everett puts on a tough-guy front, and I think the feminine traits one associates with a case like this are missing because, well, he simply

never had any feminine influence whatsoever. But the
result is the same. I've talked to the prosecutor, incidentally, along with the investigating officers on his
last case. There had been a string of child molesta-
tions, an unknown man carrying little girls out of their
bedrooms at night and . . . They caught Everett in the
act of climbing in a little girl's window. He accepted
the burglary sentence in a plea agreement. According
to the prosecutor, since he'd never been caught in the
act of molesting one of the children, it was the best
the state could do. Both the prosecutor and the inves-
tigators are convinced that he was the culprit. The mo-
lestation incidents ceased once Everett went to
prison.''

"Hey, isn't this the guy . . . ?'' Lincoln allowed the
papers he was holding to drop back into the open file
folder. ''Yeah. Yeah, this is the guy that told me he
used to be a football player. I didn't think he looked
much like one, tell you the truth.''

"He was a good all-around athlete in spite of his
strange physique,'' Anna Matthews said. ''They did
reconstructive surgery on his penis before he entered
the home, but I think his injuries are quite repugnant
to look at. He's awfully reluctant to talk about them,
even though he's pretty glib on every other subject.
When he was older, the kids at the home were allowed
to attend public school in Pasadena. You know, the
Houston suburb. Everett was a very good defensive
lineman and even had some chances for football schol-
arships. Do you have any idea what happened to those
chances?''

"According to my file,'' Lincoln said, ''his first trip
to the joint was when he was eighteen. I guess that
ended them.''

"Not exactly, his first burglary sentence was after
he'd graduated from high school. But there was another incident which happened in school, and frankly
it's difficult to get the school administration to talk

about it. A teacher. He beat her up and put her in the hospital. For some reason no charges were ever filed, and from my interviews with Everett I sort of, well, suspect that what happened was that the teacher made some sexual advances to him and he went berserk. If she was the aggressor, that would explain why she didn't go to the police even though he broke her jaw and arm. But word got around, and that's why the colleges were no longer interested in him as a football prospect. I suppose the University of Oklahoma never heard about him.'' She smiled at her own little joke, then composed herself. ''He's still terribly strong, even now at forty.'' Anna Matthews intertwined her fingers, the clinical psychologist now completely at home, right in her own ballyard with what she was discussing. And just a little bit smug about it, Lincoln thought, thinking she's talking over my head.

''It's pretty interesting that you should come up with all that on him,'' Lincoln said. ''Especially when the whole state of Texas couldn't. This file looks like a case history on a plain vanilla burglar to me. A guy stealing TVs and stuff.''

''Oh, he steals things,'' Anna Matthews said. ''And swaggers around and talks out of the side of his mouth, and does everything a tough convict should do. He's absolutely rabid about wanting everybody to think he's one of the penitentiary 'in' crowd, but the prison psychologists recognized the tics in his makeup. It's pretty easy to do once you've interviewed him a couple of times. That's why they recommended counseling in his parole regimen, that plus what the Houston authorities had to say about him. I consider Everett both unpredictable and potentially dangerous, Mr. Lincoln, even more so because of the outward veneer of normality, and I'm here to let you know that if you terminate his counseling there may be serious consequences.'' Her tone was calm and matter-of-fact, her gaze steady; the lady meant exactly what she was saying.

There she goes again, Lincoln thought, talking down to me, this pint-sized woman trying to use her education and looks in order to get the upper hand. Lincoln wondered briefly whether she'd go over his head to his supervisor. Probably would, he thought. The trouble was that Lincoln had recommended terminating the visits and had put it on the list of things he'd done to stay within the budget, and if he now reversed himself he was going to look pretty stupid. But Jesus Christ, he thought, a kid getting his tallywhacker nailed to a board. He closed the file and pretended to think it over, then finally said, "Tell you what, Dr. Matthews, I'll talk it over with my boss. Whatever he says goes, if he wants to overrule me on this one it's up to him. How's that?"

"It's better than nothing," Anna Matthews said. "But I'm going to stress the importance of time. Everett doesn't need to be walking around without help for very long. Thanks for lending your ear, Mr. Lincoln." She stood, picked up her clipboard from Lincoln's desk, and turned to go.

That ought to hold her off a couple of months, Lincoln thought.

Everett Wilson didn't like TV news. Couldn't stand it, in fact, some fucking nigger sitting up there grinning, or worse than that, some white guy who got his hair done in a beauty parlor and laid around in a tanning salon with the rest of the perverts, telling all about George Bush playing golf or, even worse to Everett's way of thinking, showing a videotape of some Iraq hostage whining for somebody to turn him loose. Those fucking Iraqis were damn sure lucky they didn't have Everett Thomas Wilson for a hostage. Everett Thomas Wilson would show the fucking sand-niggers what a real by-God ex–Texas convict thought about anybody trying to hold him for ransom. Make them sand-niggers holler uncle is what Everett Thomas Wil-

son would do. Served George Bush right, sending a
bunch of wimps over to Iraq for some fucking terror-
ists to capture.

So anytime he was watching TV and the news was
about to come on, Everett changed the channel. He
had it down to a science. It had been a little harder in
the joint because one of the perverts might put up a
bitch, but in the joint the back of Everett's hand, or
the threat of having Everett's strange-looking cock
shoved down their throats, had pretty much kept the
perverts in line. In the cellblock, Everett Thomas Wilson had ruled the dayroom.

Here in his own apartment, all he had to do was
turn the channel selector. *Click-click,* no more grinning nigger or faggy-looking white guy. Just as the
nine-to-ten network program was winding down and
was about to show five minutes' worth of commercials, Everett would get up from the sofa and switch
to Channel Eleven. Channel Eleven was an indepen-
dent, showing fifteen minutes' worth of news from
nine-forty-five until ten and then coming on at the hour
with Benny Hill. Everett didn't really think that Benny
Hill was very funny, kind of a fat British guy who did
a lot of slapstick, but Benny Hill damn sure beat the
news and had a lot of big-titted women on his program.

But on this particular night when the network came
on with the commercials, Everett's mind was someplace else. He was picturing the girl and the soccer
ball—Christ, but that bitch had had an ass on her—and
he stared off into space through the Miller Lite, Cadillac, and Eveready ads. By the time Everett snapped
to, the ten o'clock news was already on the air. He
lumbered over to the set to switch to Benny Hill, but
once there froze with his hand on the channel selector.

He heard one word that caught his attention: ''Hardin.'' Everett backed quickly away in order to see the
picture, a kind-of-pretty nigger girl giving a five-

second preview of what was coming on the news. "Major suspect" was the second phrase that Everett caught; a major suspect in the Hardin murder. He left the channel selector alone and retreated to the couch, a stumpy hairy-chested man with arms hanging to his knees, barefoot and wearing only a pair of Bermuda shorts, moving across the dirty hardwood floor, flopping down finally on the sofa cushions, picking up a bag of Cheetos from the end table and stuffing a fistful from the bag into his mouth. He chewed, crunching the salty Cheetos with crooked teeth and washing them down with Coke, and watched the news.

Which for the first twenty minutes was a lot of bullshit, more pictures of George Bush playing golf and more pictures of wimpy hostages bawling at the camera. So much bullshit, in fact, that three different times Everett got up from the sofa and nearly switched over to Benny Hill. But each time he did, the anchorperson would come on with another teaser, saying that in a few minutes they were going to show the suspect in the Hardin murder, so Everett would retreat to the sofa and put up with the bullshit.

Finally, there it was, a shot of downtown Fort Worth with an Assistant District Attorney (who looked like a fat little prick just like every other prosecutor Everett had seen) giving an interview on the sidewalk. Then the scene cut to the sidewalk outside the entrance to an office building, showing a guy with a weightlifter's build, clad in jeans and T-shirt, coming down the street with one arm around a Mexican broad.

Everett's eyes narrowed. His jaw froze with his mouth open, and crumbs of soggy Cheeto dropped from his lips and stuck to his chin. Jesus, this steady-eyed dude on television looked like somebody you might not want to fuck with, arms ridged with muscle, solid chest, and strong nimble legs like a middle-weight fighter. Everett watched as though hypnotized, watched as Lackey Ferguson strode purposefully away

from his girl and grabbed the cop by the tie, then
shoved the cop head over heels into the gutter. One
tough son of a bitch, this guy might be. The picture
on the TV screen cut quickly to a full-length shot of
the tough guy, stern-eyed gaze on the camera, as he
paused long enough to open a car door for the chili-
pepper girl and put her in the front seat. There was a
closeup of the girl, tears streaming down her cheeks
as she got in the car. Then the news segment ended.
The program continued.

The sports guy was next, giving the baseball scores,
but Everett was no longer paying attention. His gaze
was frozen on the spot on the screen where, seconds
ago, the girl's image had been, the closeup of her soft
pretty features, dark eyes and long curved lashes. She'd
been crying.

It was as though something had taken control of Everett's body. His hand dropped into his lap and his
eyes glazed. In seconds he was pulling feverishly at
his crotch. His eyes closed passionately and he
moaned.

9

One time when Lackey Ferguson had been stationed in Germany, a young corporal in the outfit had lost his mother. For some reason the boy's relatives hadn't gotten through to him on the phone, and the kid had learned of his mother's death by mail. On the night the letter had come, Lackey and the corporal had gone into Wiesbaden. There they'd found an isolated tavern where the two of them had been the only customers who had spoken English and had drunk pitchers of dark beer until three or four in the morning. Around two o'clock, the corporal had broken down. Lackey had sat there at the rough wooden table and listened to the boy's sobs and would have given anything to have been able to ease the pain that the kid must have felt. It had been a totally helpless feeling, and was the same feeling that Lackey had now, seated in his pickup in front of Nancy's apartment house at midnight, cradling her in his arms while she cried against his shoulder.

"Maybe it would," Lackey said, then swallowed a lump in his throat and said. "Maybe it would be better if you didn't see me any more till this is over. We could tell people that you don't want to go around with a guy that's, you know, under suspicion or whatever they're saying." The stereo was on low volume and Lackey had switched from country and western to an easy-listening station; the song now playing was "French Foreign Legion," an old, old oldie by Frank

Sinatra. Forty yards from the pickup, across a lawn of mowed Bermuda grass and two sidewalks, a single bulb glowed above the steps leading to Nancy's place. A block away, the lights on Loop 820 made a faint illumination on the horizon, and, heard through the pickup's open window, distant freeway traffic rumbled.

Nancy moved slightly away from him and tilted her head, looking up with her face illuminated in the glow from the overhead streetlamp. Her lashes were stuck together in a row of dark wet points. "If that's what you want," she said softly. "If that's, God, if that's what you . . ." She buried her face in the hollow of his shoulder and cried even harder, her shoulders heaving, her breath coming in brief gasps.

He spread his hand and laid his open palm against the back of her head, feeling the unsprayed softness of her hair. "Hey. Hey, you know better than that. It's just that your job, those lawyers aren't going to want anything like this. Those guys aren't going to like you being on television a bit."

"To hell with them," Nancy said, her voice muffled against him, using the tame English cussword, about the only cussword other than "damn" that Lackey had ever heard from her. "If they don't like it, I'll go to Whattaburger or somewhere," Nancy said. "That's silly, you talking like that." She backed away once more, sniffling, her despair shifting into a determined thoughtfulness. "They found her in her bedroom. Were you in there?"

"Jesus Christ, Nancy."

She placed four fingers over his lips, shut her eyes tightly and shook her head. "We don't have time to be dumb, either one of us. You're a man and all—if I have to, I can live with it. They do some criminal defense work down at the office, you know. We're talking about evidence. Now. Were you?" Her gaze was steady, no hint of jealousy in her look, just a very interested and very smart girl looking for information. Sometimes when they were goofing off, it was easy for Lackey to forget just how smart Nancy was.

"I went in that house twice," Lackey said. "Once with her and her husband, that was in the parlor. Then I went to the bank and came back. The second time it was just me and her. We went through this big den, you ought to see that room, we went through this big den into the kitchen. I went out the same way." He was really glad that he hadn't fooled around with Marissa Hardin, really glad now because he knew that under the circumstances he wouldn't have been able to lie to Nancy about it.

"Think very hard," Nancy said. "What did you touch?"

"She gave me a milkshake."

Her eyes twinkled suddenly in the moonlight. "Chocolate or vanilla?"

"There wasn't any milk. Nancy—"

"Hush. A sense of humor is important right now. What was it exactly?"

"A health kick, it was orange juice and an egg, I think. She whipped it up in a blender and I remember it tasted like an Orange Julius."

She scooted away from him on the seat, drew up one leg and sat on her ankle. A foot of tensed thigh showed below the hem of her skirt. "So you handled a glass. That means they'll have a fingerprint. What else happened?"

"You already know she wrote me out a check."

"That's right. And you cashed it, they'll try and make a big deal over that. Like you knew you had to run to the bank with the check because you knew she was dead."

He ground his knuckles into the palm of his hand. "I can't understand why they didn't put me in jail. If I was them . . ." Lackey wondered briefly how long the helpless feeling was going to last.

"They don't have to. You're not going anywhere. I wouldn't be surprised if they're following you. Just try and leave town and see how far you get. Downtown today, did they take any samples from you?"

He studied the top of the steering wheel. "I guess you have to know about that."

"Me or your lawyer. Or both, we'd better talk about retaining one," Nancy said. Nervous as he was, Lackey didn't miss Nancy's use of "we." Nancy and Lackey, in it together.

"I can't afford one of those guys," Lackey said. "Unless I used the fifteen thousand. Then they'd probably get me for stealing the money."

"What tests?" Nancy said.

"Well. Well, they took a hair."

"From your head?"

"No."

"Oh. Down there, huh?" Nancy said.

"Yeah."

"Then whoever it was must have raped her. Did they take semen?" She blinked clinically, this girl around whom Lackey was careful not to say "shit" or anything.

"Aw, Nancy," he said.

"We're getting married, Lackey. And we've been to bed together. Come on, did they take semen?"

"Yeah."

She folded her arms and pertly nodded her head. "That's good."

"That's funny, I didn't think it was so hot."

"That's the reason they didn't arrest you, dope." She pronounced *dope* more like "dop," with just a trace of a Hispanic accent. "They've got your fingerprint on a glass in the kitchen and the canceled check from the bank," she said, "but without a match on the semen and the pubic hair they can't place you in the bedroom. I'll bet they have a comparison the first thing in the morning, and if there's even a hint of a

match you'll be in the county before noon. Mr. Brantley defended a guy on a rape charge and they let him
walk around loose for three days before they picked
him up.''

He brightened slightly, getting her drift, getting into
the swing of trying to figure out what evidence the
D.A. might have. "She entered that check in her
book,'' he said.

She cocked her head. "I'm not sure what you
mean.''

"Her ledger, she subtracted it, I remember she
looked around for a calculator and then did it in her
head. I mean, if I was standing there saying, write me
a check or I'll kill you, something like that, would she
take the time to do that?''

"It's a thought," Nancy said, pinching her chin.
"But they'd just say you waited until she'd written the
check before you started to get rough with her.''

"Oh," Lackey said.

"No, it all comes down to the samples. It doesn't
mean they'll leave you alone if they don't get a match,
but they won't arrest you until they can get more evidence. Or invent more, whatever.''

"Well, I—"

Lackey stopped in midsentence, jumped slightly as
headlights shone in his rearview mirror. The car approached from behind them, coming down the dark
street at a pretty good clip, then pulled suddenly to
the curb and screeched to a halt with its nose close to
Lackey's bumper. The car's lights stayed on. Its doors
opened and slammed shut. Jesus, Lackey thought, are
they coming for me already? Nancy gasped, turned to
peer fearfully through the rear window. In the beam
of the headlights, her pupils shrank instantly into twin
pencil points.

"Stay," Lackey said, drawing a breath. "Stay put,
hon.'' His knees slightly rubbery, hearing in his mind
the metallic rasp of handcuffs as they closed around

his wrists, he got out of the pickup and walked to the rear.

He'd gone about halfway, had come abreast of the pickup's bed, when he stopped and squinted at the car's headlights. One of the lights shone brightly while the other was dim and flickering. The car badly needed a tuneup; its hood vibrated as the engine missed. Visible between the headlamps was a rocket-shaped hood ornament; the car was an Olds, fifty-nine or sixty. What the hell? Lackey thought, that isn't any cop car. What in . . . ?

Alvin Cuellar came past the nose of the Oldsmobile, approached with his square shoulders outlined in the glow of the headlights. He stopped a few feet away and said, "Ho, Lackey Ferguson."

Herman Cuellar came around the rear of the pickup to stand shoulder to shoulder with his nephew. Alvin was Nancy's older brother and had been a year ahead of Lackey in school; Herman had been full-grown when Lackey had been a kid, and had operated his own auto repair business for twenty years or so. Herman was maybe forty-five. Even could have been fifty, Lackey wasn't sure. But Herman still did all of the heavy engine work himself, and was in pretty good shape regardless of his age. Lackey leaned against the side of the pickup and said, "Hey. What's goin' on?"

"Now you and me always got along," Alvin said, holding up a hand palm out. "So I tell you the same thing I tole my mama. We don't want no chit, let's get that straight." He was a couple of inches taller than his uncle, the top of his head on a level with the bridge of Lackey's nose. Alvin was on the angular side where Herman had beefy shoulders and a thick chest. Both men wore plain white T-shirts and faded jeans.

"That's what I tell my sister, Nancy's mama, too," Herman said. "I don't want no chit wid anybody. So how 'bout you, Lackey? You want any chit?"

"Course not," Lackey said.

"That's good," Alvin said. "Nobody wants no chit wid nobody. We all in agreement, right?"

"Yeah, I guess," Lackey said. "I don't want any shit, you don't want any shit. So like I said, what's goin' on?" Alvin had been a pretty good dash man in high school, but wasn't doing any working out right now. His slightly protruding gut told Lackey that much. Lackey figured he could take either of the two alone. Both at once, he doubted it. Besides, he didn't want that. Nancy had enough problems with her family as it was.

"But if chit come along," Alvin said, "don't nobody going to run from it. Mama seen the news tonight. You got my little sister's picture on the television, huh?"

"I didn't do it on purpose," Lackey said. "And I've done nothing, I don't care what you—"

"We ain't saying you did," Herman said. "And chit like that ain't nothing the Lackey we know going to fuck with. But that ain't helping Nancy's mama none, you know what I mean?"

"Yeah," Lackey said. "I guess I do."

"We awful proud of my sister," Alvin said. "And she didn't go through no college so some dude could get her on no ten p.m. crime news, you know what I mean?"

"I don't want her on any crime report, either," Lackey said. "But that's something I can't do anything about. Not right now."

"So what we're saying is," Alvin said, "that maybe you ought to leave my sister be till you can get this chit straightened out. What you think?"

Lackey opened his mouth to answer, then closed it. Nancy was suddenly at his side, her hands on her hips, the scent of her perfume in Lackey's nostrils, Nancy slim and pretty, the legal secretary in high heels and business dress facing off against two guys in T-shirts. *"No necessito mi familia,"* Nancy said. *"¿Por que tú estás aquí?''* Lackey didn't have any idea what she was saying, but the defiant tilt to her chin was enough.

Alvin dropped his gaze to the asphalt and answered her in Spanish, and then Nancy took a step closer to her brother and said something in Spanish as well. Then Herman said something, also in Spanish, and Nancy cut him off in midsentence with a few choice words of her own. Lackey caught *''pindejo''* and tried to remember what Ronnie Ferias had told him that meant in English, and at the same time he wondered why Nancy didn't mind cussing at her own family but wouldn't cuss at her fiancé. Must have something to do with them all growing up in the same house together. Whatever she was telling them it was putting them in their place, both Herman and Alvin were looking sheepishly down at their shoes.

Finally Nancy stepped close to Lackey, put her arm through his and hugged him to her. "He's my man, *hermano y tío,*" Nancy said. "And pretty soon he's going to be my husband and part of your family. Anybody that can't live with that needs to go find themselves another relative. You understand what I'm telling you?''

10

At seven-thirty on Wednesday morning, Oscar Ferguson set his coffee cup into the saucer with a soft glassy clink. "The trouble is that the service manager's afraid to get that white coat dirty. I used to get right down into the engine with the mechanic and show the guy what was wrong with his car. That's what my customers wanted, and now I'm a customer it's what I want, too. Show me somebody that'll do that, and that's the guy that's getting my business." There were deep creases around his nose and eyes, his skin like leather from spending time in the sunlight, showing a tan the color of stained oak even though the hot season had just begun. Oscar mowed the yard three times a week, and by August he'd be hard to distinguish at a distance from one of the Mexicans. When Lackey had been a kid his dad had mowed on Sundays only, which had been his only day off from Hudiberg Chevrolet's service department.

"It's different now, daddy," Lackey said. "They got these college guys. Management degrees, they're supposed to spend all their time supervising. It's what the big corporations want 'em to do." He was seated at the white wooden breakfast table in the kitchen with Oscar at his left and Helen, his mom, across from him. Every Wednesday, rain or shine, Lackey came by his folks's on his way to the job. So far they hadn't mentioned the murder, though Helen was sniffling a bit as though she had a cold, and Oscar was really grasping to find something to talk about. The green-and-white linoleum and the refrigerator with the icemaker were things added since Lackey had joined the army. Otherwise, the kitchen was still the same. "As long as they're sending your retirement check, what do you care?" Lackey said.

"I keep cashing it," Oscar said. "But where I spend it's going to change unless they show me something different."

"Marj Stevens called," Helen said. "August they're going to Canada. Said she's sorry she won't be here." There wasn't as yet a trace of gray in her auburn hair. Everyone said that Lackey had gotten his features from Helen and his coloring from Oscar; studying his mom's prominent cheekbones and straight slender nose, Lackey couldn't disagree.

"Well at least she won't be grading my wedding," Lackey said. "She might do it like one of my English papers."

"I 'spect you'll be better prepared for getting married than you ever were for English," Helen said. She gave a nervous laugh, exchanged glances with Oscar, then regarded her folded hands.

Lackey decided he'd better move on before he had to get a kitchen knife to cut through the tension. "Well," he said. "I got to get going." He finished his milk with a gulp; to this day Helen never offered him coffee, and Lackey doubted that she ever would. He stood and lifted his hard hat from the table.

"Lackey," Helen said, and at the same instant Oscar said, "Son."

Lackey twirled his hard hat between his fingers, wanting to say something that would make them feel better but knowing that the only way to make it right with them was for him to get out of this mess. "Hmm?" Lackey said.

"We got a little savings," Oscar said. "Not much."

"Hang on to it, daddy," Lackey said. "I'm okay."

Helen began to cry, then, taking her napkin from her lap and blowing her nose. Lackey's vision blurred slightly. He went over to stand beside her, reached out and stroked her hair.

"I didn't do it, mama," Lackey said. "And if I was lying you'd know it. Wouldn't you, now?"

Lackey was beginning to understand how a fugitive felt, driving down the road glancing in the rearview mirror, waking up in the morning and peering out through the drapes like a guy whose place was surrounded. He thought about the semen and hair samples he'd given, knowing he'd done the right thing, but at the same time feeling nervous as hell. I'm no doctor, Lackey thought, how do I know they won't mix my samples up with somebody else's? He pictured himself trying to explain to Nancy how they'd gotten a match on the samples even though he'd never even been in that bedroom. Even Nancy could only swallow so much.

He didn't notice anyone following his pickup east on Loop 820, but that was something Lackey didn't know anything about, either. He doubted that the police would put a tail on him with the guy wearing a sign. Probably the tail would be disguised, Lackey thought, like the guy driving behind him at the moment, a man wearing a sportshirt and driving a blue four-year-old Ford. Or the tail could be a woman, the schoolteacher type in the green Nissan in the lane to his right, wearing conservative hornrim glasses, both hands on the wheel, her gaze on the road. He pictured himself stopped at a red light, and the woman suddenly leaping from her car, flashing a badge and pulling a gun from her purse. As she cuffed his hands behind him she'd tell him that word had just come over her radio that his hair and semen samples had matched. Lackey slowed the pickup and moved over in the lane behind the woman. A little further on, she pulled from

the freeway into a Citgo station, got out, then regarded
him suspiciously with her hand on her gas cap as he
cruised on by. Jesus, Lackey thought, now she'll be
calling the police and telling them that I'm following
her. He snatched his hard hat from the seat, put it on
and pulled it low over his eyes. See, lady, nothing
dangerous, just a guy on his way to the construction
site.

He took the Grapevine exit, leaving the rush hour
stop-and-go traffic—little foreign makes transporting
working women over to Irving and Dallas along with
a few pickups and semis carrying the blue-collar men—
and concentrated on his driving to get his mind off of
his problems. As if that was possible.

At eight in the morning it was near ninety degrees;
Lackey rolled his window down, rested his elbow on
the sill, and let the sun beat down on his arm and the
hot wind whip around the interior of the cab. The radio was still tuned to Nancy's easy-listening station;
he switched over to country KJIM and listened to Da-
vid Allan Coe's raspy tenor on "Please Come to Bos-
ton." By the time he'd driven north on Davis Boulevard
to the remodeling job, and pulled over and parked at
the curb, he was in a better mood. He was whistling
softly to himself as he cut the engine, climbed down
from the pickup and started to cross the lawn. He
stopped. The gloom returned in a flash and clutched
at his insides.

The car parked behind Ronnie Ferias's Bronco
wasn't a police vehicle, but it didn't belong here and
had to mean trouble. It was a drab gray unmarked
four-door Mercury Marquis. Lackey knew for sure that
the Merc didn't belong to one of the crew. Frank Nichols's old Buick was across the street behind Ramon
Gomez's beat-up Plymouth; the black guys rode with
Frank, and the Mexican workers came to the job with
Ramon, all eight of them piling in the two cars, some
to save on gas and others because they hadn't been out

of prison long enough to get up a down payment for a car of their own. The Merc didn't belong to the house's owner, either; the plumber was a sporty guy who went around in a Corvette and wouldn't have been caught dead in a plain vanilla four-door. Lackey sighed, then skirted the house and went back to the addition, mentally preparing for trouble. Trouble was back there, all right, beginning with a capital *T*.

Near the west side of the addition, at the corner where two sections of roofboard joined overhead, Lincoln the Parole Officer stood with hands on hips. He was talking a mile a minute, giving Ronnie Ferias a marine-corps drill-sergeant dressing-down. Ronnie wore his usual T-shirt and jeans. His plastic Texas Rangers batting helmet was tilted downward as he regarded his hard-toed shoes. Frank Nichols stood off to one side, along with Ramon Gomez and the other six workers. As Lackey approached, Frank met his gaze. Frank shook his head sadly and rolled his eyes.

Lincoln was saying, "And if you decide to break up the partnership, I got to be able to verify it. The guy can't be lurking in the wings."

"We got a deadline on finishing this job," Ronnie said.

"Not my problem," Lincoln said. "*Your* problem. Not my problem whether the guy did it or not, either, that's up to the D.A. What is my problem is where these parolees hang out, and as long as the guy's part of this company you're not using any of our people." He raised his voice and directed his attention to Frank Nichols and the other workers. "I'll be checking the other job sites, too, and the first one of my guys I catch working for this outfit can look to spend some time in the cooler."

Lackey went up and stood between Ronnie and Lincoln so that the three of them formed a triangle. "Mr. Lincoln," Lackey said. "How you doin'?"

Lincoln's eyes were hidden behind black sunglasses

and his lips were set in a rigid line. He nodded curtly. "Mr. Ferguson."

"He says we can't use no more parolees," Ronnie said.

Lackey swiveled his head to look toward the workers, then said to Lincoln and Ronnie, "I heard him. I guess you know you're putting us out of business. No way can we put together enough crews to finish these jobs we got going."

One corner of Lincoln's mouth turned up. "Like I said, not my problem. And you got bigger problems yourself, from what I'm hearing and reading."

"I haven't seen the paper," Lackey said.

"I don't blame you," Lincoln said. "If I was you I wouldn't read it, either." He took two long steps toward the workmen. "Out of here, men. Now. I'm going to stand in the front yard and check your names off, don't nobody think about staying on. You got five minutes to collect your gear." He turned on his heel and marched away, disappearing around the corner of the house with his clipboard swinging by his hip.

Frank Nichols watched Lincoln go, then glanced around him at the other workers, finally lowering his head and murmuring, "Mothafuckah." Cussing in English and Spanish, the men began to pick up their hammers and nails and canvas bags of specialty tools. They moved past Ronnie and Lackey in a disgruntled, uneven line, lugging their belongings away.

Frank Nichols paused. His gaze swept Lackey, head to toe. "Ain't over, bossman," Frank said. "Bet yo ass on that. Ain't no way you done that shit, you ain't the type. I seen too many of 'em." He lowered his head and followed the other men.

When the men had gone, Ronnie said, "That just tears it. Beats all I ever saw. What you think, *compadre*?"

Lackey looked around at the construction site, at the partially completed roof, at the pile of brick waiting to be laid. "Looks like you and me got a lot of work to do," Lackey Ferguson said.

At ten o'clock on Wednesday morning, County Detective Henley joined County Detective Morrison and Deputy District Attorney Favor in Favor's office. "The lab can't get a match," Henley said. "I would've bet a month's pay on the fucking guy." He sat down and rubbed the smooth skin on top of his head.

Favor was chewing an unlit cigar. He laid the cigar in an ashtray, used his thumb and index finger to remove a shred of tobacco from between his teeth, and thumped the tobacco into a wastebasket. "What, not enough points of similarity, or . . . ?"

"Not one," Henley said. "The hair's thicker and a different color, they even checked it for dye. The sperm count in the semen's different, so's the blood type." He propped his ankle up on his knee and pressed his shin against the edge of Favor's desk. "No match. The hair's not the guy's and neither's the jism."

Favor tugged at his own earlobe. "Well that's a fly in the old ointment." Visible through the window behind him, one off-white wall of Tandy Center was in sunlight, the other visible side of the skyscraper in shade.

Morrison bent forward in his chair and scratched his rump, then adjusted the holstered revolver on his belt. "Maybe. But it don't mean anything except that he had a buddy with him. They probably took turns. Sonofabitch push *me* down in front of all them people." Tufts of blond hair stuck out from his crown as though he'd just gotten out of bed.

"Look, Charlie, I can't blame you for having it in for the guy," Henley said. "But we got no match, which means we got no case. Shit, you can see the difference without even a magnifying glass."

"So we squeeze the guy to find out who his buddy is," Morrison said. "No big deal."

Favor stroked the side of his chubby face. "Okay, what have we got on the guy? One fingerprint, which corroborates his story that he was in the kitchen. One of Mrs. Hardin's canceled checks plus the banker's word that the Ferguson dude came into the bank and cashed it in person. Might look suspicious, but what does it prove? That Ferguson wanted cash. So what?"

Morrison straightened. "You're forgetting the woman, Mrs. Hardin's tennis partner. She says Mrs. Hardin told her on the phone that the guy was fucking her. How 'bout that?"

"Not worth shit," Favor said. "Inadmissible without corroboration, and the only one that could corroborate the woman's testimony would have to be Mrs. Hardin." He shook his head. "Not worth shit."

Morrison blinked. "Well what about *Mr.* Hardin? What if he was to have heard it? He seems like a man that would cooperate with us to help get the bad guy." He grinned in turn at the other two men.

"What, the guy's going to testify that his wife said in his presence that some other guy was fucking her?" Favor snorted. "Jesus Christ, Charlie."

"Well how 'bout if he was listening on the extension?" Morrison said.

"Charlie," Henley said, "the guy was at the golf course. That's the only reason we're not putting the heat on *him,* that we can verify his whereabouts. He can't start testifying that he was listening on the extension."

"You got a point, Roscoe," Morrison said. Then, scratching his chin, he said, "Assume he had a buddy with him. Who could that be? What about his partner, Ferias? The Mexican guy."

"He was on the job," Henley said. "Picked up some brick that morning from the supplier; he was out there at the same time Mrs. Hardin was getting hers. Believe me, I checked."

Favor stood, faced the window, shoved his hands

into his pockets and looked down at the street. His outline against the rectangle of daylight resembled a bloated parabola. "This just doesn't wash," Favor said. "We got a guy with no rap sheet, a perfect service record, no history of drugs or deviant behavior. I've put many of 'em away for no other reason than that they pissed me off, but we can't go against this guy on just what we got."

"Bullshit," Morrison said. "Whaddya mean, 'no history of drugs'? All those army guys take dope."

"I can't get up in front of a grand jury and say that," Favor said. "Some of 'em probably were in the service themselves. What I'm saying is, no way can I go for an indictment without a match on the physical evidence."

"An old lady that lives across the street saw Ferguson leaving the Hardins' place," Morrison said. "He damn near had a wreck with another guy."

Favor turned around and narrowed his eyes. "What guy?"

"According to the neighbor lady, a guy driving a little white foreign make. I wish we could run that other driver down, maybe he saw something." Morrison showed a hopeful smile.

"We don't need that, or the neighbor woman, either," Favor said. "Hell, the Ferguson guy's already admitted being over there." He bent to pick up his cigar, poked the soggy end in his mouth and chomped down. "They're on my ass upstairs, we got to put together a case. If it's not Ferguson we got to work on somebody else."

"It's Ferguson," Morrison said. "I'm telling you it is."

"Jesus, Charlie," Henley said. "The guy only pushed you down, he didn't fuck your old lady or anything."

Favor turned his back and studied the street once

more. Pouches of fat stuck out over the back of his belt. "So what's next?"

"I'm for watching Ferguson," Morrison said, "and letting him damn well know it. Make him sweat until he comes across with the guy that was with him."

Henley scratched his nose. "Well, I ain't saying it won't work."

"You fucking-ay it will," Morrison said. "From now on if Mr. Ferguson goes in to take a shit he's going to hear a noise in the next stall. Me."

"Suits me, as long as it's okay with the D.A.'s office." Henley looked at Favor. "Hey, Wilson, whatever you say," Henley said.

Wilson Favor turned from the window, mildly regarding first Morrison, then Detective Henley. He took the cigar from his mouth while Morrison fumbled and lit a cigarette. Finally Favor said, "Well on the laboratory samples we're putting 'inconclusive.' Anybody, the newspapers or anybody else that wants to know, the lab results are inconclusive. If anybody wants to know if Ferguson is still a suspect, we're not commenting. They can take that however they want to. In the meantime, you two put some pressure on this Ferguson guy. See what we can come up with."

11

At three-thirty on Wednesday afternoon, J. Percival Hardin III stood in the middle of the eighteenth fairway at Colonial Country Club and used some body English to urge his worm-burner on. He was one-seventy out from the center of the green, and he'd half-topped the ball with a three-wood. It was his third shot on the par-four hole, after his tee shot had squirted off to the right, and after his shanked four-iron second had struck a tree and bounded back into the center of the fairway.

"Go," Percy Hardin said as he moved his hips in a counterclockwise bump and grind. "Go, baby, go."

Slightly behind Hardin and to his left, Greg Norman, his golden locks down over his forehead in carefully tousled bangs, stood with hands on hips beside his caddy. "I think it's going to get there," Norman said in a thick Aussie accent. The other three amateurs besides Hardin in the group—two men in their fifties wearing navy slacks and knit polo shirts and one youngster whose father was on the club's board of governors—stood watching near the gallery ropes.

Hardin's ball was slowing as it bounded in the short grass near the green, between two yawning sandtraps. Finally the shot ran out of gas, rolling over one final time and coming to rest on the putting surface by the width of the ball.

"Good shot, mate," Greg Norman said. "You fel-

las play the bounces here, I'll grant you. Do you get
a stroke on this hole?''

"Sure do," Hardin said. "If I can two-putt from
there it counts as a bird." He handed his three-wood
over to his caddy, then hitched up his pants like Arnold Palmer on a roll and fell into step beside Greg
Norman. The two of them strolled toward the green.
Percy Hardin was wearing a pale lavender shirt, dark
lavender slacks, and white Corafam shoes with lavender inserts. Mirrored sunglasses covered his eyes,
Doug Sanders style. Behind the gallery ropes, two
teenagers, members of the Arlington Heights High
School golf team, whispered to one another and giggled into cupped hands over what a lousy golfer that
Percy Hardin was.

A portly woman in white cotton slacks and a sleeveless blouse stood behind the teenagers. She'd been
raised up on tiptoes to watch the action and now sank
down on her heels and yanked on her husband's arm.
''That's disgusting,'' she said. Her forehead was per-
spiring, and she wiped it with the back of her hand.

Her husband, a tall man with a wide rear end, wearing Bermuda shorts, was watching three girls. The
girls, all in their late teens or early twenties, wore
snug shorts and bare-midriff halters, and sported
healthy tans. They were *oh*ing and *ah*ing over Greg
Norman. The husband said to his wife, ''Huh?'' He
had thick knees and hairy legs which were turning pink
in the sun.

''That's disgusting,'' she repeated. ''His wife just
murdered and it all over the news like that, the day
before her funeral he's out playing golf. If you ever
pulled anything like that I'd climb out of the grave and
do you in.'' She fiddled with her pasteboard grounds
pass, which hung by a string from a button on her
blouse.

The husband directed his gaze toward Percy Hardin.
Hardin bent his head to say something to Greg Nor-

man, and the two men laughed like old buddies. "Tell you what, hon," the husband said. "Just don't you die anytime I got a chance to play with Greg Norman. Then we won't have to worry about it, okay?"

Around nine-thirty that evening, the band at the Colonial pro-am party yielded to pressure from the older folks and agreed to play a slow one. As the opening bars to "Twilight Time" filtered through the room, hip young women in mod slacks and designer jeans led tanned up-and-coming stockbrokers and insurance agents in knit Ralph Lauren and Vito Domici golf shirts from the dance floor and formed a line at the portable bar. Behind the bar, red-jacketed blacks and Hispanics mixed highballs, whipped drinks to a froth in twelve-speed blenders, and shook specially ordered cocktails in chrome interlocking cups. As the younger folks gave way, statuesque graying women with two-hundred-dollar hairdos led balding, paunchier men onto the floor, where the couples embraced and did hesitant box-steps together.

Near the center of the floor, Luwanda Monroe danced with her just-widowed son-in-law. "We should go home after this," she said. "I'm getting enough dirty looks as it is." She wore a navy slack-suit with a filmy pink scarf at her throat. Her silver hair was blued, and faint rays from the bandstand footlights glinted from the diamond barrette positioned above her ear. Her neck was firm from cosmetic surgery and her body was slim, though Hardin's hand on her back was touching loose skin. She'll be into lipo-suction pretty soon, Percy Hardin thought.

"I'm having a tough time keeping upbeat," Hardin said. "I keep telling myself it's what she would have wanted, and I think I'm right about that. They're dedicating the club tennis championship to her, I thought that was quite a gesture."

"That it was," Luwanda said, blinking. She wore

thick mascara and eye shadow along with bright pink lip rouge. "We still have Betty, that's something. If she stays the fuck in town." She bumped gently into the couple behind her; Hardin steered her away from them while throwing an excuse-me glance over his shoulder.

"She's been here what, six months?" Hardin said. "Probably ready to settle this time."

"I damn sure hope so," Luwanda said. "It's the longest she's been here since college, and every time I think she's home for good she's farting around off to France or someplace. She's almost twenty-six, she should be finding herself a husband."

"How's Ross taking it?" Hardin said. "I haven't talked to him much."

"Getting by, you'd never know if the bastard had terminal cancer, the way he's ate up with being so fucking tough about everything. What time are we due tomorrow?"

"They're hauling Marissa over to the church around eleven. Twelve, I suppose. Thereabouts." Hardin drew Luwanda abruptly closer, avoiding a collision with another couple by a hair. Luwanda stumbled slightly and gripped Hardin's shoulder for support.

"I need some more champagne," Luwanda said. She giggled and burped. "Twelve'll be fine, my hair appointment's at nine-thirty. Do you remember the last time you danced with me?" She pressed her cheek against Hardin's chest.

"I'm thinking," Hardin said, wincing as Luwanda stepped on his toe.

"It was at your high school graduation, and it was to this same song. 'Twilight Time.' You were young and strong. Still are." Luwanda hiccupped.

"How could I ever forget, Luwanda," Percy Hardin said.

* * *

When the dance ended, Percy steered Luwanda back to the linen-draped table. She was listing some. As they approached the table, Ross Monroe stood while Betty Monroe kept her seat, her elbows resting on the linen, her slim fingers intertwined, her classic chin resting on her interlocked hands. "It's time we're going," Ross said. He was square-shouldered and erect, a man of sixty still in shape, and who could break eighty if he made a few putts.

"Yeah, head for the house," Luwanda said, thick-tongued. "Where's the car?"

"Nigger's gettin' it," Ross said. He cupped his hands in front of his mouth and yelled in the direction of a table which stood twenty feet away, "Pete. Hey, Pete, we got to have lunch." A rawboned man whose cuffs struck him above his wrists raised a hand and answered, "Sure, let's do it."

Percy Hardin went around the table to hold Betty Monroe's chair for her. She stood, her dark eyes on a level with Hardin's chin, her full lips set in a bored pout. She wore baggy green shorts and a Nelda DuMont cotton sweater from Neiman's over in Dallas. She nodded. "Percy," Betty Monroe said.

Hardin returned her nod. "Betty."

"Come on, daughter," Ross Monroe said. "You're gonna have to do the drivin', mama's on her ass and I don't see too good at night." He grabbed Luwanda's upper arm and guided her none too gently, skirting tables in the direction of the exit. Over his shoulder, Ross said, "See you at the church, Perce."

Betty Monroe took a couple of modeling-runway strides after her parents, then stopped and turned. The tip of her tongue flashed briefly as she licked her lower lip. She said to Percy Hardin, "I've got to wait until they're both zonked. About one-thirty?"

"Come around to the back," Hardin said. "I'll leave the porch light on."

* * *

Percy Hardin finally got away from Edna and Donald Rafferty and made his way out to the parking lot. Christ, what a bunch of insincere tripe he'd been listening to. The only reason Edna Rafferty gave a damn about Marissa being dead was that Edna would have to find herself a new tennis partner, and somebody new with whom to go on and on over the phone. And Percy hadn't missed the slight smolder in Edna's glance nor the way she kept brushing against him. Hardin's being widowed gave the old broad a new prospect for someone to hump her in the afternoons. Christ, Hardin thought, I'd as soon hump Luwanda. Would that be a fearsome twosome, or what?

And Donald Rafferty the Distributor was enough to make Percy throw up on the floor. Christ, what a bullshitter, going on and on about deals with Paramount and Universal, when the truth was that the only films Donald Rafferty had anything to do with were produced in some motel room with a guy keeping watch by the door. Percy would bet that old Donald had had to get the club picture book down before he knew which broad Marissa was. Wherever you are, Marissa, Percy Hardin thought, the truth is that you might be the lucky one.

The valet parking attendant, a young black guy wearing a waist-length gold jacket, approached at the door, but Percy waved the kid away. Hardin would get his own car; the walk across the parking lot in nighttime air might clear his head. He hadn't had *that* many Scotches, but on a near-empty stomach, and after five hours of golf in the sun, the booze had fuzzied his thinking. Jesus, what a round, huh? That shot on eighteen with Greg Norman looking on and that big gallery watching from behind the ropes, that had been one for the memory book. Would stay with Hardin forever.

The asphalt lot was half-full, the autos parked in silent, slanted rows. They were Caddies, Mercedes, and Porsches mostly, with an occasional plain vanilla

Buick or Chevy which probably belonged to some of
the middle-class proles who'd wangled tickets to the
pro-am party. Probably won the tickets in a raffle, Hardin thought, or on a KVIL radio giveaway. Hardin pictured a working stiff at an insurance company, fucking
off instead of tending to business, listening to Ron
Chapman while the boss wasn't looking and trying to
be the twelfth one to call in to win the pro-am tickets.
Well, by God, Percy Hardin had better not catch his
gardener or maid calling in to any fucking radio show
on Percy Hardin's time. Have those fucking Mexicans
running for cover, if he were to catch them at it.

Hardin's midnight blue Mercedes was four rows
from streetside, practically dead center in the north-
south layout of the parking lot. He paused for a moment behind his car, glanced both ways at thick groves
of elm and sycamore trees that bounded the golf course
and country club, then looked up at the three-quarter
moon. The moon shone hazily through the light Fort
Worth smog, and the leaves around him rustled in the
spring night wind. Directly in front of him, visible
through the trees, headlights passed one another going
in opposite directions on University Boulevard.

Hardin brushed off the front of his shirt. Lavender.
Christ, was that a perfect color for a perfect pro-am
to remember, or what? He'd checked both pros and
amateurs coming and going, and he was sure that his
was the only lavender outfit in the bunch. Christ, to
think he'd nearly worn orange. Damn near half the
players in the pro-am had been wearing orange, a
bunch of Ben-Crenshaw-Hook-'Em-Horns assholes.
Your day all around, old Perce, Hardin thought. How
'bout that three-wood on eighteen, huh?

He went up to the driver's side of the Mercedes,
fiddled with his keys, inserted the proper key in the
lock, and turned. The horn began to honk monotonously and the lights to flash. Hardin opened the door
and shut off the burglar apparatus, then after a final

glance toward University Boulevard he prepared to sink into the driver's seat.

And caught sudden movement in the corner of his eye, sucked in his breath as a big hand clamped onto his collar, grunted in pain as the hand yanked, then shoved, felt himself pushed inside the car like so much foam rubber, and watched the stumpy man climb in beside him. Hardin gritted his teeth as the stumpy man's elbow dug into his ribs and slid over by the passenger window to give the stumpy man room. Christ, the stinking breath, the hate in the stumpy man's look. Maybe it wasn't such a good day for Percy Hardin after all.

"You been forgetting me or something?" Everett Wilson said.

Hardin felt gingerly of his own ribcage. "We're, we're not supposed to have any contact."

Wilson put a thumb on one of Hardin's cheeks, a forefinger on the other, and squeezed. He put his nose just inches from Hardin's. "You don't give me one word of shit," Wilson said. "Not one, you hear? You come to me, I didn't go looking for you. Where's my goddam money?" His breath reeked of onion.

"Christ. Hey, let go, will you." The fingers released their hold on Hardin's cheeks, and he sat back and massaged his jaw. Christ, the bastard was strong. Had to be careful what you said to these types. Like jungle animals. "Money's nothing to worry about," Hardin said.

"Yesterday. You were supposed to see me yesterday, you fucking—"

"I was tied up. Business."

"Well you ain't tied up now," Wilson said. "Pay me, I ain't fucking with you."

Hardin shrank back against the passenger door. "I don't carry that kind of cash. A man in my position."

Wilson held a stumpy forefinger underneath Hardin's chin, pressing into the flesh. "Lemme tell you something about your fucking position. Your fucking position is that you told me to do something and I done it. Now. My goddam position is that I don't got no problem doing it to you, too, I don't get my money."

Hardin's throat constricted. "Look, there's a meeting."

"There damn sure is. It's going on right now."

Feet scraped suddenly on asphalt as two men in golf outfits walked by in front of the Mercedes. Wilson murmured, "Shut up. Not one fucking word, you hear?" Hardin sat straight as a ramrod and followed the men with his gaze, wanting to yell, needing in the worst way to take a piss. The men got into a Cadillac, started the engine, and drove away.

When the Caddy had exited the lot onto University Boulevard, Wilson said, "You gimme five thousand, and you owe me ten. Now, I'm telling you—"

"Insurance people," Hardin said in a high squeaky voice, then cleared his throat and said more normally, "Insurance people, they don't pay out the kind of money we're talking without a meeting."

"The fuck you talking about insurance people? You didn't say nothing about no insurance when you come to me."

"It's a big policy. Pays double on a murder."

"You rich asshole, you telling me you ain't got *ten thousand dollars*?" Wilson folded his arms and leaned back against the cushions.

Hardin adjusted his collar. His sharp-looking lavender collar. The collar was wrinkled and bunched together where the stumpy man had grabbed him. Christ, people like this. "Well, sure. Sure I've got ten grand, only I can't make a cash withdrawal like that without raising suspicion."

"You done raised some suspicion. Mine."

"You're going to get paid," Hardin said.

"You fucking-ay bet I am."

Hardin did his best to think. Christ, this wasn't like

putting off a note at Ridglea Bank, wasn't like calling up Merlyn Graham and telling old Merlyn to deduct the interest from the trust account and send over a renewal notice. Wasn't like that at all. "Look," Hardin said.

"I'm looking."

"It's just a temporary situation. My wife paid out fifteen thousand to that contractor guy, and it's run me a little short."

"That ain't my problem. If the contractor got fifteen grand, you should have got the fucking contractor to off her for you." Wilson leaned his sloping forehead against the top of the steering wheel. "I done it perfect, make it look like some pervert done her and everything. You got to come up with something, man."

"I'm going to. Just a little time."

"How much time?"

"Ten days. The check should be here in ten days."

"Jesus Christ, where they come up with assholes like you?"

"Ten days, you have my word on it." Hardin showed his best The-Check-Is-In-The-Mail expression, then felt sort of foolish because the stumpy man couldn't see the earnest look in the dark.

"Fuck," Wilson said. "I tell you something. If you're bullshitting me you ain't going to be around eleven days."

"I'm not worried about that," Hardin said as sweat popped out on his forehead. "My word is my bond."

"Fuck."

"Listen," Hardin said, "we can't keep sitting here. Let me drop you someplace."

Wilson held out his hand, palm up. "Yeah. Yeah, okay, my car's a block or so away. Gimme your keys. I always wanted to drive one of these things. And think about it. You ain't going to be driving this car much longer yourself, if you're fucking with me."

Hardin handed over the keys, tried to relax as the stumpy man cranked the Mercedes' engine. As Wilson wheeled out of the parking lot, Percy Hardin's bladder let go and he pissed in his pants.

12

Helen Taylor's smirk told Nancy Cuellar that she wasn't going to like the message even before Helen could get the words out of her mouth. "Two men out front," Helen said. "They're policemen." She spoke quite a bit louder than necessary. Up and down the corridor outside Nancy's cubicle, typewriters skipped a beat, then resumed their *clickety-clack* chatter like wagging tongues. Helen was around forty, broad shouldered and large breasted, and wore her hair fluffed out around her head like a Roman warrior's helmet. She'd had it in for Nancy ever since Mr. Brantley had chosen the younger girl as his assistant, and Helen could smirk with the best of them. She handed Nancy a printed business card and rested her ample hip against the edge of Nancy's desk.

Nancy resisted the urge to panic as she read the card: Tarrant County Sheriff's Department, Charles Morrison, Detective, Homicide Division. She wasn't really surprised; if it had been good news Helen would never have traipsed the length of the corridor to deliver it. Good news would have come through Trudy, the law firm's message coordinator, with Helen's instructions to relay the tidings to "that Mexican girl." Well, *caramba* to you, Helen, this is one Mexican girl that's not going to let you get her goat. She showed Helen her best smile of gratitude. "Thanks, Helen," Nancy said.

Helen's eyes widened slightly, and a grain of mas-

cara dropped from one of her lashes to form a speck
in her purple eye shadow. She drew in a breath and
said, "They're waiting," even more loudly than she'd
announced that the cops were outside. The chattering
typewriters skipped another beat. With a final toss of
her permed mane, Helen turned on her heel and left.
Her big rear wobbled above thick ankles and heavy
calves. Inside ten minutes everyone in the office would
know that the police had come calling on the Mexican
girl. If they didn't know already.

Nancy stood and pushed her rolling secretarial chair
flush against her desk. She took her time about
straightening things, paying more attention than normal to the shipshape alignment of pens and steno pads
on her blotter, as she flexed her mental muscles and
got ahold of herself. *Crying time's over, Nance*, the
think-positive voice inside of her said, *and even if they
should take Lackey into the death chamber and shove
the needle in, Nancy Cuellar's going to hold her head
high*. That was the message she'd delivered to her
brother and uncle two nights ago, and that's what she'd
tell the rest of the world as well.

Her desktop in order, she smoothed her skirt as she
went over to rattle the handle on Mr. Brantley's door.
It was locked, of course, and Nancy had already
known that. Mr. Brantley was in depositions out in
Phoenix (thank God for that, Nancy thought, otherwise Helen Taylor would have *screamed* that the cops
were in the reception area) which meant that the young
lawyer from the University of Houston who was doing
Brantley's wife would be late this morning. As Nancy
straightened her shoulders a tiny sob escaped from her
throat; she choked back the sob, forced her lips into a
confident smile, then strode briskly down the hall toward the waiting room, a slim young woman wearing
a green-and-gray checkerboard blouse, navy skirt, and
white high-heeled shoes with straps encircling her ankles, her dark hair cut in flippant bangs, bustling along

in a manner that would make Tammy Wynette proud. Stand by your man.

The distance from Nancy's cubicle to the reception room was about a hundred yards over light green heavy-weave carpet with three-quarter-inch padding underneath. Her journey took her past a row of side-by-side cubicles identical to her own, with secretaries seated outside lawyers' offices, typing or filing or doing their nails, and this morning the short walk seemed to Nancy like a hundred miles. Surely *everyone* wasn't staring at her, it only seemed that they were. The staff at Brantley, Nevers and Wilts, P.C., was about evenly divided, half on her side and half on Helen Taylor's, but at the moment who liked who didn't matter. The flap about Lackey in the newspapers—coupled with Nancy's own picture on television two nights earlier— had the whole office twittering, including the lawyers. That Nancy's fiancé was a sex-fiend murderer (it didn't matter that Lackey hadn't even been charged with anything, of course, everyone was assuming he was guilty because of what they'd read in the paper) had taken the place of Mrs. Brantley's affair with the young lawyer as the main coffee-room topic. Why don't they just come right out and ask me about it? Nancy thought. You can bet I'd have something to tell them. As she passed Trudy's desk, her Number-One best friend raised soft brown eyes and smiled. Nancy returned the smile with a confident wink. As she thought, I ought to take acting lessons, Nancy went through the floor-to-ceiling door and entered the reception area.

Nancy would have spotted the two cops as something other than run-of-the-mill visitors even if she hadn't known in advance who they were. After a few months around the office she'd been able to tell visitors' business merely by their postures in the waiting room. Salesmen sat upright on the chairs or sofas with their briefcases held in their laps; civil clients checked their watches over and over as they wondered

whether the lawyers' fee meters were running while
the client cooled his heels; criminal clients all appeared to be worrying. These two detectives, though,
were lounging. The big blond guy was sprawled on
the couch with one long leg bent at a near-perfect
ninety-degree angle as he rested his ankle on his knee
and flipped through a magazine. The bald one, the
older of the two, had his skinny rump forward on the
cushion as he lay practically full-length in an arm-
chair. His elbows were on the armrests and his hands
were folded over his navel. Nancy wondered briefly
whether the slob effect was intentional in order to put
her off guard. Helen Taylor sat behind a half-moon
shaped desk, pressing lighted buttons and routing
calls, and she now stopped long enough to arch an
eyebrow in Nancy's direction, then throw a knowing
look in the direction of the detectives. Here she is,
boys. Have at her.

The blond detective's suit was pale blue, the bald
one's light brown. The blond sat up on the couch and
put both feet on the floor, at the same time laying the
magazine he'd been reading on an end table beside a
shaded lamp. *Sports Illustrated,* Nancy thought, that
or *Popular Mechanics;* she'd have guessed *Playboy* or
Penthouse, but knew that the law firm didn't keep any
girlie mags around in the waiting room. Those were
for the lawyers in the privacy of their offices. The blond
detective extended his index finger, formed a pistol
with his hand, and pointed it at Nancy. "Hey. Hey,
you Nancy?" He shot a quick glance at his partner.

They both look surprised, Nancy thought. Probably
they were expecting one of the cleaning people. She
placed one spotless white shoe in front of the other
and folded her arms. "I'm Miss Cuellar," she said.

"We're—" the blond guy said, then showed an
almost-bashful grin. "Hey, I'm Detective Morrison
and this guy"—waving a hand as the bald man sat up
into an erect position—"is Detective Henley. We've

got a few questions. Is there a place . . . ?'' He looked
around expectantly.

"Sure," Nancy said. "Why not? Follow me, gen-
tlemen." She turned to lead the way back into the
inner offices. The cops rose to follow. The bald one
said something to Helen Taylor which Nancy couldn't
hear. Helen whispered something back to the guy.

The trip down the corridor with the detectives in tow
was only slightly worse than the walk up to the reception room had been. This time, secretaries stopped
what they were doing and stared openly. The two cops
grinned as though they were enjoying the attention,
and Nancy guessed that they were. As she opened the
door to the conference room and stood aside for the
cops to enter, warmth crept up the back of her neck
and settled behind her ears. She stepped inside behind
Henley and Morrison and closed the door.

"Would you like some coffee?" Nancy said profes-
sionally. She needn't have bothered; the detectives had
already helped themselves to styrofoam cups and had
surrounded the Mr. Coffee like chow hounds at the
chuckwagon.

Both men took their coffee black, just like in the
movies. Henley and Morrison carried their cups over
to take seats on one side of the long polished conference table. Nancy sat down on the other side, facing
them, and smoothly crossed her legs. Two adjacent
walls in the room were lined with bookcases which
contained black hardcovers of Vernon's *Annotated
Texas Statutes,* red-bound volumes of the *United States
Code,* and big light-brown tomes that looked like log
books and which were in reality the *Federal Reporter,
2nd Edition.* Nancy mentally held her breath and
waited for the session to begin. She briefly wondered
whether they'd take their coats off and adjust their
shoulder holsters.

Morrison hunched his shoulders and put his hands
on either side of his coffee cup. He blew lightly on the

surface of the liquid, then took a sip. "I don't guess I have to tell you this is about your old man," he said.

One corner of Nancy's mouth tugged sideways in irritation. "My father?"

"No, your . . ." Morrison grinned sideways at Henley. "Lackey Ferguson, you know," Morrison said.

"He's my fiancé."

"Yeah, him," Morrison said. He drew a small recorder from his inside breast pocket, placed the recorder on the table and pressed a button. Tiny reels began to turn. "You don't mind," Morrison said. "It saves note-taking."

Nancy's gaze flicked at the recorder, then steadied on Morrison. "Go ahead," she told him.

"Cuellar, that's . . ." Morrison scratched his eyebrow. "Hey, isn't there a Mexican restaurant?"

Nancy blinked. "El Chico. Not the same family. Cuellar's a common Spanish surname, Mr. Morrison. Not like Smith or Jones, but probably on a level with Douglas or Moore in English."

"I thought maybe there was a connection," Morrison said. "Well, hey, Nancy—"

"Miss Cuellar," she said.

"—so long as we're here and the tape recorder's laying in plain sight, and so there won't be any question that we all know what this is about, you know we've got your boyfriend—"

"Fiancé."

"—under investigation, don't you? On some pretty serious charges, specifically in connection with the murder of Mrs. J. Percival Hardin III."

"I've seen the TV news," Nancy said. "I didn't bother with the newspaper stories, but I did see the headlines. None of it's true."

As Morrison did all of the talking, Henley was alternating his gaze between the tape machine and Nancy as she sat across from him. There was a half-smile on

Henley's lips, accompanied by an alternate lifting and dropping of his eyebrows. Nancy knew that she looked all right—was proud of it, in fact—and admiring glances from men were something that she didn't mind at all. But this guy was *leering,* and her uneasiness over confronting these two was now accompanied by a creepy-crawly sensation which paraded up and down her back. She uncrossed and recrossed her legs, glanced down at her lap and then concentrated on Morrison again. Henley's grin was still visible in the periphery of her vision.

"Can you state your full name, so it'll be on the tape?" Morrison said.

"Nancy Patricia Cuellar," she said. Morrison was now leering as well, and Nancy wondered briefly if she should get up and do a couple of bumps and grinds for this pair.

"You're what?" Morrison said. "Twenty-one or two?"

"Twenty-five," Nancy said.

"Our sources tell us you went to college."

What sources? Nancy thought. There was a quick tightening in her throat, but she kept a poker face. She wasn't about to ask who they'd been talking to. Not yet, anyway. "I've got a B.B.A. from the University of Texas at Arlington," she said.

"That's a commuter school," Morrison said. "My wife took some hours out there. You work your way through?"

"Yes."

"What'd you do?"

"I thought this was about Lackey," Nancy said.

Morrison shot a triumphant glance at Henley, and Nancy mentally kicked herself under the table for giving them a reaction. Even under normal circumstances she wouldn't have liked Morrison, the big Anglo cop talking down to the Mexican girl. She thought that people with racial hangups were too dumb to waste any time with, and made up her mind not to let Morrison get another rise out of her.

"Just getting background info," Morrison said.

"I worked at Arby's," Nancy said.

"They make a pretty good sandwich," Morrison said. "You got any brothers or sisters?"

She pictured the kitchen table when she'd been a kid, and mama chiding her brothers in Spanish over their table manners. "Six," Nancy said. "Three and three. Two older, a brother and sister. The rest are still at home."

"Any of the others go to college?"

"No. Not yet."

"Our sources tell us you tried to go to law school." Morrison's interest was picking up, his eyes widening slightly. He's wondering about the best way to trip me up, Nancy thought.

His question told her their source: Mr. James, her high school counselor, who she still called once in a while, who'd talked her into taking the SAT to begin with and, upon seeing her scores, had really done a sales job on her to get her into college. Lackey didn't know about her law school apps, she'd been saving that as a surprise in case her dream came true. So they'd been nosing around Richland High, letting everyone who knew her in on the fact that Lackey was a sadist killer and Nancy was his Number-One moll. Nancy choked back her anger. "I'm *going* to law school," she said. "Just as soon as I find the right one."

"Oh?" Morrison said. He looked surprised.

"I've been accepted to three. One is too expensive, that's SMU over in Dallas, and the other two are in Lubbock and Houston. I thought about moving, but since I've gotten engaged I decided not to. There's a new one. UT Dallas is beginning a law program, and once it's in gear I'm going to see about going over there." It occurred to Nancy that she might be volunteering too much, but her education was something she was really proud of. Human nature, she decided, and if these guys wanted to know her grade-point average she'd tell them that as well—3.2, and that while holding down a full-time job. How 'bout that, Mr. Tough Anglo Detective?

The corners of Morrison's mouth turned down, the blond tough guy showing that he wasn't impressed, no way. "Okay, say you're going," Morrison said. "Well let's talk about Lackey awhile."

"I thought that's what you were here for," Nancy said.

"Yeah," Morrison said, grinning. "Yeah, it is. So how'd you and old Lackey get together?"

"You mean, how did I meet him, or how did we get engaged?" Or how often we do it together, Nancy thought, that's what these guys would really like to know.

"Start with the beginning," Morrison said. Beside him, Henley adjusted his position in his chair, his expression as though he was about to get in on the real nitty-gritty.

"Lackey went to school with my big brother," Nancy said. "He's ten years older, but you'll already know that." She hesitated; Morrison's slight nod told her that they already did. Nancy went on. "When he went to the army I was eight, going on nine."

"Then when he got out you were all grown up," Morrison said.

"He had leaves, I'd see him around. My first, what you would call a real date with him was when I was nineteen. He came by the Arby's out in Arlington where I was working." Nancy permitted herself a small grin. "I was never sure whether he just happened by or if someone had told him I was working there. Still don't know, he won't tell me."

"So you went out with him when he was in town?"

"Yes. Not *just* him. We started really, what you'd

call going together about a month after he came home for good.''

"And now, are the two of you living together?" Morrison never changed his tone of voice, the trained questioner, throwing the bombshell but making it sound like an offhanded remark.

"No, Mr. Morrison," Nancy said. "We're not common-law."

Morrison and Henley looked at one another, their eyebrows lifted, clearly getting a surprise from the Mexican girl. "You're not what?" Morrison said.

"Common-law. We're not married and we're not common-law, so you don't have any problem forcing me to testify against him if you want to."

"You know quite a bit about the law, Nancy," Morrison said. "You ever been in trouble?"

She snickered. "Of course not. I work for a law firm."

"Oh," Morrison said. "That's right."

"But you wouldn't want me as a witness anyway," Nancy said. "Since I know he didn't do anything."

"How do you know? Were you with him on Monday?"

"Just at night. I'm not an *eye*witness to anything, I just know Lackey."

Henley cut in, the first time the bald detective had had anything to say. "You probably do." Then, pausing, directing his words to the recorder. "This is Detective Henley talking here." His gaze back on Nancy, "When you two are together, he ever do any rough stuff?"

Her heart missed a beat. "I beg your pardon?"

"Rough," Henley said. "Spanking or whipping or anything."

She didn't bat an eye. "He's so gentle you'd never believe it." Which was the first lie she'd told; Lackey certainly wasn't sadistic or anything, but he knew just how aggressive to be in bed so that her eyeballs rolled up into their sockets. She didn't suppose that the detectives had been peeking in the window or anything, but with this pair she couldn't be sure.

"That's with you," Henley said. "How about with other people? Any fights or arguments, anything that makes you think he might lose control sometimes?"

"Not when he was with me," Nancy said, then decided that wasn't enough and added, "And I've never heard of any."

Henley opened his mouth to say more, but Morrison raised a hand. The blond cop reached out and turned the recorder off, and Nancy watched as the turning reels came to an abrupt halt. "I'm turning the recorder off," Morrison said, "because, to tell you the truth, we're not supposed to do anything but ask questions. But I think I ought to help you out, Nancy."

I'll bet you do, Nancy thought. She folded her arms and didn't say anything, looking at Morrison with her lips parted questioningly.

"Look, these army guys," Morrison said, then appeared deep in thought as he got out of his chair, parked his rump on the table and leaned toward Nancy in a buddy-buddy attitude. "These guys have all been through combat training, a lot of them come through it okay, but it's been our experience that some of 'em come home with, maybe a little screw loose that they didn't have before. This is a pretty brutal murder we're talking here. Guys that do things like that to women are subject to do the same thing again. He's already admitted to us that he was at the house, and we got other people that saw him. I'm wanting to protect you, you know?"

"Who else did they see?" Nancy said.

Morrison threw Henley a sideways glance. "Huh?" Morrison said.

"You're talking about neighbors and stuff," Nancy said. "Did you ask them, 'Hey, have you seen anybody?' Or did you flash Lackey's picture around and

say, 'Have you seen this particular guy, right here?'
There'd be a big difference, depending on how the
questions were asked, as to who they remembered seeing.''

"We're using established investigation procedure
here," Henley said.

"No, now that's not a proper answer," Nancy said.
"You can investigate a murder, or you can investigate
a person. If you're just asking around about a particular person, then that person's all you're going to hear
about. Isn't that right?''

"Nobody's told us they saw anybody else," Morrison said. "And I'll tell you, Nancy, your old man was
in one big hurry to get away from there. He was in
such a sweat he nearly sideswiped a little white
Volvo.''

"My *fiancé*,'' Nancy said. "And you just said, that's
what I'm talking about, that there was somebody in a
Volvo. What did you find out about the Volvo driver?''
She was letting herself get more excited than she would
have liked, but this was something to get excited about.

"The guy in the Volvo's not a witness to anything,"
Morrison said.

"That's ridiculous," Nancy said. "You say you've
got all these people that saw Lackey, saw him nearly
run into a car, now you're saying that the other driver's
not a *witness to anything*? That's a lot of baloney.''
She pushed back her chair and stood up. "I don't think
I want to talk to you people any more.''

"Now calm down, Nancy," Morrison said. "We
were just trying to do you a favor, letting you know
you could get hurt with this guy." He switched the
recorder on. "Tell you what, just a couple of more
questions.''

"No way," Nancy said, then had a thought and
leaned closer to the tape recorder. "This is Nancy
Cuellar speaking here. These policemen just turned off
the tape and told me there's another witness, but since

the other witness might hurt their case against Lackey Ferguson, they don't think they'll use him.'' She alternated a scathing glare between the two detectives. ''How's that, fellas?'' Nancy said. ''That the kind of evidence you're looking for?''

13

"Deep . . . deeper. Oh, God, God, don't ever stop."

"Jesus, babe, I'm . . ."

"Not now, not now. Slower. Easy, easier. That's . . . that's it, oh, that's it, that's my . . . *madre de Dios,* oh, God, God, God, God . . ."

"I . . . I don't think I . . . Jesus . . . now, I . . ."

"That's it, oh, yes, yes, yes, my God, I . . ."

"Jesus."

"Oh. Oh."

"It's . . ."

"Yes. Yes, it's . . ."

"Jesus, it's . . ."

"Yes. Yes. Oh, angel, yes, yes, yes. That was . . . oh."

"Did you . . . ?"

"Oh, yes. How can you ask me?"

"Was it . . . ?"

"Yes. Oh, yes."

"Do you know when you're speaking in Spanish?" he said.

"Sure. If I didn't know the difference I'd have a tough time of it. I'd look pretty dumb speaking Spanish to somebody that didn't understand me."

"I mean, when we're doing it."

She raised up on her elbows, looking down at him, at the square jaw and neat beard, the faint light from

the digital clock-radio outlining his nose in shadow on
his cheek. "Making love," she said.

"Sure. Sure, that's what I mean."

"You don't sound like it. 'Doing it,' that sounds
like a couple of animals or something."

"Sorry, I don't mean to. Do you know you're speaking Spanish sometimes when we're making love?
How's that?"

"Better. Sometimes when we are, I don't know anything. Why, did I say something in Spanish?"

"Yeah. Just a couple of words."

The FM station was playing "Send in the Clowns,"
by Judy Collins. She lifted her leg, crossed her inner
thigh over the top of his midsection, then rolled on top
of him to reach the nightstand and adjust the volume,
because she liked the words to the song. His pubic
hair was wet and coarse against her leg. "I really didn't
know I was," she said, then stretched out beside him
on sheets damp with their perspiration, and laid her
head against the hollow of his shoulder. She could have
remained like that for days, cradled against her man
while music played in the semidarkness. "Lackey,"
she said.

"Yeah? Yeah, babe?"

"We need to talk about it."

"I thought we were. I like it when you're on top and
moving side to side."

She stroked his chin with her fingertips. "Not that.
You know."

He sighed. "That's all I've *been* doing is talking
about it. To Ronnie, those cops. Everybody."

The ceiling in the dark was varied shades of gray
and beige. When Nancy had been a little girl, she used
to imagine spiders crawling on the ceiling and then
bury her face in her pillow. "Did they give you a rough
time?" she said.

"Didn't I look like it? Me and Ronnie back there
working our butts off trying to do the job without a

crew and those two cops coming around screwing with
us. Couple of grinning idiots is what they looked like.
No telling how long they had those TV cameras waiting in front of the house. I come out to my pickup and
there they are.''

''I thought you looked pretty innocent on the news,''
Nancy said. ''A hardworking man trying to get by.''

''They didn't make me *sound* very innocent, that
announcer guy. What'd he say, 'the suspect on the job'
or something? Course the two cops stayed out back so
it wouldn't look like they were the ones that set it up.
Coming on the ten p.m. news right after the bit on
Mrs. Hardin's funeral, I sure didn't look so innocent.
I looked like Jack the Ripper or somebody.''

''I thought her husband was the one that looked
guilty, a whole lot more than you did,'' Nancy said.

''You did?''

''Sure. It doesn't look right, him playing in that golf
tournament and then giving an interview right outside
his wife's funeral. A man that just lost his wife should
be more grief-stricken. He stood up in front of those
microphones like he was running for office.'' She was
quiet for a moment, and then said, ''You know what?''

''What's that?'' Lackey said.

Nancy sat upright and hugged her knees, her ankles
crossed, the warm skin of her thighs pressing against
her bare nipples. ''Well, if he was going to kill his
wife, he set it up perfectly.''

''He wasn't even home,'' Lackey said. ''I saw him
leave myself, and the guy he played golf with is his
alibi.''

''So maybe he had it done,'' Nancy said.

''I thought about that, too. But if a guy was going
to do that, what I think is that somebody'd just blow
her away. Not all of that sexual stuff.''

''Unless that's a coverup.''

Lackey suddenly laughed, his stomach muscles
tightening, his shoulders heaving, rolling onto his side

and cracking up as though he was watching a comedy show.

She grabbed a pillow and threw it at him; the pillow grazed his shoulder and toppled off of the bed to land beside the window. "What's so funny?" Nancy said.

"I'm picturing me, if I was this real cool hit man from the mob or something, and the guy asking me, 'How much extra does it cost for you to jack off on her?' "

"*Lackey.*"

"Well imagine that scene in *The Godfather,* like it was Luca Brasi and the look he'd get on his face when the guy asked him that."

"I'm having a hard time imagining that," Nancy said. "What I'm imagining is the scene with this guy I'm going to marry being led off in handcuffs while I'm crying my eyes out. Now, is that one funny, too?"

His smile faded; he rolled onto his back and clasped his hands behind his head, stretching out his legs and crossing his ankles. "No. It'd probably be funny to those two cops, though. Frick and Frack."

"What did they say to you?" Nancy said.

"A lot of stuff, most of it just to get under my skin. They asked me who was with me when I did it. I thought that was kind of weird."

"You mean, when you killed her?"

"Yeah," he said.

She pressed her forehead against her knees. "That means the physical evidence doesn't match," she said.

"That's what I thought."

"It's a good sign, but them trying to bring some unknown accomplice into it means they aren't going to leave you alone."

Lackey scooted onto his belly, stretched out his arm and lifted one corner of the windowshade. "That's pretty easy to figure out. That car out there, the two guys sitting in the front seat aren't there just to shoot the bull. Hey, one of 'em just lit a cigarette."

Nancy moved, catlike, rested her chin on his bare shoulder and looked through the window across the lawn, at the four-door car parked at the curb in the moonlight. "How long have you known they were there?" she said.

"They followed us home. Pulled up over there as I was parking the pickup in the driveway."

"And you didn't tell me?" she said.

He turned his head. There was a hint of irritation in the set of his jaw. "Why should I tell you everything, Nance? You don't tell me everything."

There was a tightening sensation in the muscles at the base of her neck. "What . . . ?"

"Those cops. They said they talked to you."

She lowered her gaze. "You had enough on your mind."

"They said you thought I did it," Lackey said.

"That's ridiculous."

"That's what I thought. But then you sort of forgot to tell me you'd been talking to them."

"You're being silly," Nancy said.

He maneuvered around to face her, reached out and laid his palm against her cheek. "I'm not trying to be silly. I can take anything except you lying to me."

"I didn't lie," she said. "I just didn't tell you about it."

His lips tightened into a line. "Bastards. They can do whatever they want to me, but messing with you . . ."

"They're just trying to get to you."

"Well," he said. "Well, they're doing it."

Her eyes suddenly misted. She studied his face, the prominent cheekbones, the picture she saw each night in her mind before she went to sleep. She stretched out and pressed against him, his chest against her nipples, his thighs against her own. "Hush. We'll make it, angel," she said.

* * *

"I had an aunt like that," Charles Morrison told Roscoe Henley, "spent years getting all that education, wound up with a master's degree, marries an old boy that barely could read. Spent the rest of her life teaching school supporting the guy, he's sitting around on the front porch sucking on a beer all the time. Women are funny, some of 'em are masochists."

Henley was scooted forward on the seat, his fly open, holding the piss container between his legs. The stream of urine made a hollow sound, echoing around inside the half-gallon jar. "This guy can read, Charley," Henley said. "Seemed like a pretty smart guy to me."

"Come on, the guy's a knuckle-buster," Morrison said. "That's why you got to figure he did that woman, she's over there in that big house and he's some construction worker. You think maybe it's a racial thing?"

Henley finished pissing, shook the final drops into the bottle, screwed the lid onto the jar, raised up to move his pelvis forward while he zipped up his fly. "Pass the coffee. What racial thing you talking about?"

Morrison poured coffee from a thermos and passed the styrofoam cup over to his partner. "You know, the Mexican girl wanting to go around with the contractor guy, her having all that education. Maybe it's like a lot of those black singers, Diana Ross and them. They make a little money the first thing you know they're marrying a white guy. This Cuellar girl here, maybe she thinks she's graduating up from her race and she's going to marry her a white boy no matter what kind of a guy it is."

Henley blew on the surface of his coffee as he let his gaze roam from the supercab pickup in the driveway to the small patch of lawn in front of Lackey Ferguson's house. The lawn needed mowing; moonlight cast little shadows here and there where clumps of

Johnson grass stood above the sparse Bermuda. "Know what I think, Charley?" Henley said.

"What's that?"

"I think you're some kind of half-assed bigot. We work a homicide over in Polytechnic you think these guys are shooting each other 'cause they're black. If two white guys get drunk and one shoots the other, you think they're acting like a couple of niggers. Now you're saying this girl's got a racial thing, well I'll tell you something. The only one's got a racial hangup around here is you."

Morrison reached for the piss container and unscrewed the lid. "Naw, hey, that ain't right. I got a lot of buddies, a lot of the black guys on the city force and me get along real good. This one guy, this city patrolman, hell, we're on the same bowling team."

"Yeah," Henley said. "He carries a one-ninety average and won a coupla trophies for you, but when the match is over you take all the white guys on the team out for a coupla beers and let the black guy fend for himself."

"It's for him," Morrison said. "A lot of the places we go the guy would be uncomfortable."

"You mean *you'd* be uncomfortable. Look, Charley, you managed to get us on this stakeout, let's just stake the guy out, okay? No more racial shit, we got enough problems without that. Besides, you get a look at that girl? She's got no problem drumming up men, I don't care what race the guy is."

Morrison paused with the piss container positioned on the floorboard between his legs, swiveled his head and showed his partner a crooked grin. "You ever had any Mexican pussy?"

"Jesus Christ, Charley."

"You're getting pretty—" Morrison said, opening his own zipper, moving forward to position himself over the piss container. "You're getting pretty touchy, Roscoe. I never knew you to be touchy before."

"You never knew me to be staking out a guy that ain't done nothing," Henley said, "just because my partner happens to have a hard-on for the guy. Why didn't you just get up out of the gutter and take a swing at the guy instead of all this?"

"Too many people standing around," Morrison said as urine spattered into the container. "You can bet he wouldn't be pushing me down like that it was just me and him. And they done the woman, Roscoe. Mr. Badass Ferguson in there, him and his buddy."

"Jesus Christ, what buddy? Look, the guy Hardin, he said the contractor come by earlier to talk about building the bathhouse and it was just him. People saw Ferguson driving away from the place, just him again. Now just because we can't get a match on the physical evidence, now there's got to be a buddy. Now I haven't said anything about all this, and I'm not going to say any more. You and Favor want to build a case around this guy, well I'm not stopping you. Just don't expect me to—"

The porchlight at the house came suddenly on, a single yellow bulb glowing above the front door. Nancy Cuellar came out wearing thigh-length shorts and a baggy cotton shirt. She was barefoot. She descended the two steps into the yard, her expression urgent, motioning toward the two cops seated in the stakeout car. She cupped her hands in front of her mouth and shouted, "Please. Help, please, he's . . ."

Henley yanked on the handle, shoved the car door open with his shoulder and sprinted across the lawn toward the girl, his hand digging for the pistol at his belt, while Morrison swore softly, capped the piss jar and set it aside, alighted from the driver's side while zipping up his fly, and took off after his partner with long loping strides. Nancy was gesturing toward the house, her breath coming in short gasps. "In the bathroom. His wrists, I think he's cut his wrists. Please . . ."

"Where is it, miss?" Henley said. "The bathroom, where is it?"

"At the back. Down the hall, it's . . . hurry. Please hurry."

Up onto the porch they charged, the slender bald cop, pistol ready, followed by the big blond guy, the blond's head revolving on his neck as he looked warily from side to side, the petite barefoot Hispanic girl close on their heels. They dashed through the living room as floorboards creaked under their weight. Henley collided with a chair in the darkness, stumbled, righted himself, cursing, as on his left Nancy threw a switch and the overhead light illuminated the room. Nancy pointed to a hallway which branched off from the rear of the living room. "Down there," she said. "It's right down there."

The detectives raced past her, following her direction down the corridor, both cops hustling now, guns drawn and ready, moving in the light spilling into the hallway from the living room. The bathroom door was open; small octagonal tiles were visible in alternating black and white. Henley entered first with Morrison close behind. The blond detective turned the light on, and the two stood shoulder to shoulder, their breathing ragged, pointing their guns around at a porcelain commode, a sink and mirror, an off-white shower curtain drawn closed in front of a tub. Morrison yanked the curtain aside, and the two cops stared at a gleaming white, empty bathtub as, behind them, the door slammed. A deadbolt slid into place with a solid click.

Morrison gaped at his partner, his jaw dropping as realization dawned. "Sonofa*bitch*," Morrison said. The sound muffled by the door, bare feet slapped on hardwood as Nancy retreated down the hallway. "Sonofa*bitch*," Morrison said. "She's locked the fucking . . ."

Henley turned the knob and pushed with his shoulder. "Sonofa*bitch*," Henley said.

"Out of the way," Morrison said. "Out of the fucking way."

Henley stepped aside as Morrison pointed his .38, *blam, blam, blam,* emptying the chambers as bullets thudded into wood and splinters flew and the bathroom was filled with the odor of burnt gunpowder. The lock shattered, the door sagged inward. Henley grabbed the edge of the door and yanked; the two cops charged back down the hallway and into the living room. The front door stood open; hot wind rustled the window curtains.

Back onto the porch the detectives ran. A block up the street, the tail lamps on Lackey Ferguson's pickup glowed red as the supercab rounded the corner, bounced hard on its springs, and disappeared behind a row of houses.

Next door, a man stood in the yard wearing a bathrobe. "What the hell's going on?" he yelled.

Morrison let his pistol hang by his hip as he stepped down from the porch. "Police," he said. "Just get the fuck back inside." He turned to his partner and shrugged.

Henley stood under the yellow porchlight, leaning against the doorjamb. He was laughing. "Guess it's a racial thing, huh?" Detective Roscoe Henley said.

14

Frank Nichols was pretty sure that the seven would go. Just enough of the green seven was visible beyond the edge of the yellow nine so that if Frank missed the nine with the cue ball he'd get enough of the seven to cut it into the corner pocket. The five was a simple straight-in on the side, but Frank wanted to try the seven because, with just a little lefthand English, the cue ball would come off the rail and maybe knock in the nine as well. That was what Frank liked about Nine-Ball, the different ways to make the money shot. He placed his tongue near the roof of his mouth, whistling softly between his teeth as he chalked his cue, circling the table like a man stalking a deer, looking over the cut it would take to knock the deuce into the far corner, considering the backup action required to bring the cue ball back to the center for shape on the five. Nope. Nope. The seven was the shot. His mind made up, Frank returned to the end of the table, stretched his lanky body full-length and put one knee up on the rail, spread three fingers of his left hand on the felt, circled the cue with his thumb and index finger, drew the stick back and forth like the bow on a violin. "Touch shot, man," Frank said. "Touch shot."

"That's what it is, man," Rock Man Bentley said. "Only by the time you touch it the afternoon be over." He beat on the floor impatiently with the butt end of his own cue stick. Rock Man wore a grimy white

T-shirt and size 48 jeans, his gut overhanging his belt and his skin the color of bittersweet chocolate.

Frank grinned as he hit the shot, hit the cue ball hard with lefthand English, watched with a bland expression as the cue ball clipped the seven into the corner, rebounded from the rail with a soft thump. The English took hold; the cue ball curved slightly as it approached the nine, bumped the nine sideways. The yellow nine crept to the edge of the side pocket, teetered there, and finally tumbled out of sight with a muted rattle. "Afternoon ain't over, man," Frank said. "The game is, though. Pay me."

Rock Man grimaced and dug in his pocket as Freeway approached from the front entrance. Freeway was around sixty, his kinky brown hair going to gray, slightly stooped as though he'd picked a lot of cotton. Which Freeway had, doing half of his life on TDC work farms. "Dude up front to see you," he said to Frank. "White dude, don't look like he's no man. No law or nothin'." Freeway picked up the cue ball from the table, looked it over as though inspecting for loaded dice, dropped the cue onto the felt where the ball thumped and rolled. "Never seen this dude," Freeway said.

Frank took the bill from Rock Man and stuffed it in his own pocket as he squinted toward the front of the pool hall. The glare from the front window outlined the bearded man who stood by the entrance, leaning on the bar. Frank laid his stick down, nodded to Rock Man, then ambled up to the bar for a better look. Damn, he knew the white guy. Frank's features relaxed. "Bossman," Frank said. "You slummin' on this side of town. If you ain't lookin' to see no *po*lice, then you *really* in the wrong spot. These streets over here be crawlin' with 'em." He tilted his New York Yankees baseball cap lower over his eyes.

"Well, you might be in the wrong place, too,"

Lackey Ferguson said. "I don't think guys on parole supposed to be shooting pool for no money."

"If you think that," Frank said, "then what you doing looking for me in a gambling pool hall?"

"I said you weren't supposed to," Lackey said. "That's why I figured to find you in here. Got a minute?"

"Parole dude say I can't work for you," Frank said, "and say I can't do no gambling. But, shee-it, I got to make a living. Yeah. Yeah, I got time. You want a beer?"

Lackey nodded and Frank motioned to Freeway. Freeway moved behind the bar, regarding the white dude with narrowed eyes as he dug into the cooler and opened two Pearl longnecks with faint hisses of air. Frank grabbed both beers in one hand, separating the necks with his index finger, and led the way to a booth in the back, moving casually, nodding left and right, saying once, " 'S okay, brudda, dude's cool," and another time, "Ain't no law, man," while black men looked up from their pool games, gave Lackey the once-over, then returned to what they were doing. At the back of the room was a long, sawdust-sprinkled shuffleboard. As Lackey sat down, a skinny kid in a Hard Rock Cafe T-shirt slid the puck to the opposite end where it halted overhanging the trough. A leaner.

Frank handed one beer over the table to Lackey and sipped from his own. "You come in a Vaughn Boulevard poolhall in the afternoon and you going to get looked at funny," Frank said. "It's the way it is. You don't look so good."

"I spent the night in a motel," Lackey said. "I didn't sleep much. Walls thin as pastrami. I can't stay at home for a while."

"I seen in the paper. You gull friend, the paper say she help you disappear. She staying wid you?"

"No, I took her home. She's at work. They got no warrant for me, she wasn't helping me escape from jail or anything. Other than get pissed off, there's not much they can do to her.''

"That'll change, bossman. Lay you odds they got a little warrant before nightfall.''

"Probably," Lackey said. "I got some things to do I can't get done with those two cops following me around.''

"Way they writing you up in the paper, the best thing for you to do is hit the highway.''

"It's a thought," Lackey said. "Hey, you know I didn't do that to that woman.''

Frank held the neck of the bottle between his middle and index fingers and swigged. "If I thought you did I don't be sitting here wid you. We just thieves around here, bossman, ain't no crazies. Guys that take pussy from women, they safer downtown in county jail than in no Vaughn Boulevard poolhall.''

"As long as the cops got me to kick around they're not going to look for anybody else," Lackey said. "That much I can figure out for myself." He lifted his own bottle to his lips, his gaze traveling to the far corner of the pool hall. A dusky, lanky chick in tight shorts was lining up a shot while a lightskinned black guy of about twenty-five watched her. She smiled at the guy over her shoulder. Lackey looked back to Frank Nichols. "Nancy thinks the woman's husband had it done," Lackey said.

"Everybody think that if it wasn't for the way the dude handled that woman," Frank said. "Might be coverup, though.''

"Look, Frank. If you wanted something done like that, kill your wife or something, where would you go?''

"Don't got no old lady and don't want one," Frank said. "But if I wanted somebody blowed away I'd do it myself. Not fuck wid no funky killer-man. Rich dude living out by Colonial Country Club think different, though. Yeah, there's a few dudes around he could talk to.''

"That's kind of what I'm getting at."

Frank grinned. He had big white piano-key teeth with one gold inlay. "Getting at what? You don't just walk up to one of these dudes and say, 'Listen, you a hit man?' People try that they wind up getting hit themselves."

"I guess you have to find somebody to arrange it with the guy," Lackey said.

"That the way it work," Frank said. "Only most people go looking they wind up either getting ripped off or talking to the law pretending like they're some killer-man. Getting somebody offed ain't no easy proposition, bossman."

"That's why I'm talking to you."

"I know a homeboy does things. You know these people not afraid to talk to me 'cause they know I'm cool. I take somebody around that's going to get these people busted or something, then I ain't going to be walking around my ownself, not for long."

"I'm not going to get anybody busted," Lackey said. "I just figure, well, if that Hardin guy went around looking for somebody to do his wife, then somebody you know probably heard about it."

"Probably did, bossman. Only they not be talking about it. That the way these people stay in business."

"Listen, I got a little money," Lackey said. "Maybe the way to find out something is to act like I'm, you know, looking for somebody to do something myself."

"Most of these dudes going to know about you," Frank said. "They read the *Fort Worth Star-Telegram* just like everybody else." A squatty guy in a jumpsuit went by carrying a pool cue in a leather case. Frank nodded to the guy and said, "Tied up now, brudda. Little bit later."

"What I figure is," Lackey said, "that if I can meet

one guy then that might lead to another guy. All these people probably know each other.''

''Yeah, they do,'' Frank said. ''But I got to tell you, bossman, you pretty much shooting in the dark. You got no way of knowing for sure that rich Hardin dude done anything. For all you know, whoever done that woman happened by on accident.''

''Not in that neighborhood,'' Lackey said. ''Over there you got to know where you're going. Plus, and I been thinking about this, Hardin let all of his servants off. He gave that gardener the day off while I was standing there holding his golf clubs, then when I talked to Mrs. Hardin about the bathhouse she said the maid was gone, too. In a neighborhood like that you'd have to know when she was going to be there alone.''

''Makes some sense,'' Frank said. ''But then I ain't no police detective or anything.''

''If you were looking for the guy,'' Lackey said, ''and figure I'm right and Hardin had it done. If you were looking for the guy that did it, where would you go?''

Frank rubbed a circle in the frost on his bottle with his thumb. Then he set the bottle aside, fished in his pocket for a crumpled pack of Pall Malls, and lit one. He blew smoke at the ceiling and scooted the ashtray closer to him on the table. He leaned forward and glanced around as he said in a near-whisper, ''Well, you wouldn't look noplace on this street here. Vaughn Boulevard they got a few gulls working around, some dudes selling twenty-five-dollar papers on the street corner, but nobody's going to do no hit for nobody. I'd go over on East Lancaster Avenue. It's on the borderline between white and black and they got people over there that'll do anything, you want to pay 'em enough.''

''Any place in particular?''

Frank dragged on his cigarette and exhaled smoke

through his nostrils. "They got one spot, a white dude owns it. No place where you'll find anything out by yoself. You better take me along."

"I don't want to put you in any problem," Lackey said.

Frank grinned, slow and easy. "You done put me in a problem, bossman. I don't have no job no more, remember?"

Lackey went outside with Frank and stood on the curb, looking up and down the street at old weather-beaten houses, at a dumpy white building across the way which had a sign over the door reading "Cal's," and listened to muffled soul music drift from the interior of Cal's while Frank said that they'd better ride in his old Buick. "That pickup you driving probably got a hot sheet on it by now. We going to see some patrol cars on the way. Bet on it."

The Buick was a '77 model, two-tone green, and was parked nose-on to the curb in a slant-in space. Lackey went around to the passenger side and climbed in. He closed the door with a creak of hinge and a solid clunk, then settled back, glad to have somebody drive him, the bone-weary tired feeling settling in, his eyelids suddenly heavy. The motel where he'd spent the night was on Belknap Street in Haltom City, and the air-conditioning hadn't worked. He'd left the window open and had stared at the ceiling for the most part, listening to the rumble of passing motorcycles through the night. He'd finally shut the window when two bikers had gotten into an argument outside, but had opened it once more when the stifling heat had gotten to him. The bikers had gotten into it for real, cussing and slugging, then had made up and ridden off together like pals forever. At five in the morning, Lackey had still been awake. He'd dozed off for an hour or so, dreaming of Nancy, missing her, and had wakened at six-thirty to the sound of bottles clanking together, and finally had watched groggily through the window while the Coke man had filled the drink machine. While he'd been using the toilet a roach the size of a mouse had scuttled into the shower, so Lackey hadn't bathed. He'd put back on the same blue T-shirt and jeans in which he'd sneaked away from the two detectives. At the moment he felt as though he'd been on a two-day march, back-pack and all, was certain that he smelled like a goat, and would have given anything to never have heard of J. Percival Hardin III— and would have given even more to have just married Nancy and spent his wedding night in a motel in Arlington near Six Flags. To hell with San Francisco. If Lackey ever got out of this, he'd never think of going to San Francisco on his honeymoon again.

Frank got in behind the wheel and cranked the engine; James Brown wailed suddenly from the dashboard speakers. Frank turned the volume down, put the Buick in reverse and backed out into Vaughn Boulevard. Lackey sat up straighter, rubbed his eyes, and slapped his own cheeks. The car's interior smelled of stale cigarettes and beer. As Frank applied the brakes and dropped the lever into forward gear, bottles rolled and clanked beneath the seat. "Got to clean this mothafuckah out," Frank said, then pressed hard on the accelerator and Lackey sank back against the cushion as the Buick fishtailed away from the pool hall. A hooker wearing heavy makeup stood on the corner in front of Cal's. She hiked her skirt and blew a kiss at Lackey as the Buick passed.

They went north on Vaughn, past the old gas station which stood at the corner of Vaughn and J, with its rusty ancient pumps, to turn right on Rosedale Street. The Buick's muffler had a hole in it, the engine noise more like a tractor than a car, and thick, carbon-filled exhaust fumes billowed from its tail pipe. It was cloudless and hot as the blazes; Lackey rolled down the window and let the wind whip around inside the car. Ashes blew from the end of Frank's cigarette and swirled in the draft like confetti.

On Rosedale Street they passed the sandy brick buildings of Texas Wesleyan University on their left and turned to the north on Miller Street. They wound a couple of miles between houses with sagging porches, finally going west on Lancaster Avenue. Lancaster was a wide boulevard with a tree-lined island in the middle and had once been a major thoroughfare. But twenty years earlier, when Lackey had been in high school, the freeways had opened and the traffic had gone to the north and west. Lancaster's shopping centers were now deserted mostly, the clothing stores and restaurants replaced by pawn shops, tote-the-note car lots, X-rated book and video places, and an occasional topless bar. The discount furniture store where Lackey's mother had once bought a dining room suite was no longer there; the building now sported a fifty-foot sign out front, showing an outline of a naked girl brandishing six-guns over the current name of the place, the Crystal Pistol. Two blocks on the other side of the Crystal Pistol, Frank pulled to the curb in front of a washateria and killed the engine; the Buick dieseled through a few vibrations and finally died with a backfire like a howitzer. "That joint. That joint right there," Frank said.

Next door to the washateria was a wooden building with swinging saloon-style doors. One wall of the building was painted black and doubled as a sign, the big white letters spelling out simply, "Herb's." A ten-year-old Eldorado was parked in front of the entrance. Frank got out and ambled toward the doorway, his head turning warily from side to side, watching for whatever it was that guys like Frank watched out for. Lackey climbed down and followed, and the two of them entered Herb's. A spring creaked as the double doors closed behind them. Lackey blinked and squinted in the dimness.

An old Wurlitzer jukebox stood in the far corner with its plastic panels lighted, and the song playing was "There Ain't No Gettin' Over Me," by Ronnie Milsap. As Lackey's eyes grew accustomed to the dimness, other shapes materialized, a stack of cardboard boxes, a long bar at the back of the club, barstools with plastic seats and cotton stuffing poking out in spots, a small stage near the jukebox, old wooden tables and old wooden chairs. The odor of must mixed with the odor of stale beer. The song ended, and while the juke's mechanical arm searched for another record, a cooler motor hummed.

The two guys seated at the bar were still as dummies. One man had his back turned and was facing the bar mirror. He wore a short-sleeved jumpsuit and had thick, hairy arms. His shoulders were hunched, his neck short, his hair thinning. As Lackey watched, the man lifted the longneck bottle in front of him and poured beer into a glass. Otherwise the guy didn't move. Visible beyond him, a lighted red and yellow sign over the register advertised Budweiser Beer.

The second guy at the bar was turned around on his stool, facing the door. He was skinny as a snake and wore sunglasses, and his nose was wrinkled as though he was squinting behind the dark lenses. He wore a short-sleeved khaki shirt open to the third button, and his elbows were stuck out behind him like vulture's wings, resting on the bar. His chest was sunken and the color of grammar-school paste. His dark hair was long and stringy, its greasy ends touching his collar. The heel of one shoe was hooked over the rung on the barstool; his opposite ankle rested on his propped-up leg with its knee sticking out at an odd angle. He appeared frozen on the stool, like a man waiting for something to happen which never did. Frank left Lackey and skirted tables as he walked halfway to the bar. He said to the skinny man, "I got a guy here. Need to talk." There was a pop from the jukebox and

Tina Turner moaned lustily through "What's Love Got to Do With It?"

The skinny guy finally moved. He took his ankle down from his knee and rose slowly, crossed the fifteen feet of space to stand beside Frank and to regard Lackey with hands on hips. The skinny guy's nose was still wrinkled, and Lackey decided that instead of squinting, the guy was smelling something awful. Lackey sniffed the air. The skinny man said to Frank, "Who you bringing here?"

"He's cool," Frank said.

"So everybody's cool," the guy said. "Who you bringing here?"

Frank's shoulders lifted, then dropped. "A man wants to talk some business. You don't want to talk no business we go someplace else. 'S cool, brudda, we can dig it."

The guy raised a bony arm and pointed to a corner, away from the bar and jukebox. "Yeah, over there," he said. "I got to turn down this fucking noise. Give a guy a headache."

While Lackey and Frank sat down, Skinny went over and adjusted the volume on the juke. Tina Turner's voice grew suddenly faint. The man at the bar continued to mind his own business, watching the back mirror, drinking his beer in silence. There was no air-conditioning in the place; a tall rotating fan beside the juke blew a warm draft. A drop of sweat rolled down the side of Lackey's neck and soaked into the collar of his T-shirt. With Tina Turner jiving faintly in the background, Skinny came over and grabbed a chair. He turned the chair around and straddled it, crossing his arms on the chairback and resting his pointed chin on his forearms. "So," Skinny said. "What business?"

Frank tilted his cap back and said to Lackey, "This dude name Dick. He can do some shit." His skin in the dimness was midnight blue.

"Depends on what you want done," Dick said. His nose wrinkled even more than it had. "And who wants it done."

"Ain't no law, bro," Frank said. "All you need to know about him. Ain't no law and got money, and wants something did to somebody. Wants you to set something up."

"Let the man talk," Dick said. He turned his face toward Lackey. "I seen you someplace?" Dick said.

"I don't know where it'd be," Lackey said. "Around somewhere, maybe, you don't look familiar." He was thinking about his picture on TV and in the papers, and was wondering if the photos had been a good likeness. Personally, Lackey didn't think so.

Dick shook the hair away from his forehead, girlfashion. "If I know you it'll come to me. Guy wanting something like you're wanting, if I think it over most times I can make 'em. I tell you something up front. Frank Nichols says you're cool, anybody knows Frank's going to buy that. But if it turns out you ain't cool you got real problems. Something else, too. This ain't the kind of deal you can crawfish on. Once you do it, it's done. So you better be talking about somebody you don't like very much, not some broad you been fucking and tomorrow you fall back in love with her and change your mind."

Only his lips move, Lackey thought, while his nose stays wrinkled. Maybe the guy's got sinus trouble. "Are you the one we're talking about?" Lackey said.

Dick's lips turned up in a grin. His teeth were rotten. "Where you get this guy at, Frank?" His grin disappeared at once, like a scene in a movie with some frames missing. He said to Lackey, "I'm nothing but a bar owner, friend, and as a bar owner I happen to know a few people. If I put you together with somebody I know, I don't want to hear nothing about your business. Understand?"

Lackey had never understood longhairs, had always

thought most of them were kind of wimpy, but this guy Dick talked like somebody used to giving orders. Must have a lot of people backing him up, Lackey thought, unless he's a whole lot stronger than he looks. "It would probably be better that way," Lackey said. "That way I could talk it over with the person."

"That's my very point," Dick said. "This middleman shit don't work, either somebody gets ripped off, or somebody don't pay, which puts the middle man in the position of being responsible for somebody's money. I guarantee nobody's credit, all I do is put people together."

"How about the other end of it?" Lackey said. "You guarantee if somebody pays somebody, something's going to get done?"

Dick snugged his sunglasses up on his nose with his middle finger. "I don't guess you're getting it. I'm going to get in touch with Frank and tell him when and where you can meet this person. That's fucking all. Then I'm through with it. People come in here wanting what you want, they got no fucking guts or they'd be doing it themselves. I can tell you, yeah, this person's always done what he said he was going to, but if it don't work out nothing comes back on me."

Lackey's neck muscles had bunched when Dick had talked about somebody not having any guts, but he decided that Dick was only stating fact, not making a personal remark. "If that's the way it's going to be," Lackey said, "then that's the way it's going to be."

Dick's chin moved up and down. "That's the way it's going to be," he said, then turned to Frank. "You still in the same spot?"

"Mostly," Frank said.

"You still on parole, huh?"

"Yeah. Going to be on it awhile."

"The last time you went down," Dick said. "I heard about that. Sounded like a bad beef to me."

"Sounded like one to me, too," Frank said. "But

I got a rap sheet, they offer me three years which I can do standing on my head. Them D.A.'s know just what to offer a dude, if they case is bullshit.''

"I had one like that," Dick said. "Three grams of coke. Grams, not ounces, but they offer me a year county time. With good time I'm on the street in what, ninety days? You got to figure the odds, you know?''

Lackey was losing interest, the two guys talking about what D.A.'s were offering everybody, so he scanned the barroom. The thick-necked man hadn't moved, as though he was a prop in a TV serial, just sitting there watching the back mirror. Lackey's eyes were now used to the dimness; he made out clusters of dust and gum wrappers and wadded cigarette packs on the floor. He decided to interrupt the guys. "How long are we talking about?" Lackey said.

Dick paused in midsentence, telling Frank about the time that he'd done in the county, and swiveled his head to say to Lackey, "Couple of days. No more than that.''

"Okay," Lackey said. "Look, we better be going. This makes me a little bit nervous, sitting here.''

"No worry," Dick said. "Everybody's nervous. You just be thinking about what you're wanting to do and making sure you're wanting to do it. You ain't talking about hiring somebody to mow your yard, you know.''

Dick stood in the doorway and watched Frank and the bearded man leave, watched them walk side by side over to the beatup Buick in front of the washateria. The bearded guy was different, not like the run-of-the-mill nervous asshole looking for somebody to do his wife or, more often, do the guy who was fucking his wife. Dick thought personally that they should leave the bitch and forget about it, but who was he to say? The bearded guy, though, looked like somebody who could take care of himself, shoulder muscles rippling under the fabric of the blue T-shirt, ridged triceps and long lean legs like a running back. Looked like somebody that if he wanted something done he'd take care of his own business. But Dick only arranged things, and why the bearded man wanted to talk to somebody was something Dick didn't want to get into. The bearded guy climbed easily into the front seat of the Buick beside Frank the black guy. The starter chugged; the engine coughed and backfired, and the Buick moseyed a half-block down the street, made a U-turn through the slot in the island, and disappeared going west on Lancaster Avenue. Dick let the doors close behind him as he went back to the bar. He moved his hair from his forehead with his fingers as he thought it over. He'd seen the bearded guy someplace. He'd have to think about it.

He went behind the bar, walking on raised wooden pallets lined up on the floor, and moved down to stand across from the thick-necked man. Dick felt of the thick-necked man's beer. The bottle was half-full but warm. Dick emptied the bottle in the sink, dropped the longneck into the trash, and dug into the cooler for a fresh one. He opened the beer with a tiny hiss of air and let the cap drop into a metal bin. Then he set the cold one up on the bar. The thick-necked man shoved over a couple of bills and some change, but Dick pushed them back. "On the house," Dick said. "You catch any of that?"

The thick-necked man frowned. He had thinning hair, a sloping weak chin, and arms the length of an orangutan's. "The white guy, I know who he is," Everett Wilson said. "But who's the nigger?"

15

Nancy Cuellar had been expecting the two detectives to come calling all day—going through the motions at her desk, glad for once that her boss was out of town, wincing mentally every time her intercom buzzed, rehearsing in her mind the response she was going to make when Helen Taylor smirked her way in with the news that the law was once again in the reception room—and when four-thirty rolled around and still no Morrison and Henley or anyone else from the sheriff's department, Nancy was just a little bit confused. As the *clickety-clack* of typewriters ceased up and down the corridor, followed by the rattling of paper, the rolling noise of file drawers closing, and the muted hubbub of going-home conversation, Nancy called the desk at the county jail. No Lackey X. Ferguson in custody at present. Well, that was a relief. She put her things away and joined the other office people in front of the elevators, avoided one car when she noticed Helen Taylor climbing aboard, and finally took a milk run with Trudy and two of the girls from the file department. The car stopped at nearly every floor to let more tired workers trudge aboard and arrived at lobby level with Nancy jammed to the rear behind an overweight woman whose shopping bag kept bumping Nancy's arm. She exited last, taking quick *clickety-clack* steps in her high heels through the lobby, and made it halfway to the parking garage elevators before she came to a halt that made her shoesoles squeal like tires. So, at last, there they were.

The two detectives were lounging around in front of the first-floor gift shop. Henley was coatless, in shirt-sleeves and tie, and wearing sunglasses. The bald top of his head was visible as he smoked a cigarette and thumped ashes into a receptacle filled with white sand. Morrison wore a powder blue sport coat and was leaning against the wall with his ankles crossed, chewing gum as he read a *People* magazine that had a picture of Madonna on the cover. The big blond cop had gotten a haircut, a burr. Henley nudged Morrison, who looked up from his reading to regard Nancy with a pinch-lipped smirk.

Nancy held her breath and quickened her pace, sweeping past the two cops as though she hadn't seen them, clutching her purse firmly under her arm. She was wearing a white pleated thigh-length skirt and a green cotton pullover sweater. As she passed by, Morrison took a step in her direction. "Nancy. Hey, Nancy."

She felt the warmth coursing up the back of her neck and almost paused, but strode firmly on.

"If you want, we can arrest you," Morrison said loudly. "You want that?"

She stopped, lowered her head while she swallowed hard, then turned. "Arrest me for what?"

Morrison fished two letter-sized folded papers from his inside breast pocket and held them up for her to see. "Come on, Nancy, we're not out to get you. Not much to this little charge here, just obstructing our investigation is all. Hell, we'd even tear it up. You know what we want."

Nancy blinked. There was a knot behind her breast-bone the size of a grapefruit. She hadn't counted on this. "Can I see that?" she said softly.

Morrison came forward and handed her one of the papers while Henley walked forward as well and stood beside his partner. Henley's hands were on his hips, his fingers near the pistol holstered on his belt. He was chewing gum, his expression masked, his eyes hidden behind dark lenses.

Nancy unfolded the paper and scanned it, feeling slightly faint, her vision blurring. The paper was a form, some fill-in-the-blanks starting with THE GRAND JURY CHARGES and ending with the printed words, AGAINST THE PEACE AND DIGNITY OF THE STATE OF TEXAS, and in between her own name—God, she thought, Nancy Patricia Cuellar, that's me, it *is* me—followed by some typewritten sentences stating that she'd knowingly and willingly interfered with two officers of the Tarrant County Sheriff's Department in their investigation of one Lackey X. Ferguson, suspected of the crime of Capital Murder. *Capital Murder,* Nancy thought, oh, God, oh, God, oh, God. She let the warrant hang at her side and looked fearfully at the two detectives.

"Hey, Nancy," Morrison said, "we understand that you got a thing for this old boy. Now let's get him in so we can clear all this up. That's all we're trying to do." Nancy's gaze was frozen on the remaining paper in Morrison's hand. Morrison glanced down, then said to her, "It's his. It's the one we got for your old man."

"My . . . fiancé," Nancy said.

Henley clasped his hands palms-out, stretched his arms, and turned his eyes toward the ceiling.

"Well, hey," Morrison said, grinning. "Well, hey, you can't get married 'til you clear this up, can you? Come on, you just tell us where to find old Lackey and we can forget about this little old warrant for you. Charges don't amount to a hill of beans. The D.A.'s done told us, you tell that nice little Nancy Cuellar girl that all she's got to do is lead us to her old man, and she's home free. Now don't make no problems for yourself, Nancy. Come on, where is he?"

They're just doing their job, Nancy told herself. Just

doing their job and . . . No. No, they're not just doing their job, either. It's more than that. Just look at that blond guy grinning. God, she hated that man. "I don't know," she said.

Henley took his gaze from the ceiling and rubbed his bald head with his palm. "That won't do, Nancy."

As part of Nancy's job at the law firm, she'd had to go down to the county jail a few times, sometimes to research records and other times to post bond for Mr. Brantley's criminal clients. It was the only part of the job which Nancy absolutely despised. She pictured the helpless look on the female prisoners as they waited in line, handcuffed, wearing light green shapeless smocks, going in one at a time to answer the in-processing questions. *Ever been arrested before? Are you lesbian? Any special medical problems we should know about?* Different images jumped suddenly into Nancy's mind, a picture of herself in line with those women, and a clear impression of what would happen to her once they locked her in the innards of the jail, in the same cell along with all those Rosedale Avenue whores. Nancy swallowed bile. "I told you," she said. "I just don't know where he is."

The two cops exchanged glances, the blond smirker and the bald deadpan, the two guys appointed to make life miserable for Nancy Cuellar. Morrison sighed. "Tell you what, Nancy." He put Lackey's warrant away in his pocket and rolled the *People* magazine into a cylinder. "Tell you what. We really ought to book you, but putting a nice girl like you in that nasty jail would stay on our conscience. What we're willing to do is—and this is up to you, if you want to go to jail we can take you there—but what we're willing to do is, we'll take you downtown and let you talk to the D.A. Deputy District Attorney Favor's his name, and he ain't a bad guy like me and Roscoe here. Now if you can convince Mr. Favor what you're telling us, that you don't know where your old man is at, then

maybe we can do away with this warrant altogether."
He smiled like he'd just shown Nancy a used car he
had for sale. "Come on, whaddya say?"

Uptight as she was, Nancy didn't believe Morrison
for a minute. She'd seen enough of the law firm's criminal clients handled by the Tarrant County Sheriff's
Department to know better. The plan was to get her
downtown in the D.A.'s office, grill her with the Assistant District Attorney in on the questioning, and if
she didn't have anything to tell them—or, rather, if she
didn't say what they *wanted* her to say—they'd whisk
her away up the street to county lockup. Don't pass
go. Still, she'd rather have that than . . . She folded
her arms and firmly planted her feet. "Can I drive
myself?"

Henley shifted his wad of gum from one cheek to
the other. "Well, you got to understand that we can't
really go for that. Officially we're supposed to put you
under arrest. But we'll stretch it this far. You can drive,
as long as Mr. Morrison here rides in the car with you.
I'll follow in the county vehicle. That way, if Mr. Favor gives the word, you can drive yourself on home
once we're through. How'll that be?"

Through her fear, Nancy was beginning to get just
a little bit mad. The way that Morrison was leering,
Nancy would as soon go downtown in the paddy wagon
as ride in the car with him. It wouldn't surprise her if
the grinning blond cop decided to cop a feel from the
Mexican girl on the way. Wouldn't surprise her at all.
It would be her word against his. And the only reason
they were willing to let her drive her own car downtown was to save them the trouble of sending a tow
truck for it later. This Mexican girl's not as dumb as
she looks, Detective Morrison, Nancy thought. You're
a *cabrón,* detective, I'll bet you've heard that before.
"My car's on the seventh floor, over in the parking
garage," Nancy said.

"Hey, that's good, we'll walk with you," Morrison

said. He took a couple of steps toward the garage elevators, then stopped and looked at Nancy over his
shoulder.

Nancy kept her gaze on the floor as she went along
with them, walking beside Morrison with Henley a
couple of steps behind her, seeing passersby in the
lobby in the periphery of her vision. They're not really
staring, she thought, it's just the old imagination
churning. To prove to herself that people weren't staring, Nancy lifted her gaze. Two men in tailored suits
passed going in the opposite direction. Both men
glanced at Nancy, then in turn at Henley and Morrison, then stopped and did double-takes. Nancy's
cheeks flushed and she lowered her gaze once more to
the tiled floor.

Just as always at this time of day, there was a noisy
crowd in front of the elevators. Nancy stood between
the detectives while the two chatted casually over the
top of her head. She wasn't a tall girl to begin with,
and standing between the two cops made her feel about
two feet high. Not under arrest, she told herself. *Not
under arrest?* Well, what in the name of Jesus am I,
then? The center elevator door rumbled open. Henley
stepped quickly forward, holding a small black wallet
open over his head, flashing his badge. ''Stand back,''
he told the crowd. ''Stand back please. Sheriff's Department, stand away.'' The crowd parted like the Red
Sea as Morrison took Nancy by the arm and escorted
her aboard the elevator. Morrison and Nancy stood to
the rear of the car while Henley got on and held his
finger poised over the button panel. ''Seven, huh?''
Henley said. Nancy shot the detective a look that would
wilt flowers and nodded her head. Morrison laughed
softly beside her as the doors closed. Sudden increased gravity sank Nancy's feet deeper into the carpet.

After the hubbub of the lobby, the silence on the
seventh floor of the garage pressed on Nancy's ear-

drums. Cars, minivans, and small pickups stood in rows in slanted parking spaces. Henley paused outside the elevator and said, "Which one, Nancy?"

"Up there, the . . . green Mustang. The little green . . . the green one." Nancy's feet were numb and there was a tingling sensation in her calves. Morrison used his palm in the center of her back to nudge her gently out of the elevator car as though he was escorting her to the prom. At his touch, her insides twisted.

Henley led the way to the Mustang, his footsteps echoing from uninsulated concrete. Three sides of the garage were open air, and a warm spring breeze blew on Nancy's cheeks. Inside, she was cold as ice. She couldn't let this happen. Couldn't. In the fifteen seconds it took to cross the floor to the Mustang, she made up her mind.

Her car was parked in between a Ford Bronco and a brown Mercury Marquis. Henley held back while Morrison took Nancy in between the Bronco and the Mustang to the Mustang's driver's side. The big blond cop stood with his hands in his pockets, a half-grin, half-leer on his face, as Nancy fumbled for keys. Finally she found it, a long silver key with a personalized head, the Ford symbol superimposed over a cursive *N*. She unlocked and opened the door, and drew in her breath. Morrison was whistling softly between his teeth.

Suddenly, moving faster than she would have dreamed possible, Nancy tossed her purse into the back, clambered behind the wheel like a petite gopher into a hole, slammed the door and hit the lock button. The plungers engaged with two simultaneous *thunks*. Morrison moved as if in slow motion, his jaw dropping, reaching for the door handle from outside. As he yanked, the cop's features twisted in rage. The door didn't give a fraction and the Mustang rocked on its springs. Morrison yelled something that Nancy couldn't understand and pounded his fist on the Mustang's roof. Her heart thudding as though it would tear through her ribcage, Nancy groped the key into the ignition, and twisted the key so hard that pain shot through her thumb. The starter chugged briefly; the engine caught and raced. Visible in the sideview mirror, Henley was now coming forward, his eyes hidden behind dark lenses and his lips set in a rigid line. Nancy popped the lever into reverse and floored the accelerator. Rubber squealed as the car leaped backwards. The two cops flashed by on Nancy's left. She was in the aisle now, rolling back, her neck popping as she shifted to drive and the Mustang reversed directions. The two detectives were now coming at a dead run, clutching at the holsters on their belts.

God, would they shoot her? Would they? Nancy pictured bullets smashing through the windows and drilling into the sides of the car, and gave a nervous giggle as the death scene from *Bonnie and Clyde* flashed through her mind, the old touring car rocking on its springs while the bodies of Faye Dunaway and Warren Beatty danced like grisly marionettes. Nancy shut her eyes tightly as she floored the accelerator. The Mustang careened forward with Nancy fighting the wheel, very nearly sideswiping the rear bumper of the Mercury in the next parking space, straightening the Mustang's forward path, leaving the two cops in her wake. Henley and Morrison, pistols drawn, were now framed in the rearview mirror. Morrison actually leveled his gun at the Mustang as Nancy held her breath. Henley grabbed his partner's arm, stopping him, and the two cops sprinted for the elevators. They disappeared from view as Nancy rounded the turn, the Mustang's nose slanted downward, and headed for the exit six floors below. Concrete beams flashed overhead like ties under a speeding train.

She barreled downward, fishtailing as she rounded the sixth-floor turn, and passed the elevators. She dared to glance at the lighted panels above the cars.

One elevator was stopped at the lobby, another on three. The third car was in motion upward, passing the sixth floor, headed for seven, so it would be a few seconds before the cops boarded the elevator. Nancy returned her gaze to the front, pressed on the brakes just before the Mustang nearly rammed a concrete barrier, and careened onto the fifth level. Two women in business dresses stepped from the row of parked cars. Nancy jammed the heel of her hand against the Mustang's horn; the blast of the horn vibrated through the parking garage as the women leaped back to safety and mouthed curses as Nancy sped past them. The lighted fifth-floor panel showed that the elevator had stopped on seven and reversed its direction, the cops were now passing the sixth level.

Nancy steered the Mustang through the fourth floor and down onto the third. A panel truck was backing out into the aisle directly in her path. She couldn't stop. No way could she stop. She whipped the Mustang to the right and went around the panel truck, missing its bumper by inches; the panel truck's horn blasted and, visible in Nancy's rearview mirror, the truckdriver shot her the finger. The lighted panel told her that the cops' elevator had stopped on the fifth level, and she pictured Henley flashing his badge and stopping other stunned passengers from boarding. Nancy careened onto the second level. Only two more turns to go, she thought. Two, God, two more.

As she wheeled past the second floor with walls and beams flashing by in a series of dull gray blurs, she thought for the first time that she might actually be going to make it. When she'd made the snap decision to run from the cops, she'd acted out of sheer desperation and had been certain that her plan would never get off the ground. But now it was possible. One more turn. More than possible, it was . . .

Nancy made the final turn at ground level and threw on her brakes. Her heart sank into her belly, and any hope that had been building within her flew out the window like winging sparrows.

The three exit booths were busy, and a line of four or five cars waited before each drive-through slot. The drivers were taking their time about it, the daily parkers fumbling for their money, and monthly contract people holding plastic cards out their windows. Nancy checked the first-floor panel on her right; the detectives were passing the third level. In moments the door would slide open and out they would dash, guns drawn, the big blond bastard with a smirk on his face. Nancy wasn't giving up. No way. As she firmed up her mouth and scanned the three exit lines, a small red foreign car—a Z or a Porsche, Nancy didn't know one from the other—pulled to a stop behind her and tooted its horn. The detectives were passing the second level. Nancy had a few precious ticks of the clock, no more, before they'd be on her.

She had stopped in the neck, at the place where the slanted drive widened into three exit lanes, and the booths were perhaps thirty steps from the Mustang's nose. The lefthand booth was flush against a concrete wall, but on the right of the three lanes—sweet savior, on the right, Nancy thought—there was clearance. Not much, fifteen feet at the most from the right side of the Ford Taurus, whose driver was now passing money to a bored attendant, to the door marked ''Employees Only'' which led to the interior of the building. And the fifteen feet wasn't level, either, a few feet to the right of the Taurus was a raised curb. Beyond the booths the drive exited onto Throckmorton Street; visible through the yawning portal, cars, trucks, and buses crawled in a rush-hour hodgepodge. On Nancy's right the elevator opened and the detectives came out. Henley headed straight for the Mustang with his pistol ready; Morrison stopped in his tracks and showed Nancy a crooked grin through the windshield. She curled her lip. Behind her, the little red car tooted its horn a second time.

As though acting on its own, Nancy's small foot jammed the gas pedal to the floorboard. At the same time her hands twisted the steering wheel to the right. The Mustang leaped forward and hesitated, and for a heart-stopping instant Nancy was sure that the engine was going to stall. Then the Mustang screeched ahead, tires burning rubber. Henley's slender body and bald head flashed by on her right. Nancy crossed the thirty steps to the exit booth in what seemed milliseconds. Heads turned in her direction. A toll booth attendant— a Hispanic girl who looked to be around Nancy's age— let her mouth drop open and her gum come out and roll down her chin. The steering wheel jolted in Nancy's grasp as the Mustang jumped the curb; the Mustang's left side clipped the Taurus with a protesting squeal of metal.

And all at once Nancy was clear of the exit booths, fighting the wheel as the Mustang fishtailed among the rush-hour traffic on Throckmorton Street. A small blue pickup loomed in her path; Nancy whipped the Mustang to the left, dodged the pickup, and did a forty-mile-an-hour squeeze between a yellow city bus and an old Riviera with less than a foot to spare on either side. She risked a glance at the rearview mirror; Morrison and Henley charged from the parking lot onto the sidewalk to stand with their hands on their hips. Seen over the Mustang's hood, the light at the intersection of Throckmorton and 7th switched from amber to red. Nancy held her breath as she ran the light, turning left on 7th with a squeal of rubber and a cloud of flying pavement dust. Pedestrians who had started to cross the street leaped backwards and shook angry fists.

Five minutes later, Nancy stopped at the traffic light where 7th crossed University and joined at an angle with Camp Bowie Boulevard. No one was staring at her, not the bald man in the Cadillac on her right nor the white-haired lady in the Imperial directly behind the Mustang's bumper. No sirens sounded in the distance and no red rooflights flashed. Ahead of Nancy and to her right, two teenage kids stood before the box office at the 7th Street Theatre, glancing furtively around. Directly above them, the marquee advertised *The Cook, the Thief, His Wife and Her Lover.*

Nancy Cuellar rested her forehead against the top of the steering wheel and gently closed her eyes. She was shaking like a leaf and her pulse was racing like a Geiger counter at White Sands.

16

Percy Hardin wondered whether it was doing it in her
dead sister's bedroom that turned Betty Monroe on.
Christ, that had to be it. Anywhere else—in the luxury
suite at the Green Oaks Inn, on the daybed in the back
of Percy's customized van, even once at midnight in
the froghair around the seventh green at Colonial
Country Club—he'd found Betty to be only a slightly
above average piece of ass. But here, Christ Jesus,
here in the canopied four-poster with the scent of
burning incense filling his nostrils, Betty was something else. She bucked and strained against him, her
lips pulled away from perfect teeth in an earthy grimace, her long legs tightening around his midsection
as though she was trying to squeeze the very breath
from his lungs. He pounded into her, tried to hold
back but couldn't, groaned as he spurted semen and
she screamed lusty screams. Christ, it was good.
Christ, it was . . .

They lay intertwined as their breathing subsided. Finally Betty said, her face just inches from his, "Was
it different with her?"

He rolled from on top of her and sprawled on sweat-
dampened sheets. "Different? Christ, yes."

"Better or worse?" Betty said. She favored Daddy
Ross more than Marissa had, Betty's features sharper,
her complexion lighter. In the past few years Marissa's
increasing resemblance to Mama Luwanda had made
it more and more difficult for Percy to get it up.

"Oh, better," Percy said. "Yes, hell, yes, better."

"A *whole lot* better?" Betty rolled onto her side and raised up to lean on her elbow, her small, well-formed breasts drooping toward rumpled silk sheets. *Tell me how good I am.* Christ, Percy thought, that's all she wants to hear.

"How many times do I have to tell you?" Percy said.

"Until I believe it."

"Well, if you don't believe it by now, you may never."

She threw back her head and laughed. "Even when she was alive? I know I'm better now."

Christ, what a morbid sense of humor, Percy thought. "Better than then," he said.

"Than when she was alive? Say it."

Did he have to? Christ, he already knew the answer to that one. She'd keep after him until he did. "Better than when she was alive," Percy said.

"That's more like it." Betty got out of bed and pranced naked over to the vanity. She sat down, picked up a tiny spray bottle with a gold-colored bulb and read the label. "Daphne," she said. "I sent it to her from London. Did she use it before you two fucked?" She squeezed the bulb and there was a tiny hiss. Betty sniffed the air like Bambi. "Did she?"

"Christ, Betty, I don't know. What makes you so obsessed with it?"

"I just want to know." She crossed her legs and twisted her head to look at him. A crease formed in the skin on her slender back. Her brown hair was center-parted and at the moment disheveled. "A guy I knew in England. It turned him on."

"Probably it was you that turned him on," Percy said. "Not the perfume."

She wrinkled her nose. "Maybe I'll go back over there. Would you like that?"

"I doubt it. I wouldn't try to stop you."

She swung her legs around and pointed her knees in his direction. "Probably you would like it. It would solve part of your problem." Her shoulders hunched closer together as she gripped the edges of the bench on either side of her thighs.

"What problem is that?" Percy said.

She lowered her head and looked at him from underneath long brown lashes. "That someone knows."

He stood and picked his Jockey briefs up from a chair. "You'd know no matter where you were. Jesus Christ, are we going to talk about it again?" He stepped into his underwear.

"Again?" she said.

"What's done is done. Why keep bringing it up?"

She showed a peeved smirk. "I'll talk about my sister if I want to."

He was pulling up white cotton slacks and buttoning them. "Suit yourself."

"Doesn't it bother you that I know?"

"Why should it? It was your idea."

"Having an idea, that's nothing," she said. "I didn't *do* anything."

He zipped up his fly. "Christ, what is it with you? Before, you didn't even want me to mention her name. Now she's all you want to talk about."

She stood and did a little pirouette, examining her body in the vanity mirror, pressing her fingers tenderly into a purplish mark between her hip and ribcage. "I'm bruised. I just don't want you to forget what I know."

"I can't believe you people. Your whole family. Couldn't you just fake some sorrow or something?"

"No different than you, dear one," Betty said.

"I had a reason not to like her. I had to sleep with the woman every night. The rest of you, she was your own flesh and blood."

She found a second small bruise, this one on her fanny, and poked the bluish-purple spot with her index finger. She made a sour face. "You want to know something?"

"What's that?" Percy said.

"I think my father knows, too."

He put his hands on his hips. "Jesus Christ, did you tell him?"

"Of course not. I can just tell. I think you're going to hear from him once you get the money."

"I expect to," Percy said. "Everybody that comes into any money hears from old Ross, he's trying to get his hands on whatever he can. If he finds out you've got any money, look out. That doesn't mean he knows anything about . . ."

"He knows that you're broke," Betty said. "I've heard him say."

Percy froze with his arms through the sleeves of a blue knit golf shirt. "Say to who?" He lifted the collar over his head, shrugged and wriggled, and adjusted the shirt's hem around his hips.

"I don't know. Somebody over the phone."

Percy found his Piaget watch on his dressing table and slipped the band around his wrist. "My financial situation is temporary. Only temporary."

She snickered. "It wouldn't be if you hadn't—"

"Betty."

"Well, it wouldn't."

He sat down, lifted his knee to pull on one white cotton sock. "If Ross knows I'm broke he knows more than my banker."

"Dummy. It's Merlyn Graham that told daddy you had to borrow the premiums for Marissa's life insurance," Betty said.

"Christ. Well, I'll sure take *that* up with Merlyn."

"Daddy's a bigger customer than you are," Betty said. "Merlyn Graham tells daddy everything about his relatives' business. You having to make sure the insurance was paid up, that's how daddy figured out what you did."

Percy jammed his foot into one spotless white Reebok and snugged up the laces. "As long as he doesn't know it for a fact."

"Aren't you afraid he might have you killed or something?" Betty pulled up black bikini panties and adjusted the elastic at her waist, and modeled the panties in the mirror, softly touching her own long thighs.

"Ross?" Percy said. "If I'd beaten him out of some money, maybe. Not just over his daughter. If he knew it for a fact, though, had some proof, he'd probably hold it over my head so he could get his hands on some of the insurance money."

She picked up a wispy black bra, shrugged into the shoulder straps, reached behind herself to fasten the clasp. "You think he'd mind if he knew you were fucking me?"

He pursed his lips. "Well, yeah, come to think about it. I can't figure out how a man can worry so much about one daughter and not give a shit about the other. Or seem to."

"She started it," Betty said.

"I know all about that. Christ, that was fifteen years ago."

Betty tossed her head and picked up a hairbrush from the vanity. "She exposed him. He never forgets anything like that."

"Jesus Christ, Betty, the man was screwing around with his daughter's college roommate. He deserved to be exposed. What I don't understand is, why did it turn Luwanda against her?"

She sat and brushed her hair with firm strokes. "You don't know? You should. Besides, what's the difference between his daughter's roommate and your wife's sister? Are you saying somebody ought to expose you?" Betty's accent was back-East Greenbriar with just a hint of Texas twang mixed in.

He ignored the barb. "What don't I know that I should?"

"Daddy's been screwing around ever since I can remember," Betty said. "I knew it when I was five years old. Mother knew it, too, but she didn't want anybody throwing it in her face. Especially not her own daughter. He made it with a girl I knew in Italy, I didn't come running to tell mother about that. Marissa should have had more sense." She laid the brush down and went over to lean on the windowsill and look down at sculpted hedges, at pruned Chinese elms, at aqua water shimmering in a pool shaped like a teardrop. "Three o'clock in the afternoon and we're up here doing it. About the same time the guy was doing it to Marissa."

"No, Betty. No, earlier. Around one in the afternoon was when it happened. Even earlier, before noon. I was making my eleven-thirty tee time, remember?"

Betty undulated back to the vanity, picked up khaki Jamaica shorts and stepped into them. "Next time we'll have to do it earlier, then." She buttoned and zipped the shorts, and reached for a T-shirt that had a cartoon of Bart Simpson on its front.

He grabbed the laces on his second shoe and jerked the ends into a bow, then raised up and rested his forearms on his thighs. "I still can't believe all this."

"Well," she said, "I've got to admit I didn't think you'd get away with it. Probably you wouldn't have, either, if it hadn't been for that contractor guy."

"I'd feel better with him in jail," Percy said.

She sat back on the vanity bench, reached for light blush makeup and applied it with a brush. Marissa's makeup. Christ, Percy thought. "Are you kidding?" Betty said. "As long as he's a fugitive it looks even worse for the guy."

Percy studied her, her back straight as a ramrod, her legs crossed in a finishing-school posture. "I suppose that it does,'' Percy said. "But what if he should come here?''

"Then he'd scare you shitless," Betty said. "Why don't you hire the apey-looking guy as a bodyguard?''

"That man makes me shudder, just thinking about him," Percy said. "Christ, getting involved with somebody like that.''

Betty paused with a lip brush inches from her mouth. She laughed, a silvery, tinkling sound like crystal. "Why, you haven't paid the apey guy, either.''

"Now why would you say something like that?''

"Because I know you. You'd do anything for a bodyguard, you're so afraid of the contractor, and the only reason you wouldn't call the apey guy for protection is if you owe him money." Betty dabbed rouge onto her lips.

"I take care of people," he said. "I can afford it.''

"*Could* afford it," Betty said, "before you pissed your father's money off.''

He stood abruptly and went to the door. "I don't have to listen to any more of this.''

"Well, you're going to until the money comes," Betty said. "Once you pay me off and I can get the hell gone from this town again and not have to depend on daddy for anything, well, then you can listen to whatever you want.''

He pulled the door open. "I'm going down and fix a drink.''

She screwed the tiny brush back into the cylinder of lip rouge, watching his reflection in the mirror. "Nothing for me, thanks," Betty said.

"I didn't offer you anything," he said. "Christ, how can you go on like this?''

She picked up her small purse, came up with a vial of white powder, a mirror, a razor blade and rolled-up dollar bill. She sprinkled powder on the mirror and scraped it into a line with the razor blade. "Because

I'm decadent,'' she said. ''Just like you're decadent and my father's decadent.'' She used the dollar bill to snort powder up her nose. ''Decadence, that's what keeps us going. Come to think about it, I do want a Scotch. Fix it for me, will you, love?''

17

Frank Nichols had a pretty good afternoon playing pool. He collected eight different times from Rock Man Bentley and four times apiece from a couple of mulatto dudes over from Stop Six. Man, Frank had that cue ball walkin' and talkin', and times like this were what convinced him that the parole people were full of shit when they said that everybody needed a job. Frank thought that the parole people needed a job because they didn't have no talent to do anything else, but for a first-rate pool-playing man a job only got in the way. Things were panning out in spades, and as long as the hard-ass parole dude kept Frank from working the construction job, Frank was going to keep his pockets full. End of discussion.

The only trouble with playing pool in the afternoons was that a man needed a few beers to stay loose, and drinking beer in the afternoon gave Frank a headache. But the headache was nothing a nap wouldn't take care of, so around five-thirty Frank hung up his cue stick and called this girl Monette that he knew. Monette worked the day shift, delivering meals and handling bedpans at John Peter Smith Hospital, and had her own place off Rosedale near I-35. Her brother Stu had been a pretty good hand in the tractor shop, Eastham Farm Unit, TDC, and Monette and Frank had met in the visiting room. She wasn't the only girl he was fooling with, not by a long shot, but Frank guessed that you could call her his main squeeze for now. He told her over the phone that he'd made a score playing pool, and that as soon as he went home, took a nap and cleaned up, he'd be over and take her out to get something to eat. Finally he bought a round for Rock Man and the Stop Six mulatto dudes, rapped with them for a few minutes, and went out to where his Buick was parked. There was an ugly white dude with a sloping forehead sitting in a Volvo across the street, but Frank was so busy thinking about Monette's smooth milk chocolate skin and proudly stuck-out ass that he didn't pay the white dude any mind. The Buick's battery was getting slightly low, and Frank was afraid for a moment that the car wasn't going to start. Finally, though, the engine caught, and Frank drove east toward Miller Avenue.

Life on the streets plus a couple of beefs at TDC had taught Frank not to truck with anybody else's problems, but he was making an exception where Lackey Ferguson was concerned. Lackey was an okay dude, pretty different from the usual honky boss, plus Frank was pretty sure that Lackey was taking a bum rap where the dead woman was concerned. No way had Lackey Ferguson done that woman, and helping Lackey out was going to make Frank feel pretty good about himself.

Frank steered the Buick into the driveway of the duplex where he rented on Miller Street, bumping slowly over raised cracks in the cement, and wondered whether his landlord had come by. The rent was due today, Wednesday, every week, but sometimes the landlord didn't come until Thursday, depending on which of the days he could get his nephew to drive him around. The landlord was an old white dude, eighty if he was a day, and the state had revoked his driver's license because he'd had a couple of wrecks and didn't see too good. But Frank knew that the lack of a driver's license didn't have anything to do with why the old dude brought his nephew along on rent collection days. In fact, just that Sunday, Frank had seen the old landlord driving his Cadillac on Berry Street, going about twenty miles an hour and straddling the median with two Stop Six colored whores in the front seat along with him, so not having a license didn't keep the old dude from driving. The reason he brought his nephew along to collect rent, though, did have to do with the landlord's eyesight. The nephew would stand beside the old man and examine each and every bill handed over by the renters, just to make certain that the renter didn't try to slip the half-blind landlord a ten and claim it to be a twenty. Old fucker don't trust nobody, Frank thought. Today Frank was hoping that the landlord showed up to take the rent on time, because Frank's pockets were full of pool-playing money, and he'd as soon not have to hang on to enough bread to pay tomorrow in case tomorrow at the pool hall didn't go so good.

Frank left the Buick and ambled across the rock-strewn yard, tilting his Yankee baseball cap forward and shoving his hands into his back pockets, all the while whistling the opening bars to ''I Just Called to Say I Love You,'' by Stevie Wonder.

Across the street, a porch swing was suspended from the limb of a tree, hanging by two rusty chains. Two hookers that Frank knew were sitting in the swing with their legs crossed and their leather skirts hiked up. As Frank climbed the two steps onto his own porch, a Volvo cruised slowly by on Miller Avenue. A white dude was driving, and Frank did a double-take. It was the same guy with the sloping chin who'd earlier been parked across from the pool hall. One of the hookers climbed down from the swing across the way and whistled at the Volvo. The driver ignored her, continued up Miller and disappeared around the corner. Weird dude, Frank thought, if I'd been the hooker I'd have thought the dude was out to buy some pussy, too.

He pulled his screen door open and entered, let the screen slam shut, and dropped the latch through the eyehole.

Frank passed through his sitting room, skirting a faded green sofa and a standup TV which operated off a rabbit-ears antenna with tinfoil wrapped around its stems, and entered the kitchen. In the kitchen stood a stove with grease-encrusted burners which smelled of bacon and cooking oil. Frank looked in the icebox. Two open six-packs were sitting on a shelf, one empty, the other holding one lonely Pearl. He opened the beer and dropped the cartons on top of the overflowing garbage underneath the sink. The cracked linoleum needed mopping, and Frank decided to let Monette spend the night with him so that she would clean up the place in the morning. Sipping beer, feeling woozy, he left the kitchen and entered his bedroom.

The bedroom contained an iron bed with filthy sheets and grease-stained pillows, a nightstand, and a rocking chair with one back-slat broken. There was an old Amana window air conditioner which hissed and creaked but blew frigid air, and above the window unit the Venetian blinds were closed. Frank set his beer on the nightstand, lay down on the bed, and watched a small brown spider crawl on the ceiling. He thought about finding a newspaper or magazine with which to swat the insect, then changed his mind. Fuckin' spider wasn't hurting nobody and wasn't no poison spider anyhow. Frank's mind wandered and his eyelids drooped. He began to snore, dreaming of Monette, the way she'd looked the other night in a red shortie gown. Suddenly, a faraway banging noise shocked him awake.

The pounding ceased for a couple of seconds, then resumed. Paper thin walls vibrated and the lampshade on the nightstand wavered. Fuckin' old landlord, Frank thought, standing out there on the porch while his fuckin' nephew beat on the door. Old dude waiting until somebody was about asleep and then hassling them for the rent. Frank sat groggily up and checked his windup Baby Ben alarm clock. Quarter after six. About the right time, the old dude usually collected the rent in the early evening, when those with jobs would be home from work and those without jobs hadn't hit the streets to prowl as yet. Frank took his baseball cap off and scratched his head.

Just as he did every week, Frank was having second thoughts about paying the rent. He'd never missed ponying up altogether—the old landlord would throw him out in a New York minute, and Frank damn well knew it—but the idea of handing over his pool winnings no longer seemed like such a good idea. Paying the rent would shrink Frank's bankroll by a half-inch or so, and he'd like to have a wad of money to flash when he took Monette out to eat later on. Women went for that, a fat roll of bills with a couple of hundreds showing. Frank stayed still on the mattress and waited for the pounding to stop.

But whoever was knocking on the door was more determined to roust Frank than Frank was determined not to be rousted. The pounding continued, hesitating occasionally as though drawing its breath, then resuming in earnest. Shee-it, Frank thought, my Buick's parked in the fuckin' driveway; the old dude's going to know I'm home. Probably half of the people the landlord collected from gave him shit about coming to the door. Frank removed his shirt and shoes and went through the kitchen, yawning and scratching his armpit, doing a pretty good imitation of somebody who'd been asleep awhile. He padded into the living room. The door stood open and there was a squatty white dude standing on the porch.

For an instant Frank was relieved that his caller wasn't the landlord after all, but then Frank's eyes narrowed warily. Shee-it, this dude again, the same white dude who'd driven by ignoring the hookers, and who

earlier had been parked across from the pool hall.
Come to think about it, Frank had seen this dude
someplace, squatty guy with thinning hair, a parrot's
beak for a nose which gave his face a pinched expression, arms hanging to his knees like a monkey at the
zoo. Ugly dude with crooked yellowed teeth, wearing
a khaki-colored shirt whose sleeves were too short and
green army pants whose legs were too long. The cuffs
on the pants were rolled up a couple of turns. White
dude fucking around in this neighborhood might be
the law, might be the census taker, might be the re-
possession dude, might be any fucking thing. Where
the hell had Frank seen this guy. He stepped closer to
the inside of the screen.

"Yeah?" Frank said. "Hey, yeah, bro', I'm hearing
you." The Volvo which he'd seen earlier was now
parked in the drive behind Frank's Buick. A tingling
sensation began at the base of Frank's neck and spread
upward into his scalp.

The squatty man paused with his fist cocked, ready
to knock, and eyeballed Frank through the screen.
Frank snapped that the guy was wearing rubber gloves.
The fuck was this? Didn't no white dudes come to
Polytechnic to rob no black dudes, it was supposed to
be the other way around. The squatty man's lips
twisted into a sneer. "Yeah, nigger, I know you're in
there. Ain't no use to try and hide."

Frank cocked his head as anger boiled up in his
throat. Crazy white mothafuckah running around
Polytechnic hollering racial shit. "I done told you I'm
home, man," Frank said. "The fuck you want pound-
in' on my door?" The beer-buzz was wearing off and
Frank's mind was clearing in a hurry.

The man on the porch pointed a thick, latex-covered
finger. "I want a piece of your ass, nigger. Open this
fuckin' door." He grabbed the handle and rattled the
screen.

Frank's eyes widened. He had it now, he was placing this dude. Down on Eastham Farm, crazy white mothafuckah they'd kept in the hole all the time. Some kind of baby-raper or pervert, dude that went around acting like . . .

"Hey. You that Monkey Man, aintcha?" Frank said.

The man balled his free hand into a fist and rattled the door even harder. "You fucking crazy? Don't no nigger call me that, boy. You come out here and call me that."

If Frank had thought it over he would have known better. Would have known there was a method to this, the racial slurs, the pounding on the door, all designed to keep Frank from thinking straight. But thinking straight had never been Frank's thing to begin with. He flipped the latch and pushed open the screen.

Frank was able to say, "Man, you looking for—"

Before the Monkey Man brought a thick knee up in Frank's crotch, before blinding pain shot upward through Frank's belly and paralyzed him in his tracks. Before a leather sap appeared in the Monkey Man's hand and slapped Frank's jaw, accompanied by the slight pop of breaking bone. Before Frank tasted his own blood as it ran over his tongue and between his lips, and before Frank went down on the sitting room floor with the Monkey Man on top, kicking and swinging the sap, and before the Monkey Man's knee jammed into Frank's ribcage and forced the air from his lungs. As his vision blurred, Frank had a closeup view of the Monkey Man's ugly face. As Frank passed out, the Monkey Man was showing crooked teeth in a triumphant grin.

If there was one thing that Everett Wilson knew, it was how to get a nigger to acting dumb. Worked the same way out on the street as down in the Texas Department of Corrections, just call the dumb black bastard exactly what he was, get the bastard to pissing all over himself about how somebody was calling him down for being a nigger. Then when the dumb son of a bitch made his move, lower the boom on the fucker. Worked every single time.

Everett left the nigger laying on the floor as he went over to peer through the screen at the street. No one stood in any of the yards or porches gaping at what was happening over in the duplex. The two hookers who'd been sitting in the swing across the way were long gone; Everett had seen to that. When he'd parked his Volvo behind the nigger's old Buick, Everett had gone over and showed the hookers the Smith & Wesson .38 which now nestled in his hip pocket, and the whores had run for cover with their asses jiggling under skintight leather. Nobody was around but Everett Thomas Wilson and this nigger that Everett was fixing to have a little talk with. That was good. That was good.

Everett grabbed Frank by the collar and dragged him into the interior of the house like a fifty-pound sack of sorghum on Eastham Farm. Everett hauled his cargo through the kitchen (Jesus Christ, Everett thought, but that greasy bacon leaves a stink) and into the bedroom. Halfway into the bedroom, the nigger groaned. Everett released the collar and hunched over his victim, ready with the sap, breathing slowly and evenly. He studied the chocolate-colored face, the swollen lips and jaw, the trickle of blood running from the corner of Frank's mouth. If Frank's eyes should pop open, Everett was going to swing the sap and put the bastard back to sleep. Frank rolled over on his side and began to snore. Everett hauled his cargo over to the bed, grunting and straining, lifted Frank onto the bed and spread-eagled his arms and legs. Everett dug in his hip pocket for the nylon rope he'd bought that afternoon in the hardware store. The rope was cut into five-foot lengths. Working fast, his armpits oozing sweat, Everett lashed the nigger's hands and feet to the bedposts, then stood back. The dumb black bastard was dead to the world.

There was a nearly-full bottle of beer on the nightstand—Pearl, Everett thought, the cheapshit bastard drinks Pearl—and Everett parted Frank's lips and poured from the bottle into the swollen mouth. Frank coughed, spewed beer from between his lips, and moved his head around. Everett poured more beer in Frank's mouth, and Frank opened his eyes. His pupils danced from side to side in his head. Now Everett turned the bottle up and emptied the beer full in Frank's face. The liquid hit Frank's nose and mouth and splashed onto the pillow. Frank gagged and spit. His gaze riveted itself on Everett's face and his swollen lips parted. Everett had the nigger's full attention. He sat on the side of the bed. The springs creaked under his weight.

"We're going to talk, Frank," Everett said. "That's you, ain't it? Frank?"

"Why you want to come fucking wid me?" Frank said. "I ain't done shit to you." His look showed fear. Only his lips moved as his swollen jaw remained rigid. His stretched-out arms were taut and sinewy and tiny hairs sprouted from the chocolate-colored flesh around his nipples.

"Well, yeah, you did do shit, Frank," Everett said. "You called me a name I don't like, and you been out on Lancaster Avenue asking questions."

Frank's eyes widened. He didn't say anything.

"And them questions you been asking," Everett said, "they ain't really what you're trying to find out, you and that construction man. Are they? You and that construction man looking to find somebody, ain't you? He ain't really looking to hire nobody, is he?" He placed a thumb and forefinger on either side of Frank's jaw and squeezed. Frank whimpered and his body stiffened. Everett released his hold and picked up the sap. Fresh blood ran from the nigger's mouth, dripped

onto his ear and dropped onto the pillow to mix with
the beer. Frank was trembling.

"See, Frank? I can hurt you." Everett's lips were
inches from the nigger's ear, and Everett was whis-
pering. "Now what I'm thinking is, if that construction man wants to talk, then maybe I ought to see him.
So tell me something, Frank. You know where to find
this guy?"

Breath escaped Frank's lungs with a noise like a
death rattle. He fixed his gaze on the ceiling. "Don't
know nothin' about no construction man," Frank said.

"Now, that's too bad, Frank. Hey, that's too bad,
'cause as long as you don't know I got to hurt you."
Everett raised the sap, quarter-inch steel stitched inside smooth brown leather, and brought the sap down
on Frank's ribcage. There was a flat slap and a sound
like the breaking of a twig. Frank grunted, strained
against his bonds, then relaxed. His eyes glazed and
his lids drooped. Everett's brow furrowed. No way did
he want the nigger passing out. Break the nigger's jaw
and maybe crack a rib or two, but Everett needed the
nigger awake to talk to him. "Stop being dumb,
Frank," Everett said. "See, I did something for somebody, and then that contractor got his hands on some
money that should have went to me. And I aim to have
it even if I got to bust your arms and legs, you hear?
Now tell me where this—" Everett paused and cocked
his head. There was a faraway pounding noise.

At first Everett thought that someone was building
something a block or so away. But the sound was closer
than that, and wasn't the noise of a hammer. *Rat-a-
tat-tat.* Stop. *Rat-a-tat-tat.* Someone knocking on the
outside door. Somebody calling on the nigger. Might
even be the construction guy.

"Who you got coming over, Frank?" Everett said
softly.

"Don't know nothing about nobody coming over.
That's the truth, boss, don't . . ."

"Oh, hey, I'm going to work on you some more,"
Everett said. "Yeah, I am. But first I got to take care
of your caller. Don't run off, now." He got up, left
Frank, and went out through the kitchen, dropping the
sap into his back pocket and digging for the Smith &
Wesson. Everett flattened against the doorjamb in the
kitchen and peered through the sitting room. Somebody out there, all right. Somebody visible through
the screen door, somebody out there on the porch
banging away like—

Everett's jaw dropped in surprise. Jesus Christ, was
it . . . ? Yeah. Yeah, Jesus Christ, it was. Everett's
fingertips trembled and there was a tightening in his
groin. He squeezed at his crotch through the coarse
fabric of his pants. His breath quickening, dropping
his pistol into his pocket along with the sap, Everett
Wilson grinned and stepped around the doorjamb into
the sitting room, standing in full view of the porch.

Nancy Cuellar discontinued her knocking to check
the slip of paper in her hand, then to compare what
was written on the slip to the numbers affixed to the
lower panel on the screen door. She was sure that this
was the right house; she'd had Ronnie Ferias repeat
the address three times—twice in English and once in
Spanish to be certain—while she'd stood in the phone
booth and written it down. There couldn't possibly be
any mistake. Nancy had never been to the Polytechnic
section of Fort Worth in her life, so she'd had to use
the Mapsco in her glove compartment to find the street.
Get in touch with Frank Nichols, Lackey had told her,
and he'll know where to find me. Well if Nancy had
ever needed Lackey, now was the time. She glanced
from the porch across the weed-infested yard at her
Mustang where it sat at the curb. The old Buick in the
driveway was Frank Nichols' car; she'd been by Lackey's remodeling job where Frank had been working a
couple of times, and she was sure that the Buick was

the same one that Frank had driven on the job. The white Volvo parked behind the Buick tickled something in Nancy's memory. Hadn't one of those county cops told her something about a Volvo the first time she'd talked to them? Yes, they had, something about a Volvo that Lackey had nearly collided with as he'd left the Hardin home. Sure of herself, and determined to raise Frank from whatever nap he might be having inside, Nancy raised her fist to knock again.

Someone was standing inside the house, on the other side of the screen, watching her.

Nancy moved in closer and squinted to peer inside the house. She was looking into a sitting room with an ancient standup TV against one wall. The rabbit-ears antenna had its feelers encased in tinfoil. To the left of the TV sat an old cloth chair, and right beside the chair were two scarred black work boots. Above the boots were ankles clad in white socks and green army pants with turned-up cuffs. Two big male hands hung beside the legs, practically to the knees. The man's head and shoulders were hidden in shadow.

"Hello," Nancy said. "Hello in there."

The man stepped into the light. He had a sloping forehead and thinning hair, and was grinning. His teeth were crooked, and his smile sent a crawling sensation up Nancy's backbone. "Yeah," the man said. "Yeah, you looking for Frank?" He pulled the screen door open. A spring creaked like inner sanctum.

The man's breath smelled of onion. He was only an inch or so taller than Nancy's five-three, was burly and barrel-chested, and there was something about his eyes. His smile seemed friendly enough, but his eyes were dead black holes in his face. Nancy mentally recoiled, and if she hadn't needed Lackey so badly she would have made a lame excuse and left. But she had to find Lackey. *Had* to. She took one hesitant step across the threshold. "Frank. Frank, yes, is he . . . ?" Nancy said. Visible through an open doorway beyond the man, a rickety table and an old refrigerator with a yellowed finish sat on cracked linoleum.

The man's grin broadened as he stepped aside and extended his hand toward the kitchen. "He's jest restin', little lady. You go right on back, now."

A warning voice somewhere inside Nancy told her that she should turn around and run. There was something *not right* about this, this strange man answering the door in Frank Nichols's house. Think of Lackey, Nancy thought. She nodded and smiled timidly as she went past the man toward the kitchen. The afternoon sunrays filtered in through the screen and made a rectangle of light on faded carpet. Halfway across the sitting room, Nancy's foot slipped. She'd stepped in something. Conscious of the man's bulk near her elbow, his onion breath in her nostrils, Nancy backed up a step and looked down past the snow-white hem of her pleated skirt. She gasped.

It was blood. She was *certain* it was blood, a big glistening drop clinging to the carpet and beginning to soak thickly in. A few feet further on was another drop, then more drops which formed a trail through the kitchen. In the kitchen some of the blood was smeared on the linoleum. Her pulse racing, Nancy started to turn back toward the porch.

The man grabbed her from behind. Thick strong fingers dug into the back of her neck; an arm like twisted ocean liner rope encircled her chest and he hugged her to him. "Back there, little lady," he whispered fiercely into her ear. "Back there, I said."

Oh, God, Nancy thought, oh, God, oh, God, oh, God. She opened her mouth to scream, but a rough hand clamped over her mouth and stifled the sound.

Christ, she smells good, Everett Wilson thought, and that TV news program didn't do her looks no justice, either. Smells good and *feels* good, smooth skin over vibrant muscle, firm buttocks pressed against his

crotch, bouncy young breasts moving against his arm.
Christ, what a . . . You're going to like me, girl, he
thought, before this is over. I got plenty of time for
you.

He put his lips close to her ear. "Your name, girl.
What's your name?" His voice was like sandpaper.

She struggled and squirmed in his grasp. Feisty. Everett liked that. His erection swelled until he thought
it might tear through his pants. He kept his left arm
tight around her as he fished in his back pocket and
drew out the Smith & Wesson. He showed her the gun
by holding it in front of her face, then placed the barrel
just below her ear. Her struggles ceased; she was rigid
as stone.

"Your name. I ain't going to hurt you lessen I have
to. Your name."

"Nancy." Her voice was soft and cultured with just
a hint of a Spanish accent. Highbrow pepper-belly gal,
Everett thought.

"Nancy. Nancy." He repeated her name like a sixth-
grader struggling to memorize a lesson. "You looking
for your boyfriend, are you?" Everett said.

Her chin lifted. "Lackey? Is Lackey here?"

"Well, no he ain't. Not exactly. Come on, straight
back yonder. Somebody back there wants to talk to
you." Everett shoved her in front of him toward the
kitchen.

Slowly, one faltering step at a time, Everett herded
Nancy back through the kitchen and into the bedroom.
He kept the barrel of the pistol against her head and
his arm tight around her. Her movements were
wooden. He'd liked it better when she'd been fighting
him, but he'd have more time for that later on.

As they approached the bed, Frank Nichols's head
lifted and his eyes widened like twin cue balls. He
strained against his bonds. Waste of your time, nigger,
Everett thought.

"Lackey said you'd know where . . ." Nancy's tone

was subdued, even apologetic. She trailed off and her chin sank toward her chest.

Everett released her and stood back, holding the gun loosely in her direction. "You sit awhile in that corner, Nancy. I got business to finish with old Frank here."

She looked around, confused.

Everett motioned with the pistol. "The corner. Right over there, this won't take but just a minute."

She backed slowly into the corner of the room, pressed her shoulders against the adjacent walls, and sank down to a sitting position. Her skirt rode up to show a foot of thigh covered by transparent nylon.

Everett stood still for seconds as his gaze shifted from Frank to Nancy and back again. Frank's bare chest moved up and down with his breathing. Nothing personal with this nigger, Everett thought. Just something I got to do. Finally Everett said, "I got this lady here, Frank. I can't think of nothing else you and me got to talk about. Can you?"

Frank watched the pistol, his look uncertain, not sure what was coming but suspecting. Deep down inside, Everett thought, they all know. Frank shook his head slowly from side to side.

Everett grabbed the pillow from behind Frank's head, brought the pillow up, pushed it down over Frank's swollen face. Then Everett pressed the Smith & Wesson's barrel into the softness of the pillow, felt the pillow's downy inside give, felt the shock of recoil as he pulled the trigger. The gun's discharge was like the popping of an air-filled paper bag. The pillowcase around the barrel changed as if by magic from dirty gray to sooty black. Frank's body jerked once, raised to strain against the ropes, then relaxed. Breath came out of the lungs in a sigh. The odor of burnt gunpowder mixed with the stench of feces. Jesus Christ, Everett thought, they all got to shit all over themselves. He looked to Nancy.

She cringed back into the corner. Her mouth was twisted in fear.

Everett smiled. He reached down and untied the length of rope from Frank's lifeless ankle. "See, Nancy," Everett said. "That didn't take long. Now we got nobody to mess with us. We got all the time we need, Nancy."

18

Once, during the Panama invasion, Lackey Ferguson got lost from his seven-man unit. The mission had been a house-to-house search, supposedly in search of General Badass Noriega, but what they'd really been doing was walking down peaceful city streets in full battle gear, knee-high boots laced tight against calf and shin, M-1 rifles nestled in the crooks of their arms, wearing pants and shirts of dull green camouflage cheesecloth, while the near-the-equator sun beat down and olive-skinned men and women stood in doorways and on curbs and stared at the *gringo* soldiers as though they were a bunch of monkeys in the zoo. Which was exactly what they had looked like, Lackey supposed.

Somewhere he'd taken a wrong turn. One minute he'd been part of a squad of battle-ready troops; the next minute he'd found himself stalking alone down streets the width of bicycle trails with two- and three-story buildings crowding in on both sides, and while muffled shouts of *"Chingarro"* and "Yankee go the fock home" had come from balconies and doorways all around. He'd come within a hair of laying down his rifle, going into one of the bars that he passed, bellying up to the rail and ordering a cold one.

Suddenly he'd been face to face with a woman. It was as though she'd materialized. He'd rounded a curve and there she'd been, eyes flashing, frizzy hair sticking out like an uneven frame around her face, grimy bodice cut low and shapeless skirt molding around strong brown legs. She'd looked him over head to toe, no fear in her gaze, a hooker measuring him up, deciding whether he might be a john or was just a no-money dude and a waste of time.

Apparently she'd decided the latter. Her upper lip had curled as she'd said in perfect English, "Sonny, you want to play G.I. Joe, you need some toy tanks and trucks and shit." Then she'd flounced away while hoots and catcalls had come from all around. Ten minutes later, Lackey had sat down on a bench in front of the Panama Hilton Hotel and resigned from the war.

It had been the same feeling that he had now, wandering around in the Polytechnic section of Fort Worth, Texas, looking for a needle in a haystack. Aside from asking Frank Nichols, Lackey didn't have the slightest idea how to go about finding a hit man, and if he *should* run across a hit man, what were the odds against it being the right guy? A hundred to one? More like a thousand.

And then there was the empty feeling in Lackey's stomach every time he saw a patrol car, and in Polytechnic it seemed that every other auto had a cop behind the wheel. How long before somebody recognized him from his picture in the paper? He didn't have any doubt that by now there was a full-fledged manhunt going on, and his pickup standing behind the Sleep Inn on Berry Street coupled with his being the only white person registered at the motel was sure to point the finger in his direction.

More than anything else, Lackey missed Nancy. In the six months since he'd come home from the army he'd never been away from her for twenty-four hours in one stretch, and he guessed it had taken the previous night and day for him to realize how much a part of his life she'd become. The second she'd left him last night, taking her short confident steps up the sidewalk, pausing in the glow from the gaslight to turn and wave, then ascending the staircase with her small hand grip-

ping the rail every few feet, a lump of sadness had
lodged firmly in his throat. The lump was still there.
Maybe if he could talk to Nancy he'd feel better. Sure
couldn't do any harm.

Springs creaked as he rose from sitting on the motel
bed and went over to the window. He parted the drapes
to look outside, his gaze falling on old pickups, seventies and early-eighties model cars as they paraded
back and forth on Berry Street. It was near dusk; about
half of the cars that went by had their lights on. A
seventies model Ford with one headlamp glowing
bounced through the intersection of 10th and Berry;
the dead light winked on, then off again as the Ford
negotiated the double dips. Catty-cornered from the
motel was a 7-Eleven; burglar bars made grid patterns
across the convenience store's windows, and, seen
through the windows, overhead neon reflected from
rows of potato chips, laundry detergent, and every
brand of candy known to man. As Lackey watched, a
stoop-shouldered black woman in a shapeless flowered
dress came out of the store, struggling along as she
carried a stuffed-to-the brim grocery sack. She very
nearly stumbled and fell a couple of times as she made
her way down the sidewalk. At the front of the store,
on the far righthand side, was a single open-air phone
booth. This time of evening Nancy was generally doing her situps. Lackey dug in the pocket of his jeans
and found three quarters.

He shrugged into a navy blue T-shirt which showed
a silver star on its front underneath the script letters
spelling "Dallas Cowboys," slipped his bare feet into
dirty white Reeboks, and left the room and entered
the parking lot. Two women—a fortyish black-skinned
lady with close-permed hair, and a light-skinned colored chick wearing skintight jeans—got out of an old
Plymouth and entered the room next door. The women
ignored Lackey, which suited him fine. He crossed the
asphalt lot and went around to the front of the motel,

crossed Berry Street and did a column-right through
the crosswalk on 10th, circled the gas pumps at the
7-Eleven, and approached the phone booth.

A teenage girl was talking on the phone, one elbow
leaning on the shelf, her lips moving nonstop. She
wore bright pink lip gloss, which contrasted sharply
with the chocolate color of her skin. She cut her eyes
in Lackey's direction, showed him a disapproving grimace, then clutched the receiver tighter and turned her
back. Lackey jammed his hands in his pockets and,
doing his best to appear casual, strolled over to the
newspaper rack. He spun a quarter into the slot, lifted
the plastic cover and took out one late edition of the
Star-Telegram. He spread the paper open, then felt his
throat constrict as he gazed on his own picture on the
front page beside a large reprint of Nancy's high school
graduation picture.

He glanced quickly up and down the street. There
were no pedestrians in sight, and other than the teenager on the phone there was no one else standing in
front of the convenience store. Nonetheless, Lackey
held the newspaper up to shield his features from view
as he read the story. They'd indicted Nancy. Jesus,
they'd *indicted* her, and according to the article—which
was preceded by the italicized caption, *"Exclusive to
the Star-Telegram"*—she had eluded the police in a car
chase and was still at large. The picture of Nancy was
one he'd seen a thousand times, and as far as Lackey
was concerned the photo didn't begin to do her justice.
He skimmed the parts of the newspaper story which
were about him—most of it was a rehash of the same
things that had been in previous editions of the paper
and on TV, and, what the hell, he'd known all along
they'd be coming for him eventually—then rolled up
the newspaper and stuck it under his arm. He went
back to the phone, where the teen-queen was just finishing up. She dropped the receiver into its cradle and
sauntered away with her rear end twitching, and with-

out so much as a glance in his direction. Lackey dropped a quarter into the phone with a rattle-and-jingle and called Ronnie Ferias. They'd made the arrangements earlier; Nancy's phone could be tapped, so Lackey would call Ronnie, who would drive the three blocks to Nancy's place and give her the number of the phone booth where Lackey now stood. Then she'd call Lackey from a convenience store near her apartment.

Lackey said to Ronnie, "You read about Nance?"

"I don't got to. She's all over the TV. You, too. Them two cop assholes been by already, but I don't tell 'em shit."

"Well I need to talk to her. I'm at—"

"Nancy ain't home, man," Ronnie said.

"How you know?"

"She call me. Wanted to know how to get to Frank Nichols's place."

Lackey thoughtfully regarded his shoes. Nancy was looking for him if she'd gone to Frank's place. "I'll go meet her there," Lackey said. "Look, Ronnie, I might be leaving town. *We* might. Me and Nancy, I got to think about this."

"You ought to, man. You ought to get the hell outta town and I need to find me a job. That plumber dude that owns the house, he come by today and told me to stop work. Says he don't want people like us working over there. I told him, hey, ain't nobody said *I* done shit. He say, tough, we don't like it we can talk to his lawyer."

Just a few days ago the news would have put Lackey in orbit. Now it just didn't matter. "What time did Nancy call you?" Lackey said.

"Little after five. She was in a booth out on Camp Bowie Boulevard."

Lackey said, "Thanks, pardner," and started to hang up, then had a thought and said, "Listen, Ronnie. You still got my Army .45 I give you?"

"In my truck," Ronnie said. "Why, you need it?"

"I could. Yeah, I might," Lackey said. "I might come by later for it."

He was concentrating on whether or not he should take Nancy and run, so much so that he forgot about the hot sheet that was doubtless out on his pickup. He waited at the light on the corner of Vaughn Boulevard and Avenue J, ready to turn right onto J and cut over to Miller Avenue, when a squad car cruised slowly around the corner to go north on Vaughn. The patrolman really gave Lackey the once-over, squinting against the glare from the pickup's headlights, slowing abruptly, the black-and-white listing in the direction of the curb. The driver's partner, visible through the squad car's rear window as it went past, was alternating his gaze between the pickup and something he was holding in his lap. Lackey's palms were suddenly damp. He turned onto Avenue J, really struggling with his foot to keep from jamming the accelerator to the floorboard, his heart up in his mouth until he'd gone a full block and the squad car hadn't followed. He was going to have to ditch the pickup at his first chance and find some different transportation.

Nancy's car was parked behind Frank's Buick in Frank's driveway. The sight of the green Mustang, neat as a pin, washed and polished and sporting spotless whitewall tires, lifted Lackey's spirits. He breathed a relieved sigh; as long as he could talk to Nancy, maybe hold her close for a while, everything would work out. He angled across Miller to park at the curb in front of Frank's place, got out and eagerly crossed Frank's yard. Halfway to the porch Lackey halted in his tracks. He cocked an ear, listening, as there was a tightening sensation between his eyebrows. There was something out of place.

The sun had been behind the horizon for a half-hour now, and the earth beneath his feet was warm. This time of year the daytime temperature hovered around ninety, and nightfall would lower the thermometer about ten degrees. The half-moon overhead was partially hidden behind a wisp of cloud. There was a thick-trunked oak standing in the yard, and in and around the tree, crickets *chirrup*ed. At the house next door a couple sat on the porch in a swing, rocking back and forth beneath a yellow light. Up the street a lawnmower chugged as someone mowed with their yardlight on. Light shone from behind window shades up and down the block. Not at Frank's, though, and that was what was wrong. If Nancy was here, there should have been some lights on inside, but Frank's place was dark as a tomb.

Lackey retraced his steps to stand alongside Nancy's Mustang and thumbed the doorhandle. The latch clicked and the door swung easily open. The interior lights came on, both overhead and underneath the dash.

Lackey's flesh crawled like a thousand earthworms. If he knew anyone in this world he knew Nancy Cuellar, and leaving her car unlocked—particularly in this unfamiliar neighborhood—was something she wouldn't have done in a million years. Lackey bent to look inside. The key was in the ignition; the green plastic letter *N* which Lackey had given her dangled from the chain. Her purse was on the seat.

She hadn't been intending to stay. Lackey had always kidded her because, in spite of her determination to lock her car and apartment as though expecting the Indians to attack if she was going to be gone for any extended period, Nancy thought nothing whatsoever about leaving her key in the ignition in front of the grocery story while she "just ran in for a few things." He'd told her over and over that ninety percent of the car thefts happened while people were "just running in for a few things," but he might as well have been talking to a tree.

So she hadn't intended to stay at Frank's at all. No, she'd meant to run in for just long enough to ask Frank about Lackey's whereabouts.

But she had stayed, hadn't she?

But the lights were out inside Frank's, and the place was silent as death.

Lackey went back to his pickup, rummaged around and located a steel L-shaped lug wrench, and hefted it. It wouldn't be much of a weapon against anybody with a gun, but it would have to do. Gripping the wrench firmly, he went across the yard and up on the porch. The screen door was closed, but the front entryway to the duplex stood open. His teeth grinding, Lackey knocked, then stood back and waited for a full minute. No one came to the door and there was no sound from within. He knocked again. More silence.

He pressed his nose against the screen. Spotlighted in a rectangle of moonlight was one end of a couch along with a small table. There was a big dark spot on the rug, a six-inch irregular circle of . . .

Lackey yanked the screen open and went inside, then bent and ran his finger over the spot. The spot was damp, and the sticky residue which adhered to his index finger appeared black in the moonlight. Slowly, as though walking on eggs, his gaze darting left and right, a warning knot between his shoulder blades, Lackey walked to the kitchen entrance, reached around and found the switch, then clicked on the kitchen light.

The kitchen was empty save for a yellowed stove, a refrigerator, and a rickety table, but there were more spots on the linoleum. These spots had dried to a ruddy brown. Lackey hefted the tire tool and went through the kitchen to the doorway leading to the bedroom. He kept his body inside the kitchen and stuck his head around the doorjamb.

He detected no movement, heard no sound other than the ticking of a clock. He blinked in the dimness, groped on the wall for a switch, found none. On the gray whiteness of the bed was a dark shape, someone or something, he couldn't tell. The outline of a lamp materialized as his pupils dilated, a lamp and a night-stand by the head of the bed. He stumbled slightly as he entered the room, went over to the lamp, felt under the shade and located a button. A sharp click vibrated his thumb as the room was bathed in muted light.

Frank—at least he assumed it was Frank, though the face above the sinewy chocolate-colored chest and arms was covered by a dirty pillow—was spread-eagled limply on top of the mattress. There was a singed hole in the pillow; Lackey held the pillow by one corner and slowly lifted it. He had a brief glimpse of Frank's face, lips pulled back in a permanent scowl, saw in an instant the hole in the cheekbone and the splash of drying blood around the back of Frank's head. Lackey dropped the pillow like a hot poker; Frank's tortured features disappeared from view with a soggy, downy *plop*. Lackey stepped to the foot of the bed and examined the floor.

Protruding from underneath the bed was one petite, dark green high-heeled shoe. Size 4, Lackey thought. It's a size 4.

He murmured, "Jesus. Oh, sweet Jesus."

He knelt to pick up the shoe, bent down to look under the bed. Nothing. Nancy's other shoe was in the corner beside a closet, and Lackey picked it up as well. He backed into the corner and looked hopelessly at Frank. Lackey's vision blurred and there was a dull ache in his throat.

He made a quick check around the duplex for her body, but, as he thought, there was none. A cheap brown handset phone was on the nightstand. Lackey put Nancy's shoes on the bed, keeping his gaze averted from Frank as much as possible, picked up the receiver and punched the buttons. There were two quick rings, followed by a click, then a soft female voice said, "Nine-one-one, your emergency?"

"I'm—" Lackey said.

Jesus, he couldn't do this. There was a capital murder warrant out for him. He hung up quickly.

Lackey managed two steps in the direction of the kitchen before the phone began to ring. Jesus Christ, he'd done it now. That would be the emergency operator calling the number automatically registered on her computer screen along with the address of the caller, and if she didn't get an answer by the fourth ring there'd be a squad car on its way in seconds.

Panic nearly caused Lackey to bolt, but he fought for control of himself. What had he touched? Nothing, nothing save for the phone, Nancy's shoes, and the handle on the front screen door. He let the tire tool dangle as he dug in his back pocket for a handkerchief, went to the phone and wiped at the handset. The ringing ceased; now the computer would be flashing the address to a police cruiser. Lackey scooped up Nancy's shoes and held them under his arm as he dashed out through the kitchen and sitting room to bang the screen open with his shoulder. On the porch, he used the handkerchief to wipe frantically at the doorhandle, then ran across the uneven yard to the pickup. In the distance, a siren *hoot-hoot*ed.

He tossed the shoes and tire tool into the front seat, then dove in behind the wheel and started the engine. As he pulled away he froze his gaze on the speedometer, let the needle creep up to thirty-five and held it there.

He was stopped for the red light at Miller and Rosedale when the black-and-white came into view, siren blaring and rooflights flashing, squealed around the corner and headed for Frank's. Lackey waited for the light to change, then drove slowly through the intersection.

He was halfway to Interstate 30, staying well within the speed limit on tree-lined streets, when a flashback came to him. The picture was of himself, standing in

Frank's sitting room and reaching around the door-jamb into the kitchen. Jesus, he'd thumbed the light switch. The lamp in Frank's bedroom, too, he'd gripped its base with a sweaty hand as he'd turned the lamp on.

Panic welled in his throat. His hands trembling, Lackey pulled to the curb, stopped, and rested his forehead against the top of the steering wheel.

After he'd pulled himself together, Lackey took the long way around in driving to Ronnie Ferias's house. He avoided the interstates and poked along amid stop-and-go traffic down Beach Street and onto Belknap, and out through dusty Haltom City to cross underneath Loop 820 on the Grapevine Highway. It was a fifteen-minute drive on the freeways, twice that by the route that Lackey took, but the chances of some patrolman with nothing better to do running a make on the pick-up's license plate were greater on the interstate. He kept his gaze on the road, certain that stares were focused on him from each car that he passed, and by the time he crept down the rutted alleyway which ran in back of Ronnie's, Lackey's fingers were numb from gripping the steering wheel. Ronnie lived in a frame two-bedroom house with a waist-high cyclone fence enclosing the small back yard. A thick hedge ran along the fence with its top portion clipped even with the fence's top iron rail. Lackey left the engine running and the lights on; he didn't like the idea of blocking the alleyway, but would rather chance that than leave his truck in front of the house, in full view of anyone who happened along. He entered the yard through a swinging gate, ducked under a clothesline that was no longer in use since Ronnie had bought a washer-and-dryer combo the previous fall, and walked up to the back window which opened into Ronnie's bedroom. He leaned over a flower bed to knock loudly on the sill. Slats clacked together as the Venetian blinds lifted, then Ronnie's round Hispanic face appeared and blinked its eyes. "What the hell are you doing?" Ronnie said. His voice was muffled by the closed window.

Lackey crooked a come-here finger, and Ronnie nodded. Then Ronnie dropped the blinds back into place, and in a couple of minutes he descended the two back steps into the yard. He was shirtless and barefoot, wearing yellow Bermuda shorts. A soft roll of fat poked out over the top of his pants, and his chest was hairless between puffy nipples. "Man, you getting my old lady in an uproar," Ronnie said. "She already got it figured out that they going to put me in the same cell with you and she going to wind up on relief with these two kids." There was a kidding-around tone to his voice, the old buddy doing his best to be cheerful, but there was just the slightest bit of anxiety as well. Ronnie folded his beefy arms.

Lackey wasn't in any mood to joke. "I'm going to need that gun."

Ronnie squinted in the moonlight to study Lackey's face. "I took it out of the truck," he said. "It's right here in my pocket. I had it figured you might want it. You ain't fixing to get in trouble, are you?" His right-hand pocket was bulging and weighted down from within.

"You kidding?"

"Yeah. Yeah, okay, I guess you already in trouble. You get ahold of Nance?"

Lackey hesitated. He wanted to tell Ronnie, but didn't have time to get into the details. "No," Lackey said softly.

Ronnie dug in his pocket, held the .45 service automatic heavily in one hand while he fished out a box of shells. He turned the gun flatwise, stacked the bullets on top, and offered both to Lackey. "How long since you shot that sonofabitch?" Ronnie said.

Lackey put the bullets away, then held the .45 at arm's length, released the lever and slid the clip from the butt. The clip was loaded, brass jackets in a row like a miniature stack of pipe sections. He replaced the clip and slid it home with the heel of his hand. ''Not since firing range, in the army,'' Lackey said. ''At least a year, I never unholstered it down in Panama.''

''Yeah, well it's a little off,'' Ronnie said. ''Goes to the right, so you got to aim a little left. I was going to adjust the sight, but I ain't had time.''

Lackey squinted down the .45's barrel at the ground. ''Yeah. Yeah, thanks. Listen, I got to be going.'' He turned to leave.

Lackey had gone five steps when Ronnie said, ''Lackey?''

Lackey stopped, turned, and cocked his head.

Ronnie shuffled his feet and jammed his hands into his pockets. ''Hey. Hey, pardner, you ain't ever shot anybody, have you?''

Lackey was suddenly calm. He raised his eyebrows. ''No, I haven't,'' Lackey said. ''Not yet, anyhow.''

19

Nancy Cuellar lay in the back seat of the killer's Volvo under a coarse painter's tarpaulin, feeling every bump in the road, her weight shifting with every turn. She was hogtied, her wrists and ankles bound with a line stretched taut in between. If she tried to straighten her legs the rope cut painfully into her wrists; if she lay still there was an awful cramping of her calf muscles and in the backs of her thighs. A dirty strip of cloth was tight over her eyes; a filthy rag was stuffed into her mouth and secured by a second strip of cloth which was tied behind her head. The gag tasted like sour milk. She thought, oh, God, will this ride never end? Then fear stabbed through her at the thought of what might happen when it did.

At least she was still alive to thank her lucky stars, which was more than she could say for poor Frank Nichols. At the moment the crazy had jammed the pistol against the pillow covering Frank's face, had pulled the trigger and filled the air with the stench of burning gunpowder, Nancy had given up hope. She'd been sure that her life was going to end, right then and there, and she'd even said a silent Our Father followed by a quick Hail Mary. As the man had loosened the rope from Frank's ankle, all the while grinning and cooing at her, Nancy had drawn what she'd been certain was her final breath.

But he hadn't shot her. Instead he'd told her with a strange faraway look that now they had all the time they needed. All the time that they needed, Nancy and this maniac, all the time in the world for him to . . . Not me, you bastard, Nancy thought as she bounced around under the tarp. She'd already made a solemn vow that if he tried anything sexual, he was going to have to kill her to have his way. *No way are you going to touch me, you freak. Not while I have breath you're not.* She tried to separate her wrists. Her bonds didn't give so much as a whisker.

She'd at first thought that he was going to try to rape her right there in Frank's bedroom, just nudge Frank's body aside and have his way with her right beside the corpse. He'd held the ropes in one hand and yanked her to her feet with the other. God, the man was strong. Nancy's upper arm still throbbed where he'd grabbed her, and he'd pulled her toward the bed with such force that she'd actually stepped out of her shoes. He hadn't seemed to notice. She was still in her stocking feet, in fact, right at this moment, and therein lay the one ray of hope that she had left. Lackey had been with her when she'd bought those shoes. If Lackey should call Ronnie Ferias, and if Ronnie should send him to Frank's place to look for her, and if Lackey should find those shoes, then . . .

And if elephants could fly, she thought, and if an ant could find a pot of gold at the end of the rainbow, and if the little blindfolded Mexican girl could hit the *piñata* with a stick. Oh, God, God, God.

He'd given her a shove and she had sprawled headlong onto the bed alongside Frank, had felt the cooling flesh against her body, had silently gritted her teeth and waited for the crazy man to come at her. But he hadn't. He'd turned her roughly over, her nose pressing against Frank's bare dead shoulder as he'd tied her hands and feet, brought her legs up behind her and secured the line between her wrists and ankles. "Don't spect we better be hanging around here, girl," was what he'd told her, then had left her in that cramped position, her face buried in Frank's shoulder, while, heard but not seen by her, his footsteps had retreated and he'd left the room.

She had no idea how long she'd lain there with the dead man. Not over ten minutes, surely, but to her it had seemed like hours, while the sweat of terror dried on Frank and the dusky odor of his body filled her nostrils. She remembered wondering, crazily, how long it would be before rigor mortis set in, how long she would have to lie there before Frank was stiff as a board. Then the maniac had returned, had said to her in a chatty tone, "See? Didn't take long. I pulled your car in the drive behind old Frank's. He ain't going noplace, and a cop might ticket that Mustang in the street."

The maniac had blindfolded and gagged her then. The blindfold had come first, the filthy cloth strip over her eyes, and when he'd tried to stuff the gag into her mouth she'd resisted by clamping her teeth together. He'd only laughed at that, then placed the hinges of her jawbones between his thumb and forefinger and squeezed. The pressure had been so hard she'd felt that her face might cave in, and her mouth had popped open. In had gone the foul-tasting gag, followed by the second strip of cloth. Then, laughing softly and humming an off-key tune, he'd rolled her onto her back.

Not knowing what was coming next had been the worst part for her. As he'd rolled her over, the ropes had cut into her wrists and ankles and she'd whimpered into her gag. He'd stood over her for a few seconds, grinning and looking her over as though he was proud of himself, then he'd reached down to the floor and held up the tarp. The tarp was off-white, with spots of red and blue and green paint dried on its surface in places. He'd thrown the coarse cloth over her body, then wrapped her up like an animal carcass, grasping the ends of the tarp and throwing her over his shoulder, Santa Claus fashion, with no more effort than if she'd been made of foam plastic. He'd carried her out of the duplex that way, with Nancy swinging helpless inside the tarp, across the porch, down to the yard, and across the yard to his car. The tarp and blindfold had shifted a bit when he'd dumped her into the back seat, and she'd caught a glimpse of the Volvo's padded ceiling. The crazy had tightened the blindfold and adjusted the tarp, and since then Nancy had seen nothing.

They had never left pavement, she was sure of that, there'd been no crunch of gravel or whisper of dirt beneath the tires. And they hadn't driven on any freeways, either; the entire journey had consisted of a block or so of gentle acceleration followed by a shifting forward of Nancy's weight as the Volvo had stopped for a traffic light or stop sign. The fading of the light penetrating her blindfold told her that night had fallen. The lunatic had his radio playing, on Country KJIM—one thing the guy's got in common with Lackey, she thought with a silent hollow laugh, I *told* Lackey he was crazy for listening to that awful music—and the voices of Willie, Waylon, Merle Haggard, or Jessie Coulter were interspersed with patches of crackling static. KJIM operated from a low-watt tower in the southwest part of the county, and the weakening of the signal told Nancy that the crazy was traveling away from the radio station. So, great, Nancy thought, we're not in southwest Fort Worth. Might be anyplace else in the county, though.

The Volvo pulled abruptly to the right and stopped. The engine died; the music quit with a final pop from the radio speaker. Well, Nancy thought with a quick tightening sensation in her throat, we're here. We're finally here, and now he's going to . . .

The front driver's side door swung open; the car rose on its springs as the crazy got out, then the door slammed. In a few seconds there was a metallic rattle near her head followed by a slight rush of air over the surface of the tarp as the rear door swung outward. The coarse cloth tightened about her as the crazy lifted her up and out. He's strong as an ox, Nancy thought, strong as an ox and crazy as . . . She shut her eyes tightly as he threw her over his shoulder and hauled her away.

Nancy twisted painfully onto her back as she dropped to the bottom of the pouch. The bonds cut into her wrists and the cartilage in her knees stretched to the tearing point as her weight came down on her shins. Her skirt bunched up around her waist. Her pantyhose were torn; the rough tarp brushed the smooth bare skin of her thigh. She pressed her tongue outward against the wad of cloth between her teeth and whimpered.

The crazy carried her across a path of uneven ground and mounted a flight of stairs. His footsteps clunked on metal steps as he climbed. He reached a level place, a landing of some sort, and stopped. The faint jingle of keys reached Nancy's ears through the tarp. A latch clicked. The man carried her across a threshold and a door thudded closed. Nancy counted his steps as he carried her inside, and after twenty-three paces he halted. There was a sudden weightlessness, an empty sensation in the pit of her stomach, then she fell onto a mattress as the air whooshed from her lungs. He yanked the tarp from beneath her and tossed it away. There was pressure behind her head as thick fingers worked at her blindfold, a quick tightening of the cloth covering her eyes, then a sudden loosening as he stripped off the blindfold. Nancy blinked in the sudden glare.

She was on a double bed with a single bulb glowing overhead. The sheet-covered mattress beneath her was lumpy. The sprayed-on ceiling plaster was cracked in places and there was a cobweb in one corner. Nancy was on her left side, which eased the pressure on her

wrists and ankles but increased the throbbing in her
knee joints. The bedspring creaked as the crazy sat on
the mattress and grinned at her. His gaze was on her
exposed thighs. God and Jesus, Nancy thought, I can't
even pull down my skirt. He stroked her leg where her
pantyhose were ripped. Her flesh crawled, her eyes
widened, and she struggled against her bonds. His grin
broadened.

It was Nancy's first good look at his face. He had a
narrow face and a big crooked nose. His eyebrows were
thick and untrimmed, his forehead wide and sloping.
He had thinning brown hair combed straight back. His
grin showed crooked, yellowed teeth. Gently, he
brushed her bangs away from her forehead. Not me,
you freak, Nancy thought. No way are you.

"Now, Nancy," he said, "you and me, we need to
have us a talk. I ain't wanting to hurt you none, but I
got to ask you some questions. I'm going to take that
gag off, and I'll tell you there ain't nobody here but
you and me. If you yell, nobody's going to hear you,
plus you're going to make me knock you around. Hey,
girl, I don't want to do that. So tell me, you going to
yell?"

Yell, she thought. *Yell?* You bet your filthy boots I'm
going to yell, you . . . Her dark eyes wide, Nancy
shook her head.

"Well I'm sure hopin' you don't," he said. He lifted
her head to untie the knot at the nape of her neck. The
strip of cloth fell away, then he pulled the wadded rag
from her mouth and dropped it on the bed.

Nancy worked her tongue across her palate, then the
insides of her teeth, then licked her lips. Finally she
threw her head back and screamed at the top of her
lungs. The noise was deafening, Nancy thought, loud
enough to wake the dead. Even the walls seemed to
vibrate. She stopped to catch her breath while she
watched the crazy man through challengingly narrowed eyes. How 'bout that, you crazy. . . ?

His grin faded and he shook his head sadly. "I told you, girl," he said. Then he grabbed the waistband of her skirt and yanked downward. Nancy flinched as cloth ripped and buttons popped. The crazy pulled her cotton sweater up; her abdomen was suddenly cool as air flowed on her bare stomach. His touch like emery cloth, the man dug his fingers into the flesh around her navel and squeezed.

The sudden pain froze Nancy like a statue. His grip was like pliers, digging, bruising. Tears leaped into her eyes and ran down her cheeks. Her arms and legs thrashed against their bonds; more pain razored through her wrists and ankles. She tried to scream, but all she could manage was a whimper.

He released her and stood back. Nancy's head sagged and her tears dropped on the bed. "How come you don't listen?" he said. "How come, huh? Now, girl, you going to answer some questions?"

The crazy reached out and touched her midsection. Her gaze averted, her teeth digging into her lower lip, Nancy moved her head up and down.

He sat down on the bed. "Hey, that's good. That's real good, Nancy, we're going to get along fine. What I want to know is, your boyfriend's been looking around for me. I think I'd like to meet him, face to face. I want you to call him in the morning. Think you could do that?"

Nancy thought dully, Lackey? Why would Lackey want to see this creep? Lackey didn't know any people like this. What Lackey was supposed to be doing was finding out who . . .

It dawned on her. The Volvo. The big blond cop had said something about a man in a Volvo. This guy. God.

Nancy's head hung as she said, "I have," then drew a tortured breath and said, "I have to go to the bathroom."

The crazy man smiled. "I ain't surprised you do after that." He glanced at her midsection. "It ain't my fault, Nancy, I warned you. Now. You think you can behave yourself if I let you up? I'd just as soon not be hauling no bedpans around.'' He laughed softly, a man making a joke for an audience of one.

Nancy softly closed her eyes. ''Yes.'' Her tone was docile, her voice tiny like that of a little girl's.

He pointed a thick forefinger. ''You know what? I believe you. I ain't no bad person, Nancy. So I'm going to let you loose to use the toilet. But you got to behave, you hear?''

''I have to,'' Nancy said. ''Please.''

He stood and lumbered around the bed, then quickly undid the knots at her wrists and ankles. ''There. See how easy it is?''

Every bone in Nancy's body ached and her midsection was on fire. She scooted painfully to the edge of the mattress and sat up, rubbing her wrists. There were deep red creases in her skin where the ropes had been. Her fingers tingled with sudden increased circulation. Her gaze on the floor, she said, ''Where? Where is it?''

''Right in front of you. See?'' He crossed the room, pushed a door open, reached around the jamb and flipped a switch. Sudden illumination revealed a tiled floor and one end of a grimy porcelain tub.

Nancy held the front of her torn skirt together as she limped in stocking feet to brush by the crazy man as she went into the bathroom. Her head was lowered like a slave's. She went over and looked down at the commode. The seat was streaked with grime and there was a brown ring around the bowl at the waterline. She tore a long strip from the toilet paper roll and separated the individual squares, placing them carefully around the perimeter of the seat. Got to be tidy, she thought, got to be clean and tidy and not sit on any dirty old toilet seats. A voice inside her laughed a hollow laugh. After she'd covered the seat as best she could, she turned to the doorway.

The crazy hadn't moved. One thick shoulder was pressed against the doorframe and one thumb was hooked inside his pocket. There was an expression on his face as though he was waiting for a show to begin.

Nancy was suddenly mad. Mad as hell. She forgot her aches, forgot the pain in her belly. Forgot everything except this evil sonofabitch who was wanting to watch her sit on the toilet. She took two defiant steps toward him and balled her hands into fists. "I'll tell you something," Nancy said. "You may be big and strong, at least strong enough to beat me up. But you're not going to watch me go to the bathroom, I don't care what you do to me." Her resolve faltered slightly and she waited for him to come at her.

His grin faded. His cheeks reddened and his ugly features sagged into an aw-shucks expression. "Well, okay. Listen, I ain't no leering pervert or nothing. You just take your time, you hear?" As he backed out of the room, his feet shuffled like an embarrassed schoolboy's. He closed the door.

Nancy was suddenly light-headed. She touched her forehead with her fingertips and shut her eyes tightly. Bile erupted upward into her mouth, and for long seconds she was certain she was going to vomit.

Nancy pressed the lever to flush the toilet. As the water gurgled and swirled in the bowl, she pulled up her white bikini briefs and adjusted the elastic around her hips. Then she bunched the front of her skirt together and let the pleats fall down to cover her thighs. She'd already dropped her torn pantyhose in the wastebasket to rest on wadded Kleenex, disposable razors, and two *Hustler* magazines. She went to the filthy sink, turned the tap and splashed cold water in her face.

There was no window in the bathroom. Surprise, surprise, she thought, no way for her to see outside or to signal anyone. If there had been a window, Mr. Murderer out there would have never let her stay in the bathroom alone. He would have stood right there and given her the choice of squatting on the toilet in plain sight of him, or holding her urine until her bladder erupted.

She had to be right, the guy outside was Mr. Murderer. There wasn't any other answer for what was happening. She pictured him with Marissa Hardin as, shuddering, she opened the door. "I'm finished," she said in a dull monotone.

The crazy was sitting on the bed. He uncrossed thick legs and put both feet on the floor. "Yeah. Yeah, and behaving yourself. You'll see I ain't no bad person, Nancy, long as you behave. You climb up on the bed, now, I got to tie you up."

She rubbed her wrist and said in her best you-can-trust-me tone, "Do you have to?" Fat chance, Nancy thought.

The sloping forehead smoothed into a look of apology. "I got to for now. Maybe not, when we get to know each other." He stood and picked up the ropes and let them dangle from his fingers.

Once we know each other? Nancy thought. Once we *know* each other? Why don't I go ahead and get it over with? He's going to kill me anyway, maybe I could put one of his eyes out before I'm gone. Maybe I could . . .

Docilely, her head bowed, Nancy crawled up on the mattress. She put her hands behind her back and held her ankles together. As the crazy trussed her, he hummed a tune. When he'd finished, he turned off the lights and stretched out beside Nancy on the bed. He scooted over close to her. God, Nancy thought, is he going to . . . ?

He yawned, assaulting her nostrils with onion breath. "We need some sleep," he said. "We got a lot to do tomorrow." He moved his head so that his thinning hair lay against her cheek. "You my baby, Nancy. 'Night, now."

In seconds he was snoring. Nancy strained and wriggled to move away from him. He opened one eye, smiled at her, then put his arms around her and hugged her close. Her ankles and wrists tingling as feeling left them, Nancy Cuellar whimpered in the dark and said a silent prayer.

Everett Wilson lay down beside his baby and went to sleep, glad he could control himself, glad he wasn't like one of them perverts down in the Texas Department of Corrections. First things first. No way was he going to lay a hand on his baby until the contractor guy came up with the money. Jesus, five minutes earlier and the Hardin woman would have never given the money to the contractor asshole to begin with. But now things were going to work out fine. Everett was going to get the money, then he was going to kill the contractor guy. After that, Everett and his baby would have all the time in the world.

He'd never had a woman of his own, but Nancy was going to change that. He'd buy her nice clothes, take her to all the spots, whatever she wanted. She'd see.

Once long ago, he'd thought his high school art teacher was going to be his baby. Miss Halfern had been her name, and Everett had called her that, never knowing her *first* name, not even on the day she'd taken him to her apartment. It hadn't mattered to Everett that she was forty years old, nor that she was short and on the dumpy side. What had mattered was that she was soft and gentle with him, that she never gave him funny looks when she thought he wasn't looking, and that she hadn't cared that he was an orphan who rode the bus every day to public school. That Everett had wanted her so badly—and had known she'd wanted him as well—had made the hurt so much deeper inside him on the day at her apartment when she'd showed him that she wasn't going to be his baby at all.

There in the afternoon cool of her living room, with

the shades drawn and the television's volume turned down low, she'd reached for him on her couch and unzipped his trousers. Everett had closed his eyes and waited for it to happen.

But after a single touch she'd released her hold on his member, and Everett had opened his eyes to find her staring at his crotch. Her lips had been parted in shock. She'd uttered a tiny gasp. Then she'd tried a forced smile, but it had been too late. She hadn't really liked him at all.

Everett didn't remember everything that had happened after that, just a few fuzzy and fragmented mental images. Miss Halfern on the floor was the one clear picture in Everett's mind, Miss Halfern on the floor with blood streaming from her mouth and nose, Miss Halfern begging, telling him if he'd only stop she'd do anything that he wanted. She wasn't no good, Miss Halfern, and she didn't understand that all Everett had wanted was for her to be his baby.

Now, at last though, Everett had found his baby for sure. Nancy was going to be different.

He dropped off to sleep, and to dream a beautiful dream. In the dream he and Nancy walked hand in hand down a long corridor, and her head was tilted at a saucy angle as she smiled and talked to him. As they rounded a corner there was a bad guy, a guy out to hurt Everett's baby. Everett took care of the bad guy in seconds, knocked the bad guy cold as a mackerel with a left-right, one-two, then took Nancy by the hand and led her away. Her look at Everett was one of pure worship.

The bad guy had had a mean look about him, thick eyebrows set close together, lip curled in an evil snarl. But his features had been familiar. Aside from the mean look, he'd been the spitting image of Lackey Ferguson, the contractor guy.

20

Lackey left his pickup downtown, sitting at the curb in front of Juanita's Restaurant, catty-cornered across from the Worthington Hotel, and took a cab to the west side. He'd been bucking long odds for two days, driving his pickup, and he couldn't believe that a passing squad car hadn't picked up his license number from the hot sheet. Parking right in front of Percy Hardin's house would *really* be asking for it. Besides, with what Lackey had in mind, he wasn't going to need his own transportation anyway.

He sat back in the taxi and kept his face in shadow, out of the rearview mirror's line of vision for the driver. He needn't have worried. The cabbie, a Mexican guy with a bushy mustache, kept his hands on the wheel and his gaze straight ahead of him. The drive west on I-30 from downtown consumed a quarter of an hour.

He'd given the driver a made-up address a couple of blocks from Hardin's, and hoped he hadn't made a mistake. He knew the street and the approximate hundred-block, but for all Lackey knew the address didn't exist at all. Hell, what if the place was a vacant lot or something? He breathed a sigh as the cab pulled up in front of a two-story Gothic home. The driver turned expectantly around as Lackey glanced over the seat to check the meter. Eight forty-five. He had to be careful with the tip. A too-small tip would serve to piss the driver off; too big of a tip would be just as bad. Either one would cause the driver to remember him. Lackey handed a ten over and told the guy to keep the change. The driver stuffed the bill in his pocket and did an eyes-front. Lackey got out of the taxi, walked up the sidewalk toward the Gothic house until the cab had rounded the corner, then retraced his steps to the front and took off down the walk toward Percy Hardin's place.

A hazy half-moon shone overhead, accompanied by a few softly twinkling stars, and a faint warm breeze was blowing. Lackey passed under a streetlamp where moths and June bugs whirred their wings and banged against the glowing bulb, then crossed the wide street and walked by a house with a lawn the size of a ballpark. Somewhere in the distance a golf-course sprinkler spit and hissed. Just ahead, a woman waited patiently, leash in hand, while a white poodle pissed on a lightpole. Lackey lowered his head and quickened his pace as he went by. His thick hair was dirty and wild and he hadn't been able to trim his beard or shave his neck. He still wore his Dallas Cowboys T-shirt and dirty sneakers without socks, and a guy wandering around this neighborhood in his condition was likely to prompt a call to the law. The woman barely glanced at him. The .45 weighted down his back pocket and bumped against his rear end; he reached around and adjusted the gun so that the handle pointed upward and the barrel sideways.

He wasn't sure what he was going to do once he reached Hardin's house, and didn't even know why he was going there. He didn't even know for sure that it was Hardin who'd done his own wife, but that was Nancy's theory. Lackey had known a lot of people in his life who thought they had all the answers—Jesus, the army had been crawling with those guys—but Nancy wasn't one of them. Nancy was the type to keep her opinions to herself, and when she *did* have something to say, Lackey had always found her ideas to be pretty accurate. Hell, Lackey thought, it's *got* to be Hardin. Why else would he give all the servants the day off and leave his wife at home by herself?

Lackey was smart enough to know that even if Hardin was the guy who'd hired the snuff man, that didn't necessarily mean that Hardin knew anything about what had happened to Nancy. That could be unrelated. But one thing which Lackey was sure of, if Hardin hadn't had his wife killed (and, Lackey thought with a slight wince, Lackey Dumbass Ferguson hadn't tried to get rich quick by getting that high-dollar bathhouse job), then Lackey himself would be happy as a clam doing cheap northside remodeling jobs, and Nancy wouldn't be out there in God knows what danger. Mr. Percy Hardin owes us for this, Lackey thought. He quickened his pace in the moonlight, hustling through another intersection. Only a half-block to go. Lackey's eyes narrowed and he touched the butt of the .45 through the fabric of his pants.

The sprinkler system at Hardin's place was running, hissing and spraying tiny droplets; the fine mist dampened Lackey's cheeks and beard as he made a 90-degree left-face off of the sidewalk and marched across the yard. He passed the bush where, just a week ago, the Mexican gardener had been working with pruning shears. The twin brick spires towered overhead as Lackey went between them and entered the patio. The hissing of the sprinklers grew faint behind him. Lights were on in the foyer and shone from two windows on the second floor of the house. Lackey had skirted a quarter of the fountain in the direction of the porch when he stopped in his tracks, put his hands on his hips, and regarded his sneakers. Visible in the corner of his eye, the goldfish underneath the surface of the water were twisting dark streaks.

What the hell was he thinking about? He couldn't just walk up and knock on the door. He had a big picture of that—old J. Percival Hardin pumping Lack-

ey's hand in greeting and asking if he wanted a beer
or something. The truth was that if Hardin even suspected Lackey's presence in the neighborhood, he'd be
on the phone to the law quicker than the Rangers could
blow another one. End of rescue mission, probably the
end of Nancy. End of Lackey X. Ferguson as well. He
could talk to the two detectives, Morrison and Henley,
until he was blue in the face and they'd just laugh their
asses off while the jailer led him away. Lackey retreated at a half-walk half-jog into the front yard and
stood in the sprinkler-generated mist.

Lackey had been in Hardin's backyard one time, and
now called up a mental image of the quick tour on the
day—Jesus, only a week? it seemed like years ago—
when he'd come by to talk about the bathhouse. Hardin
had been really swaggering and strutting as he'd
showed Lackey around, the rich guy rubbing the
northside guy's nose in it, and the rich guy had been
especially proud of the ten-foot smooth plaster wall
which enclosed the backyard and pool. Without a ladder, Lackey thought, that wall would be hell to climb.
But he seemed to remember some trees. Yeah, some
trees, some leafy elms or sycamores—Lackey wasn't
a nature-lover and didn't know one tree from another—which stood outside the backyard with their
branches extending above the wall. Ignoring the mist
thrown by the sprinkler system, his sneakers slogging
through wet Bermuda, Lackey jogged around to the
side of the house.

There were trees, all right. Three of them, side by
side at twenty-foot intervals along the western perimeter of the wall. But the trees weren't quite *flush* with
the wall; there was about five feet of yawning open
space between the tallest of the trees and the ten-foot
dropoff into the yard. From his angle looking upward,
Lackey was pretty sure he could make the jump; he
clambered up the trunk into the lower branches with
his rubber soles scraping bark. Jesus, from this new

height perspective he wasn't so sure any more; it
looked to him like one helluva long way. He drew a
deep breath, closed his eyes and pictured Nancy as
she'd looked the last time they'd made love, shoved off
with both feet and launched himself into thin air.

He hung suspended like Batman for what seemed
like minutes as the wall's top edge crept toward his
fingers in painful slow motion. He wasn't going to
make it. No way was he. He was going to slam into
that fucking wall and ooze down the side like some
kind of Humpty Dumpty, and then Hardin was going
to find him the next morning and carry him away in a
garbage sack. He'd never see Nancy again, either, he
was going to—

Lackey's hands scraped plaster and went over the
top of the wall. His toes banged into the side and the
pain made Lackey wonder if he'd broken something.
He twisted and wriggled, threw one leg up and over,
hoisted himself on top and sat with his legs dangling
down inside the perimeter of the yard and his breath
coming like a five-thousand-meter runner's.

Jesus, his right big toe was killing him. He wiggled
the toe inside his shoe, and it moved up and down.
Lackey held his hands up in front of his face. His
palms were bruised and there was a drop of blood on
his left index finger. He sucked on the finger, watched
the back door of the house, and halfway expected
Percy Hardin to come out shooting. No one came. As
his breathing subsided, Lackey put both hands down
beside his hips and vaulted from the wall to drop into
the yard. His legs gave way as he landed and he rolled
painfully over twice. Then he climbed to his feet and
looked around.

From where Lackey stood, the land sloped downward forty feet or so to the bank of the teardrop-shaped
pool. The underwater lights sent aqua shadows rippling, both on the surface of the wall and the south
side of the house. The diving tower stood at the near

end of the pool like a hangman's scaffold. Lackey's feet were planted exactly on the spot where the spa at the back of the bathhouse would have been. Moving carefully, limping and grunting at the pain in his toe, he went down the slope, circled the pool, and moved past four pruned, expensive trees. Chinese elms, Hardin had told him smugly. Great, Lackey had thought, if you're a Chinaman. He climbed three redwood steps and stood on the deck. On his right was a sunken spa covered by molded blue tarp; the thermostat kicked in and the spa's heater made a humming sound.

A sliding glass door opened from the deck to the house. Lackey crossed over, gingerly moved his toe inside his shoe as he bent to peer through the glass. The aqua shadows from the pool wriggled over the refrigerator and standup freezer in the kitchen, and the same table where he'd sat down across from Marissa Hardin. She'd fixed him an orange-and-egg shake and had written him a check. He tried the door. It wouldn't budge. He backed away a few steps and looked upward.

There was a suspended balcony about ten feet overhead, extending from dead center in the house's wall and running outward for about fifteen feet on either side. Lackey backed up further and winced slightly as he stood on tiptoes. About half visible over the balcony railing, a second sliding door led into the house. The master bedroom, Lackey thought, and the balcony's a spot where Percy Hardin can sit and drink cognac while he keeps an eye on the gardener, probably interrupting his reading of the paper once in a while to yell and point the finger at the Mexican guy. Lackey wiped sweat from his forehead with the back of his hand. His palms stung where he'd scraped them climbing the tree and scrambling over the wall.

Once upon a time, Lackey Ferguson had been a pretty good basketball player. He would have been a cinch to make the high school team, in fact, if he hadn't had to work every day after school. Even today he liked watching the Mavericks, in person when he could get a ticket and on TV when he couldn't, almost as much as he liked keeping up with baseball. Back when he'd played, Lackey hadn't been a very good shot. But he'd been the best rebounder around, mixing it up under the boards with shoulders and elbows, and he'd been able to outjump everybody in school, even though a lot of the guys had been several inches taller. At one time he could handle a one-handed dunk from a flat-footed start, and give him a couple of steps in the free-throw lane and he'd show you a two-hander with no effort at all. But Jesus, Lackey thought as he looked upward at the balcony, I was eighteen then. It had been ten years, minimum, since he'd even thought about . . .

He sucked in his breath, rotated his shoulders to loosen the muscles, took two running steps and sprang from the balls of his feet. More pain shot through his big toe, and he missed by a hair. His fingers scraped the bottom of the balcony; he came down hard, stumbled, and righted himself just in time to keep from smashing through the plate-glass door into the kitchen. He gathered himself, backed a couple of extra strides away from the balcony this time, and had another run at it.

This time there was more spring in his legs and more arc to his jump. His hands came into stinging contact with one of the posts which supported the balcony railing. He grabbed ahold and dangled while his feet swung back and forth in small decreasing arcs. Almost there, buddy, he thought. Just a little more.

Now his thoughts traveled back to army boot camp, and he pictured the hand-over-hand rope climb, and himself, arms aching as though they might come out of his shoulder sockets, shinning up the rope like a monkey on a string with the big-gutted drill sergeant cussing a blue streak underneath. "You look like an

ape fuckin' a football, Ferguson,'' was what the bastard had told him, and Lackey had a special hate for
the drill sergeant even today. But Jesus, he thought,
what wouldn't I give to have old sarge here right now.
He kicked his feet and pulled himself up. Blood surged
into his throbbing toe and he scrambled up and over
the rail, finally standing erect on the balcony, not be-
lieving himself that he'd made the climb. He touched
his shoulder joint. Be sore in the morning, Lackey
thought.

On the balcony was a wrought-iron breakfast table
surrounded by four matching chairs. The iron was
molded into a leafy vine pattern. Lackey skirted the
table and approached the sliding entryway, walking
softly. The soles of his sneakers, not quite dry after
the wet grass in front of the house, left a trail of damp
grid-patterned prints. Just outside the glass panel he
halted in his tracks. He was looking into the master
bedroom, at a French Provincial vanity and four-
postered, canopied, king-size bed. On the bed sat a
woman, and she was watching him.

There wasn't any doubt about it, she was looking
directly at him. Her eyes were bright and there was a
tiny smile on her face. She was brushing her hair, her
head tilted at a slight angle as she pulled the brush
through her hair with long firm strokes. She wore a
filmy pink shortie gown, and her crossed legs weren't
half bad. Were damn good, in fact, as was her face,
with its slim straight nose and soft feminine cheeks.
He couldn't say that she was as pretty as Nancy—
nobody in the world measured up to Nancy, to Lackey's way of thinking—but this woman would run Nancy
a close second. There was something about the eyes,
though, that Lackey didn't like. Where Nancy's eyes
had a straightforward, honest look about them, this
woman's gaze was narrowed slightly, and there was a
tightening around the corners of her eyes which made
her look like someone you wouldn't trust. He had a

feeling that he'd seen her somewhere before. He searched his brain. Nothing. Never mind, it would come to him.

Lackey dug in his back pocket, came up with the .45 and pointed it at her through the glass. Her gaze flicked at the pistol, then zeroed in on Lackey's face. Her smile broadened.

Lackey decided that this was the weirdest goddamn female he'd ever seen, smiling at a guy in dirty tennis shoes who was pointing a gun at her. He gestured with the pistol and pointed at the handle on the sliding door. She dropped her hairbrush, gracefully uncrossed her legs, then crossed the room to let him in. The door made a swishing noise as it moved sideways.

She stood to one side. "Don Juan, right? Where are your tight britches, Don?" Her voice was cultured, with a slightly nasal twang, and her speech was slurred. Her eyes were twin bright points.

Lackey hadn't seen near the amount of cocaine in the army as everyone had told him he would, but he had seen quite a bit. He'd never touched the stuff himself, and was glad of it, but he'd learned to spot a user. A faint powdery residue clung to the woman's upper lip and the skin below her nostrils was inflamed. "I need to see Mr. Percy Hardin," Lackey said.

She took a couple of steps in the direction of the bed, then regarded him over her slim, uplifted shoulder. "Well, I'll tell you, Don. The last time I saw old Perce he was downstairs getting drunk on his ass. He might still be coherent, fifty-fifty I'd say, but if he's passed out, you're in deep shit as far as talking to him." She ignored the gun pointed at her as she pranced the remaining steps to the bed, crawled up on all fours beneath the canopy, and peeked at him around her upraised fanny. "So, Don. You like it doggy style?" She wore pink bikini briefs and had a generous, well-proportioned ass.

Lackey glanced down at the pistol, then at her up-

lifted behind, and finally lowered the gun to dangle at
his hip. What was he going to do, shoot her in the butt
or something? He'd say one thing for her, if she was
trying to make him feel like a jackass she was doing
a helluva job of it. And he sure wasn't doing Nancy
any good by standing here pointing a gun while this
coked-up woman stuck her ass out at him. He went
over and grabbed her upper arm, then hauled her to
her feet. "I told you, I got to see Mr. Hardin," he
said.

She stuck her tongue out at him. "You're no fun,
Don."

He moved toward the bedroom door with a gentle
push. "I got to say you're not, either. Let's go downstairs, okay?"

She gave an irritated "oops," then shrugged and
led the way with the hem of her nightie popping from
side to side in rhythm with her hips. Like a parade,
Lackey thought as he followed her out of the bedroom.
Like she was the majorette and I was playing the sax-
ophone. They passed by a standing suit of armor in
the corridor, then came to the head of the staircase.
Lackey stopped her with a hand on her shoulder, then
looked down the wide steps into the den.

He'd never been upstairs in the house, but from his
angle looking down at the mammoth den, everything
below seemed just as he remembered it, the baby
grand piano and rear-projection bigscreen TV, the
double french doors on the right which led into the
sitting room. It had been in the sitting room where
Lackey had first laid out his bathhouse plan to Percy
Hardin, while Mrs. Hardin ran back and forth in her
robe, bringing them coffee. Overhead were the vaulted
ceiling and curtained skylights. Lackey gave the
woman a gentle nudge forward, then stayed two steps
behind and above her as they descended. She touched
the banister on her right every few feet, and there was
a saucy rotation to her shoulders as she went down. In

the den, a stereo was playing an old Sinatra album,
"New York, New York." There was no one in sight
below. The woman descended the final step and took
off at a slight angle toward the sitting room. As Lackey
followed, he caught sudden movement in the corner of
his eye.

The movement was a shadow on the floor, something outlined in the faint beam of overhead hidden
fluorescents, something which detached itself from the
shadow of the staircase and moved quickly forward.
Lackey flinched sideways and raised his arm to protect
his head.

A bottle smashed into his forearm; Lackey's shoulders and chest were suddenly wet and his nostrils filled
with the odor of whiskey. Shards of glass flew into his
hair, past his face, and tinkled on the carpet. Lackey
went to his knees. His arm was numb and the shock-
waves traveled like lightning into his shoulder and
neck. The .45 flew from his grasp, thudded to the
carpet, and bounced in the direction of the sitting
room. From behind him, a slurred male voice said
loudly, "Get it." The woman spun on her heel and
dove for the pistol; the shortie gown flew up to show
her tanned midsection. She was giggling. Jesus,
thought Lackey, she's *giggling*.

He rose into a crouch and went after the gun like a
lineman after a fumble, driving off at his instep, ram-
ming the woman with his left shoulder and encircling
the pistol with his body, then wrapping his left hand
around the handle. His right hand was numb and use-
less and blood seeped from a gash on his forearm.
Breath whooshed from the woman's lungs as she stumbled backwards; her knees hit the corner of a long
leather sofa, and she sprawled headlong onto the cushions in a flash of arms and shapely suntanned legs.

Lackey rolled over on his side and leveled the .45
in his left hand. Percy Hardin was holding the shat-

tered bottle aloft, ready to strike, but now froze in his tracks and let the bottle fall to his side.

For long seconds no one moved. There was no sound other than the crooning of Sinatra and Lackey's ragged breathing. Hardin was dressed as though for his tee time, in a purple Ralph Lauren knit, matching slacks, and snow-white canvas shoes. His blond hair was combed and sprayed. Lackey had never seen Hardin without his sunglasses before. Hardin's eyes were pale blue and the skin across the center of his face was fishbelly white in contrast to his tan.

Finally, Hardin said, "You take money? How much?"

The woman snickered. "What money? He'll have to wait in line with everybody else."

"Shut up, Betty," Hardin said, then directed his gaze once again to Lackey. "How much you take to just go away?" Hardin said.

"I don't know what you're talking about," Lackey said. The climb over the wall and up on the balcony plus the bottle smashing down on his arm had left him weak; the pistol in his grip seemed to weigh a ton.

"Can't you hear?" Hardin said. "I'm talking about money. And you just walking out of here."

Lackey steadied the gun. "You don't have enough money. There isn't enough anywhere. Where's Nancy?"

Hardin glanced at Betty, then cocked his head. "Where's who?"

Lackey's jaws clenched. Just as he'd told Ronnie Ferias, Lackey had never shot anyone. Shooting Hardin would be easy, though. "I'm not fooling around with you," Lackey said. He rose to his feet and aired back the hammer with two sharp clicks. The muscles in his forearm tensed in preparation for the recoil.

"Good God, man." Hardin extended a hand, palm out. His fingers were trembling. The bottle slipped from his grasp and fell on the floor. "I don't know any Nancy. I swear to God."

"Somebody knows her," Lackey said. "Somebody's got her. Why not you, you fuck? You killed your wife." His right arm throbbed as a drop of blood fell onto the rug. The wound was only seeping, so the arteries were still intact.

"I wouldn't do that," Hardin said. "I wouldn't ever."

"He means he wouldn't have the guts," Betty said, scooting around and sitting up on the sofa. "That much is true."

Lackey backed up a step and leveled the .45 at a spot midway between Hardin and Betty. "I tell you something, Mr. Hardin, you got me in a helluva mess here. I'd just as soon have the law on me for something I did as something I didn't. Now wherever Nancy is, she's there because of you. I think you better start talking to me."

Hardin's jaw thrust forward like a spoiled kid's. He pointed at Betty. "*I* didn't do anything," Hardin said. "It was her."

"Oh, Jesus, Percy," Betty said.

"It was, too," Hardin said. "She found the guy. *She* did."

The way Hardin was pointing reminded Lackey of Pig Newton, a kid Lackey had known in grammar school who went around telling the teacher on everybody. "Right now I don't care who did what," Lackey said. "What I want is for you to lead me to this hit guy, wherever he is."

"Well you'll have to ask *her*," Hardin said. "Go on, ask her."

Lackey swiveled the gun around to point at Betty. Would he shoot a woman? If it would help Nancy, he damn sure would.

Betty nervously licked her lips. "I don't know where the guy *lives*. I just set the meeting up. You ask Mr.

Hardin over there where he lives, he made all the arrangements with the guy.''

Lackey's right arm was hurting like the blazes, and he was having trouble getting his thoughts straight. *He* did. *She* did. What did it matter *who* did, with Nancy somewhere out there and probably—

Lackey tightened his grip on the pistol and swung it back and forth in arcs. ''First we're going to do something to fix this arm.'' He raised his right hand and clenched it into a fist. ''Then we're going for a ride, the three of us. You two'd better hope I find what I'm looking for. You damn sure had.''

Lackey didn't like the idea of having a woman on cocaine bandage his arm, but he didn't see any way around it. He herded the woman (Betty, he thought, her name's Betty) and Hardin upstairs into the huge master bath, and kept the gun ready in his left hand while Betty dabbed alcohol on the cut and then rolled gauze around his right forearm. Hardin sat on the marble counter with one hip hanging off the edge, keeping his gaze steadily on the gun. The bathroom fixtures were shiny brass, and there was a big parabola-shaped sunken tub. Betty stood back and looked at the bandage, then broke into a nervous giggle. The gauze was loose and twisted in places.

''Sure you won't reconsider?'' Hardin said. ''About the money.'' He had calmed down and now sounded as though money was the answer to everything. In this guy's world, Lackey thought, it probably is.

''No way,'' Lackey said.

''There's a lot of it.''

Betty snickered. ''Not now there isn't. Maybe when the insurance check arrives.''

''Keep out of this,'' Hardin said.

Betty cut a strip of tape from a roll—Lackey swung the .45 in her direction the second that she touched the scissors—and plastered the gauze's end into place.

With the top of her head near Lackey's mouth, she said, "I'll tell you something, Mr. Muscleman. Percy-pooh over there is full of it. If he's got two cents he owes it to somebody. And the part of the money he's talking about giving you? Let's see, I think that makes a hundred and fifty percent he's got committed to people."

"Damn it, Betty," Hardin said.

"Four banks," Betty said, "plus the mortgage company, not to mention a couple of bookmakers and the guys he plays golf with out at the country club. He hasn't even paid his old hit man, can you believe it? And me. And as soon as the money shows up, my daddy's going to be lurking around for a piece of it."

Lackey couldn't believe this, the woman standing here bandaging him and telling this stuff. "Your daddy?" Lackey said.

She wrinkled her nose. "Percy-pooh's father-in-law."

Now it dawned on Lackey why she'd looked familiar. He'd never seen her before, it was just the resemblance. "Jesus Christ," Lackey said. "You're her sister?"

Betty got an Ace elastic bandage from the cabinet and began to wrap over the gauze. "Decadent, huh?" she said.

Hardin folded his arms and regarded his own swinging foot. "Just go right on, Betty. I guess you know what you're talking us into."

She raised a plucked eyebrow. "To him? You can't exactly call the police, Mr. Muscleman. Can you? You going to tell on him?" She jerked her head in Hardin's direction.

"On *us*," Hardin said.

"On *him*," Betty said.

The two glared at one another while Betty secured the elastic with two metal clips.

Lackey clenched his fist and flexed his arm. The

bandage was a shoddy-looking job, but gave more support than he'd expected. "Well maybe I can't call the cops," he said, "but I'll tell you something. If Nancy's not a hundred percent okay, you're going to wish I had." He showed Betty a businesslike wink. "Get a coat on, lady. You might feel funny, running around town in that outfit."

If it hadn't have been for the throbbing in his arm and his worry over Nancy, Lackey might have enjoyed the feeling of being a westside guy, sitting in the back seat of a midnight blue Mercedes and getting chauffeured around by J. Percival Hardin III. With the plush leather seats cradling his back and buttocks, the .45 resting in his lap and the outline of Hardin's head directly in front of him, and with Betty Monroe, wearing an olive green raincoat over her nightie, batting cocaine-glazed eyes at him over the back of the passenger seat, Lackey still thought that guys who drove Mercedes were getting screwed. Yeah, the ride was soft, and, yeah, the interior had a lot of doodads—a wraparound stereo with what sounded like about ten speakers, an automatic sentinel that turned the lights on and off, and a built-in phone, the receiver of which now lay disconnected beside Lackey on the seat in case Hardin thought about trying any funny business— but sixty thousand dollars' worth? No way.

He was glad that Hardin had finally gotten the point and quit offering money. In fact, if Hardin had offered money one more time, Lackey didn't know if he could have kept from beating the shit out of the guy. If getting a lot of money meant losing Nancy, Lackey Ferguson would just have to figure out how to get along without a dime, and if getting to be a westside guy meant having to be a wimp like Percy Hardin, then Lackey Ferguson would stick to being a broke.

As the Mercedes left Camp Bowie Boulevard and made the gentle climb onto westbound I-30, Hardin said over his shoulder, "You know we can't guarantee to find this man, don't you?"

Lackey glanced out the tinted back window, at darkened trendy shops and restaurants along Camp Bowie. "That'll be bad for you," Lackey said.

"You've got to be reasonable, man. All we can do is go to the place where Betty found him to begin with. I don't have the slightest idea where he lives, or even if he's still in town."

"He's in town," Betty said. "Percy owes him money, along with a big percentage of the rest of the population." She was coming down from her high and her words were beginning to slur. As they'd come from Hardin's kitchen into the connecting garage, she'd tried to slip a vial of white powder into her pocket. Lackey had taken the vial away from her and washed the powder down the sink. Without the cocaine to bolster her, Betty was more subdued, and she was beginning to act just as jittery as Hardin was. That was okay with Lackey. He wanted them to be afraid of him.

"How did you find this guy?" Lackey said.

Hardin chuckled, the first time he'd laughed since he'd brought the bottle down on Lackey's arm. "Tell him, Betty," Hardin said.

Her gaze dropped as overhead freeway lamps made patches of moving light across her cheek and one side of her nose. "You go to hell," she said.

"No, go ahead and tell him. You've been getting a charge out of putting *me* down, tell him all about your dope connections."

She flashed a painted-on smile. "Sure, love. Let's start with how you started screwing around with your sister-in-law."

"Yeah, okay," Hardin said. "Let's talk about that. Let's talk about how my sister-in-law came over and seduced me one day while my wife was playing tennis."

"Like you weren't thinking about it," Betty said.

"Of course I was. What man wouldn't, when a woman goes around hiking up her skirt so he can see her panties?"

Lackey couldn't understand these two, how if they hated each other this much they could stand to get into bed together. Sex with Nancy was great, but just lying beside her in the dark was about as much of a kick as the sex itself. He decided that these two were really missing something in life and even felt just a little bit sorry for them. The cut on his arm was beginning to sting. He looked across the freeway at headlights going by in the opposite direction like a parade of spooky yellow eyes. Hardin was making the slow curve from I-30 onto I-35, headed south. Lackey wasn't surprised, most of the illegal stuff he heard about seemed to originate on the south side.

"Let's talk about," Hardin said, "a woman that will jump into bed with anybody that'll furnish her drug money. You hear that, Mr. Contractor? That first time, that first time she came over we hadn't even begun to get it on before she was asking if I had a connection to buy cocaine. It was her fucking coke dealer that introduced her to the hit guy, what do you think about that?"

"I think maybe you shouldn't have been screwing around on your wife," Lackey said.

"I'll grant you that," Hardin said. "I'll admit that was wrong."

"How benevolent of you," Betty said.

"But I'll say I'm no different than any other man."

Oh, yeah, you are, Lackey thought. He pictured Marissa Hardin, the day she'd come on to him, the day he wished had never happened. As good-looking as Marissa Hardin had been, Lackey wouldn't have touched her with a ten-foot pole as long as he had Nancy. If he hadn't had Nancy, well, things might have been different, but to Lackey's way of thinking that didn't make Percy Hardin any less of an asshole for screwing around with his sister-in-law. These westside guys are really fucked up, Lackey thought. The Mercedes had left the freeway and stopped at the red light at the intersection of Lancaster Avenue. The left turn signal bonked monotonously.

"You're damn sure different in bed," Betty was saying to Percy. "They should have named you Peter Cottontail."

"That's a good one," Hardin said. "Hey, Betty, really funny. Hey, back there, you really want to know how I came to hire this killer guy?"

"I guess. If you want to tell me," Lackey said.

"Well, sweet little Betty sold me on the idea. She'd been hassling me to divorce Marissa anyhow—"

"Now don't start that," Betty said.

"Oh, don't worry. She didn't really mean it, not when she found out I was out of money. Before she found that out, I think she really did. But when she found out my divorcing Marissa would cut sweet Betty off from her coke money, she changed her mind."

"He was living off my sister's money," Betty said. "Sweet guy, huh?"

"My wife's money," Hardin said, "which translates into her father's money. Who is also Betty's father, but you want to know why Betty can't get her hands on any more of daddy's money?"

"Fuck you, Percy," Betty said.

Jesus, but they hate each other's guts, Lackey thought. Even Frank Nichols and those convicts on the job had *liked* each other.

"Why, Betty's an addict," Hardin said. "That's why she's home right now instead of screwing around someplace in Europe, so daddy could put her little butt through a treatment center. You know Betty likes her dope so much that one time she even pimped for her own father so he wouldn't cut her money off? Fixed daddy right up with this friend of hers."

They're all a bunch of loonies, Lackey thought,

every one of them. There was a wad of bills in Lackey's pocket, the fifteen thousand dollars Marissa Hardin had given him, less what he'd spent of it. A bunch of loony money, Lackey thought, and also thought that if he ever got out of this he was either going to turn the money over to the law or throw it in the nearest trash can. Right now, he didn't care which. They were driving east on Lancaster now, in the lane nearest the island median, cruising along in the Mercedes with topless bars and X-rated bookstores on both sides of them. Two hookers—a black girl in tight jeans and a blond white girl in a leather mini and knee-high boots—lounged on the curb and gave the Mercedes the once-over. You can have the fucking Mercedes, Lackey thought, and the westside crowd and the horse that they rode in on. All that Lackey wanted was Nancy. And if he hadn't tried to make a big score on Percy Hardin's bathhouse job, instead of being satisfied with what he had, Nancy would be safe now. Lackey softly closed his eyes.

"So what Betty did," Hardin said, "was come to me one day and tell me she knew a way out for us. For *us,* she said, when she really meant just for her. Just hire this guy to do away with Marissa, collect on her insurance, and on to the good life. Isn't that the way you put it?" He swiveled his head to sneer.

"I just said I knew someone," Betty said. "The rest was your own doing, don't be putting it off on me." She faced the front and hugged herself inside her raincoat. Lackey suspected that with the wearing off of the cocaine, Betty was getting a chill. On the left, the lights inside the washateria were now visible across the median. Lackey wouldn't have noticed Herb's unless he'd known where to look, next door to the lit-up windows with all the washers and dryers standing in a row.

"You're going through the turnaround in the median up there, aren't you?" Lackey said.

Hardin had already slowed down, pulled over to his left and applied the brakes. "Christ, you knew where we were going all along."

"I didn't," Lackey said. "But now I do. I just figured out a couple of things."

Lackey didn't know what he would have done if the Mercedes trunk hadn't been roomy enough. But it was, big enough for Percy Hardin and Betty Monroe to lie nose to nose, their legs drawn up behind them with their knees touching and even some room to spare. They didn't look very comfortable, and Lackey wondered briefly whether he should place them back to back, or maybe both facing the same direction, one behind the other. He decided against it; Percy and Betty needed to be face to face so they could carry on a conversation. Maybe work out their differences. Hardin's lips were pulled back in a grimace, and Betty looked even less happy about the arrangement than Hardin did.

Lackey closed the trunk lid with a solid thunk and jammed the .45 into his back pocket. He skirted the Mercedes to mount the curb, looking warily right and left. A yellow Nissan was parked nose-on to the curb, the same car that had been there before, and Lackey decided that the Nissan had to belong to Dick the longhair. At least he hoped so. An old Ford Ventura was parked beside the Nissan. Lackey didn't like that; he'd hoped to catch Dick alone. No matter, though, Nancy didn't have any time for Lackey to waste. He pushed the door open and entered Herb's.

Dick was seated exactly as he had been on Lackey's last visit, on the same stool, in fact, with his elbows behind him on the bar, his ankle resting on his knee, and his shin stuck out at an angle. He was dressed the same, too, in a khaki shirt open to the third button. He was wearing the same sunglasses and the ends of his greasy hair were touching his collar. His nose was

wrinkled the same as well, as though he were squinting behind the dark lenses. His nose must be frozen
that way, Lackey thought. Jesus, it was as if the guy
was roosting on the barstool.

On the stool beside Dick sat a hooker. At least that's
what the girl looked like—a hooker, a shade on the fat
side with oversized hips, showing thick calves and
heavy thighs in too-tight blue shorts which molded into
the contours of her crotch. She also wore a sleeveless
red and white–striped knit shirt that was about two
sizes too small for her, showing big pillowy breasts
and chubby upper arms. She was a bleached blond and
badly in need of a touchup; a full inch of mouse-brown
hair showed near her scalp. Lackey wondered if she
was over eighteen. It would be a tossup. The jukebox
was playing a rap number, either Vanilla Ice or M. C.
Hammer. Lackey didn't know one rap musician from
the other and wished they'd all go out and get a job.
The blond was vacantly chewing gum and rocking her
foot in time to the music. She wore sandals with medium heels.

Lackey skirted the tables and approached the bar.
No one was visible except for Dick and the blond, and
Lackey was pretty sure there was no place inside the
club for anybody to hide. There might have been a
back office, but there didn't seem to be any interior
doors. The odor of stale smoke mixed with the odor
of stale beer.

Dick allowed his jaw to slack for a heartbeat, then
resumed his deadpan look. The girl regarded Lackey
with a mild curiosity in her gaze. Dick raised a hand
in her direction. "This dude ain't after no trim,
Paula." The girl lowered her gaze and chomped down
on her wad of gum. When Lackey had stopped a few
feet away, Dick said to him, "I told you I'd get back
to you, friend."

The guy's pretty good, Lackey thought. But what
had happened at Frank Nichols's place had only one

explanation, this longhair had been talking to somebody. If Lackey had thought things out, he wouldn't
have gone to Percy Hardin's to begin with, he'd have
come straight here. But he was sort of glad he hadn't;
if anything bad had happened to Nancy, both Hardin
and this longhaired bastard were going to pay.
"Yeah," Lackey said. "You were going to get back to
me. Through Frank. You got back to somebody else
first, didn't you?"

Dick scratched his sunken, hairless chest. "I don't
know who you mean."

Lackey touched his forearm through the bandage; it
was sore as hell, but he thought he could still throw a
righthanded punch. "I think you'd better figure out
who I mean," Lackey said.

Dick lifted his narrow rump from the stool and
hooked one heel over the stool's rung. "You pushing
me? Man, I'm just in here running my business. That's
fucking all." He flattened his hand, palm down, and
made a sideways, that's-the-end-of-it motion.

"Well, let's say I am pushing you," Lackey said.
"And let's say that if you don't start talking to me,
I'm going to do worse than that."

Dick glanced at the hooker and snickered, then said
to Lackey, "I think you better go back where you come
from. You don't know what you're fucking with."

Lackey grabbed Dick's collar in both hands and
yanked the skinny guy forward, holding Dick's nose a
half-inch from his own as he said, "You probably already know your buddy killed Frank Nichols, but you
might not know about the lady he took. I don't have
any time to fuck around with you, Dick. Understand?" Visible in the corner of Lackey's vision, the
hooker's jaw dropped. Her gum clung to her lower
teeth.

Dick lightly placed his hands on Lackey's wrists and
smiled, a narrow smile without much friendliness.

"Hey, cowboy, take it easy. You want to know something, just ask nice. There ain't no need for this shit."

Lackey had expected the guy to pull a knife or something. He released the collar and lowered his hands. "The guy you talked to. I want to know how to find him."

Dick raised both hands, palms out. "Sure. Hey, sure, no problem. Problems I don't need. I got the guy's name and address right back here." Still smiling, his expression earnest, Dick circled around behind the bar. "Right under here, I got an address book." He bent down and reached underneath a counter.

The stunt nearly worked. Lackey had been expecting a fight, and the longhair's attitude was something he hadn't been ready for. It was the hooker who gave the stunt away. As Dick bent over, her gaze flicked at Lackey, then instantaneously downward. It was just enough.

Lackey put both hands on the bar and vaulted over; a dull ache throbbed in his injured forearm. As he came over the top, he lashed out with both feet and kicked Dick in the ribs and side of the neck. Dick uttered a startled grunt and both men fell headlong into a stack of empty beer cartons. The boxes scattered like bowling pins. Dick had been bringing a little revolver up from under the counter, and his gun now dropped from his fingers and clattered down between two of the wooden slats which lined the floor. As he went down on top of the longhair, Lackey dug for his .45, brought the big army pistol out, pressed the end of the barrel against the longhair's chin. Dick froze with his fist cocked beside his ear.

"You fuck," Dick said.

Lackey rose to his feet and glanced over his shoulder. The blond's fat bottom jiggled as she made for the exit. "Hold it, sweetie," Lackey said. She halted, then retreated to the bar and sat down. Her eyes were wide and round as dinner plates.

Lackey grabbed Dick by the arm and hauled him to his feet. The longhair nervously rubbed the back of his neck. Lackey bent down and picked up the revolver from between the slats. It was a chrome-plated .38 with a bone-white handle. Lackey dropped the extra gun into his pocket.

"So you'll know," Lackey said, "I'll shoot you in a heartbeat. I got things at stake you wouldn't understand. Now, you found out who I was the second I left here yesterday, if you didn't already know, and then you told the guy that did the things I'm taking the heat for. Now the guy's got a woman with him. Where is he?"

Dick's upper lip curled. "Man, I ain't worried about no cunt."

Lackey pistol-whipped Dick across the jaw. Dick's head snapped back and an ugly red welt appeared. "Well, let's say you'd better start worrying about her," Lackey said. "You got two seconds." He put the .45 against Dick's chin and clicked the hammer back.

The glance that Dick gave was almost bored and showed no fear at all. The longhair was measuring the odds. Lackey'd say this, old Dick had some guts. Finally Dick said, "Everett Wilson. Two blocks north of Sylvania, half a block from Northeast Twenty-eighth Street. There's an apartment building. Up the front stairs, second door on the right. The building's about to get condemned, there ain't nobody else living there except two old women on the first floor."

Lackey put more pressure on the .45. The barrel pressed deeper into the longhair's skin. "You're dead if you're lying to me," Lackey said.

"I ain't lying. You're too fucking tough for me to lie to." Dick's tone said that he didn't think Lackey was tough at all.

Lackey stepped back and let his gaze roam from

Dick to the hooker and back again. "Well, now I got to figure out what to do with you two," Lackey said. "No way can I have you calling anybody."

Lackey sort of hoped that the blond teenage hooker bathed regularly. He found a quarter in his pocket and dropped it into the phone slot. The pay phone was in a small strip shopping center on Lancaster, a half-mile east of Herb's, attached to a wall outside a Wyatt's Cafeteria. The midnight blue Mercedes sat behind him at the curb with its engine running. Faint trails of exhaust rose from its tailpipes.

He didn't really have any reason to think that the hooker *didn't* bathe, but as she'd climbed awkwardly into the Mercedes trunk he'd glanced down at her feet. Her thick ankles and the portions of her feet visible between the straps on her sandals were grimy. If she hadn't had a bath lately, things inside the trunk were going to get pretty ripe. Lackey had turned Betty Monroe over to face the hooker because it hadn't looked as though Betty and Percy Hardin were getting along too well. With Betty, Percy, and the hooker in the trunk, Lackey had measured the trunk's interior walls with his gaze, then done the same to Dick the long-hair. He'd decided that Dick wasn't going to fit. He'd had them unload, then had stood by with his gun ready while Dick muscled the spare tire out and set it on the curb. It was still a tight fit, but they'd made it. He'd almost put Dick and Hardin together, but when the longhair had said to Percy, "Man, you rich pricks are really fucking dumb, running your mouths," Lackey had decided against it. If he'd laid the two down together, Dick might've bitten Hardin's nose or something. So, while Lackey was now using the pay phone, Dick lay at the front of the trunk, nearest the back seat, with Hardin at the rear and the women in between. Lackey hoped to hell that the Mercedes didn't have a flat. He called the sheriff's office, asked for

Homicide, then told the detective in Homicide that he wanted Morrison's home telephone number.

"We don't make a practice of that. Something I can do for you?" The voice was deep, with a heavy good-old-boy accent.

Lackey decided that he didn't have time for a bunch of red tape. "This is Lackey Ferguson. So you'll know, I'm in a phone booth and I'm not going to stay on the line long enough for you to get a position on me. I got to talk to Morrison. Or Henley. Either one'll do. But I got to talk to one of them, nobody else."

After the barest hesitation, the cop said, "I can't give you the number, but I can patch you through."

"No soap," Lackey said. "If the next words out of your mouth aren't one of them's number, I'm hanging up."

There was another half-second pause, then, "Here's Morrison's. Three-five-eight, six-four-oh-two. Listen, Ferguson, maybe you should—"

Lackey disconnected, found another quarter, and punched in the number. As the ringing sounded over the phone, he stuck his free hand into his pocket and crossed his ankles. Finally there was a click and Morrison's talking-down-to-you tenor said hello.

"This is Lackey Ferguson. How you doin'?"

"Well I'll be damned. I'm not doin' too good, Lackey. I'd be doing a lot better if you'd quit screwing around and come see me."

"Well I might just do that," Lackey said.

"Now you're talking, bud. Hey, I'd even come downtown right now, if you'd meet me."

"Not exactly that," Lackey said. "Listen, I got a lot of trouble right now because of all this. I think you know I never touched that woman." He glanced toward the street. A forty-foot trailer rig rumbled west on Lancaster; across the median in the eastbound lanes were a little foreign car and a city bus. The bus driver applied the air brakes and stopped at a passenger loading zone.

"Well, sure, that's something we got to talk about," Morrison said. "Whether or not you did it. Anything you got to say, believe me, I'm all ears."

"I'll bet. Listen, I'm driving a Mercedes, license number"—he squinted toward the curb—"six-seven-two–TWD. It's blue, but so dark it's probably going to look black at night. In half an hour I'm going to come through the intersection of Sylvania Avenue and Northeast Twenty-eighth Street. North, I'll be going north on Sylvania. Why don't you bring a few guys and wait for me?"

"I'll be glad to," Morrison said.

"I'll bet on that, too. Oh, yeah, Detective Morrison, I got a few hostages. A couple of them, well, they might not be worth much ransom. But you got to take what you can get, you know?"

21

Nancy Cuellar lay wide awake in the dark, her ankles and wrists aching and her knee joints stiff as rusted hinges. The crazy's head lay inches from her face on the mattress. He was snoring gently. His onion breath made Nancy want to gag. Nancy worked her fingers, straining for some sort of grip on her bonds for the umpteenth time, even though rationality told her she was wasting her energy. As she bit her lower lip against the pain in her wrists, someone knocked loudly on the apartment door.

Nancy froze. God, could she be off her rocker? Nobody could possibly be coming here. Maybe she'd finally gotten so bone-weary and sick of hoping that she was having a dream.

The knocking resumed, *bang, bang, bang*. Nancy opened her mouth and sucked in her breath to scream.

Quick as thought, a rough hand clamped over her mouth. The scream died in her throat. Her breath flowed slowly out between thick rigid fingers. The crazy kept one hand over her mouth as he raised up on one elbow. The knocking continued.

In a gruff whisper, the man said, "Use your head, girl. I don't want to hurt my baby." He shifted on the mattress, reached down to the floor and brought up a snubnosed pistol. His head was cocked in an attentive attitude. The knocking quickened in tempo and increased in volume.

The bedsprings creaked as the crazy climbed to his

feet. He reached once again down to the floor, then stood squattily erect. Before Nancy had time to wonder what he was doing, he'd laid his pistol aside and stuffed the rags back into her mouth, and was knotting the strip of cloth behind her head. She'd forgotten how foul the gag tasted; she pressed her tongue helplessly outward. The crazy finished tying the cloth, then stood back and retrieved the gun from the mattress. "Be just a minute, girl," he said, then crept noiselessly out of the bedroom.

Prison had made a light sleeper out of Everett Wilson; in the joint, a guy never knew when some stinking lousy pervert was going to sneak up and grab his pecker or something. Everett moved quietly out of the bedroom on stocking feet and closed the door gently behind him. Who in hell would be knocking on somebody's door at this time of night? He crept to the front of the apartment, stood close to the door and turned his ear to the wood.

The knocking paused, and then resumed. Some nutty bastard trying to beat the door down. Trying to pester Everett while Everett was with his baby. Everett stood back and leveled the Smith & Wesson at chest level. Blow the fucker away if he had to.

The knocking ceased abruptly, and a tenor voice out on the landing said, "I know you're home, Everett. Your car's outside. It's me, Sam Lincoln."

Everett's sloping forehead bunched. The voice had sounded like a nigger's. Lincoln, Lincoln, Everett thought. Oh, yeah. Jesus, the parole officer.

Everett jammed the pistol into his back pocket. "Hey, yeah. Yeah, sure, I 'as asleep."

"Well you sure go to bed early," Lincoln said. "It's only nine. Open up."

"Sure. Sure, just a minute." Everett clicked on the overhead light and looked hastily around him, letting his gaze linger fleetingly on the rickety breakfast table, the couch, the ancient black-and-white TV like a blank unseeing eye. Nothing of Nancy's laying around. Everett moistened his palm with his tongue and slicked back his hair, then clicked the latch and opened the door.

It was Lincoln, all right, tall and thin, his hide the color of a chŏcolate malt, shaved clean, wearing a short-sleeved white shirt and dark slacks. A beeper hung from the parole officer's belt. Lincoln swept Everett head to toe with an uppity-nigger, I'm-suspicious gaze. "You took your time about it," Lincoln said.

There was a woman standing beside the parole officer. A little-bitty good-looking thing she was, short dark hair done at the beauty parlor, an alert erectness about her, wearing a dark blue sleeveless dress and white high-heeled shoes. Matthews, Everett thought. Sure, Dr. Anna Matthews, the psychiatrist broad. Old Everett had damn sure fooled her. Had her thinking Everett Wilson wouldn't hurt a fly. She'd quit seeing him just when Everett had been pretty sure the psychiatrist was about to offer him a little pussy. Ain't got time for you no more, girl, Everett thought. My baby's right in the next room.

"Good evening, Everett," Dr. Anna Matthews said. Her gaze was cool and confident, the all-business professional lady. Bet she's one hot bitch in private, Everett thought. Sometime he just might try some of that. Would have to be sure his baby didn't find out, though.

Samuel Lincoln was already more than a little pissed over having to go with the highbrow psychiatrist to Everett Wilson's apartment, and Wilson letting them cool their heels while he took his time about coming to the door hadn't helped Lincoln's mood one bit. If Dr. Anna Matthews wanted to go over Lincoln's head to get her way, that was one thing. Lincoln figured that everybody had to make a living, and he really couldn't blame the psychiatrist for not wanting to give up the easy money from the state. But going so far as to have Lincoln's supervisor order him to go to Wilson's apartment with her—the business about Anna Matthews being afraid to go alone was a lot of shit, all these fucking feminists wanted to act like a man until falling back on their gender suited their purpose better—making him go with her was pure harassment. Nothing but an I'll-show-you attitude from the highbrow psychiatrist, just because Lincoln wouldn't approve any more state-paid counseling sessions.

Sam Lincoln had already made up his mind what he was going to do about it. Actually, he was going to do *two* things. The first thing had to do with the completed application that at the moment lay in Lincoln's top desk drawer, the application for a transfer to the Texas Department of Corrections as a prison guard. The pay was about the same—more, in fact, when you counted the overtime hours one could log sitting up in the guard tower listening to the radio, subbing for somebody who wanted to take off to visit a sick relative or knock off a little strange or something—and there weren't a third of the headaches. If some guy who was in the joint gave you any shit, all you had to do was lock the bastard up in solitary. None of this running around in the middle of the night with some uppity female psychiatrist who had something to prove, and none of the mountains of paperwork to justify the reason you wouldn't let your parolees work for some sex pervert like that Lackey Ferguson guy. Lincoln had known there was something funny about that contractor the moment he'd laid eyes on him, and the fact that Mr. Lackey Ferguson was a pervert murderer came as no surprise to Samuel Lincoln.

The second thing that Samuel Lincoln was going to do was cut Dr. Anna Matthews's water off where Parolee Everett Thomas Wilson was concerned. Shut off the psychiatrist's easy state money for good. How you like that, Ms. Highbrow Feminist? Teach you a thing or two about going over Samuel Lincoln's head. Dr. Anna Matthews was going to find out something about getting fucked around within the system, and nobody alive could do a better job of fucking with somebody than a State of Texas parole officer.

What Lincoln was going to do was pretty simple: He was going to turn Parolee Everett Thomas Wilson back into *Inmate* Everett Thomas Wilson, Number Whatever-the-fuck. Poof, shazam, quick as a flash. All Sam Lincoln had to do was figure out what violation Parolee Wilson had committed, and that was going to be easy as pie. Every parolee alive had a joint laying around their place, that or a pistol, little things that a parole officer didn't pay any mind unless he wanted to fuck with the guy. And if the parolee didn't have any dope or any guns, he was a lead-pipe cinch to be out drinking coffee or beer with some other ex-con. Who the hell would drink coffee or beer with one of these assholes but another asshole, huh? Consorting with felons was an easy rap to hang on a parolee, all you had to do was follow the guy. It was tough shit that it wasn't Parolee Wilson's fault that he was about to have his parole revoked. That was just the way the cookie crumbled. See how this Dr. Anna Matthews liked having to visit old Wilson down at Eastham work farm. Let her do a little driving to earn her fucking money, huh?

So, as Dr. Anna Matthews was saying, "It seems we're going to be working together again, Everett," and flashing her office-visit smile—

and as Parolee Everett Wilson was giving her a dumb-convict grin while saying, "Hey. Hey, that's nice, Miss Matthews," and holding a chair for her to sit at his rickety table—

Parole Officer Samuel Lincoln was having a look around, casting his gaze into the tiny kitchen, looking up at the overhead cabinets which showed cracked and yellowing white paint. The kitchen was always the best place to start. Likely there'd be a lid of grass hidden in the cabinet or behind the sink. A lid, or even a bottle of prescription medicine that poor dumbass Wilson had borrowed from some other asshole instead of going to the doctor on his own, that was all Lincoln needed to start the ball rolling. Goodbye, Parolee Wilson, and goodbye, Dr. Anna Matthews, once and for fucking all.

Lincoln paused just outside the kitchen and said, "While you two are visiting I'm going to look around some. Just routine. No objections, huh?"

Parolee Wilson said quickly, from his seat at the table across from the psychiatrist, "Naw. Sure, sure, go ahead."

Which Lincoln knew was what they all said, but there'd been a quaver in Wilson's voice and a slight shiftiness about him that said it really wasn't okay at all. None of these bastards wanted Big Daddy poking around. Lincoln felt a surge of satisfaction as he strolled into the kitchen. The guy was hiding something, okay, and it was up to Lincoln to find it. And Samuel Lincoln hadn't missed the disapproving glance that the petite psychiatrist had thrown in his direction, either. That's okay, too, little lady, Samuel Lincoln thought. That's okay, you're about to get yours.

So while Dr. Anna Matthews was saying, "Now I don't really think we have anything particularly difficult to deal with. We're just trying to make your adjustment easier on you," as she sat primly erect with her legs crossed—

and while Everett Wilson was saying, "Hey, I understand. That's what I'm wanting to do myself, make sure I don't do nothing wrong no more" (which Lincoln understood was the standard ex-convict response, and also knew was a lot of bullshit)—

Samuel Lincoln was opening and closing overhead kitchen cabinet doors, having a looksee at clay plates and saucers in untidy, cylindrical stacks, at unmatched glasses and cups turned upside down on spread-out newspaper which served as cabinet lining. Standing up behind the plates was the standard ex-convict half pint of whiskey—Roaring Springs Kentucky Bourbon, Lincoln thought, how do they drink that rotgut?—but nothing else. The rules were pretty clear on drinking, the parolee had to be boozing *excessively* for it to be a violation, and a half pint wasn't enough to make a case. Lincoln decided to leave the whiskey alone for the time being. If all else failed, though, it was likely that he could drop by late at night sometime and catch Parolee Wilson drunk on his ass. That should do the trick. They *all* got drunk, one hundred percent of the bastards. Lincoln closed the door on the whiskey and opened the next cabinet. Jesus, was it . . . ? Lincoln smiled. Yeah, it was.

A prescription bottle, half-full of capsules with the label turned toward the back of the cabinet. Lincoln stood on tiptoes, withdrew the little vial and turned it around. Christ, no good. Parolee Wilson's name was right there on the label along with the daily dosage and the physician's name and phone number, just like it said in the Parole Board Manual. Lincoln glanced quickly over his shoulder. Dr. Anna Matthews had her back turned, speaking slowly and earnestly, but the parolee was watching Lincoln. Was watching the parole officer, and one corner of Everett Wilson's mouth was twitching. Think it's funny, huh? Lincoln thought. Well, just you wait. He replaced the prescription bottle inside the cabinet, closed the door and retreated from the kitchen into the sitting room.

Anna Matthews droned on in her trained clinical monotone, and Everett Wilson hunched thick shoulders and pretended to be interested in what the psychiatrist was saying, while Lincoln strolled casually around the sofa and ran his hand along the back of the TV set. Sometimes they'd tape something back there. But that wasn't the case with Parolee Wilson. All that

Lincoln got for his effort was a dusty palm. As he distastefully brushed his hands together, Lincoln walked to the rear of the apartment, taking his time, his gaze roaming. He stopped. Aha. The bedroom door was closed.

As Dr. Anna Matthews was saying, ''I think you'll enjoy some of the tests. They're sort of fun, really—''

and Parolee Wilson was scratching his neck underneath his collar—

Samuel Lincoln interrupted by saying loudly, ''Hey. Mind if I have a look in there?'' And pointed toward the bedroom.

Everett Wilson's head swiveled toward the parole officer as if in slow motion. Wilson was smiling, but his eyes were lumps of burnt coal.

Everett had known it was going to come down to this ever since he'd let Lincoln and the psychiatrist in. Had been hoping that it wouldn't, but had known inside that it would. Underneath the white shirt and tie and phony education, Lincoln was just another nigger and too dumb to let well enough alone. Too dumb to keep from poking around in shit. It was too bad about the psychiatrist lady, she hadn't been doing nothing but trying to get to know old Everett a little better. Because of this stupid nigger parole officer, she wasn't going to get the chance.

Everett leaned slightly forward, his hand going behind him, sliding inside his back pocket to touch the handle of the Smith & Wesson. Dr. Anna Matthews was visible in the corner of Everett's eye as he said to Lincoln, ''Sure. Sure, go on in. I ain't hiding nothing.''

Nancy Cuellar lay in the dark, her knees aching, her wrists on fire, her arms feeling as though they might pull out of her shoulder sockets. She strained her ears, but try as she might she couldn't decipher a word of what was being said in the other room. There had been a man's voice, a soft tenor that was easy to distinguish from the crazy's hoarse basso, and, just briefly, there had been a woman's voice. And there had been movement, the scraping of a chair or chairs on the floor.

Whether the newcomers were friend or foe, Nancy didn't have the slightest idea. For all she knew, the man with the tenor voice was the lunatic's sidekick, and at any moment the two of them might burst into the bedroom and take turns raping her. The idea of that happening caused Nancy to whimper into her gag.

There was sudden movement just outside the bedroom, and the tenor voice said something that Nancy couldn't understand even though the voice was louder than before. Then the handle turned with a click and light slanted into the room and the door swung inward. A hand—Nancy wasn't sure in the semilight, but thought it was a black person's hand—felt its way around the jamb, fumbled with the wall switch, then flicked the switch upward. Nancy blinked in sudden illumination.

It was a black man, a tall, slim, businesslike fellow in a short-sleeved white shirt and dark slacks, and he was staring at Nancy as though he was seeing a ghost. His jaw dropped. His eyes widened.

The man said, "What are—?"

A loud crack sounded, like a mallet striking hardwood. Something slammed into the side of the black man's neck; he pitched sideways into the doorframe as if he'd been kicked by a horse. Blood spurted from a wound in his neck and coated his white cotton shirt with grisly red. He sank to his knees and held out his hands to Nancy in supplication. His mouth formed silent pleadings.

The crazy man, eyes wild, stumpy-ugly body in a crouch, materialized in the doorway behind the black man. In one hand the lunatic carried a pistol; his other

hand was clamped onto a woman's wrist. The woman
was tiny and attractive, wearing a navy blue dress and
high heels. Her short hair was trimmed like a cover
girl's, and her eyes were wide in terror. The crazy
dragged his captive along behind him as he deliber-
ately circled the crouching black man. The black man
raised a hand, palm out. The crazy shot him in the
chest. The black man tumbled over backwards, kicked
violently, then was still. The odor of burnt gunpowder
hung in the air.

As Nancy watched helplessly from the bed, the
crazy stroked the tiny woman's hair. Tears were
streaming down the lunatic's cheeks and he was sniffling.

As Everett Wilson raised up from the table and shot
the parole officer through the neck (dumb nigger son
of a bitch, you just couldn't let it alone), a red haze
formed over his vision. He watched Lincoln pitch
sideways into the doorframe as though watching a
movie with a color filter over the projector lens. Everett closed his eyes and shook his head, then looked
around. Where in hell was he?

A small woman (man?) seated across a table was
staring at him, a woman (man?) whom he'd never laid
eyes on before. Wait a minute. Yes he had seen her,
but . . . Oh, it was his mother (father?), he'd finally
found her. Had known he'd find her someday, had felt
it in his bones. Where are your long pants, mama, and
how come your hair's fixed like that? How come your
hair's not an inch long and sticking up like quills, the
way Daddy Eli told me?

Was mama going to punish him? He didn't think he
could take that. Just like Daddy Eli, with the woman
pinning his arms while Daddy Eli tied his feet to the
foot of the bed and yanked his Tuffy corduroy trousers
down around his knees. *No, no, please, I'll be good.*
But pleading hadn't stopped Daddy Eli, had it? Hadn't

stopped him from sliding the inch-thick piece of wood in between his little dingus *(Oh, I promise, I'll never call it my dingus again)* and his scrotum, steadying the nail with grimy fingers, raising the hammer while he glared his hatred, then bringing the hammer down. Everett could never take that again. He had to stop mama from hurting him.

He'd show her. He'd show her what he could . . . He grabbed her by the wrist *(Come on, mama, I'll show you how good I can be)*, and pulled her behind him into the bedroom. *What's that nigger doing on his knees?* Everett thought. *Down on his knees in our house, and Daddy Eli told me mama don't cotton to niggers nohow. I'll show that fucking nigger.* He shot the nigger through the heart, watched as the nigger fell over dead, then turned to mama and stroked her hair. Maybe she wouldn't hurt him now. He was crying. Jesus, sometimes Daddy Eli would hurt him just for crying.

"Please, mama, don't hurt me," Everett said.

Mama (Daddy?) lifted her gaze, not saying anything. She hadn't made up her mind whether she'd punish little Everett or not. She wanted more proof that he was serious. She wanted more . . . Well, he'd show her. He knew what she did near every night, knew because Daddy Eli had told him how his mama used to get down on her knees and suck on them things. She hated to suck on them things, Daddy Eli said, but them men used to give her money.

He placed a hand on mama's shoulder and lowered her down into a crouch. He was afraid at first that she'd stop him, expected mama to grab him any minute, throw him down on the bed and begin tying his feet to the posts. But she didn't. Silently, without a word of protest, mama knelt in front of him. That was good. Maybe she wouldn't hurt him after all.

Everett looked at the pistol in his hand as though he'd never seen it before, then gently stroked mama's cheek with the barrel. He moved the pistol slowly toward her mouth and touched its end to her lips. Finally, joyfully, Everett slid the barrel in between her teeth to touch her tongue. "It's for you to suck on, mama," he said.

Her gaze met his as she drew her lips tight around the gun. She liked it. Oh, she liked it, did she ever. Did she . . .

Everett closed his eyes in rapture as he squeezed the trigger.

As the crazy's arm jerked with the gun's recoil and the back of the tiny woman's head exploded, Nancy Cuellar whimpered into her gag. She tasted bile as it erupted into her mouth and further soaked the wadded cloth which was packed against her tongue. Bone splintered and fragments sailed through the air. A hot red mist dampened the sheets; something wet clung to Nancy's forehead. The tiny woman disappeared below the foot of the bed as she fell to the floor.

The lunatic seemed confused. He raised the pistol to squint down the barrel, and for an instant Nancy thought—oh, God, was hoping against hope—that he was going to shoot himself. Then he lowered the gun to dangle by his hip as he approached the bed. His movements were wooden and the tears rolled down to fill the crevices in his face like gutter runoff.

22

Lackey had expected a few cops, but the mob scene
waiting at the corner of Sylvania and Northeast 28th
nearly blew his mind. As the Mercedes left Airport
Freeway to go north on Sylvania, the flashing rooflights were visible from two blocks away. Swirling red
reflections danced on the neighboring buildings like
searchlights at a Hollywood opening. Jesus, Lackey
thought, there must be twenty patrol cars down there.
He pictured a SWAT team, just like the ones he'd seen
in the movies, clambering upward on cables like Green
Berets, running across the rooftops to stretch out in
the prone position, squint through infrared scope-
sights, and train high-powered rifles on the Mercedes.
Lackey told Percy Hardin to pull over.

After Lackey had gotten off the phone, he'd positioned Dick the longhair and the blond teenage hooker
in the front seat with Hardin, with the girl in the middle. He didn't want the hooker by the door because
she was close to freaking out. Lackey didn't know if
it was the tension or the need of a fix—it could have
been either one—but he couldn't chance her throwing
the door open and diving out into the road. Dick the
longhair, though, acted like the whole thing was a
stroll in the park, sitting back with his knee propped
against the dashboard. Betty Monroe was in the back
seat with Lackey where he could watch her from the
corner of his eye as he held the .45 trained loosely on
Percy Hardin. As the Mercedes moved over to stop by

the curb, Dick the longhair said, "Jesus Christ, Fourth of July. You really are into some *shit*."

Lackey reached down to the floorboard and picked up the phone. He held the receiver and handed the end of the spring-coiled cord to Betty. "Run this up front to Mr. Hardin," Lackey said, then got a firmer grip on the .45 as he said to Hardin, "Plug in this doodad when she hands it to you."

Betty leaned forward and passed up the cord. As Hardin reached behind him to pull the connector over the top of the seat, Betty let the front of her raincoat fall away to reveal her legs, batted her eyes in Lackey's direction and ran the tip of her tongue across her upper lip. She'd gone through the same routine four or five times since Lackey had let her out of the trunk, and Lackey supposed that it would never occur to her that some guys might not be turned on. He'd almost felt sorry for her a couple of times, then had recalled that a big part of the trouble that he—and particularly Nancy—were in was Betty's doing, and hadn't felt sorry for Betty anymore. He pressed a button on the phone and heard a dial tone. He punched in the number for the sheriff's department.

Dick the longhair was watching him and now said, "That's some deal, that phone. They got any way to wiretap that? Shit, I may get me one."

Lackey told the sheriff's operator to put him through to Homicide.

"Hey," Dick said. "Hey, rich guy."

Hardin's chin moved to one side. "Huh? Yes?"

"That phone," Dick said. "They got any way to wiretap that sonofabitch?"

"No," Hardin said, "they'd have to record the person you were calling. This car phone's wireless, they couldn't tap in on it unless they got on the same frequency. I'm no radio buff, but that's what they tell me. Of course, they could get a court order and have the phone company record you."

"I ain't worried about that shit," Dick said. "I'm talking about them tapping you without no court order. Jesus Christ, could I use a safe phone. What's it run you a month?"

Over the phone, the same good-old-boy voice that Lackey had heard earlier now said into his ear, "Homicide."

"Depends on the usage," Hardin said. "There's a basic fee, and then you—"

"Hey." Lackey flattened his palm over the mouthpiece. "Hey, you guys mind?" Dick looked out the window and Hardin shifted in his seat while Lackey said to the homicide detective, "Excuse me, a couple of guys were talking. Hey, this is Lackey Ferguson."

"Yeah. Yeah, Ferguson, I thought you were meeting Detective Morrison."

"I'm looking at him," Lackey said. "Him and half the police force. Listen, put this call through to Morrison in the county car. Oh, yeah, I'm on a car phone, sitting in the back seat of Mr. Percy Hardin's Mercedes a half-block up the street from where all those cops are parked. Don't fuck around trying to trace me, huh?" He never would have used the *f*-word around Nancy, but he didn't suppose Betty Monroe would mind, and knew good and well that the hooker wouldn't.

There was a slight hesitation, and Lackey pictured the homicide guy thinking of putting on a trace, then changing his mind. A series of clicks followed.

Dick snapped his head around to face Lackey. "You holding, huh?"

Lackey nodded.

"How much it run you, rich guy?" Dick said.

"Well, there's an installation fee," Hardin said, "then it's about the same as a phone in your house."

"Pretty slick, huh?" Dick said. "Jesus, I got to get me one of them. They got a deposit? My credit at the phone company ain't so hot, tell you the truth."

On the line, Morrison's voice said, "Ferguson?" His tone was urgent.

Lackey said, "Hey, you guys." Then he said to Morrison, "Hi." He sat up straighter in the seat to peer over Hardin's shoulder through the windshield. The squad cars were lined up on both sides of the street, rooflights flashing, and illuminated in the swirling red glow was an ambulance. Lackey supposed that there was a fire truck nearby as well. Uniformed policemen milled around and stood in small groups near the squad cars.

"We guarantee your safety if you'll surrender," Morrison said. He sounded as though he were reading from a manual.

"No way," Lackey said.

"Yeah? Well, what're you up to?"

"Right now I'm looking at you. We just pulled over to the curb, two blocks south of you on Sylvania."

"That's you, huh?" Morrison said. "Yeah, we saw you. What you got in mind?"

"Well, I got in mind doing something that I need you to back me up on," Lackey said.

"Ferguson, you're crazy as a loon. Just a minute."

There was static on the line, then a new voice that Lackey didn't recognize at first said, "Ferguson, this is Assistant District Attorney Favor. Now I'm not offering any deals, but I assure you it'll go a lot easier on you if you'll quit fucking around and just come up here quietly."

Lackey blinked. Oh, yeah, Favor. The chubby young D.A. who'd recorded the interview, the first time Morrison and Henley had taken Lackey downtown. Lackey said, "Hold on a minute." He offered the phone over the seat to Hardin. "Talk to this guy," Lackey said. "Tell him I might blow your head off." Hardin shot a wide-eyed glance over the seat. Lackey gestured with the .45.

Hardin took the phone. "This is Percival Hardin. If

you do anything to endanger me, I'm holding you responsible."

Hardin cocked his head and held the receiver jammed against his ear. Lackey imagined that Favor was giving instructions on how to handle the lunatic desperado in the back seat. After Hardin had listened for a few seconds, Lackey said, "Gimme the phone back."

He took the receiver and heard Favor say, "—and above all, don't act like you're afraid. These guys all—"

"This is Lackey again," Lackey said.

There was sudden stony silence.

"I got a whole car full back here," Lackey said. "Now here's what I want you to do." He'd seen a movie a few years back, *Dog Day Afternoon,* where Al Pacino had held a bunch of hostages in a bank and kept the police at bay. Lackey wondered if he sounded anything like Pacino.

"You're really piling up the charges, Ferguson," Favor said. "Endangering citizens."

"Yeah, well, I used to be a citizen myself, before you started fucking me around. Now I got Mr. Hardin, you just talked to him, and I got Miss Monroe, that's Mrs. Hardin's sister, and some friends of theirs." Lackey was getting really hot under the collar. Nancy didn't have much time, if she had any at all.

"What friends?" Favor said. "We need to know."

Lackey covered the mouthpiece. "What's your name, teen queen?"

The hooker said in a small frightened voice, "Paula White." Probably an alias, Lackey thought.

"You, Dick," Lackey said. "You, too."

Dick sneered. "Man, I got a rap sheet long as Johnny Wadd's dick."

"Yeah," Lackey said. "Yeah, you got a point." Then, into the phone, "Mr. and Mrs. Richard White. Couple of socially prominent friends of the Hardins, you hear me? Now first, you tell those guys to douse those roof flashers. No more lights, you hear me? Or else." Lackey wasn't sure "or else" what, but thought he sounded pretty good. "You got thirty seconds to get it dark up there," Lackey said.

"Now listen, Ferguson," Favor said.

"You got twenty-five seconds," Lackey said.

"You don't go around telling—"

"Twenty seconds."

"Now hold on," Favor said. "We're doing it. Yeah, we're doing it, right now."

"I'm watching you," Lackey said. Up ahead there was a flurry of activity as cops disbanded their huddled groups and sprinted toward squad cars. One set of rooflights stopped flashing and went dark, then another. In a few seconds there was nothing visible over the nose of the Mercedes other than the tall illuminated streetlamps at Sylvania and Northeast 28th Street. The darkened outlines of the squad cars and ambulance blended and mixed with other darkened shapes. "That's better," Lackey said.

"Glad you approve," Favor said.

Lackey let it pass, the fat little D.A. being cute. "So now," Lackey said, "we're about to drive past you, real slow. You-all get in line behind us and follow."

"Follow where?" Favor said.

"We're going to surround a guy."

"What guy? You're not really in a position to be funny about this."

You're not, either, Lackey thought. "I don't have time to go into it. Just follow." Lackey pressed the button to disconnect, then glanced at Betty Monroe—who was still showing a lot of thigh and shooting sultry glances in Lackey's direction—as he said to Percy Hardin, "Okay. Now we're going to drive. Not over twenty miles an hour, Mr. Hardin. I'll be watching the speedometer." Lackey bent slightly forward and now directed his words to Dick the longhair. "Dick, you give Mr. Hardin the directions. We're going to make a couple of blocks, and then we're going to park in front of your buddy's apartment house. Those cops are going to follow us."

Dick was watching Lackey. The longhair's expression was respectful. "I'll say this," Dick said. "You got some cods. Say, what you going to do if old Everett ain't home?"

Lackey hadn't thought of that. He bunched his eyebrows together. "Worry about it when the time comes, I guess," Lackey Ferguson said.

23

Lackey had been improvising as he went along, and as the caravan approached the condemned apartment house he had still another idea. He told Hardin to pull over, and after the line of cars followed by the ambulance were parked at the curb, one behind the other, he called the sheriff's department and told the homicide detective to put him through to Morrison again. As he listened to the series of clicks and buzzes on the line, Lackey scanned the apartment building with his gaze. It was a two-story brownstone with a second-floor landing. Streetlamps illuminated a ragged, unkept lawn with stalks of Johnson grass waving here and there and with runners of Bermuda infesting the sidewalks. An iron staircase bisected the front of the building and led up to the landing. Light streamed from the window of the second-floor apartment, two doors to the right of the stairs. Be in there, babe, Lackey thought. There was a final click on the line, and Morrison said, "Yeah?"

"This is Ferguson. I got problems."

"You ain't shittin'," Morrison said.

"I got to get inside that apartment up there," Lackey said, "without getting shot by you guys." Visible ahead of the Mercedes, a dark sedan was parked across the street from a little foreign car. A white Volvo, Lackey thought. Bingo.

"That's easy," Morrison said. "Just get me to

promise that we'll leave you alone while you go in. Hell, I'll promise. That ain't no problem.''

"Stop being funny," Lackey said. "What's going to happen is, I'm going to release these people here and send them back to you."

There was a rustling inside the car, a slight intake of breath by Betty Monroe on Lackey's right, a nearly inaudible click as Percy Hardin undid his seatbelt. Dick the longhair said in a stage whisper, "Man, you fucking *crazy*?"

"Except one," Lackey said. "Mr. Hardin up here's staying with me."

Directly in front of Lackey, Percy Hardin froze like a statue.

"This is Favor," a different voice said, and Lackey pictured the porky D.A. grabbing the phone, taking charge, and suspected that Detective Morrison wasn't too in love with Favor at the moment. "Now, no deals unless you release all of 'em, Ferguson," Favor said.

"You're not getting it," Lackey said. "I'm not looking for any deals."

"Tell you what," Favor said. "How about if Detective Morrison takes Mr. Hardin's place? How about that?" Muffled and in the background, Morrison's voice said, "Fuck *you*."

"No soap," Lackey said.

"Well, then," Favor said, "no deals. Safe passage back here to give yourself up. That's all I'm guaranteeing, and you're lucky you're getting that."

Lackey gently closed his eyes and listened to static crackle. Finally Lackey said, "Listen, you dumb bastard. I'm going in that apartment house because the guy you're looking for is in there, and if he hasn't already he's about to hurt my girl. Now, you shut up. Not another word until I'm through talking, you hear?"

There were five seconds of static-punctuated silence, after which Favor said, "Go ahead."

"Now after I let these people go," Lackey said, "we're pulling on ahead a little bit. You stay parked right where you are. Then Mr. Hardin and me, we're going in. You don't get out of your car, any of you, until we're on that second-floor landing up there. If anybody's door opens before then, Mr. Hardin's a dead guy. After we get up there, I don't care what you do."

"What the hell are you going to do once you get up there?" Favor said.

Lackey thought that one over, then said, "If I knew I'd tell you. Depends on what I find. I'm signing off, now. See you, huh?"

Lackey disconnected. Except for Percy Hardin, who remained frozen in place with his gaze to the front, the passengers looked at Lackey expectantly. Dick the longhair's nose was wrinkled below his sunglasses. The hooker's jaw was moving from side to side. Betty Monroe actually looked a little bit disappointed.

"Okay, time to unload," Lackey said. Then, as Dick opened the front passenger door and the interior lights flashed on, Lackey said, "Wait a minute." Then, he said to Betty Monroe, "You ought to think about some things. You really ought to. Now, if I go up there and find . . . well, the worst thing I can find, then Mr. Hardin's not going to have a thing to worry about, ever again. I'm going to kill him. But if things work out and Nancy's all right, then that guy up there's going to match the physical evidence they've got on your sister's murderer. Not even Morrison and Favor can get around it, he's the guy. Now you can do what you want to, Betty, but if I was you I'd be telling those cops a few things. Kind of cover your fanny, you know?"

Understanding crossed Betty's classic features. She glanced to the front as Percy Hardin turned in his seat and said, *"Betty."*

She grinned an impish grin. "It's something to think about," she said. "Bye, bye, Percy. You have a good time, you hear?"

* * *

About halfway up the walk in the direction of the staircase, Lackey began to wonder if Percy Hardin was going to make it. Percy had refused to budge from the car until Lackey had aired back the hammer on the .45, and now Lackey wondered if Hardin wasn't more afraid of the guy in the apartment than he was of Lackey shooting him. Hardin moved as if in a trance, shooting glances back to where the squad cars were parked, his breathing ragged and his eyes wide in fear or shock. His blond hair was falling down and partially covering his eyes, but Hardin didn't seem to notice.

As they approached the foot of the stairs, with Lackey keeping Hardin between him and the squad cars, Hardin shied away and held back. "Anything," Hardin said. "Anything, you name it." He sounded like a man with laryngitis.

Any pity that Lackey might have felt for this guy had died when he'd found Nancy's shoes in Frank Nichols's bedroom. Lackey glanced toward the waiting police cars; he'd have bet all he had at that moment that a scope sight was hidden somewhere and trained in his and Hardin's direction. He grabbed the back of Hardin's knit shirt and bunched the material up in his fist. "I'm taking you up there one way or the other," Lackey said. "Get a move on." He shoved Hardin bodily onto the bottom stair.

Stumbling, grabbing the banister for support, his feet grappling for purchase with a series of metallic thuds, Lackey half-dragged Hardin upward. Hardin wheezed like a cardiac patient. Lackey's arm and shoulder grew numb from the effort, but he wasn't about to release Hardin's collar. The two men had almost reached the top of the stairs when a gunshot sounded.

There wasn't any doubt that it was a pistol shot, a muffled explosion coming from within the lighted

apartment two doors down from the head of the steps.
Lackey's blood was suddenly icewater. Hardin recoiled as though hit with a sledgehammer. Jesus,
thought Lackey, oh, sweet Jesus. He doubled his effort
and yanked Hardin with him up on the landing. Lackey
glanced down at his bandaged forearm; two red wet
spots had soaked through the elastic from underneath.
He hauled his gasping hostage over in front of the
apartment and stood with his back to the door and his
nose an inch from Hardin's nose.

"Be still, you fuck," Lackey snarled. "I'm letting
go of you, and if you move one step I'll shoot you. I
hope you try me, tell you the truth."

One look at Hardin's face told him that he didn't
have to worry about his hostage going anywhere. Hardin's jaw was slack and his eyes were glazed; he didn't
seem to know where he was. Lackey turned his back
on Hardin and leveled the .45 at the doorlock. He
didn't have the slightest idea where to aim, but by God
Lackey Ferguson was going to shoot that fucking lock
until he hit something that knocked the door open.
Come hell or high water, he was going inside that
apartment and tear it apart until he found Nancy.
Without really thinking about it, he reached out and
tried the knob.

The handle turned easily in his grasp and the door
swung inward.

For an instant, Lackey couldn't do anything except
stare at the partially open doorway. He'd been so
charged-up to splinter the wood with bullets that he
nearly fired the pistol anyway. At last, realization
dawned. He turned back to Hardin, who hadn't moved
a muscle. Lackey grabbed the rich man's son by the
upper arm and used Hardin as a shield, shoving the
blubbering hostage in front of him toward the apartment, conscious that he was now in the police line of
fire for the first time since he'd dragged Hardin from
the Mercedes.

Far below and from across the ragged lawn, a voice amplified by a bullhorn said, "Hold it, Ferguson. Right there."

Simultaneously, Hardin clutched both sides of the doorframe and wheezed, "No. Oh, Jesus, please don't."

A rifle cracked and echoed. Something whined past inches from Lackey's ear and thunked into the doorframe below Hardin's clutching hand. Splinters flew. Tiny pieces of wood danced before Lackey's eyes.

Lackey murmured, "Shit." He backed off, raised his foot and placed its sole dead-center between the cheeks of Hardin's butt, and shoved with all he had. Hardin stumbled forward; his head banged into hardwood and the door swung open wide. Lackey put the heel of his hand in the small of Hardin's back and pushed even harder. Hardin fell across the threshold and went down in a heap; Lackey dived inside behind his hostage as the rifle cracked again and more splinters whistled through the air. He had a whirlaround glimpse of a table, chairs, an old TV set as he rolled over, climbed to his feet and slammed the door. A third rifle bullet whined through the door and buried into the wall at the back of the apartment. Lackey had barely drawn his breath, and had bent over to check on Hardin, when movement in the corner of his eye caused him to turn. A man was coming from an adjoining room, a stumpy-ugly man whose nostrils were flared and whose lips were pulled back from crooked teeth in a grimace of hatred.

Helpless, her hands and feet still bound, Nancy Cuellar said a prayer as the crazy left the fallen woman and approached the bed. Please God, Nancy prayed, let me have one shot at his eyes. Just one free hand is all it would take. Please, Master. Hail Mary, full of grace, the Lord is . . .

The lunatic was sobbing, dragging one foot behind

him, his pistol flopping loosely by his side. Nancy shut
out everything from her mind, the dead black man in
the doorway and the tiny woman whose highheeled
shoes were visible below the foot of the bed, and concentrated on just one thing. Her right hand. Her right
hand, as she twisted her wrist and gave her all to get
the hand free from the ropes. Please, God, *please*.

From outside the bedroom came the sound of the
front door banging open, followed closely by the faraway noise of a gunshot. Or it could have been a firecracker. Nancy looked quickly toward the bedroom
door and into the sitting room beyond.

The crazy stopped in his tracks and slowly turned
toward the noise.

Everett's mama (daddy?) was gone, and all he had
left to live for was his baby. That's what he wanted to
tell her as he approached the bed, that he wasn't never
going to leave her side, and that everything was going
to be all right. Jesus, if he could only stop blubbering
and tell her that. Jesus, if he could—

More noise behind him. A door crashing open and
a gun going off. Somebody wanting to hurt his baby.
Everett turned and moved woodenly toward the
sounds, walked outside the bedroom and stared. Who
were these two guys? One face-down on the floor, another climbing to his feet. Everett had seen these two.
Where? Didn't matter none, they were here to do
harm.

His vision blurred by his own tears, his brain swirling like a kaleidoscope, Everett screamed and charged.

The man who had come through the door and was
now bearing down on Lackey wasn't normal. No way
was he normal. He was squatty and powerfully built,
with arms that hung practically to his knees, and had
a sloping forehead and thinning hair. His lips were
pulled back from crooked yellow teeth in a snarl. He

wore a ripped khaki shirt and green army pants. He was growling. Jesus, thought Lackey, the guy is *growling*. Percy Hardin had raised up on all fours on the floor, and now said breathlessly, "Oh, Christ."

The apish man was quick as a cat and moved low to the ground like an express freight train. He carried a revolver in one hand, but made no move to raise the gun. He kept on coming, snarling and snorting. Lackey had just begun to lift his own .45 into firing position, when the wild man slammed into him like a strongside linebacker.

Backward Lackey flew with the stumpy man's weight propelling him. Pain stunned Lackey's chest as he banged into the wall. The .45 slipped from his hand and clattered to the floor. The stumpy man's gun went also, banging the wall and rebounding downward. Lackey fell on his side and rolled onto his back, the breath knocked from his lungs, and waited helplessly for the crazy to jump on top of him and finish him off. Lackey couldn't move a muscle. Couldn't breathe. Couldn't . . .

Nothing fell on top of him. Off to his right, Percy Hardin said, "No. No, please," and followed that with a gargling sound.

Lackey gritted his teeth, drew a painful breath, and sat up.

Hardin was on his back with the stumpy man's knees pinning his upper arms. The man's powerful hands were around Hardin's neck, throttling him, and Hardin's face was turning purple. The crazy squeezed tighter and tighter, and lifted Hardin's head to bang it down on the floor.

Lackey decided to let Hardin die. The bastard deserved it, didn't he? Just let that monkey-looking sonofabitch choke Hardin to death while Lackey searched the apartment for Nancy. She had to be here someplace. Jesus, she had to be.

Lackey sighed. Hell, no, he couldn't. Not even

Percy Hardin, Lackey couldn't sit by while the nutty bastard choked Hardin to death. The .45 lay just feet away, and Lackey now crawled over and picked the gun up. He raised into a kneeling position and held the .45 in both hands to level it at the crazy's head.

Lackey said, "Hey." He was still short of breath and could barely get the word out of his mouth.

The stumpy man ignored him and went on strangling Hardin, as if Lackey Ferguson wasn't even there and it was just Hardin and the crazy, one on one. Hardin's face was turning from purple to dark blue, and his eyes had rolled back in his head.

Lackey said again, "Hey."

Still no sign that the crazy heard. The hands closed even tighter around Hardin's throat.

Lackey shot the stumpy man in the back. The .45 jumped and the recoil jerked Lackey's hand toward the ceiling. The slug tore into the crazy just below the shoulderblade and exited through his chest. Red splattered across Hardin's face and shoulders. The crazy's insane face turned in Lackey's direction and the hands relaxed their grip on Hardin's neck. The stumpy man toppled sideways, rolled over, kicked his feet, and was still.

Lackey stood and gingerly touched his ribs. He bent over the stumpy man and felt for a pulse. There was one faint beat, then nothing. The crazy's eyes were wide open and stared at the ceiling.

Hardin was coughing, his color going now from purple to red. He sat up holding his throat. "Christ," he croaked. "Christ, he would have killed me."

Lackey sighted down the .45's barrel and put Hardin's nose between the crosshairs. "If Nancy's not all right," Lackey said, "you might just wish he had."

There were two dead people in the bedroom, a black man and a tiny white woman. Lackey didn't bother to check for pulses. There was a gaping wound in the black man's neck and another in his chest, over the heart. The back of the woman's head was gone. Lackey averted his gaze from the corpses, skirted around them, and sat down on the bed beside Nancy.

She looked to be asleep. Please let her be only asleep, Lackey thought. She was tied and gagged, and her eyes were softly closed. He reached behind her head to untie the cloth which held her gag in place. As he did, her lashes fluttered.

Once, twice, then a series of rapid flutters. Finally, Nancy opened her eyes. She gasped and flinched away from him; then recognition spread over her face, and her taut cheeks relaxed. He removed the cloth and gently removed the rags from her mouth. Her makeup was worn off and her lips were pale. As far as Lackey was concerned, she'd never looked better. He wordlessly kissed her mouth as he reached behind her to untie her hands.

She said weakly, "Is he gone?"

Lackey worked at the knot between her hands. "All over. All over, babe," he said.

She buried her face in the hollow of his shoulder. In seconds his shirt was wet, and her shoulders were shaking in rhythm with her sobs.

Lackey tried once to take Nancy out of the bedroom while the bodies were still there. After two faltering steps, her gaze fell on the dead woman. Nancy screamed. After that, Lackey didn't try to lead her outside again. He just sat on the bed with her and cradled her face between his shoulder and neck until uniformed paramedics had come with gurneys and the corpses were gone. It was a good three-quarters of an hour before the way was clear. Lackey didn't care about the time; if it would keep Nancy from screaming anymore, he'd sit there and hold her for days. Finally, they went into the sitting room. Lackey kept his arm around her waist, and she leaned on him for support every step of the way.

Betty Monroe was seated on the couch, talking a mile a minute to Henley and Morrison while Assistant D.A. Favor stood nearby with his arms folded. Percy Hardin sat on a straightbacked kitchen chair in the corner. His wrist was cuffed to one of the chair's legs, which told Lackey all he needed to know about what Betty was telling the detectives. Betty was getting a whole lot more mileage out of her leg show with the cops than she had with Lackey; Henley and Morrison were practically drooling. She'll do okay for herself, Lackey thought. Nancy was crying softly as he herded her in the direction of the exit.

Two uniformed city cops were standing guard, and now stepped together, shoulder to shoulder, to block Lackey's path. One of the policemen shot a quizzical glance in Favor's direction.

Favor pinched his own fat cheek. "We're going to need to examine the girl. Did he, you know, molest her or anything?"

An angry pulse jumped in Lackey's neck and he opened his mouth to tell Favor off, but Nancy beat him to the punch. She raised her face from Lackey's shoulder with sparks shooting from her eyes. "He didn't," she said to Favor. "And if he had, you wouldn't touch me, anyway."

Favor met her gaze briefly, then folded his hands in front and regarded the floor. "Yeah, okay. Yeah, okay, let 'em pass."

The cops stood aside. Lackey took Nancy by the arm and started to escort her over the threshold onto the landing.

From the sofa, Morrison said, "Hey, Ferguson."

Lackey stopped and turned.

Morrison grinned, formed a pistol with his thumb and forefinger and fired an imaginary shot. "No hard feelings, Ferguson. Just part of the job, huh?"

Lackey didn't answer. He marched Nancy out into the warm night air, led her down the steps and onto the sidewalk. Halfway down the walk he stopped and kissed her, and she kissed him back. After a final glance back toward the apartment, at the two cops still standing by the door, Lackey Ferguson picked up his lady and carried her away. He was practically running.

We invite you to preview the forthcoming A.W. Gray novel, *Killings,* available from Dutton.

A custodian named Herbert Trevino, as he reported for four A.M. duty on the SMU campus, found the second victim under a tree. At five in the morning he told Dallas County Investigator Hardy Cole that the nude body of the girl would have gone unnoticed if it hadn't have been for the noise.

"Wait a minute," Cole said. "This is the first I've heard about any noise." He was lean and angular, with a permanent what-you're-telling-me's-a-lot-of-bullshit set to his mouth, and at the moment was more than a little pissed over the call at his home at four in the morning. He hadn't shaved and had wolfed down a doughnut and a cup of 7-Eleven coffee on his way to the campus.

The custodian said, "That's 'cause this is the first time anybody ask me. All these cops tramping around here don't do nothing 'cept put up them barriers and then stand the fuck around. I try to tell them what happen three or four times, they just say, 'wait a minute,' and then throw some more cigarette butts down for me to clean up after." He wore a gray broadcloth short-sleeved uniform and hard-toed work boots. His thick hair was graying, his weather-creased skin the color of a tamale wrapper.

Cole and Trevino were sitting in the front seat of Cole's gray four-door county-owned Chevy, parked at the curb on Airline Road. Across the way, flashlight beams stabbed here and there as the University Park Police and the Dallas County Sheriff's Department poked among the bushes and shrubs around the Fondren Science Building. In the distance, the dome atop Dallas Hall blotted out a large portion of the northwestern horizon. In another half hour, a late September dawn would streak the darkness with pink and gold.

"Let's get this straight," Cole said. "You understand how important it is for me to get this right, huh?" He was bracing a steno pad on his thigh and had a flashlight clamped between his left arm and his rib cage. The flashlight's beam was directed at the page on which Cole was taking notes.

"I s'pose," Trevino said. "I got some of my people wish them poleez would fuck around like this when they out off Harry Hines Boulevard hassling Mexican brothers."

"I ain't here to talk about that," Cole said, "You're coming to work at four o'clock' right?"

"Quarter to. Twen'y-six year I don't be late a time. My wife, she let me off right over there." Trevino pointed across the street, toward a row of old brick houses with tree-lined yards. The houses were built before World War II, without central air or heat. Most of them had rickety wooden floors which creaked underfoot and, in this Park Cities neighborhood, carried price tags of two hundred grand and up. Cole pictured his own home, a three-bedroom Fox & Jacobs which had run him forty-five thousand ten years earlier, and decided that for the money he'd made a better deal.

"Okay," Cole said. "So you came across Airline and crossed that little asphalt parking lot toward the science building. Notice anything out of line?"

"No, man, not til I go up the walk toward the building. Around them big trees over there."

"And you say you heard a noise?"

"That's what I say, man, Trevino said.

"Well, *man,* what did it sound like?"

"Like somebody giving somebody a blow job," Trevino said.

"Jesus Christ, I can't put *that* in my report," Cole said.

"Well, lick-lick, slurp-slurp, then."

"A slurping noise?"

"Yeah," Trevino said.

Cole held his pencil between his first and middle fingers and tapped it on the steering wheel. The a/c fan was on low; ice-cold air drifted from the vents. "One thing's bothering me, Herbert," Cole said. "This naked body was only five feet from the walk, and you say you didn't see it?"

"She was under the blanket," Trevino said.

"I don't have any information on that."

"Man, you don't got no information on chit."

"Listen, you want to talk about this downtown?" Cole said.

"Huh? Well, what you asking about you don't got no information on?"

"Any blanket," Cole said.

"I done told you, man," Trevino said. "Them fucking cops."

"The *police* took the blanket?"

"Yeah. Prob'ly took a nap."

Cole wrote down the information, leaving out the witness's opinion as to what the officers had done with the blanket. "So where were you when you first heard the slurping noise?" Cole said.

"I just turn up the walk and go for the building," Trevino said, pointing. "Maybe twen'y steps."

"Any idea what was making the noise?" Cole said.

"Yeah. The dude under the blanket with the dead gorl."

Cole couldn't say anything for a couple of seconds, then said, "Are you putting me on, Herbert?"

"No, man, I telling you. I thought they was a couple of kids fucking on the lawn."

" 'Engaged in sex,' " Cole said. "That's what I'm writing down."

"Yeah, okay. I go over and I say to the blanket, 'Hey, you can't do that chit around here.' That when the dude jump up and run off."

"Jesus Christ, you *saw* somebody?"

"I told you, man, them fucking cops. They don't listen," Trevino said.

"Well what did he look like?" Cole said.

"I can't tell. Eighty degrees, man, that dude had on a snowsuit. Had dark hair, maybe black or brown. Fucker run like hell."

"Let's get back to the slurping noise," Cole said. "Any idea what it was?"

"Sure," Trevino said. "It was the dude under the blanket. I ain't lying, man, he was under there sucking all over that dead gorl."

Cole's lips twisted as he pictured it, the guy crouched down underneath a blanket hungrily sucking at the lifeless flesh. "Lick-lick, slurp-slurp, huh?" Cole said.

"You got it, man," Herbert Trevino said.

By seven A.M. a meeting had convened at the University Park Police station, a red brick, Colonial-style building on McFarlin Boulevard. Ancient elm, sycamore, and weeping willow trees surrounded the building, and up and down the street rolling lawns fronted seventy-five-year-old homes the size of small English castles. Across the street from the station were four tennis courts which belonged to the city of University Park.

The meeting took place in the police conference room adjacent to the municipal courtroom. Present and seated at the conference table were Dallas County Assistant D.A. McIver Strange, Detective Ben Lewis and

Captain Will Utley of the University Park police department, and Vernon "Shoesole" Traynor of the Dallas County coroner's office. The last to come in was Hardy Cole, a day's growth of beard on his face, wearing his plaid sport coat and slacks as though he'd rather be dressed in slouchy jeans and T-shirt. Cole sat down.

"Detective Cole," McIver Strange said. "Glad you could join us. By the way, who's your tailor?" He was wearing a pressed navy suit, a white shirt with a starched collar, was round and soft like a formal penguin.

Cole favored Strange with a shit-eating grin, scooted down in his chair, and propped his knee against the edge of the table. "Hi, Mac," Cole said. "Early, ain't it?"

The two University Park cops exchanged glances. Captain Utley kept his gaze on the table as he said, "We haven't talked to any newspaper people. We have to ask you. Before you do, check with us, huh?" Captain Utley was tall and thin and also wore a navy suit. He had short brown hair, neatly trimmed, with a hint of gray in his sideburns, and wore thick bifocals encased in dark plastic frames.

Cole's chin lifted slightly, then dropped. "Yeah, we know. Park Cities, Allah, Mohammed, and all that shit."

Detective Lewis was short and thick, in his thirties, with a wide face and a thin brown mustache. He folded his hands on the table. "We just work here, Hardy. Something you can't do in this jurisdiction is play the tough monkey."

"Naw," Cole said. "Frank Sinatra already did that. *From Here to Eternity.* Well I don't work here, and what I'm interested in doing is busting one sick son of a bitch. If we got to use the papers, these uppity folks out here are just going to have to lump it."

"The mayor's going to have something to say about

that," Lewis said. "He does have a little stroke where you come from."

Cole snorted. "I don't give a fuck about—"

"Hardy." Mac Strange lifted a hand, his eyes half closed as though he was bored. "Just knock it off. We can be here a week with all that. What we need to talk about here is that we've got a real doozy on our hands."

Utley looked relieved, glad to get around the conflict for the time being, at the same time showing by the twitch at the corner of his mouth that he knew the problem would come up again. "No doubt about it," Utley said. "That first one could have been a drifter or somebody pissed off about something. This one makes it look like a bona fide nut case. So. So far, what's anybody got?"

Cole used the forefinger of each hand to rub his eyelids. "Oh, not much. Only that the body was originally under a blanket that nobody seems to know anything about. Oh, yeah, and the custodian that found the body just happened to see the guy—not that anybody bothered to ask him about it until an hour later. Just little shit like that." He tossed a blink in Strange's direction.

"There's a lot going on at a crime scene," Lewis said, his gaze lowered.

Mac Strange opened his mouth as if to say something, but Cole bulled ahead. "Look," Cole said, then held up a hand, palm out, in Strange's direction. "Hear me out, Mac." Then, glancing alternately from Utley to Lewis and back again, "Listen, you guys got some facts to face. This ain't exactly the corner of Oakland and Martin Luther King out here. You people don't get many homicides. What you get is maybe some high school kids shitting in a bag and then setting it on fire and putting it on somebody's front porch and ringing the doorbell. Somebody knocking somebody's under-age daughter up, if the guy don't flash his bankroll around and grease a few palms to hush it up. What you're into this time is some heavy bullshit. Well, when the next one comes down how about calling us first, before your kiddie-cops get out there and mess up the scene. That might step on somebody's toes, but if it does, it does." He settled back with a defiant tilt to his chin.

Captain Utley folded his hands and stuck out his narrow jaw. "We have our people."

Cole rolled his eyes. "Jesus Christ."

Mac Strange pointed a finger. "No more, Hardy, I'm not kidding."

"I ain't kidding either," Cole said. "All this fucking around these people are doing, they're going to wind up with the FBI out here shoving their noses in. That's the next step. You guys probably haven't had the feds fucking with one of your investigations, but Mac and me been through it before."

"Hardy." Strange said.

"Okay." Cole said. He regarded his knee.

"First things first," Strange said. "Any ID on the victim?"

"She was nude," Detective Lewis said. "No belongings or anything. Blond, eighteen to twenty-five"—he took a small notepad from the pocket of his brown suit coat and looked at it—"right at five-six, around a hundred and twenty. Tattoo of a rose on her left cheek."

"Of her ass?" Strange said.

"Yeah. Well-nourished female. Well-built," Lewis said.

"Well-built?" Cole said. "Who came up with that statistic?" He showed another shit-eating grin while Lewis did his best to stare the county investigator down. It didn't work. Lewis dropped his gaze.

Captain Utley leaned forward and said, "No positive identification as yet. We're checking all the dorms to see what female students are missing, but that's pretty much of a bitch. A whole bunch of 'em are missing, all they have to do out there is sign out for the night. Plus a big portion of the student body lives off campus, in apartments.''

"Things have changed since I went to college,'' Strange said.

"Haven't they?'' the University Park captain said. "Classes begin at eight, we can narrow it down better when we see who's not in class. But that's not easy, either, everybody doesn't have an eight o'clock Plus a lot of them cut, and classes don't meet every day. It'll be tomorrow before we get a full roll call.''

"If she's a student,'' Cole said.

Four heads swiveled as one to look at Cole.

"Yeah,'' Cole said. "Just because you found her on a college campus don't mean she's a student. How about around the body? Any signs that maybe the guy did her someplace else and then dumped her?''

The University Park officers exchange more looks.

"Well, how 'bout this?'' Cole said. "I guess somebody did bother to take some fingerprints.''

"Hardy,'' Strange said.

"That's what I'm talking about, Mac.'' Cole folded his arms and regarding the ceiling.

"The prints are taken and already shot to Washington,'' Lewis said. Utley gave Lewis a that's-telling-'em nod.

"Okay,'' Strange said. "How 'bout it, Shoesole?''

Deputy Corner Shoesole Traynor had a thick head of graying hair and a good-sized belly, which poked out against the front of his white shin-length smock. He had a Sherlock Holmes–style briar pipe clenched lightly between his teeth. The pipe wasn't lit, but the bowl was filled with tobacco. He'd been listening to the proceedings with the barest hint of a smile. He sat forward, removed the pipe from his mouth, and cupped the bowl in his palm. "No autopsy yet, of course—maybe we'll know more then. All appearances are like the last one, same bite marks, same cuts, same kind of mutilation. Like I said, nothing official till we can slice her open.'' His smile broadened.

"What mutilation are we talking about?" Cole said.

"You mean there's something you don't know?" University Park detective Lewis said. Alongside him, Captain Utley snickered, then quickly regained his composure.

"The worst one," Traynor said, "that's the peg. A sharpened four-inch hard maple spike, actually, driven into the pelvic bone through the wall of the vagina. On the last victim, the bruise patterns in the flesh show that the guy used a hammer, or something like it. Drove the peg in with a series of sharp blows. Odds are we'll find the same thing on this one." He looked down at his pipe, then raised his gaze. "The peg wound on the last one was post mortem. Something like that would almost have to be, given that the victim would have to be lying still."

"I'd think so," Cole said. "Jesus Christ."

"Then there are the same cuts as the last one. Horizontal incisions bisecting the arteries on both sides of the throat. The cuts were made while the last victim was alive." Traynor spoke in a monotone, as though he was speaking into a recorder.

"What in hell killed her?" Coles said.

"Hardy didn't work the last one," Strange said. "He was on vacation."

"Indirectly, it was the cuts," Traynor said. "That last girl was missing almost three pints of blood."

Cole sat bolt upright, his eyebrows lifted. "Well, if she bled to death . . . How much blood was around her, where they found the body?"

"None, or almost none," Traynor said.

"Well, Jesus, that means she got it someplace else," Cole said.

Traynor shook her head. Detective Lewis was grinning openly at Cole while Captain Utley looked as though he was trying not to grin. "Not necessarily," Traynor said. "I said 'indirectly.' Indirectly, the cuts were the cause of death."

Cole frowned. "What the hell are you talking about?"

Traynor put his pipe between his teeth and let it dangle from one corner of his mouth. "Teeth marks around the wounds," he said, "plus the outward swelling of the surrounding tissue would indicate that whoever it was cut the arteries and sucked out the blood."

Cole searched the faces around him. They had to be putting him on.

Finally, Strange nodded. "That's right, Hardy. The guy probably drank it. It seems we got some kind of vampire here."

27 million Americans can't read a bedtime story to a child.

It's because 27 million adults in this country simply can't read.

Functional illiteracy has reached one out of five Americans. It robs them of even the simplest of human pleasures, like reading a fairy tale to a child.

You can change all this by joining the fight against illiteracy.

Call the Coalition for Literacy at toll-free **1-800-228-8813** and volunteer.

Volunteer Against Illiteracy. The only degree you need is a degree of caring.